SECRETS OF A DANGEROUS WOMAN

SECRETS OF A DANGEROUS WOMAN
by p.m.terrell

Published by
Drake Valley Press
USA

This novel is a work of fiction. Any resemblance to actual persons, living or dead, is entirely coincidental. The characters, names (except as noted under "Special Thanks"), plots and incidents are the product of the author's imagination. References to actual events, public figures, locales or businesses are included only to give this work of fiction a sense of reality.

Published by Drake Valley Press

Cover photographs by Glenda Sue Chapman,
www.wix.com/glendachapman/glenda-chapman-photography

ISBN 978-1-935970-05-7 (Trade Paperback)
ISBN 978-1-935970-06-4 (eBook)

Author's website: www.pmterrell.com

Other Books by p.m.terrell

Black Swamp Mysteries:

Exit 22 (2008)

Vicki's Key (2012)

Secrets of a Dangerous Woman (2012)

Dylan's Song (March 2013)

Other Books:

Kickback (2002)

The China Conspiracy (2003)

Ricochet (2006)

Take the Mystery out of Promoting Your Book (2006)

Songbirds are Free (2007)

River Passage (2009)

The Banker's Greed (2011)

What Critics Say

Suspense Magazine says p.m.terrell's books are "powerfully written and masterfully suspenseful; you have to hang on for the ride of your life."

Midwest Book Review says, "Terrell is a master at skillfully combining drama, action, suspense and romance to engage the reader in an adrenaline rush of page turning adventure."

Between the Lines Reviews says, "Terrell has become a force of nature!"

Syndicated reviewer Simon Barrett says, "As a reader you are swept along on a magic carpet ride of writing wizardry."

The Book Blues says, "Just when you think p.m.terrell is the best she can be, she gets better!"

Bengal Book Reviews says p.m.terrell's books are "riveting… spellbinding… sexy, intense, stay-up-all-night until you are done thrillers!"

Special Thanks to

Glenda Sue Chapman for her modeling and photography for the book cover and trailers;

Mickey Gregory, Executive Director of the Lumberton Visitor's Bureau, for information on Lumberton, the Lumber River, and Robeson County;

Drina Hedgpeth, Bucky Miller and Neill Thompson for the tour of the Caldwell House and background information;

Pamela June Kimmell for her valuable input during the writing and editorial stages;

Karen Luffred, my thriller expert;

John W. Neelley, Sr., retired FBI Special Agent, for information on crimes and charges;

Beth Freeman Powers for her valuable input;

Rebekah Thompson for her vision of turning an old water filtration plant into a regional art center and for the tour of the Southeastern Waterworks Regional Art Center and background information;

Arnold West for permission to use The Village Station throughout this series.

Book 3 in the Black Swamp Mysteries Series

1

The only proper thing to do after finding Aunt Laurel's dismembered body in the freezer was to open the house for a visitation.

Vicki Boyd walked through the downstairs hallway, inspecting the home one last time before guests arrived. The house felt cavernous, empty and sad. She'd never intended to live in a three-story, five bedroom historic home by herself but here she was, the sole occupant and the only one prepared to put Aunt Laurel's ashes on display for the neighbors and friends.

She glanced into the dining room, where plates of heavy hors d'oeuvres were neatly arranged. Benita, the housekeeper and cook, walked in with a purposeful stride, carrying pitchers of super-sweet iced tea and lemonade.

"Everything looks good," Vicki commented.

"Gracias." Since Benita had begun working for Vicki, she'd discovered the Hispanic woman understood quite a bit of English, though she chose to speak Spanish and preferred for people to think she couldn't understand a word they said.

As a group of ladies parked on the street in front of the home, Vicki made her way past the living room, in which a special table had been set up in front of the fireplace to hold the urn. The table was covered with a burgundy tablecloth but it was conspicuously empty. She glanced at her watch and hoped Sam would arrive soon.

She opened the screen door as the ladies arrived on the porch. She greeted each one in turn, shaking their hands and accepting their condolences, even though she hadn't a clue who they were and they were just as ignorant about her.

"My Uncle Sam will be here any minute with Aunt Laurel's ashes," she said apologetically. "Please go into the dining room and help yourself to the food there."

"My name is Olympia," one woman said. She looked like a female version of Alfred Hitchcock and walked with a limp as if her ankles bothered her. "My husband is Dr. Warberstein. He's a neurosurgeon and you know, all neurosurgeons are brilliant but my husband is a genius. He just turned 102 and he's still operating. Just operated yesterday. The patient didn't make it but he wouldn't have lived anyway. And I've known Laurel Maguire my entire life and I had no idea she wanted to be cremated. It's scandalous. Absolutely scandalous."

Vicki shook her head gently. "I'm so sorry. I didn't have anything to do with the decision. Her nephew had a copy of her will and I understand her wishes clearly stated cremation."

"Where is Dylan Maguire?" another woman asked. "I heard he'd come here to help Laurel."

Vicki swallowed hard at the mention of his name and turned to face the second woman. She was dressed in her Sunday finest, her hair perfectly coifed. "Dylan was called back to Ireland due to another illness in the family," Vicki recited what she'd practiced. "Unfortunately, Aunt Laurel passed away shortly after he left and he didn't find out about it until he landed in Ireland. He's trying to take care of his relative there and get back here as quickly as possible." She hoped her words didn't sound rehearsed.

"How did she die?" Olympia asked.

"She passed away peacefully in her sleep," Vicki said in a hushed tone. Glancing out the door, she saw Sam heading up the sidewalk with the urn. "There's my uncle now," she said, grateful for the interruption. She turned back to the ladies as she opened the door. "Please, if you don't mind, give me a moment alone with her first? Help yourselves to the food in the dining room."

Sam entered the hallway with a quizzical glance at the ladies as Benita led them into the dining room.

"Apparently, Aunt Laurel did have a few friends," Vicki whispered as they entered the living room together.

"Where were they all those months she was in the freezer?" Sam mused, placing the urn in the center of the table.

"So, that's Aunt Laurel."

"Actually…"

"It's *not* Aunt Laurel?"

"We couldn't find her. We know she's there somewhere, but…" Sam stroked his chin. His eyes always appeared as though he was bored with the conversation. It was as if he'd seen everything there was to see and nothing interested him anymore.

"Who's in the urn?" Vicki asked.

"Not who. What. It's talcum powder."

"You've got to be kidding me."

"Afraid not."

"You really think we can pull this off?"

"Why not? It isn't like anybody's going to open it up and look inside. I just added it for the weight."

"Unbelievable."

Sam turned toward the urn with his hands crossed in front of him. "Better look somber. We've got eyes on us."

Vicki placed a hand on the urn. "I am somber. But for different reasons."

"I'll take you to dinner after this."

"I'm not in the mood."

"You will be."

They were interrupted as Olympia joined them. She held her hors d'oeuvre plate in one hand while placing her other hand on the urn. Sam and Vicki backed away as the other ladies joined her.

"Oh, Laurel, Laurel," Olympia moaned. "I can smell your perfume right through the urn." She turned toward the others. "I'm psychic, you know. I can communicate with the dead. And I hear her voice calling out to me."

Vicki glanced at Sam. He continued staring straight ahead with a disinterested expression.

"I can feel her presence here, in her final—resting place." Olympia rubbed the urn. "She's so happy we've all come. I can feel her love for us pouring out."

"That must be the lavender," Sam muttered.

A woman who looked surprisingly like Aunt Laurel snorted. "Laurel Maguire never felt love for anybody. Not even her husband Jon." She turned to Sam and extended her hand. "My name is Caroline Rauch Taft. My father was Harold H. Rauch, not to be confused with Harold M. Rauch, who was his father before him."

"Pleased. I'm sure," Sam said, shaking her hand ever so slightly.

She turned to Vicki. "Laurel Maguire and I go all the way back to the first grade. Before that, even. We were neighbors. We used to slide down the banisters together."

"Nice to meet you," she said dutifully. She tried to picture the woman as a child but couldn't.

"Laurel was a hateful, vengeful person. Always was. She got it from her mother. She was always looking for people's faults. Could never find a nice word to say about anybody."

"What's that, Laurel? What are you saying?" Olympia said, continuing to rub the urn as her voice rose. "She says you're just sore because she always beat you at Wednesday Bridge."

"Well, I never," Caroline said, crossing to the other side of the room.

"I'm gonna have to leave," Sam muttered.

"Oh, no, you don't," Vicki whispered hoarsely. "You're the one who arranged this and you're staying with me until the last person leaves."

"I've got a lot of work to do."

"The CIA can wait two hours."

The screen door opened and an attractive woman with blond hair popped her head in the door. "Vicki?" she said.

Vicki sighed with relief when she spotted her next door neighbor, Sandy. They met in the middle of the room as they exchanged a quick hug.

"I'm very sorry about Aunt Laurel," Sandy said. "I know how much you were looking forward to working for her."

"Yes," Vicki answered, "well, her nephew asked me to stay on and take care of the fish and the house."

"Where is Dylan?"

At the mention of his name a second time, she blinked back a tear as she recited the story she and Sam had agreed upon.

"Oh, what awful timing," Sandy breathed. "He must feel absolutely horrible that he wasn't here when she passed."

"Yes."

"He doted on her so. When I think of all he did for her... So, will he be returning to Ireland to live now?" She glanced around the room. "Will he be liquidating everything? Selling the house?"

Vicki swallowed. "I don't know. For now, I'm to take care of the fish operation—"

"Oh, that's right. The fish. What will happen to her angelfish breeding business?"

She shrugged. "It's all up in the air." She glanced at Sam. "I'm just taking it a day at a time right now."

Sandy hugged her again. "Of course you are, dear. You poor thing. Please let me know if you need anything at all, okay? You know I'm right next door."

The screen door opened again and a sheriff's deputy made his way into the living room.

"Alec," Vicki said, hugging him. She stole a glance at Sam. "You haven't met my uncle, have you? Uncle Sam, this is Sandy, my next door neighbor, and her boyfriend Alec."

Sam shook their hands and exchanged pleasantries.

"The porch looks fantastic," Alec said. "Dylan did a terrific job of replacing that whole porch railing. Makes it look like a brand new house."

"Yes, it does."

"There's one spindle missing, did you know that?" Alec ran his hand through his sandy hair. He had a pleasant expression, though he appeared very tired.

"Oh." Vicki purposefully did not look at Sam.

"Yeah, I don't know if he ran out of spindles? Miscounted or something?"

"No. It's upstairs. I think it didn't fit right or something. He needed to do something with it."

"If you'll give it to me, I'll put it in. That'll be one less thing for him to worry about when he gets back."

"Thank you. I'll do that."

They stood awkwardly as they listened to Olympia crying and speaking to the urn.

"So, that's Aunt Laurel?" Sandy asked.

"Yep," Vicki answered.

"I guess I should pay my respects."

"Or you could eat," Vicki said. "Looks like she's going to be busy for a while."

Alec laughed a bit nervously. "Yes, it does." He turned to Sandy. "Shall we?"

As she made their way toward the dining room, Vicki turned to Sam. "Hold down the fort for a minute, will you?"

"Where are you going?"

"Upstairs. To get that spindle."

"Are you serious?"

"Dead serious. I washed it but didn't know what to do with it. Now I do."

"You're going to give it to a sheriff's deputy?"

"Can you think of anything better to do with a murder weapon?" Vicki whispered. "How many folks do you think will be looking for the weapon among the spindles?"

"Good thinking," Sam said admiringly. "Dylan teach you that?"

"Please." She started to say more but thought better of it. As she made her way up the stairs to the second floor, she glanced below. She caught a glimpse of Alec with a full plate, his wide girth ready to pop open a button on his uniform shirt. Sandy was chatting incessantly to Benita, who acted like she didn't understand a single word. And down the short hall were four women in the living room carrying on a conversation with talcum powder.

2

Vicki leaned back in the booth and watched Sam sip his black coffee. He'd recently begun wearing reading glasses, which were perched on the end of his nose. He watched her over the top of them for a long moment. His eyes had always been dark brown but now she noticed the slightest tint of blue was forming around the outer edge.

"So, that's over," he said finally.

"That's over." She tapped the edge of the table absent-mindedly. They were sitting in a corner booth at The Village Station. They'd begun to visit the restaurant so frequently that Arnold, the proprietor, referred to it as "their regular table." Now a folder lay between them, a folder Vicki longed to open, but she knew Sam would broach the subject when he was good and ready.

He watched her stare at the folder while he drank his coffee. Finally, he pushed it toward her. "So, here's your next assignment," he said.

She opened the folder but instead of reading it, she looked back at him.

"Aunt Laurel's nephew plans to sell the house and everything in it," he said. He waited as if gauging her reaction. When she didn't respond, he said, "How do you feel about that?"

"Sad," she said immediately. "I know it's probably hard for you to understand with everything that happened there, but I've grown to like it. I enjoy working with the angelfish, though I don't know if I'm any good at it. And I wish there weren't so many memories there…" Her voice faded as she looked away.

"But you would like to stay anyway?" he asked.

"For some reason I can't explain, yes. I would."

"I was hoping you'd say that."

"Why?"

"The CIA can arrange to make an offer. It'll look like it's coming from someone in town, somebody who knew Laurel Maguire, knows she recently died, and would like to buy the whole thing, lock, stock and barrel."

"What would the CIA do with everything?"

"It's the perfect front for you, Vicki. I don't care what you do with everything in the house. Sell it. Trash it. Burn it. But keep the fish operation and try not to let too many of 'em die so you can at least appear like you've taken over the business."

"Wouldn't there be questions from Aunt Laurel's nephew about the fish business?"

"He never saw it as a business. Just as a silly little hobby to keep his aunt busy. Frankly, in our conversations with him, he acted like she was nothing more than a nuisance to him."

"That's too bad," Vicki said. "I've not met anybody who had anything nice to say about her, but… She didn't deserve to die like she did. Or be lost somewhere at the CIA." She said the last sentence with a bit of an edge, but Sam acted like he didn't pick up on it.

"So," he said, "we'll buy the place. You continue living there, work your fish business and work your assignments with the Agency."

"Speaking of which," she said, glancing at the folder.

"Yes. Speaking of which," he repeated, "here's the run-down."

She leaned forward as he spoke. He glanced around the restaurant but the other patrons were on the other side of the dining room. "You've met Christopher Sandige," he said.

"Yes."

"You know he works for Congressman Willo."

"Yes."

"Last November, he spent the weekend in Lumberton. He met a woman and got himself in a bit of hot water before the weekend was over. Seems there'd been a double homicide that turned out to be related to this woman somehow or other. She was involved in a computer scheme involving oil."

"Do we know this woman's identity?"

He flipped to a page with a black and white photograph paper-clipped to the edge. Vicki leaned in to look. The picture was taken from afar as if from a surveillance camera. As she stared at the grainy image, Sam continued, "Name's Brenda Carnegie. She doesn't have a criminal record—yet—but they seized her computer. Turns out she's been involved in a long string of illegal schemes."

"Why does the CIA want her?"

"We want her because Congressman Willo wants her. He wants her because he sits on a subcommittee overseeing the oil industry. Turns out, there was evidence on the computer that some senior members of Congress and the Administration could be major shareholders in some Middle Eastern oil companies."

"Is that illegal?"

He shrugged. "Would it be illegal for John Doe to own stock? No. Would it be illegal for a member of Congress to own stock and then deny oil drilling in the US? That's another matter."

"Is that what's happening?"

"There's evidence to suggest it."

"What do you need from me?"

"Chris was here that weekend with her," Sam said, "and—to cut to the bottom line—she escaped. She knew about the double homicide, she was wanted by local law enforcement, but when they closed in, she simply disappeared."

"Into thin air?"

"Into thin air. They even got dogs to track her and they couldn't find her. The scent just vanished. Local law enforcement put out bulletins, enlisted local media, watched airports, train stations, rental car companies—they got nothing. It was as if she'd never existed."

"Which brings me right back to… Why is the CIA involved? Wouldn't it have been more appropriate for the congressman to bring in the FBI or some other agency?"

Sam shrugged. "Possibly. But recent evidence has surfaced suggesting she's out of the country. The CIA is better prepared to go in and extract her."

"So what you want me to do is try to find her."

The server returned, filled Sam's coffee cup and left the check. He pulled out his wallet and began counting out bills. "Think you can do it?"

Vicki peered at the photograph. "You don't have a better picture than this?"

"We're working on it."

"Is she wanted internationally?" she asked.

"We don't want to raise suspicions of members of Congress," he said. "So this is all being done quietly, behind the scenes. Chris is your point of contact. Whatever you tell him, he'll give to the congressman, and he'll take it from there." He cleared his throat. "You're our best psychic spy, Vicki. Always were. Probably always will be. Congressman Willo could be the sole reason we're all still in the business of covert psychic operations. He's made sure we continued getting funding no matter what was happening with the federal budget."

"I know."

"So I need for you to hone in on her. Give us a country, a location, a latitude and longitude like you're so good at. Give us an address so we can get some boots on the ground to extract her."

She nodded. "Are satellites available?"

"Anything you want is available." He placed his palm face down on the table. "Tomorrow. My office at Fort Bragg. We'll have a remote viewing session. Chris will be there. And we'll see what shakes out."

"Time?"

"One o'clock. I know how you like to take care of the fish in the morning."

"It's not so much that I like to, but I have to…"

"I understand. It's your cover." He stood and dropped some money on the table. "See you then?"

She slipped out of the booth and they walked through the restaurant together. "I'll be there," she said as they reached the parking lot.

He half-waved. She watched as he approached his dark blue sedan. With a lonely heart, she walked in the opposite direction to her own car. She slid into the front seat, placing the folder beside her as Sam pulled onto Roberts Avenue and immediately took the first turn onto Interstate 95, whisking him north to Fort Bragg and his hotel.

She sat for a long time without starting her car. She stared at the stars and the moon in the cloudless sky, feeling like a tiny speck in the universe. After a while, she watched the front door of the restaurant, remembering another time not all that long ago when she'd left the restaurant with Dylan. She'd been head over heels, blindly in love with him. And now he was gone. And now there was an aching hole in her heart where love had once blossomed, and she didn't know how she was going to continue putting one foot in front of the other.

3

Vicki grabbed an apple on her way through the kitchen. "I'm going to Fayetteville to run some errands," she said to Benita.

"Will you be home for dinner?" she asked in a thick Mexican accent. She was short and stout with an erect posture and squared shoulders; the kind of shoulders, Vicki thought, that could stand up to anything life threw at her.

"Can you leave something in the frig for me to heat up?"

"Sure. Oh," Benita added as Vicki's head disappeared around the corner.

Vicki stopped and leaned into the doorway. "Yes?"

"Mister Alec fixed the porch railing."

"That was fast," Vicki said. She started down the hallway toward the front door. "See you tomorrow."

She closed and locked the front door behind her before inspecting the porch railing. It was impossible to tell which spindle Alec had installed. She'd been careful to clean off all the blood. And she'd noticed the recycled milk carton composite was so strong and so thick, it hadn't even dented when it bashed in her assailant's head.

She checked her watch. It was twelve o'clock on the dot. In one hour, she'd be entering the CIA office at Fort Bragg, settling in for a remote viewing session.

She made her way to her car and started it as she stared through the windshield at the garage. It was leaning so badly now that she was afraid to park inside it. She wished Dylan was here. He'd know what to do. He'd have it repaired or replaced in short order. Her eyes moved from the garage to the house, with its new paint and shutters, the rotting eaves completely restored.

She missed him. She missed pulling into the driveway and seeing him atop a ladder, shirtless, his skin glistening in the hot summer sun. She missed him telling her in his adorable Irish brogue that he was doing it all for her. She missed the feel of his arms around her; they'd been muscular arms that had proven they could protect her.

She turned on the radio as *Just the Two of Us* began to play. She stared at the dash incredulously. That was their song. *Their* song. How ironic that it should play now, of all times.

Though the music wrenched at her heart, she kept it on as she backed out of the driveway and headed toward Interstate 95.

She'd just entered the traffic on the interstate when the song stopped. There was a brief moment of silence before *Just Another* began to play.

She glanced at the radio. Her soft drink can, nestled into the cup holder, blocked the display and as she drove down the highway, she transferred the can to a spot between her thighs.

When she glanced back at the display, the song was ending and *Superman* began playing.

The radio wasn't on. It was a CD.

Though she continued her drive toward Fort Bragg, her mind quickly moved back in time. She knew she had never put that CD in her car. She would have bet her life on it. In fact, she realized, to her knowledge it had never left Dylan's bedroom. It was the CD he always played when they were together.

She reached the turn-off to Fort Bragg twenty minutes and five songs later. Once off the interstate, she pulled into the first parking lot and ejected the CD.

The tears rolled down her cheeks unchecked. If Dylan was here, she thought, he'd say in his Irish brogue, "What are you cryin' for, Woman?" followed by a reminder that he could never abide a woman crying.

She sat for a full five minutes, wailing. She couldn't listen to any more of it, she thought. She turned on the radio as the chorus for *It Must Have Been Love* began to play:

It must have been love, but it's over now
It must have been good, but I lost it somehow
It must have been love, but it's over now...

Her body was wracked with pain as a sob was wrenched from the depths of her heart, and she turned off the radio. She put the CD back in the player and started the songs over again as she cried the rest of the way to Fort Bragg.

"Are you okay, ma'am?" the officer at the gate asked as he checked her ID.

She pointed to the music, which was still playing, as she sobbed, "He made this CD for me. And now he's gone!"

The young man appeared stunned.

Vicki could almost see the possibilities rolling through his head—that her husband was overseas, serving in some war-time capacity or that, God forbid, he'd been killed in war. Before he could respond, she started wailing again, rolled up her window, and continued onto the post.

She found the familiar CIA building nestled among the trees through blurry eyes, its brown brick and matching trim blending so well into the surrounding terrain that she imagined most people didn't even realize it was there.

Then she blew her nose and made her way into the building.

She found Sam in his office, sitting comfortably in an aged wing-back chair, his feet propped up on the government-issue coffee table. Christopher Sandige sat on the sofa. His legs were long as they stretched out casually in front of him. She spotted a dark blue suit jacket draped over a nearby chair; now he sported the matching slacks and a lighter blue denim shirt that was opened at the neck as if he and Sam had been kicked back for a while.

"You okay?" Sam said, taking his feet off the table.

"I'm fine," she sobbed.

He grabbed a box of tissues from his desk. "You remember Chris, don't you?" he said hesitantly.

At the sight of her, Chris stood. He was taller than Vicki remembered; now he seemed to tower over Sam, who was not a short man by any means. His physique was lean, the type of body that was blessed with a high metabolism. As he made his way around the coffee table to stand in front of her, he moved with uncommon grace.

"Hi," she said, shaking his hand as fresh tears started down her cheeks. When she began to pull her hand away, he held it in a muscular grip until she was forced to look into his eyes. They were warm brown with a single vertical crease between them. It grew deeper as he kept his eyes on her.

"Is this a bad time for you?" he managed to ask between her sobs.

"No," she answered, "It's a great time."

Through her tears, she saw the two men staring at each other with confounded expressions. Then she realized that Chris still had a firm grip on her hand. "I'm okay," she sniffled.

He placed his other hand on her shoulder. "I don't think you are," he said in a hushed tone.

Sam walked around his desk and grabbed a pad of paper. "What the hell, Vicki." His voice was brusque. "Get a grip. Sit over there and dry it up."

Chris held onto her hand as he led her to the sofa. He was so very tall and his hands so firm and muscular; yet he was also very gentle, she thought, and obviously very concerned. In one respect, it made her feel guilty for appearing so high maintenance. But it also made her want to put her head on his capable shoulder and cry even more.

As she sat down, she looked up at him and smiled through her tears. "I'll be okay," she said. "Thank you."

He reluctantly released his grip on her but continued standing beside her, studying her. He ran his hand through warm brown hair that was slightly long, causing one lock to drop onto his forehead. One small swath of silver at his temple looked premature but also gave him an air of dignity.

"Really," she said as she grabbed for another tissue, "I'm fine." She took a deep breath. "Let's get started."

4

She lay on the sofa, her head resting comfortably on a pillow and her swollen eyes closed. She placed one forearm over her eyes as if to block the light, but the room was so dim the corners were cloaked in shadows.

"Chris," Sam was saying, "I'll give you some background on remote viewing before we get started. I know you've read the files but it's quite different when you're watching it."

She knew they were observing her as she tried to clear her mind.

"There's a belief among some people that each of us is born with a sixth sense. Some think of it as intuition; women's intuition, in particular, is a mainstream concept, for example. You probably know at least one person who had a feeling or a hunch that something wasn't quite right. And when they followed up, their hunch was proven correct."

"Yes," Chris said. His voice was deep and confident. "That's happened to me before."

"A lot of people ignore that feeling," Sam continued. Vicki could picture him shaking a cigarette out of a pack and putting it in the corner of his mouth, even though he knew the entire building was no smoking. "But there are others who pay attention to it. And there are still others, like Vicki here, who have been trained not only to listen to it but to cultivate it."

"I understand," Chris interjected, "she's been doing this for several years now."

"Counting her time in training, it's been just about sixteen years. Since she was twelve years old."

They talked about her as if she wasn't there, which Vicki found slightly disconcerting. But at least her crying had stopped, she thought. She was ready to get on with it and get back home.

"Vicki has been trained not only to listen to that intuition but to travel to where it takes her," Sam continued. "For example, you could have a loved one out of town and you might picture them at their hotel or sitting in their conference or enjoying their vacation… But Vicki here has been trained to project her consciousness into that precise location and report back exactly what she sees."

"How do you know that she's seeing things that are really there?" Chris asked. "And it's not her imagination?"

"Men on the ground," Sam responded instantly. "This afternoon, she'll tell us what she sees. And we'll get operatives to that precise location. They'll confirm or deny it within minutes."

Vicki felt Sam making his way to the chair nearest her head. The chair creaked as he sat down and let out a weary sigh. She knew he had his note pad in his lap and pen in his hand, and that even while he was patiently explaining the process to Chris, his customary bored expression would be permanently etched on his face.

She tried to clear her mind of their presence, tried not to think of Chris watching her intently with those liquid brown eyes or Sam monitoring her breathing.

"Can you hit that switch for me?" Sam asked Chris.

She heard the switch and knew the audio and visual equipment was now on and everything she reported would be recorded. The recordings would then be sent up the chain to analysts, who would painstakingly watch and listen to every second.

Their voices faded as she cleared her mind. She focused on a bright white light until all the thoughts that threatened to push their way into the forefront of her mind were gone and her head was clear. Experience had taught her that her own thoughts could hijack the mission; only when she was as clear as a blank sheet of paper was she receptive to psychic energy.

She soon felt herself soaring upwards like her soul was leaving her body. She felt like an eagle rising into the skies as she peered down on the North Carolina topography. She could see all of Fort Bragg: the buildings, the cars and the people. But as she focused on Brenda Carnegie's presence, she felt whisked away from the army post in an instant.

Soon she was watching events unfold before her eyes, events she had a strong feeling had already happened.

"Tell me what you're seeing," Sam said. Though she knew he was physically located beside her, his voice sounded disembodied, as though he was speaking into a communication device. She felt like the eyes and ears of a covert operation.

"A barn of some type," she answered. "I'm not in the present, but in the past. The leaves are off the trees. The grass is brown. There's a man making his way around the barn. He has a gun."

"My God," Chris breathed. "The assassin."

"I see you there, Chris," Vicki continued. "You're inside the barn. You're watching him through the breaks in the outer wall. She was with you. Brenda was there."

"Yes," Chris said, his voice sounding incredulous, "that's right."

"Then she left the barn. I'm seeing some sort of animal with her. A horse, I think."

"Where did she go when she left the barn, Vicki?" Sam broke in.

"I see her driving through the night in a compact white car. A medium blue sports car. Now it's a silvery blue minivan. She's changing vehicles every few hours."

"Stealing them? Renting them?"

"She knows how to hot-wire a vehicle. She continues until she's almost out of gas. Then she leaves the vehicle in a parking lot off the interstate and finds another nearby."

"Which interstate?" Sam asked.

She hesitated. "She was driving west," she added, "but she wanted to be south."

Chris and Sam remained silent as she watched Brenda in her mind's eye driving across the country. Then she saw a sign. "Houston Intercontinental Airport," she said. "She's been driving for twenty hours. She has a ticket in her hand." She looked down at the ticket as though she was the passenger boarding the plane. "Guadalajara."

She could feel Sam noting the drive to Texas and the flight to Mexico.

"Now she's landing in Mexico," she continued as if the flight was no longer than the blink of an eye. "She's buying another ticket. Buenos Aires."

She placed her hand near her throat as if she was wearing a turtleneck and needed to loosen it. "It's so hot there. She's renting a car. Driving to a small apartment. Little more than a studio apartment—a bedroom, living-dining-kitchen are combined. On the beach." She sighed. "It's beautiful there."

"Which beach?" Sam asked matter-of-factly.

She looked for a street sign, anything that would give her a clue. "Mar de las Pampas," she said finally. "She spent the winter there. She's sitting on the beach in a lounge chair, dressed in a heavy sweater wrap, looking at the ocean."

"Is she alone?" It was Chris' voice she heard.

"No. Someone is bringing her a drink. Hotel staff, perhaps? She seems to be very well known there."

"Going on twenty minutes," Sam said. "Is she still there?"

"Wait a minute. While she's accepting the drink she's slipping a piece of paper to the waiter."

"Can you read what's on it?"

She followed the man as he crossed the beach and walked up a few short steps to the hotel. Instead of returning to the bar, he entered the men's room and slipped into a stall. She followed and watched him as he opened the paper.

"There's an email address." She recited it, spelling it as Sam copied it.

"That's a local carrier," Sam said.

Vicki continued as if she hadn't heard him, "There's a message for him: 'in case anything happens, the password is ssergnoc.' The hotel employee is pulling out his iPhone and sending the message."

"We've got to seize Brenda Carnegie. Do you see a physical address?"

Once the message had been sent, the hotel employee flushed the paper. Then Vicki moved back outside and tried to decipher the street signs. "Villa de Mar Careyes. Top floor, corner unit."

"That's enough, Vicki. Come on back."

She didn't want to leave. She felt a chill in the air even though it was summer; but the beaches were pristine and the cabana serene. She felt drawn to Brenda. She could almost see the wheels turning in her mind as she contemplated her next move.

"Return to Fort Bragg, Vicki. That's an order."

Reluctantly, she felt the sofa underneath her and the scent of the musty room.

As she opened her eyes, Chris turned to Sam. He was clearly disappointed. "We could have gotten more."

Sam looked at him with tired eyes. "She can't stay gone more than thirty minutes, tops."

"Why?" Chris cut his eyes toward Vicki.

"It's hard to explain," Sam said as she sat up, "but it's akin to jet lag. Actually, more like traveling at warp speed. There's only so much the body can take."

"But her body didn't go anywhere."

"The effects are the same. Even though she lay right there in front of us, the physical effects are the same as if she'd been driving for twenty hours, then transferring from one flight to another, and finally ending up on a beach."

Chris turned to Vicki. "So, what you're telling me," he said thoughtfully, "when Brenda and I were separated that night in Robeson County, she drove more than halfway across the country, caught a flight to Mexico and then another flight to Argentina. And she's spent the last eight or nine months living on the beach?"

Vicki nodded. "That's where I feel she is right now. But she's got this restlessness about her. Like it's time to move on."

Sam switched on the light. "Then we'll have to move fast. I'll send this up the chain and our operatives in Argentina can pick her up."

"Can she be extradited?" Chris asked.

Vicki's and Sam's eyes met. "The CIA doesn't bother with that," he said. "Most likely, she'll be put on a government plane and flown back. No one will know she's gone until she's back in our custody."

"Where will you take her? To Washington?"

"Anywhere you want her. We have facilities right here at Fort Bragg, if you need them."

Chris nodded. "So, just like that, she's ours?"

"It depends."

"On what?"

"On whether she's still there when our guys get there."

Chris nodded. He ran his hand through his hair again; his fingers, like his legs, were long.

Vicki put her head in her hands. She felt incredibly tired. Sam was right; she did feel like she had been awake for two days straight. Her back ached as though she'd been the one driving and then sitting in the cramped airline seat. And now she wanted nothing more than to close her eyes and sleep on the beach with the ocean breezes wafting over her.

"Go home," Sam said, as if reading her mind. "Get some rest."

"Can I take you to dinner?" Chris asked, helping her to her feet. There was something sensual about the way he looked at her, something so caring about the way he smiled.

"Thanks," she said, "but I think Sam's right. I need to get home. I feel completely drained."

As she looked at him, she saw the disappointment crossing his face. He had a kind look about him, she thought. He struck her as the type of man who always held the door open for a woman, was always attentive, always thoughtful. She felt guilty. Now he needed someone; he was alone and lonely. And he wanted to talk about Brenda. He was in love with her, of that she was certain. What a lucky woman, she thought. He would no doubt want to know more details about what she'd seen. And she was bone tired.

"Sam," she said, "would it bother you if I laid here on your couch for a bit?"

"Suit yourself." He turned to Chris. "It's a common side effect of remote viewing. She'll sleep for a few hours; then she'll be good enough to drive home. Tomorrow she'll be back to normal."

Sam motioned for Chris to follow him into the hall. As the door gently closed behind them, Vicki flipped off the light and lay back down. Within minutes, she was sound asleep.

5

By the time the car pulled into the driveway, the sky was already dark. Vicki sat in the driver's seat until their song finished playing. The tears were gone but in their place was an overwhelming emptiness.

The sprawling three-story home was nothing more than a void. Her footsteps would echo through the hallway, perhaps joined by the hum of the refrigerator or the air conditioner. Each room would be uninhabited, consisting of nothing more than furniture without a soul.

She wanted to back down the driveway and do what Brenda had done: drive to some distant airport, get on a plane and disappear only to reappear at an exotic beach in a glamorous city, surrounded by men without Irish accents.

Vicki took a deep breath as she contemplated her evening. Shower. Wander into the kitchen and see what Benita prepared for dinner. Maybe turn on the tube and catch an episode of… anything. Anything that put words into the air and made her feel as if someone was there with her. Anything that would make her feel less alone. And lonely.

Entering through the kitchen, she stopped at the refrigerator to find a cherry cobbler and homemade chicken pot pie with heating instructions in Benita's broken English. She pulled out the cherry cobbler, found a large spoon and prepared to carry the entire dish upstairs with her. It wasn't as if she'd have to share it with anybody anyway, she thought glumly.

She turned on the hall light as she made her way to the front of the house. It had become her custom to leave every light on. Somehow, it made her feel less alone.

Reaching the bottom of the staircase, a fragrance tickled her nostrils: Dylan's cologne. She inhaled it, her heart quickening and her stomach turning somersaults. It had no doubt been there all along but perhaps it took leaving the house and coming back for her to detect it again. She knew she'd never be able to smell that scent again without thinking of him.

She sat on one of the steps and peeled back the cover from the cobbler. Taking a small bite, she thought for a moment before pulling out her cell phone and calling Sam, who answered on the first ring.

"What's up?" his voice was curt.

"When are you letting Dylan out of Langley?" she asked.

There was a pause. "He's been gone a week, Vicki."

Vicki knew she needed to respond but each time she opened her mouth, the words wouldn't come. Finally, she clicked off the phone as a sob was wrenched from her body. She sat on the stairs and cried until the grandfather clock chimed the nine o'clock hour.

Spent and exhausted, the cobbler was left on the stairs as she made her way upstairs. She stopped on the second floor and stared at the flight leading to the third floor.

She hadn't been on that floor since that fateful night. Sam had whisked her away before Dylan's unconscious body was removed from the attic space, Aunt Laurel's dismembered corpse was carted away, and before the cleaner did his work. When he'd brought her back two days later, all the blood had been cleaned up from her bedroom and bath, the place was spotless, and Dylan was gone.

Continuing to stare at the third floor landing, she wondered what should be done with that floor. It could simply be left alone. She could pretend that floor didn't exist; it wasn't as if the extra space was needed.

In a fraction of a second, her mind was made up. She was sleeping in his bed tonight.

She wasn't going to sleep in her own bed, staring at the ceiling fan rotating above her but in his bed, surrounded by his scent. She could pretend he was still there if she wanted to. She could pull his pillow into her arms, bury her face into his sheets and hopefully find solace.

When the door opened, it felt as though he'd never left. Everything was exactly as it had been: the neat stack of *GQ* and *Coastal Living* magazines on the coffee table, his cologne bottle on the dresser, his clothes still hanging in the closet, arranged by season and color. Clothes, she now suspected, he'd obtained with Aunt Laurel's money. She buried her face in a flannel shirt and breathed deeply, trying to lose herself in its scent.

She sat on the edge of the bed and stared at the room, at the sitting area where they'd dined, at the entertainment center where he'd played such romantic songs. She lay back on the mattress, her sobs filling the air as the shadows lengthened and nighttime beckoned. And still she lay there, staring at the ceiling, tears streaming down her cheeks onto the silver and burgundy comforter beneath her.

It was too quiet. Making her way to the entertainment center, she found an exact duplicate of the CD she'd found in her car queued up.

Walking into the bathroom, Vicki turned on the shower, left her clothes in a heap on the bathroom floor and stepped into the steaming water.

As the water began to stream down her body, she began to cry again. This time, they were tears of anger.

She'd told him once it was as if she'd been bottled up all these years. And that he had uncorked the bottle, not just allowing but forcing her emotions to pour out. And she didn't know if she could ever put the genie back in the bottle again.

It would have been far better if they'd never met. If she'd never heard his smooth voice, never fallen for his lies, never felt his lips on hers. It would have been far more preferable to the pain if she'd simply continued her life bottled up and alone.

A sob was wrenched from her body. She hated what he'd done to her. Hated the way he built this perfect world around her, just to have it come crashing down. Hated the way he thought he could simply move to America, assume another's identity and take charge of another's bank accounts, and live the life he wanted to live without any regard to what was right or wrong. Hated the way he'd chosen her as part of his plan, to live with him here when he knew nothing here belonged to him. And hated the way he'd destroyed her own plans for starting over and leaving the CIA.

The sobs had turned to wails now that echoed in the close confines of the shower. She hated the way he'd seduced her. Hated the way he made himself appear so perfect when he was anything but. She hated him with every bone in her body, every muscle, every fiber—and would always hate him for what he'd done.

And now he'd be put behind her. It was time to move on to a real life with a real man and real love. And allow him to become just a distant memory and eventually, not even that.

And if he ever showed his face to her again, if he ever dared come near, she would tear him apart. Every ounce of hatred welled up now as her hands balled into fists and she leaned into the shower, blubbering with the knowledge that no one could hear her.

Finally, she turned off the shower and watched the final drips as they poured down the drain.

Reaching for the towel, she realized in her foggy state of mind, she'd neglected to bring one with her. There would be one hanging on the towel rack, and it was her house now and who cared if the floor got soaking wet.

She whipped the shower curtain open as a fresh wave of cries escaped, doubling over with the pain of a heart too large for her chest, too heavy, too burdened. She bent to her knees and bawled as she never had before.

Vicki began to feel a strange sensation, an impression that someone was watching. Raising her head, her swollen eyes blurry with her tears, she realized someone was standing just a few feet away, leaning against the bathroom vanity. Cowboy boots came into focus; boots with steel toes. Blue jeans. A light blue shirt with short sleeves from which muscular biceps emerged. A large, tanned hand holding a bath sheet in front of him, hesitantly holding it out to her.

As her eyes continued upward, she was afraid to look him in the face, afraid he would be only a figment of her imagination. But as her eyes swept upward, his dark hair came into focus. His expression was immobile, his emotions completely hidden.

"What are you cryin' for now, Woman?" he asked.

A fresh wail escaped her lips, her arms flailing to her sides, her voice once again echoing in the confines of the small room.

He was beside her in two quick steps, wrapping the bath sheet around her and drawing her close to him. "Don't cry, Darlin'," he said in his soft Irish brogue, "you know how it wrenches me heart in two. I can't stomach a woman's cries. Never have. Most likely, never will."

Vicki leaned into him, the sobs turning from those borne of hatred and sadness to those of gratitude that he was there, he was back, and he was standing there with her.

"It's all right now," he was saying as he wrapped his arms around her, the water soaking his clothing, "don't cry."

She pulled away from him and looked into his eyes. Then she blurted, "What took you so long?"

6

The moon rose high above the streets of Lumberton as Vicki lay on her side atop the bed, her head near the foot of it against a comforter balled into her hands in the throes of ecstasy. Dylan raised her head to tenderly slide a pillow underneath her before grabbing another one and lying beside her.

She stared into his eyes, not wanting to succumb to the sleep that now threatened to overtake her, afraid of closing them for even a second for fear they'd open to find him gone.

He placed his hand on her shoulder and gently stroked her skin.

Her fingers explored his jawline, caressing his five o'clock shadow. She wanted to forget everything that had gone before and everything that might happen after this one moment, and just revel in the way she felt right now, right here. She didn't care anymore what he had done or why he'd done it. Then she heard her voice as if it belonged to someone else. "Are you here to stay?"

Dylan studied his hand as it traced her shoulder and proceeded down her arm toward her torso. The longer he took to answer, the more frightened she became. When at last he looked her in the eyes, his own were misty but he quickly blinked them dry. "I didn't know if you ever wanted to see me again," he said softly.

Vicki took his hand in hers. "What took you so long to come back to me? Sam said you left Langley a week ago."

"I did." He took a deep breath. "But the last time you laid eyes on me, you shot me. You shot me not once but you shot me twice and you would'a shot me a third time if you'd a'been a better shot."

"I didn't know who you were."

"I told you the truth. Me name's Dylan Maguire. Always has been, always will be."

"But I thought—oh, you know what I thought. What you wanted me to think."

He squeezed her hand. "I was wrong. And I apologize. I never meant to do you harm."

"Did you come back to stay?"

"The truth?"

She steeled herself. "Yes."

"I came to get me clothes." He avoided looking at her, focusing his attention instead on her long, slender fingers. "I didn't think you'd want me. But when I entered the house, I could hear you cryin' all the way down the stairs. Three floors were filled with your wailin'." He kissed the tips of her fingers. "And I knew I couldn't just get me clothes and leave. I had to see you again. If you wanted nothin' to do with me, I needed to hear it from your own lips while you looked me in the eye." He took a deep breath. "So. Here's your chance, Woman. What'll it be?"

"I don't want you to go. But…"

"Yes?" he said hesitantly.

"You lied to me. We built this whole relationship based on your lies."

Dylan rolled onto his back and stared at the ceiling. He squeezed the bridge of his nose and furrowed his brows as if deep in thought. Then he abruptly sat up.

Just as she thought he was going to climb out of bed and put on his clothes and she readied herself to plead with him to stay, he turned toward her. "Aye," he said, "let's have this chat, shall we?"

His voice had changed and she opened her mouth to respond when he placed a finger on her lips. "I seem to recall a certain young lady who introduced her 'Uncle Sam' to me, knowin' full well that he wasn't her uncle. The same young lady who told me this uncle might have experienced a heart attack and left me frettin' half the day while she supposedly took off to attend him."

She opened her mouth for a second time but again he silenced her, this time with a wave of his finger, "The same young lady," he continued, "who dragged me to the hospital facilities at Fort Bragg and had me babysat by a woman she introduced as her 'Aunt Julia' but whom she'd only known a few weeks and was never related to her. All whilst she was purportedly tendin' to her dear uncle who now, on top o' a heart attack, was sufferin' from prostate cancer."

She groaned and looked away.

He placed a finger under her chin and directed it upward until she looked him in the eye. "The same little wench who told me the man I ended up murderin' for her was a stalker, all the while knowin' exactly who he was and that he'd followed her here due to her job. Which, incidentally, she never told me she had. No, instead, this little filly led me to believe she was all alone in this world and all she wanted to do was tend angelfish and live a sweet little life in a sweet little town."

"But—"

"I'm not finished with you yet," he said sternly. "I was here in this house before you. And Bennie and I had a nice little thin' goin' here, we did, nice and comfortable and easy. And then you show up and a'fore I know it, I've got an Uncle Sam and an Aunt Julia and a stalker. And then I've murdered a man in cold blood to keep him from murderin' *you*. And what do I get for me troubles? After romancin' you and lovin' you, you shoot me!"

"But—"

"And then I find meself two states over, drugged and with bullets in me and Sam standin' o'er me, tellin' me I can spend the rest o' me life in prison or I can join you and spend the rest o' it in more lies."

This time, she kept her mouth closed and waited for him to continue.

"So, you want to talk about weavin' a web o' lies, Woman? Is that what you want to discuss now, is it? Because it seems to me that we're just about even in the lyin' category."

He stopped speaking and stared at her, his eyes wide and his face flushed.

"I was doing it in the interest of national security," she said in a small voice.

He snorted. "Oh, that makes it okay for you, then, does it, because you have some political ideology, eh? You lied to me, you knew you was lyin' to me, and you still did it. So now, *now, Darlin'*," he emphasized, "don't throw it in me face that I told a lie or two to you."

The room grew silent. Dylan sat on the side of the bed and placed a hand on either side of his legs, as if to hold himself up. She watched his profile, her eyes moving over his body until she saw the bruised shoulder with an incision that hadn't yet healed, followed by a bruised thigh and another incision.

"I'm sorry I shot you," she said.

He made a sound like a grunt and turned away.

Vicki placed a hand on his back. "I really am. If I could take it back, I would. I was scared and I didn't know what else to do."

He looked at her out of the corner of his eye. "Do you know now?"

"Yes." She sat up and crawled to the side of the bed. She gently pushed him back so he was lying across the bed and then she straddled him. When she was staring him in the eyes, she said, "I know I'm madly in love with you. I know I don't feel complete unless you're in my life. And whatever relationship you claimed to have had with Aunt Laurel, it doesn't change who you are inside. And I love you for who you are. When you were gone, I've never felt so much pain in all my life."

"You're not gonna start cryin' on me again, are you now?"

"I hope I'm done crying. I hope I spend the rest of my life in your arms. Because that's where I belong."

"Do you, now?" he asked with a slow smile.

"I do."

"Then I have a little proposition for you."

"Oh?"

"If you have anythin' else you're harborin' ag'nst me, then let it out now. Let's just 'ave a real row with it, if that's what you want to do. Hit me, scream at me, curse me. But when the sun comes up, it's done. And it'll ne'er be brought up again. We put every bit o' it behind us and move forward together."

She remained sitting on top of him, looking him in the eye. He had small bags under his eyes and for the first time, she realized just how tired he must have been. If the tables had been turned and he had shot her, she knew she would never have come back. And yet here he was, ready to put it all behind him.

"So," he said, "from where I'm layin', it looks like you've got the upper hand here." He rubbed her thigh as it rested across his hips. "Go ahead. Give me your best shot. Without a gun this time, preferably."

She stared into his eyes for a long time. "I don't want to have 'a row' with you. How could you even suggest it?"

"I was hopin' you wouldn't care to take me up on it."

He placed a hand on the side of her waist and another one behind her back. With one effortless movement, he rolled her off him and onto her back. He was so large, especially in comparison with her petite figure, that he easily could have crushed her. Yet he rested his weight on his forearms, one on either side of her head, and on his knees as they brushed her legs. Then he swept his lips across hers. "Then let's pretend," he whispered, "that we've had our row. And now we're puttin' it all behind us. And there's nothin' left to do but the makin' up."

7

Vicki finished changing the water in the last tank and peered across the room at Dylan. The angel fry had reached the size of a nickel and it was time to cull them. She was so relieved that he'd returned, not only for the personal reasons she'd made quite obvious to him, but also for guidance in the fish house.

She watched as he patiently netted a fish, trapping it against the glass. Then he studied it for a brief moment before transferring it to one of two tanks that had been set up temporarily in the aisle.

He caught her watching him and said as he netted the next one, "Cullin' is considered the worst part o' the job. It's when a breeder takes a critical look at each little fishie and determines whether it should live or die." He motioned for her to join him. When she did, he gestured to the fish he had trapped against the glass. "This is a perfect specimen," he said.

As they looked at the beautiful black and white marbled angel, he continued, "It's twice as tall as it is long. Its fins are well formed, and it shows no signs o' damage." He transferred it to one of the other tanks.

"Now this," he said, trapping another one, "would be an argument in favor o' cullin'. The body is football shaped. The fins are translucent, which means they won't show up well in a display tank." He transferred it to a different tank.

Vicki peered into the tank, where half the fish had been placed. "You're not going to kill these fish, are you?" she said, feeling sick in the pit of her stomach.

He laughed softly and paused to look at her. "Don't worry, Darlin'," he said. "I can't kill the poor creatures. Most breeders would've put a chemical in that tank so when they went in, they'd die. But who am I to say that because the little fella's fins lack color or his body's a bit squat, that he doesn't deserve to live?"

"So, what will you do with them?"

"I'm puttin' together a list o' retailers who'll buy 'em, five for a dollar. Plus shippin', o' course. They'll most likely sell 'em for full price. Somebody'll buy 'em and be quite pleased."

"You have a good heart," she said as she watched him catch another fish. He didn't answer and after a moment of silence, she said, "So, would you mind me talking to you as you work?"

"O' course not."

"It won't break your concentration?"

"What do you want to talk about?"

Vicki took a deep breath. It was a subject she'd wanted to broach ever since he'd returned, but never could find the appropriate time. She was beginning to get impatient with herself, and knew she had to get this off her chest.

"Well?"

"Are you going to work for the CIA?" she asked.

"That's the plan."

"What will you be doing?"

"I don't rightly know, to be quite honest. But they're payin' me good money to do nothin'."

She felt a chill racing across her skin. "They don't pay you for nothing," she said hesitantly. "Sometimes the price of working for them is quite high."

"Is it now?"

"Did Sam tell you what I do?"

"He did." He kept his eyes on the fish but seemed to study it a moment longer than he had the others.

"Do you think I'm crazy?"

He transferred the fish into one of the other tanks and paused to look her in the eye. "Not at all. I take it you've never been to Ireland?"

"No. What does that have to do with—?"

"There's a thin' in Ireland called 'fey'—ever heard o' it?"

"No."

He returned to the original tank, where he snared another. As he studied it, he said, "For generations, the Irish 'ave believed in the powers o' some people to do—well, to do the unexplained. What you would call psychics, I suppose."

"Have you ever known anyone—personally, that is—who had psychic abilities?"

He caught a couple of fish without answering her. Though he seemed to focus on the tiny angels, she got the sense he was weighing his words from the way he held his mouth and avoided her eyes.

There had to have been more than a hundred fish in the tank, and he'd already done at least a hundred in another tank. As he wiped his forehead with the back of his arm, she grabbed a hand towel and dabbed at the perspiration.

"Seems to me," he said, "it's mostly women who 'ave the gift. Me gran'mum had it. So did—someone else I knew. Though I thought she was bonkers at the time. Turned out, she knew more than I did." His last sentence was said with a sigh and more than a hint of sadness.

"Did they ever go into trances?"

"No. Thin's just kind o' came to 'em. Hunches, intuition. Though it often turned out to be much more than that."

"Well," she said, taking a deep breath, "my 'gift' if that's what you want to call it, is my soul can travel anywhere in the world. I can see things that we can't see standing right here in the fish house. But they're very real and they're really happening."

"Like?"

She swallowed. "I don't know if you remember the time when I first came here and you found me talking to Sam in here?"

"I do."

"I was coming out of a trance. I was gathering intelligence."

He paused for a moment, stood up and stretched his back. "This is back breakin' work," he said. "You wouldn't think it, lookin' at one little fishie after another. But it is." He rested the net on top of one of the tanks while he looked at her. "So the American government, they believe in this, do they?"

"Not everybody. There are supporters in Congress. And there are detractors."

"I see."

"So, what Sam wants me to do is continue this work for the CIA. I'd stay here, live here and work here, just like I've been doing… But every now and then, he'd come by or have me go to Fort Bragg and I'd have a mission."

"A mission, I presume, is when you do your magic."

"It's not magic."

He shrugged. "Call it what you will."

"I sketch what I see. They send the sketches up the channels, some analyst deciphers it and adds it to other intelligence, and it forms a picture or a story that helps our government."

He nodded. "And they pay you good money for this, do they?"

"They do."

"Hmm." He returned to catching fish. "So, you really feel as though you can travel to another place, see somethin' hundreds o' miles away?"

"Yes."

"Then tell me somethin', Darlin'." He transferred a fish and then rested with his hands on the edge of the tank as he looked at her. "When I was at Langley, did you visit me there?"

"Would you be angry with me if I had?"

"That's not answerin' me question. Now is it?"

She looked at him silently.

"If I said I wouldn't be angry, would you tell me the truth?" he asked.

"Yes."

"Yes, you'd tell me the truth or yes, you visited me?"

"Both."

"I thought so."

Her heart quickened. "Could you see me?"

"No. But I thought I felt you one night. I was layin' in bed, thinkin' about everythin'. Thinkin' about us. And I felt like I wasn't alone anymore. Like you were there, beside me."

"Did that bother you?"

"Only in the sense that you'd shot me."

"We agreed not to talk about that."

"Well, you asked." He gestured toward the back room. "Get some bags, lass. We're gettin' these fish ready for the post."

She disappeared into the storage room, emerging a minute later with several sturdy plastic bags and a cooler. Grabbing a large plastic container and joining him, she filled the container with water from the tank and then hung it on the outside edge. He netted each fish again and placed them into the container. Once it was full, she poured the fish and the water into a plastic bag, added a spritz of de-stressing liquid and used the aerator to add oxygen before sealing it up and placing it into the cooler.

"You've gotten quite good at that," Dylan said.

"So, did it bother you that I was there?"

"As I recall," he said, his eyes focused on catching the fish, "I was in me skivvies. I knew you'd seen more o' me than that." He glanced up. "And to be quite honest, it was comfortin' to me."

"I watched you," she said softly. "I wanted you to feel me there beside you."

"You watched me, did you?"

"Yes."

He paused to look at her. Then, "We must hurry now, if we're to get these fishies to the post today."

She transferred the next batch of fish into a plastic bag, aerated and sealed it. Yes, she thought, it was good having him back.

8

An insistent ringing roused her from a deep sleep.

Vicki felt Dylan's arm leaving her as he rolled over and answered his cell phone. With his warmth gone, she felt an immediate chill. "Aye. No. Just sleepin'," he said as she rolled over. He was rummaging around on the nightstand, pausing when he found his wristwatch.

She peered over his shoulder. It was a quarter till midnight.

"Sam," he mouthed. Then he said into the phone, "Now?"

He glanced toward the front of the house. Then he made his way to the front windows and pulled back the drapery just enough to look outside. "Aye," he said. "I'll be down straightaway." He clicked off the phone and walked to the dresser.

"What's happening?" she asked groggily.

"Go back to sleep, Darlin'," he said. "It's just Sam. He's downstairs waitin' for me. I guess I'll find out what it is that I do tonight."

"But it's the middle of the night."

"I'm sure I shan't be long." He slipped on a pair of underwear and grabbed some socks before disappearing into the walk-in closet. When he returned a moment later, he was clad in blue jeans, a denim shirt and cowboy boots. He leaned over the bed and kissed her. "Keep the bed warm for me. And I promise I'll be back as soon as I can."

When he entered the hallway and closed the door softly behind him, the air had changed. Where they'd been sleeping peacefully just minutes earlier, she was now unable to relax. The front door closed downstairs and a car started up outside. Then it was gone all too quickly, and she was left alone with the void.

Snuggling into the covers, she found herself tossing and turning. The grandfather clock in the downstairs hallway chimed the midnight hour and then one o'clock and two o'clock. She rose several times and looked out the window, hoping they'd returned and were sitting out front talking. But the street was empty.

They converged on the tiny manufactured home with surgical precision, parking the vehicles a block away and making their way through the woods under the soft moonlight. Dylan's eyes swept over the terrain as they neared it: a clothesline stretched across the back yard and train tracks ran diagonally just beyond the house. It was so close to the storage shed that it was a wonder the trains' vibrations didn't knock it down.

They separated as they left the woods and entered the yard. Sam and two other men went to the front of the house. Two more were positioned on each side. Only Dylan was left in the back. He leaned against a large metal trash barrel and waited.

The lot was pie shaped, perhaps only thirty feet deep from the back of the house to the railroad tracks. Directly beyond those was a wide ditch. He knew why he was the only one stationed here. If the suspect tried to escape, he reasoned, he would most likely run to either side because to flee to the rear would be sheer folly. He'd have to run down the railroad tracks, which would be slow and laborious, or he'd cross them and end up in the ditch. He'd have to wade to the other side, a mere six to eight feet, but enough to slow him down. Once on the other side, he'd have to climb out of it, which would be no easy feat.

Aye, Dylan thought, he was in a good spot to observe but chances were that's all he'd do. Then they'd transport the suspect and with any luck at all, he'd be back home straight-away and breathin' in the perfume of Vicki's long, soft hair.

He heard the men breaking through the front door, followed by shouting as they entered the house.

A train whistle blew about a mile away. He watched the bold white light as it snaked through the countryside and wondered how the inhabitants around here ever achieved any sleep.

Then a back window opened and a man crawled out. Dylan glanced around him but he was the only one within sight of him. He shouted to the others as he raced toward him. But instead of dropping to the ground as he expected or giving up and climbing back inside, he scampered to the roof. Then to Dylan's astonishment, he jumped to the storage shed and was poised to jump on the train as it passed by.

Dylan continued shouting as he hurried across the yard but the train's whistle drowned out his voice. Reaching the shed, he tried to scramble to the roof but the sides were made of vertical vinyl siding that made it impossible to gain a foothold.

In his peripheral vision, he was vaguely aware of an agent popping his head out of a window and of another running toward them. He gave a fleeting glance around but he realized he wouldn't have time to pile anything against the building to assist him in climbing up. The train was approaching too quickly.

He rushed to the side closest to the tracks and got ready to grab him as he jumped. It was only a few feet but if he held his arms above his head, the man would have to clear Dylan's hands to make the leap. And that would be next to impossible.

At the last moment as the train rounded the final bend and headed toward the shed, the man ran to the opposite end where another agent was clambering to the roof. Dylan dropped his arms and peered around the side of the building, ready to grab him if he jumped down. But as the train came alongside, he took a running start across the roof. In seconds, he was airborne.

Dylan could feel the gust of wind between the train and the shed as he threw his arms in the air. His fingers grasped the man's baggy pajama bottoms and he held onto them, trying to grab his foot. But as the man continued like a projectile, the pants slipped off. As the train rolled past, Dylan was left with the material in his hand as he watched the now naked man running across the top of the train toward the front.

Dylan swore under his breath as he ran after the train. Coming alongside it, he managed to clutch a ladder. Just as he thought he'd be unable to keep up the pace, he lifted his feet onto the bottom rung and held on.

All he could see now was the boxcar staring him in the face. The train was picking up speed as it continued further into the countryside. Glancing behind him to see if any of the other agents had managed to also climb aboard, he saw them converging next to the train tracks. At least two of them were moving their mouths and waving their arms but he was unable to hear them over the roar of the engine.

He climbed up the ladder and peered over the top. The man was two cars ahead of him, lying prone, clutching a piece of metal protruding from the roof.

Dylan moved onto the roof and looked ahead. They were heading into a straight piece of track but shortly beyond that, it took a sharp turn. If he was going to catch him, he had to do it now.

He took a deep breath and lumbered across the train roof. Reaching the next car, he jumped to that roof, crouching as he landed to keep from rolling off. The man was now just one car away.

The bend was coming up too quickly. He redoubled his efforts, finally jumping to the car where the man lay prone.

The man held onto the metal roof but turned his head in Dylan's direction, obviously realizing he would need to move from his position or be overtaken.

Dylan continued moving up on him as the man came shakily to his feet. Both of them moved clumsily forward. As they passed between a row of trees, Dylan thought he would try to jump into the branches but thankfully they sped past and the trees were soon behind them.

There were only a few feet between them now. Four more steps and he would be upon him. Three. Then two.

He thrust his hand out, grabbing onto the man's forearm just as the train blew its whistle. In the corner of his eye, Dylan could see a railroad crossing approaching fast and a car stopped at the tracks. As Dylan tried to close the gap between them, the man jumped.

Dylan's hand instinctively closed tighter around his forearm. He heard the bone crack as they both went airborne. The man yelped in pain, his arm twisted grotesquely behind him. Then he was landing on the windshield of the car, his head crashing through the glass.

Dylan landed on his side squarely on top of him, pushing both of them further through the windshield amidst the screams of a carload of people. The air was knocked out of him and he gasped as pain shot through his chest and ribs. Glass was flying around them and he was covered in blood.

Then both of them were pulled out of the car onto the hood.

With every breath, he felt a sharp pain radiating through his body. He was vaguely aware that he was being half-carried to another vehicle. He heard someone moaning and it took him several seconds to realize it was his own voice he heard. As the car door slammed behind him, he doubled up in pain as they sped away.

It wasn't until the first rays of sunshine lightened the room that Vicki fell into an exhausted sleep.

She found herself in a hallway where the floor and the walls were stark white. The overhead lights were intense, reminding her of the type of lighting used in surgery. It might have been a hospital except the rooms on either side contained picture windows to the hall.

Vicki moved at a snail's pace. Each room was set up identically, containing a centered metal table with two chairs on either side. They were bathed in white light that illuminated the tile floor, the stark walls and a sterile-looking counter that ran along one side.

A single door monopolized the end of the corridor. She held her hand against it. He was there. She knew it.

Her hand melted through the door, followed by her arm and then her body. Reaching the other side, she hesitated and tried to orient herself.

A man was slumped in the center of the room, his wrists and ankles cuffed to a metal chair, the strands of his dark hair matted with blood.

Sam tilted his chin up with one gloved finger and examined his face. His eyes, as always, were impassive. His forehead was lined and the bags under his eyes had grown larger and puffier, the only evidence that he was tired. He spoke but Vicki couldn't make out the words. When he removed his finger, the man's head slumped forward again.

Vicki stared at the man's back, afraid to move closer to determine whether it was Dylan. As she moved one foot in front of the other, a movement caught her eye and she turned toward her left.

A counter against the wall contained a set of neatly arranged knives. They were large, formidable and glistening under the harsh lights as they rested on white cotton cloths.

In front of the counter was a barstool and perched atop of it was Dylan.

She moved toward him and studied his profile. Though his body was oriented toward Sam and the man in the chair, his head was turned in the opposite direction, as if he was purposefully avoiding watching the scene as it unfolded before him. His expression was totally blank, the immobile face of one trained not to show emotion. One foot rested on the chair slat, raising his knee higher than the other, and he had one arm casually stretched over it as if he was sitting on a street corner chatting with old friends.

In the background, she could hear Sam swearing. She knew Dylan could hear it, also; Sam was particularly loud and more obnoxious than she'd ever heard him. But Dylan's expression did not change as his eyes rolled over the set of knives.

She reached out her hand to caress his arm but before she touched him, Sam said, "It's time."

Dylan immediately rose. With the same dispassionate expression, he selected a long knife with a hooked blade. He walked toward the man as Sam stepped to the side. He was neither in a hurry nor was he dragging his feet. His steps were measured, deliberate.

He stopped in front of the chair.

Vicki awakened, gasping for air.

9

Benita was speaking Spanish as Vicki entered the kitchen. She pointed toward the sink, the dishwasher and the counter as she continued her rapid-fire speech.

"What's wrong?" Vicki asked.

Benita said a few more words in Spanish before stopping and putting her hand on her hip. "Have you seen my knives?" she asked, pointing.

She followed her gaze to the countertop where a knife block contained a lone paring knife.

"Dylan said something about sharpening them," she said, making her way toward the kitchen table.

"Where is he? I can't make food with no knives."

"He had an errand to run, but he'll be back any time now."

"Where are my knives?"

"I don't know where he put them," Vicki answered, pulling out a chair and sitting down. She sat facing the counter, her eyes riveted on the knife block. "But he'll be back long before supper."

Benita continued her rat-a-tat diatribe as she marched down the hallway toward the laundry room.

Vicki's plate remained untouched, her hands folded in her lap and her eyes glued to the slots where the knives should have been.

She barely heard the front door closing and by the time she detected the heavy footsteps in the hall, Dylan's broad shoulders entered the room. He slammed the knives into the block without turning toward her.

"Dylan?" she said.

"I don't want to talk." His voice was curt and in an instant, he had disappeared from the kitchen and was heading back down the hallway.

Vicki followed, catching a glimpse of him as he rounded the newel post at the end of the hall. "Dylan!"

"I said I don't want to talk!"

She halted, watching his boots rush up the stairs two at a time. Benita returned to the kitchen and said "Oh!" pleasantly. Vicki turned toward the kitchen, resting her hand on one of the spindles for a brief second before abruptly spinning around and making her way up the stairs. The bedroom door slammed shut on the third floor before she was halfway to the second, but she was undeterred.

Reaching the third floor bedroom, she opened the door to find one of Dylan's boots discarded by the bed. She picked it up and continued, finding the second boot at the foot and his clothes removed in a disheveled procession toward the bathroom. Her pace slowed as she gathered each article and inspected it.

The boots appeared the same as always. But the clothes were covered in dried blood.

As he turned on the shower, she stuffed the clothes under the bed. Benita couldn't be allowed to see them; when she left this evening, Vicki would either wash them or destroy them. She placed the boots just inside the closet where Dylan always kept them.

Then she made her way toward the bathroom. The door was ajar and she slipped inside.

The shower curtain was not pulled all the way and as Vicki leaned against the vanity, she had a clear view. He stood with his left profile visible, his head leaning into the water, his right hand against the far wall. He placed his left hand over his face, squeezing the bridge of his nose for so long that Vicki wondered if he was going to move. Then slowly he shifted his hand to his forehead and rubbed the area between his brows.

Dylan seemed to realize he was not alone and glanced in her direction.

"Hand me a towel, Darlin'," he said. "Please."

While Vicki grabbed a towel, he turned off the water. When she returned to the shower, he was still standing in the same position. As he leaned toward the front of the tub, his right hand slipped a fraction. A streak of watered-down blood appeared on the shower wall where his hand had been.

He glanced in her direction again. Spotting the towel, he reached out his left hand and she stepped forward and handed it to him. He did not turn toward her and she stepped back until her backside hit the edge of the vanity and stopped her.

"Be a darlin' and pull down the covers for me?" he asked.

"The—the bed?"

"I'm goin' to take a wee bit o' a nap. I was longer than expected."

"Yes. Well. I'll go turn down the covers."

She felt as though she was drifting through a dream. Her breathing was labored but the words that she wanted to say, the questions she wanted to ask, felt stuck in her throat. Realizing the bedroom door was still open, she made her way around the bed and closed the door.

When she turned back around, Dylan was already lying on the opposite side of the bed. He held the towel to the right side of his head as he rubbed his hair, drying it even as his head hit the pillow. The bath sheet covered the right side of his body.

He gestured for her to join him.

"Lie down with me, Darlin'," he said. "Please."

She kicked off her shoes and started to unbutton her blouse.

"No, sweetheart," he said, "don't bother takin' your clothes off. Just lie here with me."

She climbed into bed and leaned in to kiss him but he placed his hand on her chest and pushed her toward the bed.

"Lie down," he said. "Lie on your side. Let me cuddle up to you."

She felt as if her breath had been cut off as she turned her back to him. He slid against her and wrapped his arm around her. She started to turn back toward him, but his arm tightened around her, rendering her immobile.

She could hear his breathing against the back of her neck as he buried his face in her hair. Then she heard a muffled sound.

"Dylan?" she asked.

His arm tightened further, holding her like a steel vise. Then his body shook slightly but for so long a time that she tried to turn around again but couldn't.

"Are you crying?" she whispered hoarsely.

"No!" His voice was sharp, his answer instantaneous, as he continued holding her in his grip.

Long after he'd grown silent and still, her brain was abuzz. When his arm relaxed, she stroked it lightly. He didn't respond and she inched her way out from under him, crawling out of bed before turning to look at him.

The bath sheet had fallen away, revealing his right side. She stifled a gasp as she looked at him. His face was bruised from his right eye to his cheekbone. And as her eyes followed the curve of his body, she realized his right shoulder and his entire torso was turning deep red. Even his thigh and knee were bruised.

She put her hand over her mouth and choked back tears. Grabbing her cell phone, she left the room silently, closing the door gently behind her.

Hurrying across the hall to the opposite door, Vicki slipped inside the unfinished room and hit the speed dial.

Sam answered on the first ring. "Yeah?" he said tiredly.

"What the hell did you do to Dylan?"

He paused before answering. "Did he put you up to this?"

"Did he—? No. He doesn't even know I'm calling."

"Where is he?"

"Here. At home."

"What's he doing?"

"Sleeping. What's going on? What happened last night?"

"Look, Vicki," he said, "calm down. Do yourself a favor. And do Dylan an even bigger favor. Don't ask him any questions."

"What? Have you seen his condition?"

"He had a little mishap."

"Did you torture him?"

"Did I—? No. Absolutely not. Nobody did."

"Oh, he just did that to himself, I suppose?"

"I told you. He had a little mishap."

"That was not a little mishap," Vicki said, fighting back tears. "A little mishap is tripping on a curb. The entire side of his body is bruised. I—I don't know if he has broken bones. I don't know the extent of any internal damage—"

"He's gonna be okay, Vicki."

"Has he seen a doctor?"

"No." His voice was forceful. "And don't you dare take him to a hospital."

"What?"

"He refused to see a doctor. One of ours. He can't go to an outside doctor, Vicki. We can't have any questions raised. Do you understand me?"

She looked out the window. Sandy was watering her flowers in a skin-tight halter top and a pair of shorts that barely covered her derriere. She turned away from the window and took a deep breath. "What am I supposed to do with him?"

"Don't do anything with him. He's resting, right?"

"For now."

"When he comes to, he'll know what to do—ice, pain killers. He'll tell you what he needs. If he takes a turn for the worse, call me. We'll get a doctor there, to the house, and we'll take care of everything."

"Like you took care of everything last night? What the hell were you doing, Sam? I trusted you. *He* trusted you."

His voice sounded bored and tired. "Vicki, you cannot ask him what happened. Do you hear me? He can't tell you. He can't compromise the mission."

"I have a top secret security clearance, Sam."

"But you don't have a need to know. And you don't want to know. Just do this one thing—not for me. For him. Don't put him in a position where he has to argue with you or compromise the mission—and himself. Just be there for him."

"Just be there for him?" She wiped a tear from her cheek. "I don't know what I'm there *for*. I don't know what happened!"

"You don't need to know. You don't *want* to know."

"You swear to me, he was not tortured."

"I swear to you."

"You did not lay a hand on him."

"I did not."

"You did not allow anyone else to lay a hand on him."

"He had a mishap, Vicki. I already told you."

"I don't know what a 'mishap' is!"

"You don't need to know. Look," he said, growing exasperated. "We're running around in circles with this. Get yourself busy—do something. Your fish job. Whatever. Just let him rest. Give him space. And don't ask questions."

10

Vicki stood inside the bedroom door and tried to catch her breath. She'd been up and down the stairs at least a dozen times throughout the day; three times just in the past half hour. Now she surveyed a tray where she'd assembled assorted over-the-counter pain killers, a cooler filled with ice and plastic storage bags for makeshift compresses. Another tray contained their dinner and a bottle of wine.

The front door closed, announcing Benita's departure. Vicki had instructed her to stay out of the bedroom, explaining that Dylan was coming down with the flu. Benita couldn't see him this way. No one could.

She glanced at her watch. It was five minutes past six, which meant he'd been sound asleep for nearly ten hours.

Sitting on the bed and leaning toward him, she touched him lightly on the shoulder. "Sweetheart?" she said.

He jerked to a seated position, his eyes wide. Seeing her there, he immediately reached for the covers.

Vicki touched his arm. "I've seen you."

He groaned and lay on his back. He rubbed his hand across his eyes. "What time is it?"

"Just after six."

"In the mornin'?"

"At night. It's suppertime."

He groaned again.

She lay down beside him. "I told Benita you might have the flu. She made chicken and dumplings for you. It's on the coffee table."

He glanced toward the sitting area.

"And I brought you some pain killers—aspirin, ibuprofen, whatever you want. And ice."

He avoided looking at her. "So, you've seen me bruises, 'ave you?"

"Yes. And I'm not going to ask any questions. I'm just here if you need me."

"I couldn't answer your questions even if I wanted to."

"I know."

He reached his good arm around her and pulled her toward him. "I'm thinkin'," he said, "I'm understandin' when you said the price o' workin' for Sam can be too high."

"Are you having second thoughts?"

"I had second thoughts the moment I had the first thought." He squeezed her shoulder. "But I don't think I have much o' a choice now, do I?"

"I tried to leave when I moved here."

"Aye, and we've seen just how well that worked out."

"This is all my fault," Vicki said.

"It's nobody's fault." He was silent for a moment. "But I'm settin' a ground rule."

"Oh?"

"Don't use your fey to watch me at work. Are you understandin' me?"

"Why not?"

"Because you wouldn't like me whilst I'm workin'." He rubbed his forehead. "I don't like meself when I'm workin'."

"I won't watch you and I won't ask you any questions about your assignments. And you'll agree not to ask me anything about mine. It's not that I don't want to tell you—"

"I know," he interrupted. "It's that you can't tell me. I'm understandin' a bit more o' that now."

She lay with her head against his shoulder as he absent-mindedly stroked her back. She'd been right, she thought. The price was too high. And something deep inside her was screaming that the price was about to get even higher.

11

The ceiling fan created a lazy breeze, stirring up a fresh floral scent that surrounded the front porch. The sky was growing darker to the south and as Vicki glanced up from her seat on the porch swing, she wondered when the storm would reach Lumberton. Her view was partially blocked by a van with a sports equipment store name emblazoned on the side. It had arrived early that morning with a delivery for Dylan, and the men had been hard at work the better part of the day installing weight lifting and exercise equipment in a spare bedroom on the second floor.

She turned her attention to her laptop as she reread Sam's email. He was sending requests up the chain of command in an effort to unseal adoption records for her younger siblings, but he cautioned that it could take time. He listed each one and asked her to verify their names, dates and places of birth and her parents' names.

The first one listed was Ryan, the youngest of the four children and eight years younger than Vicki. Josh was next, who was two years younger and the oldest of the twins by fifteen minutes. Last was Annie, the youngest twin. She'd been ten years old when they were sent to separate foster homes. It had been the last time they'd seen each other, and she still remembered it like it was yesterday.

They'd been allowed to stay together for a few brief weeks after their parents' airplane accident. A neighbor had taken them in while social services tried to contact the next of kin. As brilliant as her father had been, his brother was exactly the opposite, an alcoholic incapable of hanging onto a job for any length of time. The last thing he wanted was to be saddled with four children.

Her mother's sisters were unable to take them as well. One sister had remained in Paris, too busy with her jet-setting social life to even attend the funerals. The other was in college; too young, inexperienced and student-loan-poor to raise them.

So they had gone to four separate foster homes and over the next two years, they had been adopted by four different families. The day social services had appeared at the neighbor's home had been the last time the four of them had been together. One minute they were playing touch football in the back yard and the next, they were crying as they were separated.

As the oldest, Vicki had felt it her duty to stay in touch with them, to monitor what happened to them, and to eventually pull them back together. But she'd been only twelve years old when they were separated, too young to do anything about their situation. And after the others had been adopted, she had been taken in by Sam and the CIA and trained as a psychic spy.

Now would be the perfect time to find them. She was twenty-eight, which meant Annie and Josh would be twenty-six and little Ryan, twenty. It was time to reunite them.

She verified the dates of birth and the place—all were born in Washington, DC—and her parents' names. Then the email was off to Sam. He would get it on his smartphone and hopefully he would rush it through the channels.

She closed the laptop but kept it in her lap as she swayed in the porch swing. Summer was coming to a close. The days were getting shorter; soon they would be forced to turn on the heat in the fish house to maintain the constant eighty degree temperature required.

Sam had not called her for another remote viewing session. There was a rule among psychic spies never to work on two assignments at once; the possibility was too great for two cases to become intertwined, leading to faulty results.

She remembered one case in which a co-worker was asked to penetrate a nuclear facility within Russia. As he worked on drawing the diagrams and providing information on the volume of energy produced and the number and types of warheads, unbeknownst to Sam, he was also trying to locate an old flame from his college days using his psychic gift. He found the old flame working in a hospital. The problem, though, was he drew the nuclear facilities with offices that didn't exist, laboratories and surgery rooms, and additional floors that couldn't be verified. He'd confused the hospital with the nuclear plant and the result was a total fiasco.

But now that she was between assignments, she thought, she could use her own psychic gift to locate a sibling.

Which one was an easy decision: Annie. Their parents always marveled that they were sisters at all, because they couldn't have been more different. Vicki was the good girl, always doing what was expected of her. Annie was a hellion. She seemed to have no remorse for anything she did wrong, but she could be so charming and she was so beautiful that people always made allowances for her. On many a summer night, she'd catch her climbing out the upstairs window to explore, returning just before dawn to climb the oak tree and sneak back inside. She loved reading about guns and espionage, but her real talent lay in computer technology. As brilliant as their father had been, Annie could write programs before the age of ten. The problem was she gravitated toward the dark side, to hacking and writing viruses just for the fun of it.

Her given name was Brenda Anne Boyd. But they loved the movie *Annie* and because her sister had a thick volume of wavy copper tresses, they'd all taken to calling her Annie.

Vicki wondered what her teen years must have been like. She chuckled, thinking of the parents who'd adopted such a gorgeous little girl only to find she could be the devil in disguise. They would have had their work cut out for them.

Yes, it would be Annie she'd try to locate first. While Sam was going through the conventional method of getting the adoption records unsealed, she would go the unconventional route—she'd find her through her own personal psychic missions.

The sound of men's voices wafted through the screen door, growing in volume as they approached.

"Ah, there you are, Darlin'." The screen door opened as Dylan stepped onto the front porch. He held the door open for two men, who said their good-byes on the way to the van. Dylan stepped to the porch railing and watched them drive away as Vicki studied his profile. It had been a week since his assignment. They'd watched his bruises turn a rainbow of colors and now they were barely visible. But at her insistence, Sam arranged a visit with a doctor at Fort Bragg and they'd discovered he had two cracked ribs. They had no choice but to let nature take its course. She was learning Dylan had a high threshold for pain; he rarely wanted anything more than a glass of wine to ease the soreness.

"Everything installed upstairs?" Vicki asked.

"It is," he said, resting his hand on the railing and turning toward her. "I'm quite pleased. I have what they call a home gym w' five hundred pounds o' weights, a treadmill, several other aerobic machines—but me favorite—ooh, me favorite is the boxin' equipment. I'll get plenty o' use out o' that, I will."

A vehicle pulled in front of the house and he stepped off the front porch to retrieve the afternoon newspaper as the deliveryman cordially held it out his window for him. As the car moved to the next house, Dylan made his way back to the porch and joined her on the swing. "Ah, now this is the life," he said. "Here I sit with me darlin' in perfect weather on a freshly painted porch in front o' our very own home."

"Almost our very own home," she corrected gently. "And it looks like we might get a storm. Not to rain on your parade or anything."

"You couldn't even if you tried," he said. He started to open the newspaper and then stopped and stared at the railing. "I seem to recall…" he began. He cocked his head quizzically.

"Yes, there was a spindle missing. It's been added."

"Did you—?"

"Alec. He wanted to be helpful while you were 'in Ireland'."

He started to laugh. "Well, then, we must properly thank him." He stared at it once more and then laughed again. "Imagine. A detective helpin' to hide the murder weapon."

Vicki set the laptop on the table next to the swing.

"Doin' anythin' interestin'?" he asked.

"Yes. Actually I am. I'm going to find my sister Annie."

"Ooh," he said, pronouncing the word as if it was two syllables, "I'm pleased to hear that. I think you need to find her and your brothers, too. And put your family back together."

"I'm going to use my psychic skills to find her. Will you help me?"

"I wouldn't know what to do."

"I can show you what Sam does."

"Then I could be his replacement someday," he joked.

"That could be interesting."

He opened the newspaper. "Aye, it—" he stopped.

"What is it?"

"Oh, nothin'," he said, turning the page quickly. "Nothin' at'al."

"It is too something." She grabbed at the paper but he held it just beyond her reach. "Don't do that. Are you in the paper?"

"No. I am not in the paper."

"That's a good sign."

"Aye. It is." He stood up. "I think it's just about time for supper."

As he started toward the door, Vicki scrambled after him, ducking under his arm and arriving at the screen door ahead of him. She held out her hand. "Let me see it."

"You know what? It's nothin'." He held up half of the front page. "Just the work they're doin' on the Northeast Park."

"That was not what you were looking at and you know it. Don't hide it from me."

"You don't want to see it."

"Yes, I do."

"No, you don't."

"Yes. I do."

"Trust me. You don't."

"Will you stop it?" She grabbed the paper out of his hand. Before he could take it from her, she'd ducked under his arm again. "*Teenagers Charged with Falsifying Police Report,*" she read. "This is what you were trying to keep from me?"

"I'm goin' inside and get our supper. And when you're done bein' a busybody, maybe you'll grace me w' your fine presence."

Vicki barely registered the door opening and Dylan entering the house as she read the article. When she was finished, she stood next to the railing and stared at the front lawn without really seeing it as she processed the information: seven days ago, a carload of inebriated teenagers were driving home from a party in the middle of the night. They claimed to have stopped at a railroad crossing as a train came through when they spotted two men running across the top of the train, one chasing the other. As they reached the car, the first man fell onto the car's windshield, almost tumbling through it, and the second man jumped off the train onto the car to catch him, falling on top of him. The report went on to say that another car filled with men showed up almost immediately, pulled the two men off the teens' car and shoved them into another vehicle. When the train passed, the terrorized teenagers drove home and told their parents what they'd seen.

The problem, however, was there was no evidence of any scuffle. The police arrived at the conclusion that anyone tumbling through the windshield would have required immediate medical attention, and yet no hospitals reported any injuries consistent with what the teenagers had seen. The two men seemed to have disappeared into thin air—and there were no reported sightings of any other vehicle filled with men. So they had arrived at a further conclusion: that the whole story had been fabricated to cover the fact that the teenagers themselves wrecked the car while driving drunk.

Seven days ago, Vicki calculated. Seven days.

She strolled to the recycle bin beside the garage, depositing the newspaper in it. Then she turned toward the house. Dylan would be waiting on her. And she mustn't keep him waiting.

12

Her back was pinned against the wall, her chest heaving with her exertions. Dylan held her immobilized wrists on either side of her head, and regardless how she struggled against him she could not budge either one. Her muscles were aching with the effort and she could feel her face becoming flushed.

"Let me go," she begged.

"You must learn how to defend y'self," Dylan said.

"But I can't." She looked at his hand covering her wrist. She felt small and frail while he seemed to restrain her without the least bit of effort.

"Well, you can't if all you're aimin' to do is wiggle your fingers."

She rolled her eyes. "I told you. I can't do more. You're too strong."

He leaned into her and chuckled. "Darlin', you just never know when you might 'ave a need to defend y'self. And right now, I'm seein' that all your feet are doin' is keepin' you vertical."

"But—"

"Look," he said, taking half a step back and motioning his head toward his feet. "The first thin' you could do is stomp your foot right atop 'o mine. Aim for the soft part o' the foot behind me toes, right between me big toe and the second one. Use the heel o' your shoe. Women, in particular, can 'ave such monstrous heels on their shoes. They're weapons all on their own. Go ahead. Try it."

She gingerly pushed down on the top of his foot.

He laughed. "You call that a stomp? It felt like a mosquito."

"I don't want to hurt you."

"When someone's attackin' you, you must be bloodthirsty y'self. You're tryin' to inflict real harm to the person so's they'll let you go. Then once you're free, the goal is to get away from him as swiftly as possible." He held up one foot. "Another thin' you can do is give him a solid, swift kick in the leg. Right here, in the fleshy part below the knee, is a good spot. Or in the shin."

She raised her foot against his shin.

"With your toes. Your heel on his foot but your toes against the shin."

She kicked him.

"You're not even tryin'."

"I told you, I don't want to hurt you."

He pressed his lips against the tip of her nose. "You can't hurt me, Darlin'. Many have tried."

"Let me go."

"One more. The groin. It's the most sensitive part of a man's body. A good, swift kick to the groin should 'ave him doubled over in pain. It'll buy you the time needed to get away."

"I'm tired of this game."

"It's not a game. If you want me to let you go, then you'll have to stop me."

She stared into his eyes. They were normally hazel but today they appeared very green with just a few flecks of gold scattered throughout. He smiled, causing his eyes to become half-moons accented by laugh lines.

"You have the power," he said gently.

She inhaled. Then in an instant, she raised her foot and stomped the sharp end of her heel against the top of his foot. She felt it land on the soft area just to the side of the bone. His eyes widened. As she raised her leg away from his foot, she kicked him as hard as she could in the fleshy area just below his knee.

He exhaled sharply and his hands softened their grip on her wrists. But before he could react, she pulled her leg back and thrust it forward with as much power as she could muster. Her knee found his groin with such force that he cried out. His hands instantly dropped away from her and he doubled over in pain.

Her knee jolted straight up, ramming it against his nose. His head jerked backward and he dropped to his knees, his arms cradling his body as his legs drew up to protect himself.

"Well, I'd say she learned her lesson well."

Vicki's head turned toward the door to find Sam and Chris staring at them. Dylan's low moans were constant as she knelt beside him. "Are you okay?" she asked.

He twitched instinctively as she touched him and continued moaning.

Sam strolled into the room. He glanced at the exercise equipment before turning back to them. "Of course he's not okay," he said. "That was the whole point."

Chris followed Sam. He was dressed more casually than the last time she'd seen him; a short-sleeved shirt displayed long and lean biceps.

"I'm sorry," Vicki said, turning back to Dylan. "I forgot about your ribs. I hope I didn't reinjure them."

"No, that was perfect," Dylan said breathlessly. His voice was strained. "You just do that and it'll buy you time."

Sam leaned over them. "Your nose is bleeding."

Chris grabbed a towel draped over the treadmill and handed it to Dylan. "What was that last move all about?" he asked Vicki in awe. His brown eyes were wide and inquisitive.

"Well, I don't know exactly," she said. She tried to help Dylan with the towel but he waved her away. "After I kicked him that second time, I wasn't quite sure what to do with my leg. So my knee just jerked up."

"Is your nose broken?" Sam asked.

Dylan placed his fingers on either side of his nose and twisted. "No," he moaned.

"I knew you could learn a lot from this guy," Sam said, propping his foot on a nearby weight and draping his arm over his knee to stare at Dylan. "That was very impressive."

"Will you stop it?" Vicki groaned. "He's hurt."

"He'll survive. Won't you, Dylan?"

Dylan tried to nod as he tilted his head back to stop the bleeding.

"Mind if we borrow Vicki for a few minutes?" Sam asked.

He half-waved. "Go."

"I'm not leaving him until he's okay," Vicki said obstinately.

"You gonna do that with an assailant?" Sam asked. Before she could answer, he continued, "We've got some serious business, Vicki. That suspect we were working on wasn't there."

"The—"

He interrupted her. "Is there someplace we can go where you can clear your head?"

Vicki watched Dylan as he tried to fight the pain in his groin and stop his nosebleed at the same time. "I can't—"

"Go," Dylan urged, waving her away. "Go."

Sam pulled her to her feet. "He's fine." He half-dragged her into the hallway, where he picked up a laptop case propped against the banister.

"Is he going to be alright?" Chris said, reluctantly following them into the hallway.

Vicki glanced back at Dylan, who was still waving them away. "I'm good," he managed to call out.

"Maybe I should stay—" Chris began.

"Can't. We need you," Sam interrupted.

As Sam pulled Vicki across the hall into her old bedroom, she caught a glimpse of Dylan rolling onto his side, still moaning.

"What's this all about?" she asked as Sam marched across the bedroom and peered outside. The sun was waning and he turned on the lamp in the corner before seating himself in the overstuffed chair.

"Brenda Carnegie," he said as he pulled out his laptop. She walked behind him and looked over his shoulder. He logged onto a secured CIA network and within a few minutes, they were staring at a satellite image of the beach Vicki had described in her last session.

"Within an hour of our last meeting," he continued, "we had boots on the ground. She never returned to her villa. She's disappeared again—right into thin air."

"But—"

"We picked up the hotel employee, the one we suspect was helping her. We've got his cell phone. She showed up periodically and gave him large sums of money for emailing cryptic messages. He then destroyed the paperwork she gave him and erased the message after it was sent."

Vicki sat down on the edge of the bed.

Chris was peering into the hallway.

"I told you he'd be okay," Sam said.

"But—" Chris started.

"Close the door. Please."

Somehow, he didn't strike Vicki as the type of man who took orders but rather one who gave them. But reluctantly, Chris closed the door.

Sam turned back to Vicki. "We followed the email address you gave us. Led us right here to Robeson County. We picked up the recipient."

"And he's not talking, I gather?"

"He's a bit under the weather," Sam said, glancing out of the corner of his eye at Chris. He took a deep breath and exhaled. "Best we can determine, Brenda's the brains. She appears to be the only one who knows the whole operation—"

"What operation?"

"That's what we need you to tell us."

"I see."

"She only shares a little bit of information with each person, so nobody else really knows much of anything. The guy we picked up knows a password but he has to wait until he's contacted by whoever knows the location of the file."

She crawled onto the bed and lay down. "So what do you need me to do?"

"Find her. Tell us everything you see. And this time," he tapped the top of the laptop screen, "we'll get men on the ground in real time. They're standing by, just waiting for my orders."

She nodded.

They grew silent as she closed her eyes. The room had been her bedroom when she first moved to Lumberton and Aunt Laurel's home. But it felt foreign to her now that she spent her nights with Dylan. Even her clothing and what few items she possessed had been moved to his bedroom. This bed was cold and the atmosphere vacant. She knew Sam was watching her from across the room and she knew Chris was no longer standing by the door. But as she drifted off, she no longer felt their presence and soon no longer felt the bed beneath her body.

She was soaring. She rose high above Lumberton and angled her wings like an eagle searching for prey. She instantly moved south, covering hundreds of miles in the blink of an eye, until she was flying over the Caribbean. Then she angled eastward until she could no longer see land, her eyes scanning the Atlantic Ocean until she once again turned south.

She soon found herself whisked inside a room. "I'm inside," she said.

"Location." Sam's voice was curt.

She barely shook her head. "Trying to get a reading," she said. She found herself in a small hallway. The walls were wallpapered in an ornate burgundy and green design against a creamy background. A ceiling light barely illuminated the tiny area while the light of an ebbing sun beckoned at the end of the hall. Following it, she found herself in the center of a living area.

A series of French doors opened to a balcony overlooking a perfect blue ocean. Seagulls were converging just off-shore, dipping into the waters as they spotted their prey. Vicki watched them for a moment, mesmerized by their activity. The horizon was orange but was quickly growing paler as the sun sank.

The beach was white and vacant except for a few souls wandering quietly along the water's edge.

"I'm at the same beach where I was before," she mused. "But I am inside the hotel."

A movement in the corner caught her attention. But as her body turned away from the beautiful view, she found herself sitting at a small table. Looking down at her hands, she realized they were no longer hers but someone else's, as if she now inhabited that person's body.

"Strange," she said.

"Report," Sam responded immediately.

"I am inside her body. I am seeing what she sees."

"What is she doing?"

She looked back at her hands. They were small and delicate-looking. The nails were medium length, each one immaculately polished. And they were typing.

She forced herself to look above the hands, to see the screen in front of her. It was blurry, and at first only varying shades of blue and white with wavy black lines appeared to undulate. She squinted. Where were her eagle eyes now?

She described the hands, the keyboard, the distorted screen. She knew the model and the make of the computer. Why couldn't she see the screen?

A hand reached out and picked up a glass. "Rum and coke," she said. The hand was moving the glass toward her own mouth. She longed to move outside the body and look back upon the person there, but she couldn't.

"What?" Sam answered.

"She's drinking rum and coke while she's working. But I can't see what's on the screen."

"Are you staring at the screen?"

"Yes."

"Close your eyes."

Vicki dutifully closed her eyes and felt the person whose body she inhabited, her breath, her perfume… She could taste the rum on her tongue.

"Open your eyes slowly."

Opening her eyes, she was again looking at the screen. Information was scrolling past as her hand was moving a mouse steadily across the pad.

"Lean forward."

She leaned toward the screen as if she was near-sighted.

"As you move in, focus on the text. Describe the way it looks but don't try to read the words."

"It's a list. Like a spreadsheet."

"Are the column headings stationary?"

"There are no column headings."

"Is the text remaining still?"

"No. Yes," she corrected herself as the scrolling stopped.

"Focus your eyes on the upper left corner." Sam waited several seconds before continuing. "What color is it?

"Blue. Two shades of blue. And white."

"Is there an icon in the corner?"

"It's an Internet browser."

"She's on the Internet?" Chris' voice sounded strained.

"Focus on the first word you see. The one in the first column, first row."

"Senator Billingsley."

"Billingsley?" Chris' voice seemed to have moved up an octave.

She glanced down the column. "They're all Senators and Congressmen."

"List them, Vicki." Sam's voice was brisk.

The room grew silent as her eyes scrolled through the list. She began to realize the second column listed whether they were Democrat or Republican and the third, which state they represented. She listed each one and hoped he had an audio recorder running.

The fourth column contained other names. Most appeared foreign and she found herself resorting to spelling them in lieu of risking a mispronunciation. Some were obviously Middle Eastern while others seemed more suited to a variety of European countries.

She was growing weary. As her breathing became more labored, Sam redirected her focus. "Go to the door."

Once near the hallway, Vicki tried to turn around and look at the person whom she'd inhabited, but it was as though her head was held in a vise, forcing her to focus only on the hallway.

Each step became more exhausting than the last one. Under Sam's instructions, she approached the door.

"Step through it, Vicki," he directed.

"I can't. I'm too tired."

"Step through it. I'll be on the other side. Come to me, Vicki."

She pressed her hand against the door but it wouldn't go through. Her energy was waning and she knew she would all too quickly be whisked back to North Carolina.

"Walk through the door," Sam said. "I have to know the room number."

Her hand pressed against the door but as she stared at it, she realized it was disappearing. She was leaving—the hotel room, the hotel, the woman for whom she'd come searching. And Sam was waiting for the room number, ready to dispatch CIA operatives at the exact moment she gave him the last piece of the puzzle.

As her hand disappeared completely and she felt herself whisked out of the room, she said, "Room 305."

13

Dylan slipped his arm around Vicki's shoulder as they rocked lazily in the porch swing. The sun had completely disappeared, leaving a sparkling array of stars in the cloudless sky. A cluster of lightning bugs frolicked in the front yard, their bright yellow glow a reminder of her childhood before her parents were killed and her life changed forever.

Sam and Chris remained in the house, presumably watching via satellite as CIA operatives seized Brenda. Sam had ordered her to leave immediately as if the violence of her capture would remind her of the Amazon incident.

She hadn't hesitated but left right away in search of Dylan, whom she found sipping a glass of wine on the front porch.

"I'm sorry I hurt you."

"I brought it on meself, I did," he said, squeezing her shoulder. "If ever you're attacked now, do exactly what you did today. And it'll buy you time to get away."

"I don't intend to ever be attacked."

"None of us do. It isn't like we're walkin' about plannin' it."

Sandy and Alec pulled in front of the house next door. As they exited Alec's vehicle, they waved as they continued into Sandy's house.

"Are you okay now?" Vicki asked suddenly, turning to look at Dylan's nose.

Noting her gaze, he touched his nose. "Me nose has recovered completely. But it's a good thin' I don't want children."

"Are you serious? You really don't ever want children?"

"I'd prefer to face a firin' squad."

"That's pretty extreme."

"Perhaps I just feel a might strongly about it. There are many thin's o' which a man must compromise. But that's one thin' I never will." He leaned away from her so he could look her in the eyes. "Don't tell me you've got some biological clock tickin' now, Woman."

She laughed. "Absolutely not." She leaned against his arm and they settled back into the porch swing as the bittersweet aroma of boxwood floated on the breeze.

"I suppose you were doin' your fey with Sam, 'eh?"

She half-smiled. "Yes."

"And the gent who was with him—?"

"Christopher Sandige. I'm sorry I forgot to introduce you."

"I was in no shape to shake his hand, lass."

"He works for a powerful Congressman. The mission I'm on is for him. Though I don't really understand yet what they're looking for…"

"I didn't quite understand me own mission the other night, either."

"That's the way the CIA works sometimes. We're pieces of a puzzle. And somebody like Sam puts all or some of the pieces together."

He nodded. "It's quite perplexin'."

She chuckled. But before she could answer, the screen door opened.

"I see you've recovered," Sam said dryly as he stepped onto the porch. Chris followed him and Vicki made brief introductions.

Dylan rose to shake Chris' hand and as Vicki watched, she realized they made a striking pair. Chris was slightly taller than Dylan but much leaner. And while Chris's biceps were long and lean, Dylan's appeared powerful and much bulkier.

Sam stepped toward Vicki, drawing her attention away from them. "Good job," he said.

Vicki's eyes widened. "That's the best compliment you've ever given me," she said. Before he could respond, she added, "I think it's the only compliment, come to think of it."

His face grew stern. "Don't get used to it. Anyway, we've got her. She erased her Internet history as they were coming through the door, so we don't have access to that file she was viewing. But they've got the computer and it's only a matter of time before we get to that data."

"So, that's what you're after? The data?"

"We're after what she knows. Who she knows. By the way, an analyst is typing up that list of senators and congressmen you rattled off. Should be interesting, seeing how they all relate." As Dylan turned toward Sam, he added, "Walk me to the car, Dylan." He turned back toward Vicki. "Not you."

Chris said a cordial good-bye as the three men walked to the dark sedan, but Sam never glanced back at her. He spoke briefly to Dylan, who simply nodded in response. She'd known Sam ever since the foster home and now she wondered if he'd ever cracked a smile. He was always curt, professional. But as quickly as she'd moved from Washington to Lumberton, he'd followed. Now as Chris and Sam got into the car, she wondered if Sam had a family—a wife, children of his own or even a pet.

Dylan stood on the sidewalk as they drove off. When he returned to the porch, he appeared deep in thought. "So, the fey went well, I take it?"

"Apparently they got what they were after. For now. What about you?"

He replenished their glasses of wine then settled into the porch swing and handed her a glass before raising his own.

"They tell me I should expect a call in the comin' days." He sighed. "I'm hopin' it won't be anythin' like the last."

"I hope not, too. You've been taking a beating lately."

"Aye."

"You know," she said, "something happened to me this evening that hadn't occurred since I was a child."

He cocked his head and peered at her curiously. "Did it now?"

"Usually when I'm remote viewing, I see the person I'm after. It's one of the things that make my missions successful. If they haven't yet identified the suspect, I can draw him or her in minute detail. I even know things about them that I logically wouldn't know."

"Like what?"

"Like how they got a certain affliction, scar, things like that... But tonight, I couldn't see the suspect. It was as if I was inside her. Her hands were my hands. What she viewed through her eyes is what I saw."

He shuddered. "I can't even begin to imagine how that must feel."

"It hasn't happened to me since I was a child."

"Now why are you supposin' it happened now?"

Vicki sipped her wine before answering. "I don't know. After I went into the CIA program, they taught me how to be an effective remote viewer. I always stood on the outside, looking in. Those days of being inside the person—well, they just left me. It was very odd, having that experience again."

"When you first came here," Dylan said, reaching for her free hand and squeezing it, "I recall you felt faint after your sessions."

"I don't feel that way now. Maybe I'm getting back into the swing of things. But I do feel drained."

"Do you feel like a bit of a stroll? Perhaps down to the Plaza and back. It might clear your head and help you sleep."

She gazed into his eyes. They were earnest, and she found herself tracing the laugh lines beside one eye with her finger. She shook her head. "I'm sorry, I don't feel like it."

He appeared disappointed but he reached for her hand and kissed her fingers. "It's all right. We'll do whatever you wish to do."

"Have you always been this accommodating?"

He stopped kissing her fingers and paused over her hand. His gentle smile subsided and she felt as though she'd insulted him in some way. But before she could speak again, he said, "No. And it's somethin' that haunts me each and every day of me life."

She remained silent as she watched him. His eyes grew dark as he stared at her hand. And though she longed to ask him what he meant, there was something about his eyes, his down-turned mouth and a sudden sadness that convinced her to remain quiet.

14

Dylan and Sam stood in the wide, hushed hallway as they observed the interrogation room through the one-way mirror. Inside was a metal table in the center of the room with empty chairs on one side. Against the far wall was a counter that ran the length of the room, comprised of a sink and cabinets above and below the stainless steel countertop.

But it was the single chair on one side of the table, the side closest to Dylan and Sam that riveted their attention. The metal chair was arranged so they viewed the occupant from the side. The ankles were cuffed to the slat at the bottom of the chair while each wrist was cuffed to the chair arms. As the head slumped forward, a young man tapped her chin, preventing the person from falling asleep. Thick copper hair hung in waves that reached to the person's waist and obscured the face.

"That's a woman," Dylan said.

"Very observant," Sam replied.

They stood for a moment in silence as they watched her.

"Women cry," Dylan said.

Sam crossed his arms in front of him. "Not this one. She's been in there for just about thirty-six hours. Almost constant interrogation. She's not even close to breaking. Now all we're trying to do is keep her sleep-deprived until the next team gets here."

"What's 'er name?"

"Brenda Carnegie."

"Ah, a Scottish name."

"American. Born in the District of Columbia. Raised not too far from here."

"What is it you want me to do with 'er?"

"Keep her awake, for starters." He glanced at him. "It should be good practice for you. Use some of those interrogation techniques they taught you." He pointed toward the corners of the room. "Everything you do is caught on tape, from every angle. Microphones throughout. Afterward, you can watch the tape while you're critiqued. Just like last time."

Dylan nodded as he continued to observe her. "So. You care how I go about it, then?"

Sam shrugged. "She's all yours."

They stood for another moment. Then Dylan said, "She's got blood on 'er."

"Yeah."

"You got a medical bag, do you?"

"I'm sure we can round one up."

"What is it you want to know?"

"Who she works for," Sam said as he picked up a handset beside the one-way mirror.

Less than ten minutes later, Dylan opened the door to the interrogation room and nodded to the operative seated in the room. As he made his way inside, the other man passed him on the way out, handing him the keys to the cuffs.

Dylan set the keys and the medical bag on the table and turned around to look at the woman.

"Shift change?" she said flippantly.

He opened the medical bag and retrieved a pair of surgical gloves. He took his time putting them on, flexing each finger in clear view of her. Her expression never changed. He expected to see smudges of mascara or makeup around her eyes, a sure sign she had held back tears during the interrogation, but they were completely dry.

One hand was covered in dried blood as it rested atop the chair arm. He combed her hair back from her face with his hand while she watched him.

"I'm a doctor," he said. "I'm here to treat your injuries."

"Yeah. Right," she answered. Her voice was husky and deep.

"You have quite a nasty gash on your head," he observed.

She didn't answer but watched him as he rifled through the medical bag. He turned back to her and gently cleansed the wound.

"What's your name?" he asked.

"What do you want it to be?"

He stopped and looked her in the eye. She stared back at him boldly, with neither hatred nor fear. He looked at her copper tresses falling in thick waves around her face and cascading down her back. "I think I'll call you 'Red'."

"How original."

He returned to cleaning her face. At one point, he noticed her watching him with an amused expression. "You've got one cut that's worse than the others," he announced. He hesitated and looked at her eyes for a time. Then he said, "I'm goin' to put a butterfly bandage on it instead o' stitches."

"Isn't that special."

He retrieved the bandage and squeezed the skin together as best he could while he taped the wound shut. "I've only seen eyes like yours once before," he said as he worked. "They're a very unusual color."

She stared at him until he finished working and he looked back at her eyes. "You like 'em?" she said. She raised one brow flirtatiously.

"I imagine you've seduced many a man with those eyes," he answered. Before she could respond, he turned his attention to her hand. They were petite hands, which was surprising considering her tough demeanor. The nails were immaculately polished. The band of a sapphire ring was broken, the metal cutting her finger. "They did this to you?" he asked without looking up.

"The Americans didn't. The Argentinians did."

"That's where you were picked up, is it? Argentina?"

"Yeah. That's where I was picked up. Spent two days there before they transferred me here."

He removed the ring and cleaned the blood from her hand. "How much sleep 'ave you had in the past four days?"

She tilted her head and watched him bandage her finger. "Five minutes, here or there. I've not had anything to eat. Just some water. They want to break me down."

"Are they succeedin'?"

She glanced pointedly at one of the cameras. "I've been through a lot worse than this."

He finished bandaging her hand and inspected her other hand and her forearms. There were a few cuts but nothing severe. He gathered the bloody gauze he'd used and tossed it into a nearby wastebasket.

"So, you're really a doctor?" she asked as he began to close the medical bag.

"I can't give you anythin' for the pain," he said. "Rules, you know."

She chuckled. "I wasn't going to ask you."

He noticed a fingernail that appeared to be slightly pulled up and he bent to one knee to inspect it.

"It's fake," she said. "You can pull it off."

He didn't answer. But as he began to rise again, she said, "Please."

He stopped moving and looked at her. He'd observed eyes just like hers while in the throes of passion, had seen the amber color almost glowing in abandonment and ecstasy; the black lashes thick and full. His eyes traveled to her lips. They were plump, almost pouty but also cracked and dry.

"Aye?" he said.

"I have a little cut on the inside of my thigh."

He remained on one knee in front of her, and now he placed one arm across his bent knee and gazed into her eyes. "So what is this little game you wish to play with me now?"

"If you pulled my pants down to look at this cut, my ankles would still be cuffed to this chair," she said. "And I'd be even less likely to move because my pants would be around my knees or my ankles. Isn't that right?"

He continued looking at her. "Or I could trigger a bomb that would blow you up and me, too."

She laughed. "You don't think I'd be in custody for four days without them checking me over, do you?"

He leaned back on his haunches.

After a moment, she spread her legs apart. As his eyes moved from her face to her thighs, he was surprised to see her black slacks soaked with blood and the blood pooling on the metal chair beneath her.

"I've been squeezing my legs together," she said hoarsely, "kind of an improvised tourniquet."

He looked back at her face. Her expression was detached but there was the faintest glimmer in her eyes.

"Please?" she asked.

He sat for a moment longer. He knew Sam was still outside the window watching every move, even though from this angle the window appeared to be a mirror. Every movement was caught on tape. And yet there was something sincere about the way the woman looked at him, her eyebrows slightly raised as if to say, "How about it?"

He reached to her waist and felt inside. "Are you wearin' undergarments?"

"Does it matter what my answer is?"

He unbuttoned her slacks and unzipped them to reveal black lace panties. "No," he said. "Just preparin' meself for what I might see."

Her grin was lopsided. "Spoken like a man with experience."

"Raise your bum whilst I slip these down."

"Never heard that line before." Despite her bravado, Dylan noticed she gritted her teeth as she raised herself. When she was high enough off the chair, he slid her pants down to her knees.

"That's good," he said.

"Ah," she said. She lowered herself slowly. "And I was just getting started."

He placed a hand on each knee and pulled her legs apart to reveal a slim, homemade knife holder wrapped around her thigh. Inside the sheath had been a serrated nylon composite knife, but one of the rivets had popped loose, allowing the knife to come through the sheath. Now he could clearly see nearly two inches of the blade embedded just underneath her skin.

He looked back at her face. She'd grown pale and was watching him.

"You're supposed to wear these just below the knee," he said calmly.

"Pull my pants down a little bit further."

He complied, revealing two empty knife holders, one at the top of each calf.

"They took the knives," she said.

He turned his attention back to the knife embedded in her. "I don't normally see a nylon knife worn like this."

"It won't set off metal detectors."

"How long has it been like this?" he asked.

"Four days."

"And you've been sittin' here like this ever since?"

"Well, not here," she said. Beads of perspiration had popped out across her arched brow.

He looked at the table and then back at her. He glanced toward the door but it didn't open and Sam didn't join him. Finally, he said in a louder voice, "I need permission to transport this young woman to a medical facility."

Instantly the door opened and Sam casually strolled across the room. Dylan watched his face as he walked around in front of the woman. His eyes widened. He immediately looked at her face, which remained completely dispassionate.

"Can you take this out here, *Doctor?*" Sam said pointedly.

"You want me to remove it here, without any anesthesia?"

Sam nodded.

"Are you jokin' me?"

"Can you?"

Dylan stared into Sam's eyes for a full minute before turning back to look at the knife. "I can. It won't be pleasant. But I can certainly do it, if that's what you want done."

"Then do it." With that, he strolled back to the hallway.

Dylan waited until the door clicked shut with a resounding metal clang. Then he turned to the woman. "I'm goin' to cuff you to that table there. You're goin' to lie there and I'm goin' to pull this thin' out o' you. It's not goin' to be pleasin' and I can't give you anythin' for the pain."

She nodded.

"Think you can handle that?"

"I can handle anything you want to throw my way," she said.

He retrieved the keys and when he returned to her chair, he leaned over her so his face was just inches from hers. "You can't escape this room," he said. "You and I both know there's only one way out." He nodded toward the door. "And we both know we're bein' watched. And once I take these cuffs off your legs, if you try to kick me, I can't help you. And I guarantee the next person through that door won't be helpin' you, either. You'll just make thin's worse for yourself."

She looked at him blankly.

"Are you understandin' me, Woman?"

"Yes."

He slid the chair close enough to the table to uncuff one wrist from the chair and cuff it to the table leg. Within a couple of minutes, he'd uncuffed the other wrist and legs and had lifted her onto the table, where he directed her to lie down.

She complied and he slid the slacks completely off her and left them in a heap on the floor. Then he spread each leg far enough to cuff it to opposite table legs.

"It's a little like sex, isn't it?" she quipped.

"You have sex like this, do you?" he said. As he felt the heat rising in his cheeks, he said, "Seems to me more like medieval torture." He cut the knife sheath from around the blade, untied it from her thigh and tossed it on top of her slacks. He stared for a long time at the serrated blade, the outline clearly visible just beneath the skin. Then he walked to the cabinets and banged around for a minute until he found a flat metal plate. He returned to the table and looked down at her face. "I'm goin' to pull this knife out the same way it went in," he said. "It's goin' to hurt like the dickens. I suggest you bite down on this metal plate. It'll help w' the pain."

"I won't need it."

"You'll wish you had."

"No, I won't."

"I won't offer it again."

"Good."

He placed it on the counter. Then he found two towels and returned to the table. He placed one towel across her thigh just beneath the tip of the blade and laid one hand upon it.

"Are you ready?" he asked.

She nodded.

He flexed his other hand and gripped the knife handle. Then with one quick and powerful thrust, he yanked it backwards. Her leg jerked violently, causing her whole body to come off the table. He immediately plunged the towel on top of the wound. As the knife fell to the floor, he used both hands to lean his entire weight onto her thigh. He looked at her face as her leg continued to shake and the towel became soaked with blood. Her face was pale, her nostrils were flaring but her eyes were open and she was staring at the ceiling. She'd never made a sound.

"If it had gotten your femoral artery, you'd 'ave been in a world o' trouble," he said.

She continued staring above her as if she hadn't heard.

"What are you here for, anyway?" he whispered hoarsely as he continued to apply pressure.

"Differing political opinion," she answered. She sounded winded.

"It's got to be more than that, don't you think?"

She shrugged.

"You know," he said, swapping the blood-stained towel in one swift movement for the clean one, "I work w' these mates here. They're actually a decent bunch. They 'ave wives, children, dogs. One has a cat, though he may not admit it to just anyone."

She chuckled though it sounded strained.

"If you tell 'em what they want to know, you'll make thin's much easier on y'self."

She didn't answer immediately. But as her leg stopped trembling under his weight, she said, "Here's the thing, um, what did you say your name was?"

"What do you want it to be?" he asked.

She smiled. "Here's the thing, Irish. Today your guys are in power. But with the next election, it might be my guys. In each of our camps, we have our senators and our congressmen and our supporters. So why would I tell you something today for a lighter prison sentence when tomorrow I might be a hero in another administration?"

He glanced at her wound. The bleeding was slowing. He added the towels to the heap on the floor and retrieved two more. He opened a bottle of antiseptic. "This is goin' to sting."

"Bring it on."

He shook his head and poured the antiseptic over the wound. Again, her leg came clear off the table. He glanced at her face. Her expression remained impassive. He cleaned the wound carefully. "You called this a little cut, did you?" he asked. When she didn't answer, he said, "You've got a gapin' wound here."

He returned to the cabinets and banged around for a while before joining her once more at the table. "This is not how I envisioned I'd be spendin' me mornin'," he said.

"Hey, I didn't plan this, either. I was minding my own business when they grabbed me." She glanced at him. "Thank you."

"Don't thank me yet. You might be in pain for quite a while."

She chuckled. "I can deal with the pain. Don't you worry about that."

"I'm not goin' to put stitches in you," he said. "I'm just goin' to tape this thin' shut." He grew silent as he used two large bandages across the wound, pulling it as tight as possible to close the gaping hole. "I imagine this is goin' to leave a nasty scar."

"It'll give me a new line. 'Do you want to see my scar?'" She laughed quietly.

He cut a large swath of duct tape and secured the bandages with it as he pulled it tight across her thigh. "That'll hold," he said. "But I wouldn't try removin' the duct tape any time soon."

"Let's just hope the next guy they send in doesn't," she answered.

"Anythin' you want to tell me before I leave? You could be doin' yourself a big favor."

"Yeah," she said. "You've got a great bedside manner."

He gathered the medical kit and contents and placed it on the counter, followed by the knife he'd pulled out of her. The bloody clothes and towels were left on the floor.

"Good luck to you, Red," he said as he left her on the table, cuffed to the four corners.

"See you around, Irish. Oh," she said as an afterthought.

He stopped and looked back at her.

"And, Irish, I could've made a bomb with the same type of material. Same size. Next time, be a little more careful?"

He looked at her for a long moment before turning back toward the door.

Once it clicked shut behind him, he breathed a massive sigh. Four men were now standing at the window. From their expressions, it was obvious they'd watched the entire ordeal.

"That is the toughest broad I've ever seen in my life," Sam said.

"I can't believe you 'ad me take that knife out o' 'er," Dylan said. "I can't believe you did that."

"You did great."

"I could've put 'er through immense pain."

Sam chuckled. "Yeah. If it had been me, I'd have been crying. She didn't break a sweat."

Dylan stared through the window at her, lying still on the cold metal table. "I didn't find out who 'er boss is," he said quietly.

"That's okay. You kept her awake. You found a knife *that was missed*," he emphasized to the other men, who avoided his glaring eyes, "and you left her in a hell of a position for the next interrogator." He turned back to Dylan. "Good job."

Vicki bolted upright. In front of her was tank after tank of angelfish, serenely going about the business of laying and caring for their eggs. But their images blurred as a pain seared through her leg. Her head pounded and she was so parched she thought she wouldn't survive without water and plenty of it.

Then just as quickly as the symptoms emerged, they disappeared.

As she stared into the tank in front of her without really seeing the inhabitants, she said aloud, "Annie's in trouble."

15

Vicki listened as the front door closed behind Benita. It was approaching six o'clock and Dylan hadn't yet returned home. An enticing aroma wafted through the kitchen, but her stomach was tied in knots, as it always was when Sam had Dylan on an assignment. It was different, she thought, when she was working. She was there in her mind only. There was so much more at risk when he was physically involved.

She heard footsteps and called out, "Benita?" But it was Dylan's head that popped through the door.

She let out an audible sigh. "Thank God you're home."

He walked straight to the refrigerator and pulled out a bottle of Guinness. "I 'ave just had the most bizarre day in me whole life," he said as he turned toward her. He reached out his arm for her and she slipped into his embrace.

They kissed before she replied, "You've had some pretty bizarre days. Don't tell me this one is worse than when I—?"

"No, no, you're right. That was the mother o' all bizarre days." He popped open the bottle. "I'm just thrilled to be home." He turned toward the stove. "What's for supper?"

"Benita wanted to surprise you. It's Irish stew."

"Is it now?"

She watched as he went straight to the drawer where the utensils were kept, pulled out a serving spoon and leaned over the pot of stew as he stirred it. He's more domesticated than I am, she thought. She still opened half the drawers in the kitchen before she found what she was looking for.

"Not bad," he said. He poured some of his beer into it. "Needs a bit more Guinness, it does." He stirred it some more. "Have you tasted it?"

"Not yet. But listen, after dinner, I need you to help me."

"It's still missin' somethin'. Don't know quite what it is."

"I need to look for Annie."

He took another taste. "Tonight? Oh, Darlin', I'd prefer to make sweet love to you. Or passionate love. Your choice. We could do both."

"Don't you ever have anything else on your mind?"

He stopped tasting the stew and looked at her. "Don't for one minute let me good humor fool you. I 'ave you know I'm a serious man. On occasion, I 'ave some very deep thoughts."

"Is that right?"

"It is." They looked at each other for a moment. There must have been something about the way Vicki tried to suppress a smile that caused him to continue. "If all I thought about was jumpin' bones, I'd be back in Ireland crawlin' the pubs." He finished with mock indignation, "It takes a good bit o' gumption to leave everythin' a man 'as ever known to come to a new country w' different customs, you know."

She grew serious. "Yes. You're right. It does."

He went back to tasting the stew and adding more beer to the mixture.

"Annie's in trouble, Dylan."

"Annie, your sister?"

"Yes."

"Have you been in touch, then?"

"No. I can feel it."

"You can, can you?"

"Yes. I can. And you promised me you'd help me remote view her."

"I don't recall promisin' tonight."

"She needs me. I know it."

He stopped tasting the stew and gazed at her. "Why is it that a woman must win every argument?"

"We're not arguing."

"I imagine if I said 'no' we would be."

"There is that."

"Aye," he said. "There is that."

Vicki lay on the sofa in the bedroom with her head comfortably resting on a pillow and her forearm across her eyes. The room was dim, the only light emanating from the streetlights along Elm Street. The music had been hushed and now the only sound was her own breath as she consciously breathed in and out.

"I don't see why I can't sit over there with you," Dylan said. "You could put your feet in me lap. I could stroke your leg. Keep you calm. Serene, even."

She peered out from beneath her arm. "Once more," she said, "here's how this works. You can't touch me. You have to keep your distance or your thoughts could skew what I'm envisioning. You're the supervisor."

"I've never supervised a naked lady before," he said. "I don't know if I can handle the assignment."

"Just for twenty minutes. That's all I'm asking."

"I suppose I don't have a say in the matter."

"Normally," she continued, "we'd have audio and video recordings. But we're not doing that this time."

"That's a good thin' because I don't think I'd like to have a tape of me girl naked floatin' around for just any bloke to see."

"Do you want me to put on a robe?"

"I'm just sayin'."

"You are totally breaking my concentration."

"Maybe now's not the time."

"Now's the perfect time if we get on with it."

"Well, I don't know what's keepin' you."

She sighed. "Do you have your notepad?"

He held it up. "Right here. But I've had nothin' to write."

"I'm going to start breathing deep again, and this time don't interrupt me. When it sounds like I'm asleep, I'll be moving somewhere else in my mind. Talk low, like you don't want anyone else to hear. If you talk too loud, it breaks my concentration." He didn't respond and she glanced out from under her forearm again. "Got that?"

"Got it. I just didn't want to interrupt to say I got it."

"Ask me what I'm seeing, especially if I'm quiet for too long. Ask for details. Especially things I can read—street signs, things like that."

"Got it."

"Okay. Let's start. Oh, and let me know when we've passed fifteen minutes. I need to start coming back."

"Then we do what I want to do."

"Yes. Then we'll do what you want to do." She closed her eyes and took several deep breaths, taking her time to exhale slowly and deliberately each time. She sought to rid her mind of all the external thoughts that threatened to break her concentration. She focused instead on her own breathing and a bright light that emanated from a brilliant sun, washing over her and pushing everything else further from her thoughts.

Soon she was soaring through a night sky.

"Where are you?"

She heard Dylan's soft, calm voice as if she was wearing an earpiece. It seemed strange not to hear Sam's voice. For a moment, she felt as though she was on a mission but the commanding officer had changed without any warning. Then she was whisked out of the night sky and into a vehicle.

"I'm traveling." She hesitated. "I'm sitting in the passenger seat. We're very high and it's very loud."

"What are you seein' directly in front o' you?"

"A dashboard. We're going eighty miles an hour."

"Who's drivin'?"

She looked to her left. "I don't know him. He has very curly hair, mostly gray. His beard is white on his chin but gray elsewhere. He has his eyes on the road but he's talking non-stop." She peered straight ahead. "We're in a tractor-trailer and I've hitched a ride." She paused. "I'm the one in the passenger seat. I can't see myself, can't see what I look like. But I know it really isn't me, it's Annie. But I'm feeling like we're one and the same."

"Pull down the visor and look in the mirror. Tell me what you see."

She reached to the visor and pulled it down. "It's dark. We're traveling at night." They passed under a streetlamp and a flash of light illuminated the mirror for a split second. "My eyes. I saw my own eyes. They're bloodshot and I've got dark circles under them."

"Where are you goin'?"

"I don't know." She tried to orient herself but there were no street signs, only flat, empty space that stretched for miles ahead. "We're on an interstate and it's very quiet." She caught a glimpse of movement in the side mirror and she turned to peer at it. Her heart quickened and she slid a bit further down in the seat. "Police cars, coming up behind us. No; they're unmarked. Maybe the feds. Their blue lights are on and they're passing us."

She hesitated. "One is getting off at the next exit. The others are continuing straight. All I know," she added, "is they can't catch me. I'm—I'm headed north, to Lorton. But when I get there, I'm going to wait a mile outside of the train station. As the auto train picks up on the way to Florida, I'm jumping aboard. I'll ride it back to the south."

"You're goin' north in order to go south?"

"Yes. And it will take me all night. But I'm not going all the way to Florida, when I turn around. I'm zigzagging. And then something is going to happen to make me change my plans. I'll have to lay low. I'll have to get inside and stay there. I can't keep riding the streets or they'll find me."

"Why are they after you?"

"I—I don't know. They think I've done something wrong."

"What have you done wrong?"

"I don't know."

"Yes, you do," came Dylan's voice. "You know why you're travelin' north and then south like a jackrabbit. You know why you're avoidin' the law. It's there, in front o' you. Open your eyes and look."

She turned toward the driver. He was smiling while he talked. He ran his hand through his unruly hair as if to comb it, but it only made it appear more disheveled. Her heart rate had increased and she felt hot and stifled. She turned back toward the road but the cars had disappeared in the distance. She looked into the side mirror. No one was behind them.

She hadn't slept in days and the sound of the engine was lulling her to sleep.

"How soon before we reach Virginia?" she asked. She was surprised to hear her own voice inside the tractor trailer though it was huskier. "Lorton is five hours away. I'm going to sleep now."

The driver reached behind his seat and handed her a blanket. She draped it over her and nestled into it. As she did so, she glanced down. One hand was adjusting the blanket, and it was covered in blood.

Vicki was stretched across the king-sized bed, her feet on the pillows while her head was buried in the rumpled bedcovers.

Dylan lay beside her and ran his finger along her lips. "Oh, but you are lovely," he whispered. He reached toward the headboard, retrieved a pillow and slipped it underneath her head. When he lay back down, he slowly followed the curve of her hip with one hand.

"Are you cold?" he asked as she shivered.

"Yes and no. I feel like I've got one foot in one world and one foot in another."

"No; you've got one foot on a pillow and the other foot across me rump. And I'll thank you not to move it."

She smiled. "This is the first time I've ever had sex right after remote viewing."

"Well, if it wasn't, I'd thank you not to tell me about it. That's for sure."

She rose onto her elbow. "That was the strangest feeling. Like I was two different people making love to you."

"That part I didn't feel."

"Right now, I feel hot. Flushed. But at the same time, I feel like I'm traveling at eighty miles an hour in a cab that's too cold, like the air conditioning is set way too low."

"Has the last hour and a half o' love makin' just been erased from your mind, Darlin', and now you're back in your fey?"

She realized she'd been staring at his arm as it lay across her and now she looked into his eyes. They seemed sad.

"Cause if you're tellin' me that, Woman, that would mean I've lost me touch. And that would be a tremendous blow to the ego."

"You haven't lost your touch," she said, running her hand along his five o'clock shadow. "But Annie's in trouble." She nestled closer to him. "I can feel it."

16

The phone sounded loud and rude as it roused Vicki from a deep sleep. As she opened her eyes, she realized she'd fallen asleep straddling the foot of the bed, snuggled into Dylan's arms. Now he grumbled and tried to extricate himself from a tangle of bedcovers.

"What time is it?" she asked sleepily.

He stretched across the bed and grabbed his cell phone from the nightstand. "Quarter past nine."

She groaned.

"Hello?"

She peered toward the head of the bed, where he was running his hand through his hair as he listened to the caller.

"You're jokin' me. How'd that happen, I wonder?"

He adjusted some pillows against the headboard while he listened. "Oh, that's just carelessness. That should ne'er 'ave happened."

"What?" Vicki mouthed.

He shook his head. After a moment, he said, "Really now? At a truck stop? That seems careless, too, if you want my opinion."

Vicki crawled toward the head of the bed, but he motioned for her not to listen. Sam, she thought. She pulled the bedcovers around them.

"Now?" Then, "Yes. I'll be there straight-away."

He switched off the phone. "Remember I told you what a bizarre day I 'ad yesterday?"

"Yes."

"This person I was questionin' is quite the escape artist. And they knew it. But they still allowed 'em to get away."

"Are you supposed to be talking to me about it?"

"I suppose not. Though I'm not really tellin' you anythin' in any detail." He continued sitting on the bed, propped against the headboard, deep in thought. "It makes no sense. Why would you use four sets o' cuffs on one person in a secure government facility, and then let 'em escape while transportin' 'em up the road?"

"I can't answer that."

He shook his head. Then he leaned down and kissed her. "I'm needin' to shower and go," he said. "That was Sam, in case you hadn't guessed."

"Going to Fort Bragg?"

"No. I'm meetin' him at the Cracker Barrel along the service road."

"Oh, so you get to eat breakfast out?"

"I wish. But he's gettin' us somethin' to go. And I'm hopin' it's more than toast."

As he reluctantly left her side and started toward the bathroom, she rolled over so she could continue to watch him. "Where are you going?"

"Up the road a bit. To watch a video o' the person we're after. Seems after bein' wily enough to escape, they were caught on tape at a truck stop lookin' straight into the camera."

She heard him turn on the water.

"Makes no sense," he said as he stepped into the shower.

Vicki had just begun the morning water tests in the fish house when her cell phone rang.

"Vicki."

She didn't recognize the voice and she held the phone away from her for a moment to check the Caller ID. It showed Out of Area. "Yes?"

"Sorry to bother you. This is Chris. Chris Sandige."

"Oh, yes. Chris. How are you?"

"I'm on my way to your house."

She glanced at the row of tanks. The fish knew the routine and were lining up, waiting to be fed. "What's going on?"

"You remember the remote viewing session we did together?"

"Sure. The woman in Argentina?"

"We're going to do another one. I can't really talk about it on the phone. I'll explain everything when I get there."

"Where are you now?" she asked, checking her watch.

"I left Washington early this morning. I'll be there in a few hours."

Inwardly, she groaned. "The housekeeper should answer the door. If she doesn't, come around back. I'll be in the fish house."

"Got it. See you in a few."

She disconnected the call. His voice had sounded urgent. And if he was leaving Washington for no other reason than to see her in Lumberton, roughly three hundred miles away, this mission must be critical.

Then she snapped into the present. She had a lot of work to do, she thought as she stared down the long row of tanks. And if he was already on his way, she'd better hurry.

17

Vicki paced the living room, anxiously glancing out the front window. It was mid-afternoon and she hadn't heard from Dylan or Chris since early that morning. All the work in the fish house had been performed quickly with a constant eye on the clock, knowing Chris would appear before she'd finished. But he still hadn't arrived. Now the tension mounted as she stared down the street, waiting for his car to appear. One vehicle after another had driven past the house that afternoon, and each time she'd followed it with her eyes, trying to see the driver, until it had passed her by.

Benita poked her head into the living room. "I walk to Bo's for groceries," she announced in her broken English.

"Have you started dinner yet?" Vicki asked, anxiously watching another car drive by.

"No."

"Why don't you call it a day? Go on home. You can get the groceries in the morning, on your way in."

"That make me late."

"That's okay. Dylan and I will probably go out to dinner tonight. I don't know when he'll be back from running his errands. And we can figure out breakfast if we're up before you get here."

"Okay," she said. "If you're sure."

"Yes, I'm sure." For some reason she couldn't quite put her finger on, Vicki found herself suddenly concerned that Chris was coming to the house. She found herself wondering what Benita would think about her meeting a handsome man in private while Dylan was gone. She shook her head. It shouldn't matter what the housekeeper thought. "Go. And enjoy your evening."

It seemed as though it took her forever to finish whatever tasks she'd been working on. But finally, Benita said her good-byes. And as Vicki watched her walk down Elm Street toward downtown, a dark sedan pulled in front of the house.

She met Chris at the front door, ushering him inside. Then she closed the draperies in the living room and turned on a small lamp beside the armchair.

"Sit down, please," Vicki said, motioning toward the chair. "Can I get you anything to drink?"

Chris shook his head. "I'm too torn up. I haven't eaten anything since I heard the news this morning."

"What news?" Vicki sat on the sofa across from him and studied him intently. He hadn't shaved and his hair was disheveled. For some reason, as she watched him rumple his hair with his hand, it made him seem vulnerable and in an odd sort of way, she felt connected to him. Maybe it was her own vulnerability she was feeling, she thought, as she tried to focus on what he was saying.

"She's gone, Vicki," he said, fixing her with his warm brown eyes.

"The woman in Argentina?"

He nodded. "Brenda. She's gone."

"Can you tell me what happened?"

"She escaped. No one knows where she is. She just vanished." His voice choked. "I've got to find her. She's in danger. I know it. I can feel it."

She felt a lump growing in her throat as she listened. As calmly as she could, she said, "Can you tell me anything else? Anything you know would be helpful."

"I had to get back to Washington. I didn't want to go. I knew she was being transported to Fort Bragg from Argentina. I knew she'd arrive at any moment. But Sam guaranteed me he'd have her sent on to Washington." He looked at Vicki with dark, tired eyes. "I shouldn't have gone. If I'd stayed here, none of this would have happened."

"I'm trying to piece everything together," she said slowly. She felt like saying 'you have no idea how much I'm piecing together' but thought better of it. "So they did bring her to Fort Bragg? She did arrive?"

"Yes. They had her in custody for two days. The whole time, I was kept hopping on the Hill. I couldn't leave." He leaned back and stared at the ceiling. "Why didn't they fly her to Washington?"

"They were driving her?"

"It makes no sense."

Vicki could hear his words echoing in her brain in an Irish accent.

"So, do you know what happened?"

"She escaped."

"Where?"

"Truck stop. Somewhere along I-95. Sam's supposed to be getting the particulars. But, honestly, at this point, I don't have much confidence in him anymore."

"Sam's a good guy," she said, watching his reaction. "I don't know why this happened, but—"

"There's a CIA within the CIA," he said suddenly. "Call them what you will. Rogue agents. Whatever." He waved his hand. "I don't know if Sam orchestrated her disappearance or they did. But I do know she couldn't have done this without help."

She felt her chest soar with a bit of pride, knowing she had help. It was Annie, she thought. It had to be Annie. She was going by Brenda now, but the facts and her visions were coming together. She knew they were one and the same.

"You did the right thing, coming here. For what it's worth, Sam is out there right now, looking for her. Though I'm not supposed to know that."

He nodded but he didn't appear convinced.

"If you find her first," she said tentatively, "would she still be in danger?"

"I don't know." He rubbed his hand along his unshaven cheek. "I don't know what she knows. Why she's a target. But I can tell you this." He looked her in the eye. "I'll protect her with everything I've got. I'll call in every favor, every friendship—and I've got a few friends in high places."

She returned his gaze. His eyes were wide and unblinking and there was something about the sincerity of his tone that caused her to trust him. She hoped her hunches were correct. Annie's life could depend on it.

Vicki cleared her throat and forced herself to look away. As she lay on the sofa, she said, "Give me a couple of minutes to get myself oriented and we'll see if we can find her."

Closing her eyes and trying to clear her mind, she could still feel Chris' angst from across the room. She tried to block his emotions and concentrate on the task at hand as she focused on the white light. Then she was soaring out of the room and away from Lumberton.

She found herself between Lorton and Fredericksburg on a southbound train. She knew each stop like the back of her hand, and now it was making an unscheduled one. She stepped onto the back of the train and peered outside. Dawn was breaking over a horizon framed with evergreens, casting the trees in an orange-red hue. There was moisture in the air, a thick humidity that heralded an approaching storm and made it difficult to breathe. And she was tired, dead tired.

"What do you see?" Chris asked tentatively.

"A train," she said. "It's stopping. But it's not in real time. I get the sense it happened this morning." She felt the interruption was disrupting her concentration, even though Chris was following protocol and it shouldn't have taken her out of her vision. But she was struggling to remain there. She couldn't see the person in the train, peering out. She felt as though she was there herself, and it was her own eyes she was looking through. Even as this registered on her brain, she knew in her heart she was looking through Annie's—now Brenda's—eyes.

And Brenda's heartbeat began to race and her breathing was labored. It was an unscheduled stop because they were coming for her.

"What is it?" Chris asked.

She tried to answer but the words wouldn't come. She just knew she had to escape now or risk spending the rest of her life imprisoned. As the train came around the bend squealing in its efforts to stop, she jumped.

Annie hit the ground with a force that knocked the wind out of her. Instinct took over and she rolled through the tall grasses until she came to rest at the edge of the tree line. As the train continued around the bend, she crouched as she ran through the grove of trees, her chest heaving so violently that she felt as though she was suffocating. Vicki could hear her own breathing becoming more labored as she ran into the shadows with her sister, staying close to the trees as she raced away from the direction the train was heading, running back the way she'd come, as if her life depended on it.

Because it did.

Then in the blink of an eye, she saw herself at a truck stop, her hair covered in grass and her clothes dirty and unkempt. As she brought her breathing under control, she described the scene to Chris.

"Who are you running from?" Chris asked softly.

"I don't know who they are. It's the men, faceless men. If they catch me, they might kill me."

She watched a pickup truck enter the parking lot, pulling a horse trailer. They parked along the tree line, a good distance from the building. She watched as a man and woman exited the truck, stretching their legs as they made their way toward the building, walking the laborious stride of people who had kept their knees bent and their shoulders hunched inside a vehicle for far too long.

As the couple entered the building, Annie hurried through the grove of trees toward the trailer. She raced to the back gate where the horses stared at her. It was locked, but in a few seconds she'd scaled it and landed with a thud in between the animals.

"I love horses," Vicki found herself saying out loud. "I grew up around horses." Even as she said it, she knew she'd never ridden a horse. And if she had really been inside the trailer, she'd have been terrified they'd trample her. She knew she had neither the strength nor the street smarts to scale that gate. And yet she was there, sitting in a bale of hay, breathing horse manure and feeling completely at home.

She made her way to the front of the trailer, nearest the truck bed. Then she sank into the corner and pulled the hay around her, sealing her off from the outside world.

The minutes passed until finally she heard the sound of voices. She knew it was the couple returning and she held her breath, afraid her chest rising and falling would give away her position. She prayed they would not enter the trailer and redistribute the hay. They paused to talk to the horses, a cursory check to make sure all was well.

Then the doors to the truck opened and closed and the engine started. She breathed a sigh of relief as they pulled through the lot before entering the roadway, taking the first entrance onto the interstate.

"Where are you?" Chris' voice was insistent.

She tried to see a sign, but she couldn't. Between the hay surrounding her and the metal horse trailer, she couldn't see outside at all. She had no idea which direction they were traveling.

As the engine settled into an incessant whir and she knew they were traveling a constant speed, she tried to clear more of the hay from her eyes. She found herself staring at the metal trailer as they sped past the interstate lights. And as the light caught the metal, she caught a glimpse of her own reflection—her eyes.

With a start, she realized she couldn't continue this. She struggled to get out of the vision and return to the present.

"What is it?" Chris asked, his voice growing concerned. "What do you see?"

"No. No." She kept repeating the word as she willed herself to return. "Get me back. Pull me back."

"Pull you back?" Chris asked. "I—I don't understand. Pull you back here?"

"Abort this," she pleaded as she continued speeding down the interstate.

"Stop," Chris said, his voice firm as he realized what she needed. "Stop the mission, Vicki. Come back. Come back to Lumberton. Come back to me here. Now."

He continued repeating the words, and she hung onto them. It felt like it was taking forever but finally the whir of the engine ground to a halt and she listened instead to her own breathing, her neck cramped against the sofa's arm, the light dim in the living room.

Slowly, she opened her eyes. "Oh, my God," she said, her hand shaking as she rubbed her forehead between her brows.

"What happened?"

"Oh, my God." She struggled to sit.

Chris was at her side in an instant, helping her. "What do you need?"

She was amazed to see real concern in his eyes. And as her eyes met his, she felt as though he was recognizing her; almost as though she'd been wearing a mask and now it was falling away, revealing her true identity.

He stepped back from her, visibly catching himself and forcing restraint. "Do you want some water?"

"Yes." She motioned toward the door. "Kitchen's down the hall."

A moment later, Chris made his way back down the hall. He popped open the water bottle and handed it to her before kneeling in front of her. "What did you see?"

She took a long swig of water. "Chris, I am so sorry."

"About what?" His forehead was furrowed as he stared at her.

"I—I owe you a deep apology." Vicki took another long drink and placed the bottle on the end table. Then she took both his hands in hers. They were large hands, capable hands, but now she felt as if he was the vulnerable one. "There's a cardinal rule about remote viewing," she said, trying to keep her voice even. "I can only work one case at a time."

"You were assigned to something else already?" His voice was low. His eyes didn't waver from hers, but she could see his unshaven face and his tousled hair in her peripheral vision. His appearance seemed to shout at her just how important this assignment was.

"No. I wasn't." She took a deep breath. "But because I wasn't working on anything, I was working on something personal."

"I don't understand." His eyes grew moist. He had always looked at her with such kindness, and now Vicki felt as if she was intentionally breaking his heart.

"I was separated from my sister as a child. And I've been trying to find her. I did one session last night, never dreaming you'd call today—"

He leaned back on his haunches. "And what you were seeing just now, was—?"

"It was her. My sister Annie."

He put his head in his hands.

Vicki tried to remember if she'd ever watched a grown man cry and realized she hadn't. Now as she watched Chris hunch over as if she'd just rammed a spear through his heart, she began to cry. God forgive me, she thought wretchedly.

They clutched at each other at the same time. She slipped off the sofa and as she felt his arms wrap around her, his body convulsed with his pain. He was surprisingly strong and as he tightened his hold on her, he felt like solid steel encircling her. He cried openly, his face against her hair, his day-old beard rubbing against her, his large hands grabbing her torso as if he was afraid to let go.

"I love her," he cried. "And I've got to find her. I've got to. I know she's in danger and I don't know where to turn—who to turn to."

As the time passed, her knees began to ache from her crouched position and still he cried, as if all the emotions that had been bottled up inside him were being uncorked. His hair tickled her cheekbone, sending up a sweet aroma of cedar and vetiver.

"What the bloody hell is goin' on?"

They both jerked at the same time, instinctively separating. Vicki's heart felt as though it was jammed into her throat and she struggled to her feet as the overhead light was switched on.

Dylan stood in the doorway, his stance wide, his face red and his eyes narrowed.

"Dylan," she said, wiping the tears from her face, "you remember Chris Sandige. You met him the other day, with Sam."

"Oh, well excuse me," he said, his rage mounting, "I didn't recognize you on account o' yer face bein' buried in me girl!"

"He's—he's my assignment!" Vicki stuttered.

"Some assignment this is!"

"It's not what you think," Chris said, coming to his feet.

"I've used that line m'self," Dylan said, his anger far from abating. "Give me one good reason why I shouldn't rip you both to bloody shreds."

Vicki moved between Chris and Dylan in an attempt to get Dylan to focus on her face. "Dylan, listen to me," she begged.

He pushed her to the side as if she weighed no more than a feather and motioned for Chris to approach him. "Come on, boy-o, and fight like a man."

Chris' feet remained planted firmly as he held up both his hands. "I'm no match for you," he said, though Vicki wondered if he was intentionally selling himself short. "We both know it. All you'd be doing is getting my blood all over your nice clean house."

"Good point," he said. "We'll take it outside. Close to the rubbish can so's I won't have far to dispose of yer wretched body!"

"You'll be ending a miserable existence," Chris said, "but it won't be because I did anything with your girl. Or ever hoped to."

"What kind o' a fighter are you?"

"The worst kind. Every kid in school beat me up. Even the girls."

As Vicki listened, she realized Chris was acting the role of a smooth diplomat.

"Well, you certainly know how to take the joy out o' a man killin' another."

Dylan glared at Chris from across the room while the leaner man wiped the tears from his cheeks. "Truth is," he said during the lull in Dylan's anger, "she was trying to help me find the woman I *do* love. And no offense, but it isn't her." He waved his hand dismissively toward Vicki.

"What's wrong with 'er? And why do you think you've got the right to insult 'er?" Dylan demanded.

Chris' mouth fell open. "Nothing's wrong with her. That I know of. But I'm not in love with her. I'm in love with somebody else."

"Well, you've got a dismal way o' showin' it."

"Oh, for Christ's sake," Vicki said.

"I'm sorry," Chris said, brushing his palm against his pants leg to dry it. He extended his hand to Dylan. "Please. Let me explain."

Dylan remained stone faced as he glared at him.

"Please," Chris begged.

18

Dylan popped open a Guinness and handed it to Chris. "You can imagine what I thought," he said, "findin' you in each other's arms like I did."

Chris wiped the perspiration from his forehead before accepting the beer. "Thanks for not killing me." He took a long swig and settled into the armchair.

Dylan looked at Vicki. "I imagine me secret's out. I'm an insanely jealous man."

"You think?" she quipped.

"It's just—" Chris struggled to catch his breath "—I'm in love with Brenda. I know that sounds crazy. I met her last fall right here in Lumberton. And we were only together for a weekend. One completely crazy, insane, passionate weekend. But I can't get her out of my mind. I tried. I went back to Washington. I threw myself into my work, and I tried. I tried to forget her. But I can't."

Dylan perched on the edge of the sofa next to Vicki as he answered. "Is it love? Or is it obsession?"

Vicki leaned forward as she studied Chris' face. She could feel the heat rising in her cheeks as she contemplated his words. She could envision him in the throes of passion and despite herself she still felt his long, lean and muscular arms around her.

"Anyway, you're welcome," Dylan said after a painful silence. "It would've changed me whole evenin' if I'd had to kill you."

"I just lost it, just now. Right before you came in." He looked at Vicki. "I'm sorry I touched you. Totally inappropriate. And I can understand you being upset," he added as he looked back at Dylan. "I just—Vicki was my last hope. I'm afraid I've lost Brenda forever."

"Brenda." Dylan's expression froze as he stared at Chris. "That's 'er name, this woman you're searchin' for? The one you claim to love so much?"

Chris nodded. "Brenda Carnegie. You've heard of her?" His eyes widened.

Dylan shook his head. "Afraid not, gent."

Vicki glanced at Dylan. His face was expressionless as he took a drink. She finished her water as a sickening feeling began in the pit of her stomach and moved upward.

"If anyone can help you, she can," Dylan said, giving Vicki a squeeze on her shoulder. He took a long look at her before continuing. "But I can tell that she's needin' to take care o' herself now. After one o' these—sessions—she can get quite ill, she can." He hesitated. "Have you eatin', Chris?"

Chris shook his head. "I got a call in the middle of the night. And I haven't eaten since."

"And you drove all the way here from Washington on an empty stomach?"

He nodded. "I'm not hungry."

"Well, then," Dylan stood up and politely removed the beer from his hand. "You're not needin' a brew, mate, you're needin' food. And I'm insistin' on it. I've got to feed me woman here, or she'll faint on us. And you may as well join us."

"No, I couldn't—"

"And afterward, you're not headin' back to Washington. You're stayin' right here. We've plenty o' extra bedrooms, don't we, Darlin'? The house here is set up as a bed and breakfast, though we've never operated it as such. You can get a good night's sleep. Then perhaps in the mornin' Vicki will feel like tryin' again. Worst case, you'll have had a good meal and a good sleep." He turned to Vicki. "What did Bennie make us for supper?"

"She didn't," she said hesitantly. "I told her we'd probably go out to eat. I didn't know what time you'd be home."

"Oh." He cocked his head. "Well. It's obvious that neither o' you is in any shape to go out. So. I'll just whip up somethin' for us all."

After a few half-hearted objections, Vicki watched as Dylan led the way upstairs to a second floor bedroom, where Chris could have a few minutes to himself while Dylan made supper. She knew when Dylan returned she'd join him in the kitchen and sit at the table while he whipped up something that would rival any restaurant. She'd eat, make a few pleasantries and they'd retire for the evening.

And she wouldn't be able to get Annie's eyes out of her mind. Annie, she thought. Brenda Anne Boyd. Brenda Carnegie. They were all searching for the same woman.

19

Brenda was roused from sleep as the gate opened with a resounding metal clang. The horses were being guided out of the trailer while she steeled herself for the inevitable: of being found buried in the hay with no identification and no money.

But after the horses were led into the field, the trailer gate was left open as the couple made their way across a dreary expanse of lawn, more brown than green, toward a farmhouse. Her body remained concealed until the two figures disappeared into the house. Pushing the hay from around her and half crouching, she crept out of the trailer and made her way further from the house and toward a barn.

Inside, the light was dim and the air musty and stale. Instinctively in search of the perfect hiding place, she passed two more horses and several empty stalls before arriving at a rickety ladder. She climbed upward into the hay loft, too tired to move quickly.

The bottled water the trucker had given her during the night had not been enough to quench her thirst and revive her parched body. And her stomach felt as though her throat had been slit. Moving some of the hay in the far corner, scattering mice in all directions, she tried to remember what her last meal had been. Shrimp and scallops, purchased in a swanky hotel by a handsome Argentinian. If she'd known then it would be her last meal for the better part of a week, she wouldn't have left half the stuffed zucchini uneaten and she most certainly would have ordered dulce de leche for dessert. And she might have gone lighter on the rum, though considering her capture the alcohol might have served her well. At least it had deadened the pain for a little while.

Brenda bedded down in the hay and tried not to think of the way it scratched her body and caused her skin to itch. She rubbed the area around her wounded thigh, grateful the duct tape had held. Then she stared into the rafters and watched a black snake slither around a beam.

She needed sleep. Badly. But she also needed to think.

The train had stopped somewhere south of Lorton and north of Fredericksburg. She mentally calculated the time and distance traveled until reaching the truck stop and the horse trailer. Then she tried to calculate the distance the horse trailer had traveled, accounting for one stop for gasoline.

She'd slept fitfully but attuned enough to the steady drone of the engine and the stance of the horses to have been awakened when they twice left the interstate. The first time was for gasoline; they were off and back on in no time. The second time, they'd driven here to this farmhouse.

This meant, Brenda realized with a wave of nausea, she was somewhere in the vicinity of Robeson County, North Carolina.

She'd lived in this county for the better part of sixteen years. It was like the back of her hand. She could get her bearings swiftly and get anywhere she needed to be, even if it involved tramping through an alligator infested swamp.

She owned a home here, in the county seat of Lumberton, though it had been nearly ten months since she'd last seen it, just hours before leaving the country.

Which was precisely why it was the worst place for her to be right now.

Now that they'd found her and brought her back to this country, they would assume she would return to an area she knew among people likely to help her. They would be out in force there with surveillance in the places she used to haunt.

Her eyes closed and although hay was probably one of the most uncomfortable materials in which to bed down, especially with mice crawling around her and a black snake watching her from above, she was so exhausted she didn't care. She wondered how she'd traveled from a computer programmer sitting in the comfort of her home monitoring transactions and moving money, to escaping to a far-away land and being forcibly taken back to the U.S. in the dead of night.

The most prudent course of action was obvious. After a few hours' sleep, she needed to head out of the county through the fastest route possible, which would be tricky considering the interstates would have to be avoided.

Truckers were always a safe bet. There were too many of them to check each one unless a massive roadblock was set up, which was highly unlikely. They traveled long distances quickly because time was money. They could easily be across the country in another day or two. Leaving the United States would be more complicated. By now, they would be combing through records, reconstructing her escape to Argentina. The same strategy wouldn't work again. Everything in her cabana would be gone now, seized by the feds. She could never go back there again.

That last night in Argentina had been memorable: dinner in an exclusive restaurant, a limousine ride back to a gorgeous house, bedding down with a wealthy business tycoon. Her mistake had been returning to the hotel later that night. If she'd stayed with him, they wouldn't have seized her. Or, debating herself, it would have happened the day after that or the day after that. They were onto her, and they'd stop at nothing to get her.

As she drifted off to sleep, she hoped the farmer and his wife would leave the house, at least for a short time. She needed a shower and a change of clothes.

Vicki opened her eyes to find Dylan lying on his side, one arm propped on his elbow supporting his head as he watched her sleep. When she groggily murmured "Good morning" he smiled and kissed her lightly, his lips brushing over her.

"Have you been watching me for long?" she asked, rolling onto her side.

"You were talkin' in your sleep."

"I was?"

"You were. But you needn't worry, Darlin'; you didn't call out any old lovers' names."

"Well, that's a good sign." She ran her fingers along his five o'clock shadow. "Actually, I was remote viewing in my sleep."

"How is that possible?" he mused.

"I don't know how it works, just that it does. It's the strangest thing. I feel like I am inside my sister's head, like we're the same person. I can not only see what she's doing, but I know what she's thinking and what she's planning."

"What she's plannin', eh?"

"Yes." She traced the outline of his lips. They were turned down slightly, and when she looked back at his eyes, they were narrowed and dark. "What are you thinking?"

"Do you remember the mission I was on a couple o' days ago, when I said it was so bizarre?"

"Yes."

"What if," he continued, studying her closely, "you were in my situation and suppose you suspected the person I was talkin' to was a friend o' a friend?"

"You mean the suspect was a friend of a friend's?"

"Aye. What would you do? Would you tell your friend what you suspected, possibly givin' 'em false hope? Or would you wait and see how it all unfolded? Or would you close your mind to that possibility at'al and just get on with the assignment?"

Vicki pulled the pillow closer to him and nestled next to him, burying her face in his chest for a moment. He toyed with her hair and waited patiently for her answer. She avoided his eyes but traced his bare chest with her fingers as she answered.

"I would wait," she said finally. "I'd keep an open mind and see how things unfolded." She glanced into his face, where his eyes were veiled by his lashes. "If the person ended up being someone—special—I don't think I'd want any harm to come to them."

He half-nodded. "So," he said after a long moment, "you said you knew what your sister was thinkin'. What she was plannin'."

"Yes," she said tentatively.

"How do you know this isn't your imagination? Maybe wishful thinkin'?"

She felt her insides drawing tight. "I used to think that was the case," she said softly. "Back when I was first being trained. But after a while, you begin to understand the differences between imagination and remote viewing."

"I can't pretend to understand the fey. It can be a bit disconcertin', I don't mind you knowin'."

She swallowed.

"I mean," he continued, "I could be—just hypothetically, you understand—lookin' for someone, out burnin' petrol, mountin' up wear and tear on meself, spendin' hours upon hours of me time and energy movin' from place to place."

She tried to look in his eyes but they remained shielded by his long lashes.

"Whilst, all along, you remain right here in bed, close those pretty eyes o' yours, and instantly find the person I'm lookin' for."

"What's your point?" she said gently.

"Me point is: why use me at'al? Why not just have a whole army o' people like you? Seems like it would be much more efficient, if you want me thoughts on the matter."

She waited a moment before replying. "I'm just one tool in the toolbox. And once I think I've got a 'hit', they need men on the ground to verify it."

"And that's what I am. A man on the ground. Hypothetically, that is."

"Hypothetically."

He combed her hair with his fingers. "I felt empathy for—that suspect."

"Oh?"

He kissed her on the forehead and then on both cheeks before brushing against her lips. "So, after Chris leaves, you'll want to do another session to find your sister?"

"I think," she said, "I've already found her. And I think within a few hours, I'll be able to drive to her exact location."

"You're feelin' her that strongly, are you now?"

"I am. It's the strongest I've ever felt anybody."

"Well," he said, "then today might turn out to be a very interestin' day."

20

By early afternoon, Vicki was feeling a strong pull to leave the house. It was an odd sensation like being late for an appointment and experiencing the jitters of finishing up loose ends to get out the door.

Chris left for Fort Bragg just after breakfast. He was still distressed over Brenda's escape and was anxious for a face-to-face meeting with Sam to determine how it could have happened. He planned to check into a hotel in Fayetteville where he could easily respond to Sam's office when she was located.

When Vicki explained to him she was close to finding her sister and she thought her remote viewing sessions were being skewed by that, he said he understood though she could sense his disappointment. It was impossible to miss and a glance at Dylan showed he felt it, too. But she'd quickly assured him of another session within a day or two. She was confident they'd locate her, no matter how far Brenda had traveled or where she was hiding out.

After Chris left, Dylan joined her in the fish house, where they'd worked side by side all morning. They had another shipment of fish to get out so in addition to their usual work, they were busily netting, bagging and packing.

"We're well past time for lunch," Dylan announced as he stacked the boxes on a dolly.

Vicki glanced at her watch. "One thirty," she said. "I'm a nervous wreck."

He looked at her curiously. "Your sister?"

She nodded. "I can't eat. Would you mind if I took off?"

He rested his hand on the uppermost box and studied her. "You're sure you know what you're doin' now."

"Positive."

"I don't want you faintin' 'cause you haven't eaten."

She smiled. "You're always worrying about me. I'll grab some juice on my way out the door."

"And I don't want you drivin' all over the place, tryin' to find a woman you might not know if you see her."

"I'll know her. And I'll know exactly where to find her."

"Do you want me to go with you, then?"

Vicki shook her head. "The fish need to be shipped. You don't mind doing it without me?"

"I do. But I'll manage." He took her in his arms and kissed her on top of her head. "You're sure you can't go with me to the post and then I'll go with you to find your sister?"

She kissed him before replying, "It's like I have this window of opportunity. If I wait much longer, she'll be picked up by a tractor trailer and she'll be gone. I've got to find her while she's still walking."

"What are you goin' to do with 'er once you find 'er?"

"Bring her here. Is that okay?"

His eyes widened in surprise. "Certainly. You'll bring 'er here, then."

"That's what I said."

"It's a fittin' place for 'er to be. Here." He looked at her for a moment before continuing, "Don't forget your mobile so's I can call you if I get to worryin'."

"I won't be long. I'll be home by suppertime."

With that, she was off, grabbing a bottle of juice as she hurried through the house.

Vicki found her exactly where she knew her sister would be. Although this part of the county was new to her, the roads' nuanced curves felt intimately familiar. Also recognizable was the house with the split rail fencing straddling two rural corners and an abandoned building covered in graffiti, the windows boarded up. By the time she passed a farmhouse with two horses feeding in the pasture, she knew Annie had napped in the mice-infested barn beneath a black snake that reduced the mice population while her sister was sleeping.

Two miles down the road beyond several more curves, the car passed cornstalks that had remained too long in the fields. Once past, Vicki slowed, knowing that beyond the next curve she would find her sister.

She was walking along the shoulder of the road in a pair of jeans that looked too large and a t-shirt that looked too small. From behind, it might have been a teenage boy, as her hair was pulled underneath a cowboy hat. But at the sound of the car engine, she turned around; though her face was cast in shadow, her figure was clearly visible. It was Annie. There was no mistaking her.

Vicki knew not to pass and stop ahead of her, lest she disappear in the rows of lanky cornstalks. So she stopped about fifty feet behind her. As she put the car in park, the woman turned once more and appeared ready to run.

Vicki opened the door and quickly popped out. "Annie!"

The woman stopped and looked in her direction. Though her face was still cast in shadow from the cowboy hat's bill, Vicki could feel the wheels turning.

"Annie, it's me, Vicki! I've come to get you!"

21

The bar was empty except for the bartender, who was deeply immersed in performing an inventory. It was late afternoon, too early for other patrons to begin filtering inside. The room was dark and the air still. The carpet reeked of artificial refresher meant to hide the odor of stale alcohol but it only added to the heavy aroma.

Vicki sat in the far corner with her back to the wall, affording her a clear view of the front window and a side door. The window was smoke-colored, casting the parking lot just outside in darkness as though a storm was brewing. The side door opened into a hallway that led to the parking lot in one direction and a restaurant in the other. It had not yet reached the dinner hour, so the hall remained empty and still.

Her sister sat in front of her with her back to the window and door, though Vicki knew from following her gaze that she was watching her surroundings intently through the mirror behind the bar.

"I'm not surprised you found me," she was saying as she sipped a Long Island iced tea. "I'm just surprised it took you so long."

A wave of guilt crossed over Vicki. "Annie, I—"

"Brenda," she corrected. "Annie died with Mom and Dad."

Vicki nodded. "It might take some getting used to."

"It didn't for me. The moment I was adopted, I became someone else. The name change just confirmed it."

"So instead of being Annie Boyd, you became—"

"Brenda Carnegie."

"You grew up near here."

She chuckled wryly. "I know this town like the back of my hand. Grew up on a farm a few miles from here."

"And your new family? They were good to you?"

"They didn't mistreat me, if that's what you mean." There was an edge to her voice. "They're gone now. It's old history."

"Did you ever think about me?" Vicki asked tentatively.

"In the beginning." Brenda watched the images in the mirror, though there was no activity in the parking lot or hallway.

"I cried every night," Vicki said.

"You would."

"You didn't?"

"I couldn't. Something inside—died."

"I'm sorry to hear that."

"Don't be. It's served me well."

Vicki swished her chardonnay around the glass but she didn't feel like drinking it. She wished Dylan was there beside her; he seemed to give her strength. "You're in trouble."

Brenda's eyes moved from the mirror to her sister and back again. "A little."

"I want to help you."

"Why?"

"What's happened to you, Annie? Brenda," she corrected herself. "No matter what you got into when we were growing up, I helped you out of it. You never asked me why. It was just what sisters do."

"That was a long time ago." As Brenda raised the glass to her lips, Vicki stared at her fingers. They were covered in dried blood and one false nail was missing.

"I'm sorry I didn't come for you sooner."

Brenda shrugged. "Don't sweat it."

"But I do sweat it. I felt obligated to find you. And I feel consumed with guilt that I didn't do it years ago."

"Consumed by guilt, huh?" She laughed. Her laughter was low and husky, like her voice. "You always were the emotional one. Don't tell me you still cry at the drop of a hat."

"I'm getting better."

"Good." She took a long swallow before continuing. "So where did you end up? Not here in Lumberton. I can tell by your accent."

"Washington. A single guy adopted me, actually."

She looked her in the eye. "He didn't abuse you, did he?"

Now it was Vicki's turn to laugh. "No. Sam's pretty distant. But not abusive. And I doubt he's ever thought of me as a woman."

"Sam, huh?"

"Yeah." She took a sip of her wine. "I never called him anything else."

Brenda nodded and went back to watching the mirror.

"What are you running from?" Vicki asked.

"You mean who."

"Okay."

Brenda took a deep breath. "I *am* in trouble. Big trouble."

"What did you do?"

Her eyes widened as they moved from the mirror to Vicki. "What makes you think I did anything wrong?"

"Bad assumption?"

"Depends on who you ask."

They grew silent and just when Vicki thought she wouldn't say more, Brenda took a deep breath. "I'm tired, Vicki. Really tired." Her eyes moved to the bartender, who was so busy with his inventory that he appeared oblivious to their presence. "I need to get off the street. Stay inside for a day or two. Regroup."

"I'm living in Lumberton now."

"Here? How did you manage to go from living in Washington to living here?"

"Long story. I took a summer job and it turned into a full-time gig."

"Yeah? What're you doing?"

"Raising angelfish."

"Raising what?"

"Angelfish. Freshwater angelfish."

"You're joking, right?"

Vicki shrugged. "I like it. The woman who owned the house where I'm staying passed away. Her nephew inherited it."

Her eyes narrowed. "Yeah? Where's he?"

"I live with him."

Brenda appeared deep in thought. "What does he do?"

"He inherited the angelfish business."

"So you two play house and raise fish." Her laughter was a tad louder.

Vicki remained silent.

Brenda grew somber. "So, is he good to you?"

"Better than good." She smiled. "I'm crazy in love with him."

The corner of Brenda's mouth turned up slightly, and Vicki realized despite her laughter that it was the closest her sister had come to a real smile.

"The house was remodeled to be a bed and breakfast," Vicki continued.

"How quaint."

"Come home with me. You'd have your own suite. It's a big house, three stories."

"Where?"

"Here in Lumberton. On Elm Street."

"Elm Street?" Brenda frowned as if she was deep in thought. After a moment, she said, "And it's just you and him there?"

"His name's Dylan. I'll tell you all about him on the way."

She half nodded. "He won't be taken aback by you bringing me home? I'm a bit more to handle than a stray cat."

"He'd love to meet you. I promise. In fact," she said, glancing at her watch, "he's probably wondering where I am. We have a housekeeper, and—"

"So it's you, him and a housekeeper." The edge was back in her voice.

Vicki lowered her voice though no one was within eavesdropping distance. "She's an illegal. Hardly knows any English. You have nothing to worry about with her."

"And what about him?"

"He'll take care of you."

"He will, will he?"

Vicki blushed. "He's got a strong sense of family. Besides," she said as she started to rise, "it's suppertime and you need to eat. We'll get something in your belly and you'll get a good night's sleep. Come to think of it," she said, shaking her head, "that's exactly what he said to someone else, not more than twenty-four hours ago."

"So, you do pick up strays."

"The last—houseguest—is gone. I'm so happy to have found you, Annie. Brenda. And I don't want to lose you again."

She hesitated only briefly before she rose from the table. "You sure you can handle the intrusion?"

"Positive."

As they made their way toward the door, Brenda whispered, "I wouldn't be too sure about that."

22

Dylan stood beside Benita as they stirred the pot of leftover Irish stew and debated its taste.

It was not quite six o'clock and he had hoped Vicki would be home long before now. He'd resisted the urge to follow her, which was no small feat, but he knew he'd be hard-pressed to keep his truck concealed if she were to glance in her rear-view mirror. And it would be even more difficult to explain what he was doing if she were to confront him. He'd refrained from calling her as time passed by. And it had taken a superhuman effort to avoid taking to the county roads in an effort to find her as his worries mounted.

He'd kept himself busy getting the fish shipped off and planning how to repair the garage. Finally, with his stomach in knots, he'd joined Benita in the kitchen.

He towered above the Hispanic woman by nearly a foot and now he reached over her head to open the cabinet.

"The extra Guinness helped, to be certain, but let's try this too, shall we?" he said, dropping a few pinches of onion powder and celery seeds into the stew. He stirred it, then tasted. "Oh, Bennie," he exclaimed, "That was precisely what was needed. Taste this."

As Benita leaned forward to taste the broth, they were surprised by a voice behind them.

"Vicki!" Dylan said as Vicki grabbed him from behind and gave him a bear hug. "Where 'ave you been all afternoon? I've been quite concerned."

He started to turn around, but she held him in place.

"What are you doin' to me, Darlin'?"

"I have a surprise," Vicki said.

"You found your sister?"

"Yes. And she's here."

"Well, let me go, Woman," he laughed, "so's I can meet 'er."

She dropped her arms from around him. As he turned around, she stood between him and her sister but over her head, he caught the crown of a cowboy hat beside the back door.

As she stepped to the side, a wide grin on her face, he studied the figure beside the back door. Her eyes were obscured by the hat's long, curved bill. But as he peered at her chin and her jawline, a feeling began in the pit of his stomach and worked upwards, freezing the words on his lips that he'd expected to say.

The woman stepped forward and with a jaunty sweep of the cowboy hat, removed it from her head, allowing masses of wavy copper hair to spill across her shoulders. It reached almost to her waist and was so voluminous that he wondered how she'd managed to fit it all beneath the hat.

As she stepped forward, his eyes went to the butterfly bandage on her forehead. A slow, sly smile swept across her face and as she neared him, he found himself staring into the same amber eyes shared by her sister.

She placed her hand around his neck and rose onto her toes to kiss him lightly on the cheek, her lips lingering along his cheekbone. "So you're Dylan Maguire," she said in a confident, husky voice, "and she's 'Bennie' and Vicki's 'Woman.' I just can't wait to hear what sweet little pet name you dream up for me."

Dylan's eyes met hers as he slowly reached for her hand and removed it from his neck. "Vicki, Darlin'," he said, "may I have a word with you, Dear?"

"Sure," Vicki said. She remained facing him with a wide grin on her face.

"In private?" he added.

As her sister continued to smile devilishly at him, he reached his long arm toward Vicki, lightly grasping the top of her blouse and pulling her with him into the hallway. As he disappeared from the kitchen, he called back to Benita in Spanish.

They stopped beneath the staircase. "Vicki, Darlin'," he whispered hoarsely, "where did you pick 'er up?"

"Exactly where I knew she would be. I'll probably never find it again in a million years but this afternoon, I drove straight there."

"So, this is the woman you've been seein' in your mind?"

She nodded. "Isn't it wonderful? I don't think I've ever been so happy."

He swallowed hard. "But, how do you know for absolute certain this is your sister?"

She laughed. "I'd know her anywhere. It's Annie. Though she goes by Brenda now. Long story. But other than that, she hasn't changed a bit; she's just taller and more—womanly—but her personality is exactly the same as it always was."

"Ooh," he said, pronouncing the word as two syllables, "is it now?"

"Yes. We talked all the way home. We have so much catching up to do. It's just—it's a dream come true!" Tears began forming in her eyes.

"Oh, now, Darlin', you're not plannin' to go and cry on me now, are you?"

"Yes."

"Oh, please. Don't. I'm beggin' you."

"But they're tears of happiness," she sobbed. "They're tears of pure joy!"

"Oh, she's cryin' tears o' pure joy, she is," he said. "I don't know if me heart can take all o' this, all at once, now, you know, meetin' your sister and havin' you cryin' to boot."

She grabbed his shirt and buried her face in it. "Isn't it wonderful? You have no idea how long I've dreamed of this moment, how many nights I laid awake crying for Annie. Brenda," she corrected herself. "I never knew what happened to her. I never knew where she went, who she lived with, what she did.

And now I have her." She looked at him, the tears streaming down her face. "Now I'm complete. I have my sister back."

"Ooh," he breathed. They stood there for a long moment as he held her. It barely registered that she was soaking the front of his shirt with her tears.

Finally, he took a deep breath. "So. We'd better get back to your sister then. After all, it took all this time to find 'er. We don't want to let 'er out o' our sight now, do we?"

As they returned to the kitchen, they heard two voices speaking in rapid-fire Spanish. Brenda was leaning over the stew, tasting it and laughing with Benita.

"You speak Spanish," Dylan said.

Brenda turned around. Her eyes fell first on Vicki's face, her smile fading just a moment as she registered the tears racing down her cheeks. Then she turned toward Dylan, her easy smile returning. She lifted one brow. "I just had a little vacation in South America," she said. Her lashes were long and full and for a moment, Dylan thought she intended to wink. Instead, she said, "I speak fluent Spanish. As well as several other languages. And yes, I know you told Bennie to keep an eye on me." As she walked across the kitchen, her hips swayed. "You're such a good host, Irish."

Before he could respond, she turned toward Vicki. "Sister, dear, do you mind if I change into something a little more comfortable?"

23

The pre-dawn hours found Dylan wide awake and flat on his back in bed, staring at the ceiling and listening to Vicki's soft, rhythmic breathing as she slept. The sisters had talked non-stop through dinner, reliving childhood memories and catching up on each other's lives. Or at least, Brenda had been catching up on Vicki's, who spoke as if Sam had adopted her, she'd lived in an average household in a normal suburb of Washington, and the CIA, Langley and an institutional existence was never mentioned. As for Brenda, she didn't say much about her own childhood beyond rudimentary events that might have occurred with anyone and Dylan found himself wondering if any of it was true.

Long after retiring, their giggles wafted through the door he kept slightly ajar. It sounded like a pajama party in Vicki's old bedroom on the second floor, and though he missed her terribly and the bed felt empty without her soft, warm body molded to his, he'd never heard her so happy. When she'd finally come to bed and snuggled into his arms, he'd been unable to bring up the sensitive matter of her sister's situation. And within minutes, Vicki had been sound asleep.

Now he felt like a piece of iron was wedged in his stomach. Each time he closed his eyes, the vision of Brenda in the interrogation room surfaced, her eyes pleading for help in removing the knife embedded in her. Then an image of Sam's face rose up, telling how she'd escaped and how imperative it was to recapture her. They knew she could never have engineered an escape alone; she had to have help, and it had to come from one or more of the agents transporting her. At this very moment, those agents were under interrogation, recounting every second of the time they'd spent with Brenda.

And now she was underneath his roof and he was trying to come to terms with the fact that the woman the CIA wanted so badly was Vicki's sister, the sister she'd been separated from since childhood. A sister that made her life more complete.

The door was still slightly ajar and as he lay there thinking, he heard a door open on slightly creaky hinges and softly close.

Glancing at Vicki, who was still sleeping soundly, he quietly slipped out of bed. Grabbing his jeans off the back of a nearby chair, he pulled them on while making his way around the bed to the door. Then he noiselessly descended the stairs in his bare feet, passing by Brenda's room on the second floor without hesitating.

He reached the newel post on the first floor and swung around to peer into the living room. Several African violets were arranged on a table beneath the front window and a space between them was conspicuously empty. His eyes darted to the coffee table where Vicki's pocketbook sat, the center compartment slightly open.

Dylan whirled around and silently made his way down the hallway toward the back door.

As he entered the kitchen, she was standing with her back to him, quietly removing the lock chain from the back door.

He came from behind her without a sound. She unlocked the deadbolt and the door knob and opened the door.

It had barely opened two inches before he slammed it shut with his forearm. At the moment the door had begun to close, she jerked her hand away from the knob toward her waist. Now she stood motionless, facing the door. He also remained completely immobile, his forearm across the door above her head.

She was taller than her sister; perhaps five foot seven and her boots made her a good three inches taller. His chest touched her back as he leaned on the door, her hair brushing against his face and flowing downward nearly to the top of his jeans. She smelled of Vicki's shampoo and Vicki's perfume.

"Where the bloody hell do you think you're goin'?" he said.

She didn't answer but continued facing the door. He could feel her back rising and falling with her measured but deep breathing.

"Put the gun down, Red," he said calmly.

"Aw," she said in her throaty voice, "so you do remember me. And here I was getting my feelings hurt for nothing."

"I said, put the gun down."

"Since you remember me," she said, still with her back against him, "you know I didn't have a gun. As I recall, the only weapon I had was removed by your very capable hands. *Doctor.*"

"I know," he said, his voice measured but firm, "that you've got me gun in your right hand. And I know as soon as you turn around, that gun is goin' to be pointed at me chest."

"Let me go, Irish. Don't make me shoot you."

"Well, you'd have to shoot me twice to catch up with your sister."

She laughed softly. "I don't believe you."

"Take a look above your head at me shoulder," he said, "and you'll see one o' the bullet holes she left in me."

She turned her head slightly and peered upward. "I believe you were shot," she said slowly, "but I don't believe Vicki's got it in her."

"Oh, she's got it in 'er, all right. You can ask 'er yourself."

"Let me go. You're a good guy. I really don't want to have to shoot you."

"There are two things I won't be allowin' to happen. First, you're not gonna shoot me with me own gun. And second, they won't be catchin' you with me gun on you. They won't be tracin' you back to me." He placed his other arm above her head so both were resting against the door.

"Why won't you let me leave?"

"Because it would break your sister's heart to wake up and find you gone."

She remained motionless and he could almost hear her mind racing. "I'm bad news, Irish. You and I both know it. I'd only bring trouble down on you two. It's better this way."

"It's better that you stay here. You're safe here."

"What are you saying?"

"I think I just said it."

Brenda turned so she could peer at him out of the corner of her eye. "Are you proposing that if I put down this gun, you'll let me stay here with you two?" She managed a forced laugh. "Why on earth would you risk everything for me?"

"Because Vicki loves you. And I love 'er. And I'll not see 'er hurt."

"You love her that much?"

"I do."

"You're telling me," she said, as if allowing it to sink in to her own brain, "that if I stay here, you won't turn me in?"

"I can't guarantee you won't get caught. But I'll guarantee it won't be me that turns you in. I give you me word."

"How do I know your word is any good?"

"You don't. But it's the only option you've got."

"I'm turning around," she said after a moment's hesitation. "And I'm handing you the gun."

He moved slightly away from the door, dropping his arms from around her head as she turned around. He took the gun from her hand and set it on the kitchen table beside them.

"Now I'll thank you to put 'er car keys and 'er money back in 'er purse, and the knives back in the drawer."

She blinked and cocked her head. "How did you know?"

"Because if I'd 'ave been in your situation, that's precisely what I would've done."

"Then—why did you stop me?"

"Because this time, it would've been me left behind to pick up the pieces. I've already seen 'er heart broken once. I'll not see it happen again. Not if I can help it."

"You really do love her." He didn't answer and after a moment, she added, "I wish I'd met you before she did. We would have been good together."

His eyes followed her jawline, her full lips, a slightly wide, upturned nose, her high cheekbones, and a mountain of copper hair a man could get lost in. Then his eyes moved to her perfect brows, one raised slightly, coquettishly, before stopping to peer into her mesmerizing amber eyes. "We would have been dangerous together."

She smiled seductively. "That, too." Then, "Does she know what you do?"

"She knows where I work. She doesn't know the details."

"So, you never told her about me—even before you knew I was her sister?"

He shook his head. "And I'll thank you not to tell 'er."

"Not to tell me what?"

Brenda and Dylan turned simultaneously to stare at Vicki standing in the kitchen doorway. She was wrapped in her bathrobe, her hair disheveled and her feet bare and as she watched them, she gingerly moved from one foot to the other on the cold tile floor.

"Well, now," Brenda said, smiling slyly, "it wouldn't be a surprise if I spilled the beans, now would it?" She walked across the kitchen and hugged her. "He loves you so much. You have no idea." She turned back to Dylan. "Does she?"

He looked into her face, at her cunning grin and her devilishly gleaming eyes before turning to Vicki. "Why don't I make us a bit o' breakfast?" he said. "It's Saturday and it's Bennie's day off. I could treat you both to a good old fashioned Irish meal."

24

As Vicki drove through the security gate at Fort Bragg, she wrestled with a tension that swelled as she drew closer to her destination. Shortly after breakfast, Sam had summoned her to his office. He'd been brusque and decisive about his need to have her attempt another remote viewing session.

She tried in vain to buy some time by telling him she'd located her long-lost sister, but he was disinclined to hear about her sister's sudden appearance in her life or be concerned in the least about her personal need to reconnect with her for a few days before returning to work.

And he'd made it quite clear that she could not arrive at his office soon enough.

She understood perhaps more than most, Chris' disappointment at her feigned inability to see Brenda in her mind's eye and his overwhelming need to reconnect with her. Whatever had occurred between Chris and Brenda in the past must have been powerful enough to prevent him from shaking her memory. The man was obsessed. She could envision her sister with him; he was strong and appeared so steadfast and stable. She'd need someone with a firm and steady personality to keep her reined in—if that was even possible.

But she hadn't had time to talk to Brenda about him. Or perhaps, she thought, she could have found the time. But she didn't want to spoil their reunion with talk of her sister's troubles—troubles that had compelled a government to search for her with such fervor.

It was all too complicated. And the only thing she could do was stall until she had the opportunity to talk to her sister and find out why they wanted her so badly.

She parked under the pine trees in her usual spot. She'd never before attempted to provide bad information. She wondered if there could be some way for Sam to detect the deception. Just as quickly, she knew she had to try. And if they found out—well, she'd deal with the consequences later.

Sam was on the phone as she entered his office. He was clearly agitated but he waved in Vicki when he spotted her backing away from his door.

She felt her shoulders sag a bit with the weight of his words as she entered.

"I want to know what she said, what she did, what power she had over them," he snarled. "She didn't become Houdini and slip out of those constraints on her own. She had help and they were the only people with her."

He hesitated while he listened. Then he swore. "I don't care if they're our agents. Keep them as long as it takes. Threaten to charge them." Another moment lapsed. "Take your pick. Accessories. Treason. I don't care. But they don't see the light of day until they tell us why they allowed her to—no, assisted her in—escaping."

The person on the other end of the line might have been debating the merits of the agents. Sam's face darkened and he swore again. "I don't care if they were my own flesh and blood," he growled. "This woman is important. And we're not leaving any stone unturned until we find her."

He slammed down the phone and turned to Vicki. "Sit down," he ordered.

As she made her way to the couch, she was startled to see Chris emerge from the shadows. He shook hands with her as if he was compelled to appear formal, shyly looking into her eyes as though searching for a reaction from her.

"We're wasting time with these little formalities," Sam said, nodding pointedly toward their hands. Chris reluctantly dropped his hold and backed into his chair while Vicki settled into her usual spot.

Sam turned on the video and audio recorders and sat in his customary chair near the head of the couch. He had a pad of paper in his lap and he tapped his pen against his pants leg. As Vicki began to clear her head and prepare for her session, she detected quite a bit of turmoil in the air. Sam was under pressure and his tension was permeating her psyche.

As she tried to block him and drift into her self-imposed trance, she found herself almost instantly in front of a computer screen. Her brain felt as though it was in slow motion; she was accustomed to rapidly reporting what she saw, allowing analysts to decipher it later. But now she found herself filtering every detail, weighing it for its value and its ability to lead the CIA directly to her own doorstep.

Finally, she said, "I can't see the individual. I am sitting in a chair, looking at a computer."

"What does it say on the screen?" Sam asked.

She hesitated. "Subcommittee hearing on oil prices," she read. She realized she was seeing what Brenda was studying at that very moment, and she wondered if she'd gained access to the desktop in the attic space or if she'd managed to take her laptop from her bedroom. She tried to see the edges of the screen, but couldn't—as if everything except the website was cropped out of the picture.

"Go on," Sam said after a moment of silence.

Vicki swallowed. "There are powerful members on this committee. But these same members—not all of them, but some of them—are heavily invested in the oil industry. But they use pseudonyms, so their transactions cannot be traced back to them. She's switching over to another website." She hesitated while the new site appeared, and then struggled to read the screen. "It's written in another language, maybe Spanish? I don't understand it. But I'm confident, I can feel it, that these same members of this committee are tied to the oil industry in South America. They invested heavily in oil there."

She waited a few excruciating moments as Brenda surfed through the Spanish-language websites before switching to one in Saudi Arabia. "Now she's looking at oil in the Middle East. She seems to be very focused on our laws here and how they pertain to exports and pricing throughout the world. Whoever these members are, their job is to regulate oil in the United States. But they're creating loopholes so their investments elsewhere in the world can flourish."

Chris leaned forward, his voice sounding distant. "Can you see the woman on the computer?"

She shook her head. "It's as though I'm looking through her eyes."

"Can you see the keyboard?" Sam asked.

"Yes."

"Tell me if you see her hands."

"Yes."

"Describe them."

"Petite woman's hands. Sculptured nails. One is broken; it's a bit lifted up. They're immaculate, really."

"Is she wearing jewelry?"

"A ring. It's been broken somehow. She's got a cut there, where the ring broke. Someone doctored it for her."

"That's our girl," Sam said. "Latitude and longitude."

Vicki hesitated. In her mind's eye, she could see herself looking down at a GPS. The numbers nearly jumped off the tiny screen at her, but she remained silent.

"Latitude and longitude," Sam said again. His voice was monotone but she could detect an edge to it.

"Latitude. Thirty-four point six."

"Longitude?"

She squeezed her eyes tighter, hoping the image would blur. "Minus seventy-nine."

"Are there windows in the room?"

Vicki tried to see beyond the computer screen but couldn't. "I don't know."

The minutes crept passed with a minimal amount of movement on the screen, as if the user was concentrating on the information found on each page. After a few minutes, Sam said, "We're ending this. Come on back."

Relieved, Vicki moved away from the screen, and in the blink of an eye she felt herself on the couch in Sam's office.

Sam moved to his desk where he called up a program on his desktop computer before motioning for Chris. "Vicki is the best we've got. She can pinpoint a location like no other remote viewer we've ever had." He pointed to the map. "Look at this."

"You're not saying—?" Chris said.

Vicki's mouth was parched, her lips dry as she made her way to the desk, where she peered at the map beside Chris.

"That's exactly what I'm saying," Sam said. She could feel the excitement in his voice. "This girl's a pro. She meant for us to see her at that truck stop. She wanted to be caught on film. She traveled north from the point of her escape only to turn around and head south again. And look where she's at."

"Where?" Vicki said, struggling to see. She hoped her consternation wasn't written all over her face. And just as quickly, she hoped she wasn't leading them to an innocent person's door. A scene flashed in front of her of the door being knocked down, some poor soul reading a newspaper or cooking lunch only to find the CIA surrounding them, searching their house… God, she thought, please let it be an open field somewhere…

"Right back in Lumberton," Sam continued. "It's where she grew up. She's got friends there, people who can hide her, help her escape."

"The latitude and longitude I just gave you is Lumberton?" Really, Vicki thought. She needed to get better at deception. Much better.

Sam pointed. "You gave me a coordinate that's just blocks from the courthouse."

"That's my neighborhood." She felt sick. Had she given them her own house? Had her tongue deceived her?

"I'm not surprised," Chris interjected. "When I met her, she was living in a house near there."

"We're sending a team. Her file has her last known address."

"Her last known address," Vicki said, her voice strained, "was in my neighborhood?"

Sam chuckled wryly. "Same street you live on now. How's that for irony?"

A wave of exhaustion rushed over her. Between the lack of sleep the previous night, the remote viewing session and now this, all she wanted was to go home and curl up in a ball.

"Can I go?" she asked.

Sam waved at her without looking up. "Go. You did your job."

As she made her way toward the door, he added, "Good job, Vicki. Good job."

25

Dylan stood back from the wall in the bedroom and admired the dumbwaiter. It worked perfectly. He didn't know, now that he thought about it, why it had taken him so long to repair it. All it had needed was a new pulley, and while he was at it, he installed springs along the bottom to make the landing downstairs gentler. When he thought of all the times he and Vicki had enjoyed a romantic dinner on the third floor and all the times he hoped they'd have more of them, it just made sense to make things easier on themselves.

He gathered his tools and took the stairs to the second floor. He was just about to turn the corner to the first floor stairs when he caught a glimpse of Brenda standing at the window in Vicki's old bedroom.

Soon after Vicki had left, she'd asked to borrow her laptop to check her email. And each time Dylan had made his way up or down the stairs, she'd been sitting quietly in the corner chair, the computer in her lap. She was in no hurry to leave since their early morning encounter, and he hoped she'd arrived at the conclusion that she needed to remain where she was—at least until he decided how he was going to apprehend her and bring her in. And, he thought, how he was going to break the news to Vicki.

Now the laptop was closed as it rested on the ottoman and Brenda seemed oblivious to the fact that he was behind her, watching her. As she stared out the window, her thoughts apparently miles away, he noticed she and Vicki appeared to wear the same size clothes; he'd seen that particular pair of jeans on her many times. It fit her nicely, accentuating her long legs and shapely behind. A plain white blouse was above it, but she'd rolled up the tail into a knot at the side of her waist and the collar was turned up. Instead of her usual cowboy boots, she wore a pair of heels with open toes.

He glanced down the stairs. It was quiet; the only sound that of the air conditioner clicking on and off. It was just the two of them in that rambling house. He looked back at her. After a brief hesitation, he left the stairs and headed into her bedroom, tapping on the door in a semi-knock as he passed it. "Mind if I join you?"

She peeked at him before motioning toward the window. Her cocky smile was gone along with some of the color in her cheeks.

He made his way around the bed. She remained slightly to the side of the window, as if she didn't want to be seen from the outside. He stopped beside her and studied her profile momentarily while she remained focused on something outside. Her hair still smelled of Vicki's shampoo, and he resolved to buy her the worst smelling shampoo and perfume he could find. He dragged his eyes away from her and peered outside.

"Well, I'll be," he said, breaking into a boyish grin. "Looks like Alec will be cohabitatin' with Sandy."

"You know him?" Her voice was quiet and low, which made it sound even huskier than usual.

"It's Alec Brodie. He works for the sheriff's department."

"You know what he does there?"

He shook his head. "We've seen him and Sandy socially, but never talked about his work. Never had a need to."

"Well, I can tell you what he does." She studied Dylan out of the corner of her eye. "He's a detective. He investigated a double homicide last November." She cocked her head as if gauging his reaction. "My business partner and his wife. Murders aren't the only thing he investigates. He also investigates women involved in computer—improprieties."

She turned to fully face him and he found himself unable to tear himself away from her eyes. They were like liquid pools a man could drown in. She continued staring at him, expectantly waiting for his response.

Finally, he said, "Why am I gettin' the notion that not only do you know who he is, but he is also quite familiar with you?"

"Bingo," she said. "Give the man a prize." She looked outside. "You shouldn't keep me here, Irish. It's only a matter of time before he finds me. You're harboring a fugitive. You've got to know it carries serious consequences."

He turned his attention to the activity outside and remained silent as he watched Alec and two men carry a sofa from a rented moving van into the house. "The last place they'll be lookin' is right under their noses."

"Is that so?" She sounded unconvinced.

"They think you've gone to Washington, you know."

"Is that what they think?" She cocked her head again.

"It is."

"What would make them think that?"

"Now, why do you think?"

They stared at one another for a long moment. He knew his brows were knit, his eyes narrowed, and he could feel his lips slightly turned down. But her face remained completely expressionless. She stared at him with neither malice nor friendship and though he felt as though his soul could be sucked into those amber pools and lost there, he couldn't read what the woman behind them intended to do.

"You know," he said slowly, his eyes moving from her eyes to her lips and back, "you wanted to be seen on that camera."

"What camera?" Her lips turned up slightly and one eyebrow rose.

He felt the heat rising in his cheeks and his brows knit tighter.

"Oh," she said, perhaps sensing his mood, "*that* camera."

"You wanted us to be searchin' for you northward. And all the while you knew you'd be here." She didn't respond and after a moment, he added, "And these little games you keep playin' with me are beginnin' to foul me good humor."

The gleam disappeared from her eyes as she grew serious. "I didn't mean to come to Lumberton. Honestly," she said as it was his turn to raise a brow, "it's the last place on earth I want to be right now."

His eyes narrowed further. He had the advantage of height, of tilting his head slightly backward to peer at her under thick lashes, his own eyes veiled while hers grew larger out of necessity as she looked up. After a moment, he spoke. "Now why would that be, do you suppose?"

She took a deep breath and pointed down the street. "If you were to take a nice, leisurely stroll up this street right here—Elm Street—just about nine or ten blocks, you will be standing directly in front of my house."

His eyes grew wide despite his efforts and he felt the blood drain from his face. "You're jokin' me."

"Do I look like I'm joking?" When he didn't answer, she continued, "Everybody who's looking for me knows I grew up here. My adoptive parents have a farm just outside of town, a farm I own now. And I bought a nice little house right on this street, paid cash for it."

"Whatever you were doin' must pay pretty well," he murmured.

She shrugged. "I haven't seen either property since I fled last November. Kind of hard to maintain things when you're on the run."

"You must have someone lookin' after things while you're away?" His voice sounded distant to him.

She chuckled. "You're kidding, right? Anybody who helps me is a suspect."

"What did you do, that they want you so badly?" His voice was smooth, the Irish brogue rolling over his tongue like silk.

She looked at him for a long moment, her lips curving upward and her brow raised in an amused expression. "A lot of people have been trying to get that out of me. Do you think you can just stand there and ask and I'll tell you?"

He gazed back at her without answering immediately. Then he shrugged. "No. But it was worth a try."

The air between them grew thick until she said, "It's politics, Irish. It's all politics."

"Is it now?" She didn't answer, and after a moment he asked, "Does Vicki know?"

"She doesn't know anything," Brenda said without hesitation. "She knows I was adopted. She knows I grew up near here. She knows she picked me up on a county road. And that's all she knows." Before he could respond, she added, "And I'll be thankin' you," she said in a mock Irish accent, "not to tell 'er."

A flash of light crossed through the room and Dylan turned his attention to the window. Vicki was turning into the driveway, and the sun's rays were glancing off the car's chrome. He felt his heart quicken as she parked. Sandy spotted her immediately and called out to her, waving as she met her in the driveway.

Brenda and Dylan watched them chat, though she took another instinctive step away from the window to remain less visible.

"Nice clothes," she said. Dylan didn't have to ask whether she meant Vicki or Sandy. Their neighbor was wearing shorts that didn't quite cover her derriere. Above them was a bikini top with a spaghetti halter which accentuated her ample bosom. "Those are man catchin' clothes," Brenda added.

"It appears they worked."

"Funny what sex will do." She looked back at Dylan and smiled coyly.

"I'll not be talkin' about what I do with your sister."

"I thought we were talking about Sandy and Alec."

The heat rose in Dylan's cheeks and he turned his attention back to the window as Vicki pulled away from Sandy. Her voice was light and cordial as she said her good-byes on the way to the house. A moment later, the screen door slammed. He stepped across the room and poked his head into the hallway. "Up here, Darlin'," he called.

Vicki glanced up. He watched her climb the stairs with a bounce in her step and a grin on her face.

"Well, don't you look like the cat who caught the mouse," he mused.

He leaned over the railing and as she drew near, she stopped to plant a soft, moist kiss on his lips. He reached for her across the railing but it began to give way and he teetered backward. "Ooh," he said. "I need to be fixin' that."

"Yes, you do. We don't want anybody falling through the railing to their death below."

He glanced at her, his eyes wide, but she was looking past him. Her eyes narrowed and she tilted her head. He turned to find Brenda in the bedroom doorway, an amused expression on her face and the laptop in her arms.

"How sweet," she said. "Puppy love."

"My laptop," Vicki said. Her smile had completely faded.

Brenda handed her the laptop. "Hope you don't mind. I wanted to check my email."

Vicki took it from her. "How'd you get past the password?"

Brenda's eyes widened momentarily before her cocky smile was back on her lips. She glanced at Dylan.

Vicki turned to look at him, also.

"Don't be lookin' at me," Dylan said, placing his hand on his chest. "I don't even know what it 'tis. Don't want to know."

They both turned to face Brenda.

She pointed toward the window. "Looks like you have a new neighbor moving in."

"Yes," Vicki said, making her way into the bedroom and plopping down on the edge of the bed.

Dylan glanced at Vicki and then at Brenda. It couldn't have been lost on her that Brenda hadn't answered her question.

"Alec and Sandy are moving in together," Vicki was saying. "Isn't it wonderful?"

Dylan cleared his throat. "You know," he said, sitting down beside Vicki and pulling her hands into his lap, "Darlin', it's been so long since you've seen your sister and I've not gotten to know 'er at'all. You know how I love to cook. But I never get the opportunity 'cause Bennie is always here, doin' all the cookin'. So what about it, if I whip up a wonderful dinner, just for the three o' us? Open a good bottle or two o' wine. I'll even make dessert."

Vicki looked at Brenda. "Is it any wonder I have fallen head over heels in love with this man? I could stay here forever and never even leave the house."

"Well, what about that," Brenda said, a coy smile crossing her face. "Just like house arrest."

26

Vicki lay on the sofa in the living room, her head in Dylan's lap while Brenda reclined in the chair a short distance away. The room was lit by a rainbow of colors from the television screen. Three dessert plates sat on the coffee table, the maple-apple concoction Dylan had whipped up long gone along with two bottles of wine that sat beside them.

"Where'd you learn to cook?" Brenda asked, rubbing her stomach with a pleasing grin. "You're not half bad."

"I'll take that as a compliment."

"Well?"

Dylan glanced at Vicki and ran the fingers of one hand through her hair before answering. "Me gran'mum taught me. I was on me own a lot, and she said I'd need to learn how to take care of m'self. I can cook, iron… but not sew. Me fingers are too—" he held up his free hand "—fat and clumsy."

"I wouldn't say that," Vicki said, grabbing his hand and kissing his fingers.

"Ah, aren't you two lovebirds sweet," Brenda said.

Dylan glanced at her, expecting to see sarcasm on her face, but he didn't find it.

"Didn't your 'grandmum'," she continued, "think you'd ever find a woman?"

He grew pensive. "I suppose she thought it couldn't hurt to know it, whatever the outcome."

"Fair enough." Brenda glanced at her watch. "I'm going to leave you two to your own devices."

"I think," Vicki said as her sister rose from her seat and stretched, "this is the first time since I moved in that we've actually watched television."

"Do you just have one TV?" Brenda asked.

"Why do you want to know?" Dylan answered.

"I like to watch cable news. I listen to it while I'm in bed. Wake up to it. I miss not having it."

"Why are you wantin' to watch cable news all the time?" Dylan asked.

"Why not?"

He shrugged. "Most of it's hate-filled poison, isn't it now?"

She laughed.

Vicki held up her hand. "No political discussions. Please." She raised her eyes to Dylan's. "Maybe we could set up a TV in her bedroom? That way she can watch it and we don't have to."

His cell phone rang and she reluctantly raised her head from his lap so he could pull it from his pocket. He stared at the smartphone for a moment, his brow furrowed, and then returned it to his jeans.

"What was that all about?" Vicki asked.

"Text message," he said.

They waited for him to elaborate. When he didn't, Vicki said, "Well?"

"Well," he said, hesitating so long she thought he wasn't planning to continue. Then, "It's a good thin' we planned on stayin' inside tonight."

"Why is that?" Brenda's voice was soft as she stepped toward the couch. Her eyes were suddenly wider and she appeared more awake than she had just a moment before.

"Because," he said, drawing out the word, "that was a text from a police officer friend of mine who lives down the street about ten blocks on Elm Street."

"What?" Vicki interrupted, giggling. "What police officer friends do you have?"

Brenda's eyes remained fixed on Dylan.

"It appears," he said, "that there's a group o' officers at his house on Elm Street about ten blocks down."

"Give me that cell," Vicki said, reaching for his pocket. "You don't have a police officer friend who lives ten blocks down on Elm Street. The house ten blocks down is—"

They waited for her to continue.

"Is what?" Dylan asked.

"I don't know what I'm saying," she said. "I'm tired and I'm crazy."

Though the television set continued spewing sound in the background, it felt as if the room had become deadly silent. Brenda's eyes were locked on Dylan's. His were locked on hers. Vicki placed her forearm over her eyes as if visually signaling how tired she was.

"So," Dylan said after the pregnant pause became too tense to bear, "now that we're all tired. And it's been a long day. How about if I just gather these dishes into the kitchen and we call it a night? Everybody go to bed? And spend the night in the house in nice warm beds, not lookin' out the windows or openin' the doors, just dreamin' away in our beds."

"You are making no sense whatsoever," Vicki said.

"I think he's right," Brenda said abruptly. "I'm really beat. I think I'll run upstairs, take a nice, warm shower and hit the hay."

Dylan rose from the sofa and began gathering up the plates.

"I'll do it," Vicki said. "You've done everything else tonight. It's the least I can do."

He didn't object. She placed the dirty dishes and the spent bottles of wine on a tray and headed into the kitchen. It was quiet in there and as she rinsed off the dishes and loaded the dishwasher, she relived the evening's events—the Irish dinner, the laughter and talk around the table, watching a movie in the living room while they ate dessert… It had been idyllic.

So why couldn't she shake this nagging feeling?

In one sense, it was as if she'd never been separated from Brenda. They talked about experiences growing up, things they used to do together, even sharing a bedroom and talking into the night. But on the other hand, they'd spent sixteen years apart. Brenda had a harder edge to her now and a mask of privacy.

Maybe, Vicki thought, she'd been so traumatized by their parents' deaths and their separate adoptions that it would take her awhile to adjust.

No, she thought. It's what she's running from that has her wound so tight.

She locked the back door, her fingers hesitating on the chain. They'd been standing there just this morning. Brenda had been fully clothed; that thought hadn't escaped her. And there had been a gun on the kitchen table.

When she'd left for Fort Bragg later that day, she found her car keys in the center of her pocketbook. She never kept them there; they were always in the outside pocket.

So why was Brenda standing at the back door before dawn, fully clothed, with her car keys? It didn't take a psychic to figure it out, she thought. She was leaving.

And it also hadn't escaped her that Dylan had slipped out of bed and rushed downstairs in his bare feet to stop her.

And now, she thought, she'd sent CIA operatives to Brenda's house down the street where they were probably ransacking the place looking for her or signs she'd been there… while she's upstairs taking a warm shower. She hoped she wouldn't pull back the curtains to take a peek outside.

"Are you okay, Darlin'?"

She turned to face Dylan as he stepped into the kitchen. "Has Brenda gone upstairs?"

He nodded. "Presumably to get a good night's rest."

They met beside the kitchen table. He wrapped his arms around her and she snuggled her head against his chest. He rested his chin on top of her head and they stood there in silence for a moment.

"What was that text message really about?" she asked.

"Sam," he said. "I'm on standby tonight."

"For what?"

He shrugged. "I don't know. I never know what he's gonna have me do. Sometimes I'm injurin' a man just to hear him talk. Other times, I'm doctorin' an injury—" he stopped himself but she didn't seem to notice.

He sounded tired and she thought the most thoughtful thing to do was simply go upstairs and go to bed; it might be the only bit of sleep he'd get. Instead, she pulled far enough away to look him in the eye. "We need to talk."

"Ooh," he said. After a moment's hesitation, he reluctantly pulled out a chair for her and grabbed one for himself.

"Why'd you say that?"

"I didn't hear m'self say anythin'."

"Yes, you did. You breathed strange."

"Are we micromanagin' the way I breathe now?"

"No."

"Okay, then."

"There's something on my mind."

"Ooh," he said.

"There you go again."

"It's just when a woman you're livin' with says there's somethin' on her mind in that tone o' voice, it can mean only three thin's. She wants a ring. She wants a baby. Or she wants somebody to move out. And it's usually not 'er."

"There are other reasons for wanting to talk."

"Well, then, have at it."

He grabbed her arm and pulled her to him, where she perched on his lap. He looked her in the eye. His were tired, with dark circles forming under them. But they were earnest and wide as he looked at her.

She wrapped her arm around his neck. "This morning. She was leaving, wasn't she?"

He kissed her lightly before he answered. "I think your sister is in a wee bit o' trouble."

"Why were you in here with her?"

"I wasn't leavin' with 'er, I can tell you that." When she didn't respond, he continued, "I was lyin' awake in me bed, next to you. And I heard 'er go downstairs. And I thought I'd see what she was about."

"I woke up when you got out of bed."

He nodded but didn't respond.

"And I heard you whispering by the back door. But you wouldn't tell me what you were talking about."

"I didn't want to worry you, because it was all over by then. You know," he said, grasping her tighter, "the fey thin' you do. You found your sister. And found 'er pretty easily. Drove straight to 'er, you said."

"Yes."

"I was just wonderin', is all, if you could find your sister so easily, could you not find out what's troublin' 'er?"

"I've tried. It's like I'm being blocked. She's so closed…"

"How's about sittin' down and havin' a chat with 'er then? Do you think she'd tell you anythin'?"

She shook her head.

"It's worth a try, don't you think? You're sisters, after all. Maybe she would tell you thin's she wouldn't tell anyone else."

"Can I ask you something?"

"Anythin', Darlin'."

"When I came home this afternoon, you were in her bedroom."

"I was. We were lookin' out the window. With the door open. And I called you up to us. We weren't doin' anythin', I swear to you that."

"But…"

"No buts. Nothin' was goin' on."

"You two were hiding something from me."

"No. We were watchin' Alec move in next door, is all."

She nodded but she wasn't convinced.

He gently pushed her onto her feet, then lifted her up and set her on the kitchen table.

"I was quite comfortable in your lap."

He wrapped his arms around her but stood a few inches away where he could look her in the eyes. "Well, you might end up there yet."

She reached for his shirt front and dragged him closer to her. She loved the smell of him, she thought as she buried her face in his shirt.

He kissed the top of her head and then placed his finger under her chin and lifted her face upward toward his. He kissed her lightly on her finely arched brow and then on her lid and moved slowly across her face to her cheekbones and then to her lips. As she parted them, she realized just how much she loved the way he tasted, the way his lips were so smooth and gentle while his hands were so large against her back.

He stroked his hand along her spine and then ran his hand through her hair as his other hand unsnapped her bra with one quick movement.

She pulled back from him. "My sister—"

"Oh, no, you don't," he said hoarsely. "You're not goin' to tell me you won't have lusty sex with me simply because you're afraid your sister will walk in."

She glanced toward the door. "But—"

"She'll never hear us." He started to kiss her again but stopped. "On second thought, if she does hear us all the way down the hall, up the stairs and through a closed door, I suppose it could mean we're doin' somethin' right, eh?"

He held her close and pressed his lips close to her ear. "Let's see just how loud we can get you to scream."

27

The call came shortly after two a.m. In the moment the first ring sounded in the semi-gloom, he'd thought it was the alarm clock and he was back in Ireland. Then he realized as he groaned and rolled over, he'd been dreaming of his home there, of the mists that rolled over the pond in the hours just before dawn, of the rolling green landscape with rocks jutting out and of a life he once lived that was gone forever. Even his dog, a black and white border collie, was seared into his memory, standing on a knoll, rocking from one side to the other, fixing the sheep with her hypnotic stare.

He hadn't realized until that moment how much he missed it. And now, with the insistent ringing of his cell phone urging him to wakefulness, he felt an emptiness and a longing to be home.

Vicki stirred as he stretched his arm across the bed to retrieve the phone. She was soft and warm and she cradled against him in slumber, intertwining her legs in his. She'd fallen asleep in his arms shortly after midnight, and he'd lain awake watching her eyelids flutter, feeling her breasts rise and fall against him in cadence with her breath, inhaling the sweet aroma that was uniquely hers, a scent that reminded him of lavender fields and rose petals.

He knew who was phoning him at this ungodly hour even without looking at the caller i.d. It was Sam. It was always Sam.

He wondered if the man ever slept as he groggily answered.

"Rise and shine," Sam said, though his gruff voice made Dylan want to hunker down and pull the covers over his head. "We're going in."

Vicki shifted and Dylan reluctantly extricated himself from her. He sat up, propping the pillow against the headboard and leaning back. "Where do I meet you?"

Sam rattled off the address. "Park your car at the edge of the Roses' parking lot; it's a few blocks away. Walk from there. We're going in with a stealth squad and we don't want the neighbors gawking."

"What time?"

"You have twenty minutes."

"I'll be there."

Dylan clicked off the phone. He pushed back the covers and draped his legs over the side of the bed as Vicki reached for him. He wanted nothing more than to lie back down and pull her close to him. With her in his arms, he was able to forget so much.

"That was Sam, Darlin'," he said, rising from the bed despite her groans. He turned back to her, leaned down and kissed her. Her eyelids fluttered and she mumbled something he didn't quite understand. He watched her for a few seconds. Then with a heavy sigh, he pulled the covers back around her, tucking her in, and then wandered to the closet. He was dressed quickly; he'd expected the call after receiving the text and had his clothes neatly laid out. Now it was a simple matter of slipping them on in the dim moonlight that filtered through the window and across the bedroom.

He held his boots in his hands as he came back around to the bed, where Vicki was now cuddled into the warm area he'd just vacated. He leaned over her and kissed her again, brushing his lips over hers until her eyes gently parted.

"I'll be back soon, Darlin'," he whispered.

Her eyes were closed before he had pulled away. It was just as well that she slept so deeply, he thought. It was the same every morning when he awakened before dawn. He'd shower and change and often clean up the remnants of dinner from the night before, and she'd be none the wiser. He often wished he could sleep as soundly. Demons kept him awake, he thought. Irish demons. And no matter how far he traveled from that emerald isle, there were some nights when they followed him and he just couldn't shake them.

He stopped on the second floor and hesitated just outside Brenda's bedroom. He held his hand inches from the knob, flexing his hands in indecision before quietly opening the door.

He didn't know what image might meet him and he wondered what he would do if she slept in the nude. But he knew as he poked his head around the door, he'd do the same regardless; he had but one thing to say to her.

She was sitting up in bed, her knees drawn up to her chest, a gun—his gun—resting on her kneecaps, pointed at the door. He could see the glint of the metal, though her expression was shrouded in darkness.

"It's Dylan," he said, his voice husky.

"If you wanted a tryst, you should have warned me." Her voice was silky but it caught slightly, contradicting her flip attitude.

"Don't leave this room," he ordered. "I'm goin' down to your old place. I'll be back directly."

"Raiding it, are they?" she asked. She lowered the gun.

"Somethin' like that."

"Hey, if you think about it, bring me back some fresh clothes. And I'm almost out of hairspray."

He hesitated in the doorway, watching her in the darkness. Then without a word he closed the door and continued to the first floor where he slipped on his boots. When he returned, he reminded himself, he was going to have to round up all his guns and lock them away. She helped herself to them too readily.

He silently slipped through the front door, closing it quietly behind him.

He wandered up the sidewalk, heading northward. Her house was only ten blocks away. It didn't make sense to drive. His legs were long and he was fit and he'd just as soon walk it.

The air had a dampness to it and again he felt the tug of Ireland. He'd forgotten these past few months how it rained there almost daily. He missed the rain, he realized. He missed the feel of the soft drops on his face, the mists in the morning, the dew on the grass. He missed the chill in the air as though it was always early spring.

The street was deserted. He didn't even spot another CIA operative though his sight was keen even in the darkness. But then, he reasoned, they weren't parked amid the houses. They were coming from the opposite direction, from the parking lot at the edge of Biggs Park Mall.

He noted the street numbers as he passed each home. By the time he was two blocks away, he'd calculated which one was hers.

It was narrow but deep. Set on a corner lot, it was no darker than the ones surrounding it. The grass was short and the bushes trimmed; someone was obviously continuing to care for it in her absence. A sand-colored Toyota Highlander was parked in the driveway, accessible from the side street. For all appearances, she might have been at home and asleep.

His eyes roamed over the structure, noting the front door and one window beside it, three windows down the side and two on a second floor. He knew they'd find it empty but he thought it good practice to identify means of escape.

A half block away he felt more than saw something—someone—in the shadows. He stopped immediately and peered down the shadowy side street. A figure emerged from beside a hedge; he was the same height as the bushes and in his black jeans and black jacket, he could easily have blended in and been overlooked had Dylan's senses not been on high alert.

"Very good," Sam said in a stage whisper as he joined him. "Where'd you park?"

"I walked from home."

"Even better."

They cut across the last yard and approached Brenda's house from the side street. Dylan found it interesting that on this stretch of Elm Street nearly every house had a corner lot, making each one accessible from the side as well as the front.

"Who's car?" Dylan asked, nodding toward the Highlander.

"Hers."

"She wouldn't have been daft enough to drive 'er own car to 'er own home, you think?"

Sam half-chuckled. "It was there before she disappeared."

As they passed it, Dylan glanced inside. He didn't take her for a Highlander kind of gal. But now he wasn't quite sure what he thought she'd drive. He could picture her behind the wheel of a Ford F-250 with a shotgun across the back window. Or a Jaguar XKR and she'd have five inch heels on as she stepped out. Or for that matter, he thought, a battle tank.

They met up with four more men in her back yard. Six men, he thought, to catch one woman who was curled up in bed at this very moment with his gun at her side. The thought occurred to him that she could easily take off while she knew he was gone, steal his truck or Vicki's car and head in the opposite direction. Within minutes she'd be on the interstate and in less than half an hour she'd be across state lines. And how would he explain it? How could he report that his vehicle had been stolen when he knew who took it?

He had a sudden urge to turn around and go back home, to recheck her bedroom, hide his keys and gather his guns. But instead, he looked into the shadowy faces of the men gathering under an ancient oak tree in her back yard.

"You two," Sam was saying, "will position yourselves near the front door. Gerald," he nodded toward a man with a blond buzz cut, "you watch that side." He motioned toward the side yard wrapped in murky shadows. "Max, you watch the other side."

Sam's eyes met Dylan's. "You and I are going in through the back."

Dylan nodded and waited for instructions.

Sam walked to the back of the house while the others took up their positions. Dylan followed, his eyes studying the back door. It was shielded from the street by privacy fencing that bordered the steps and small stoop. He could tell there were two deadbolts in addition to the door knob lock.

But Sam bypassed the door and stopped instead at a small window close to the ground. He pulled out a suction cup and a glass cutter. Crouching, he suctioned the cup to the glass.

"How do you know she doesn't have an alarm?" Dylan whispered.

"We checked. It's been disabled. She stopped making payments."

Sam deftly etched two vertical lines in the glass. Then he joined them horizontally. He pushed a button on an earpiece. "We're going in. Dylan will open the front door for the front team. Max and Gerald, hold your positions." He nodded. With a couple of gentle tugs, a rectangular piece of glass slid out. He set it on the ground and looked at Dylan with a self-satisfying smirk. It was, Dylan realized, the first time he'd seen any resemblance to a smile cross his face.

"I'm goin' in first I take it."

"You'll be in the laundry room. Up the stairs to the front door. Open it. Then open the back door for me."

Dylan nodded. "And in the middle o' all that I'm to look for 'er, I presume?"

"When the others are in, we fan out."

Sam handed Dylan a pair of gloves. He slipped them on, understanding their usefulness as he grabbed onto the edge of the glass and lowered himself into the gloomy basement. He stood for a moment, allowing his eyes to adjust. The basement was small, not half the size of the two floors above, and he easily found the stairs.

He reached the front door in less than a minute. The moment he opened it, two agents thrust through the doorway. One immediately went upstairs while the other investigated the downstairs with precision.

Seeing in his mind's eye the dimensions of the house from outside, Dylan quickly discovered the back door and opened it to find Sam standing on the back stoop, his eyes focused on his watch. "Two minutes, fifteen seconds," he said. "Not bad."

As Sam moved inside, Dylan hesitated only briefly. When no additional orders were forthcoming, he followed his instincts and headed toward the stairs.

He hadn't thought about it until this moment, but now he was curious what type of a home Brenda would have. And it was nothing like he expected.

It was stark, almost sanitized, as if no one truly lived there. The coffee table sported an old issue of *Offshore Magazine* while a photograph that dominated the living room wall appeared at first glance to be a beach scene but even before Dylan had passed it by, he'd seen the spires in the background—oil refineries.

Upstairs, he found the other agent rummaging through a spare bedroom. But instead of typical bedroom furniture, he found a desk and a bookshelf. He made his way down the hall to the second bedroom as Sam was coming up the stairs.

This room was dominated by a large photograph of a few people on camels making their way across the desert sands. In the background was a glistening modern city. On top of the dresser sat a hand mirror. On the chest of drawers was a jewelry box. Under Sam's curious eyes, he opened the jewelry box. It was empty.

In two strides, he was back at the dresser, yanking out drawers.

"What are you doing?" Sam asked.

"They're empty." He let them slam into the floor, helter-skelter. "They're all empty."

He opened the closet door. There was a lone pair of shoes beneath half a dozen pair of slacks and blouses. "This is a front."

Sam motioned toward the other end of the hall. "They found where a laptop had been connected down there."

"Who?"

"Local police."

"They find the laptop?"

"No."

"Just a connection? Place where it had been?"

Sam drew the word out. "Yes…"

"She didn't live here. I'm tellin' you, this is a setup."

"What makes you say that?"

"Instinct."

Another agent poked his head through the door. "All clear."

Dylan brushed past him and made his way downstairs, Sam on his heels. He strode directly to the kitchen, where he opened the refrigerator door beneath the curious stares of the other agents. He left the door open for them to see the contents—or lack thereof.

"Anybody clean out this house after she disappeared?"

"It was declared a crime scene. No one should have been here."

"But the lawn's been mowed. The bushes trimmed. No mail overflowin' the mail box. There's no food in the refrigerator. At the very least, we should 'ave been overcome with the stench o' fouled milk. Smells fresh as an Irish mornin' in there." He opened one cabinet after another. "You say a woman lived here, 'ey? A single woman?"

Sam nodded.

Dylan continued, "Why isn't there food in the cupboard? Why aren't there panties in the dresser? I imagine if I return to the bathroom, I'll find there are no tampons in the drawers or shampoo in the shower."

"What are you saying?" Sam asked, though Dylan could see the wheels turning.

"I'm sayin'," Dylan responded, "that either she never lived here and this was a front—though I don't know for whose benefit—or somebody has been here and cleaned it out."

Dawn was still a long way off as Dylan made his way out of the house. Sam was setting the glass into the window and carefully removing the suction cup. The other agents had disbursed, and the doors were closed and locked.

Dylan started down Elm Street when Sam called out to him. "Got something for you," he said, nodding his head in the direction of the side street.

Dylan followed him three blocks to Pine Street and one block over, to a small parking lot where his vehicle was backed into a spot almost obscured by the building next door.

"Get in," Sam said as he opened the door. "I'll drive you home."

"I prefer to walk if it's all the same to you."

"Suit yourself." He reached into the front seat and pulled out a manila folder.

"What's this?"

"For Vicki. Got it this morning—ah, yesterday morning, now."

Dylan took the folder from him and opened it. "What is it?"

"About her sister. The one she was looking for."

Dylan met Sam's eyes. They were shaded by the dim light and as always, his expression was unreadable. "Have you read it?" Dylan asked.

Sam shrugged. "I know Vicki found her so what's in there is probably old news now. But she should have it. I guess. I prefer to stay out of it. Nothing personal."

Dylan nodded and clamped the manila folder shut. He turned and made his way across the parking lot. But before reaching the other side, he turned back around. Sam was just climbing into the car, as if he'd been watching him walk away. "Tell me somethin', Sam."

"Yeah?"

"How'd you manage to remain at arm's length from 'er all these years?"

"Who?"

"Who do you think?"

"It's business."

"Is that all it is to you, then?"

"Don't read any more into it than that," Sam said as he slammed the door shut and started it up.

28

Dylan was deep in thought and hadn't noticed the thickening fog that had set in until he was just a block from home. As he glanced up to get his bearings he realized the house was barely visible; only the yellow bulbs on the front porch glowed eerily through the mist to beckon him home.

He halted in his tracks and looked down the street as if seeing it for the first time. The giant trees that stretched their branches from each side, meeting in the middle to form a canopy above the road, appeared like shadowy, craggy fingers. As the fog shifted with the rising breeze, the tops of the trees swayed in and out of the mist almost like apparitions.

As the fog rolled in, it cloaked the remaining houses so he felt as if he was standing in the middle of nowhere, as though he'd been transported to a remote region.

He felt an odd lump forming in the pit of his stomach as he forced his legs to continue moving. But as he neared the house, his strides became slower and narrower and his feet heavier, until just the act of moving up the steps onto the front porch were exhausting.

He hesitated at the front door, his hand hovering over the knob, before he backed away and sat in the porch swing.

It reminded him of Ireland, of the mists that rolled in during the wee hours of the morning, settling into the valleys and obscuring all in its path. He thought of the times when he stood on the small stoop of a porch, drinking his coffee or tea and watching the mists rise above the pond at the edge of the lawn. The mists of Ireland were something alive, something that could soothe a man's soul or destroy it, something that cloaked a man when he wanted to be hidden or obscured that which he needed to see.

It reminded him of the precipitation that always seemed to hover over the land. One was always looking at the sky commenting on the rains that were coming or the rains that had just left, gauging the difficulty of the day's activities by which way the wind was blowing the mist. It was the kind of precipitation that could soak into the bones in the coldest hours and sweeten the skin on the warmest of days.

And he missed it. He missed the feel of it on his brow, the ghostly way it surrounded and hugged him. He missed the way it could soften her features. No, he thought, involuntarily shaking his head as he rose. He wouldn't think of her. Not now. Not ever.

He'd left those memories behind forever when he left Ireland, and he wouldn't be going back.

He entered the house with a newfound determination, dropping the folder on the hall table. Then he took the steps two at a time, not caring if the sound of his heavy boots reverberated in the open stairwell.

He reached the second floor and immediately swung around the newel post and headed for Brenda's bedroom door. He tapped lightly on it and cocked his head to listen.

"Yes?" the voice was husky and hesitant.

He cracked the door. "May I come in?"

"I'm decent, if that's what you mean."

He opened the door and immediately shielded his eyes and turned away but the image of Brenda standing topless beside the bed had already seared into his brain. "Jesus," he said. "What does 'I'm decent' mean to you?"

"Rule number one," she said as she pulled a blouse over her head, "don't trust me. Haven't you learned that yet, Irish?"

"I have now, that's for certain." He kept his back to her. "Just thought you'd want to know your house was raided."

"Did you bring me new clothes?"

"Of course not."

"Well, what good are you, then?"

"Did you live there, Brenda?"

"Depends. Whose house did you raid?"

He rattled off the address. He caught a glimpse of her in the dresser mirror. She was sitting on the bed fully clothed now, watching him with an amused expression. He turned around to face her.

"What do you think?"

He looked at her for a long moment. "You're an exasperatin' woman."

She half-smiled.

"If you lived there, somebody's made off with most o' your clothin'. And all your food." He waited for her to answer, but she didn't. "You're not plannin' on answerin' me, are you, Woman?"

"No, Irish. I'm not."

"Then I'm goin' to bed."

She lifted one leg and placed it seductively on the bed and patted the spot beside her. "Well, what's keeping you?"

He felt his face grow hot. "You ought to be ashamed o' yourself, actin' that way with your sister's—"

"My sister's what? Fiancé? Boyfriend? Lover?" She leaned toward him. "Just what are you, Irish?"

He strode to the door as she laughed. It was a gentle laugh, low and husky like her voice, but it seemed to float on the air like a melody. Without a word, he opened the door and stepped into the hallway, her laughter continuing to follow him.

He closed the door, her voice growing muffled now, and turned toward the stairs. Something caught his eye and he glimpsed up to see Vicki standing in the doorway of their bedroom, peering down the stairs at him. As their eyes met, hers narrowed for just the briefest of moments before she backed away from the door and closed it.

He swore under his breath as he took the stairs two at a time. He flung open the bedroom door and glanced about to find the room empty. Then he caught a movement nearing the bathroom door. He was at the door in a heartbeat as she tried to close it in his face. He threw up one large hand and stopped its progress long enough to jam his boot into the opening.

"Don't close this door on me," he warned.

"Get out."

"It's not what you're thinkin'."

She let go of the door. The force of his hand on the other side knocked him slightly off-center as the door swung open. He caught himself as she backed into the bathroom, her eyes flashing. "I've heard that before."

He let the door hit the back of the wall before answering. "It was like this."

She folded her arms in front of her.

He pulled out his cell phone. "I got a call from Sam." He punched a few buttons. "See?" he said, holding up the phone.

Her eyes didn't budge from his. "Sam told you to spend the night with my sister, did he?"

"He didn't—ooh. I didn't deserve that."

"Then what does Sam's call have to do with you spending the night in my sister's bedroom?"

"I didn't spend the night there." He fought to keep his voice steady. "Do you remember me makin' love to you last night? You've forgotten that already, have you?"

Her face reddened but she didn't answer.

"You fell asleep in me arms, after midnight. I got all o' two hours' sleep, I want you to know that."

"Well, whose fault is that?"

He hesitated. "Well, it's Sam's fault, if you want to know the truth o' it."

"Go on."

"He called," he said slowly, picking his words carefully, "to tell me—order me, actually, as part of me job—down the street to raid a house."

The color began to drain from her face.

"Aye. And I told you I was goin'. I kissed you a'fore I left. Kissed you more than once, as I recall." He stopped and looked at her lips. "And I can tell you're upset just lookin' at 'em now."

"Oh?" she said. "And how's that?"

"Because you have no lips." When she didn't answer, he added, "They were there before. But they're gone now."

They stood in silence for a long moment. "I don't know what that has to do with you being in my sister's bedroom," she said.

"Well, I—it—" he fumbled for the words.

"I'm waiting."

"She thought I was a burglar when I came back in."

"Is that so?"

"Yes. That's—so."

She leaned against the bathroom counter. He could tell she was rolling her tongue over her teeth while she thought. "And then what happened?"

"Well," he said, "she's got me gun for one thin'. It seems like I lay me gun down and the next thin' I know, it pops up in 'er hand."

"I didn't hear a gunshot."

"That's cause she didn't shoot me. I told her who I was a'fore that could happen to me." He rubbed his shoulder and looked to her for sympathy. "I've already been shot once—twice—in this house. I don't really want to be shot again, you know."

She continued staring at him.

"She might be a better shot than you," he continued. "Somehow, I'm thinkin' she is. And she could—"

"So, why were you in her bedroom?"

He nodded slowly. "That's an excellent question. It is. I—she—I told her who I was, and made sure she saw me in the light and I really was only in 'er bedroom for the briefest o' time. Maybe a minute. A minute an' a half." He stepped to the side and motioned toward the open door. "You can ask 'er y'self. She's still got me gun in 'er bedroom. And if you go down there," he added, "I'll thank you to get it back for me."

"Why didn't you get it yourself?"

"Well, she was pointin' it at me, for one thin'."

"Even after she saw who you were? Why would she do a thing like that?"

He wiped his forehead. "Darlin', I can't claim to know the inner workin's of a woman's mind. And if I did know, I'd worry about m'self."

She pushed past him and went to sit on the edge of the bed. "You're not telling me everything."

He followed her and sat down beside her. "I'm not. That's true. I'm leavin' out the part about the mission I was on. As we'd agreed to do. Remember?"

She didn't answer and after a moment, he began to remove his boots.

"What are you doing?" she asked.

"I'm goin' back to bed. Whilst you've been dreamin' away, Darlin', I've been workin'. And I'm tired. You can be mad at me all you want, but if your sister tells you the truth—which I'm prayin' to the Lord she does—she'll tell you we didn't do a thin'. We talked for all o' two minutes and I left straight-away. To come up here to you, I might add." He stood and slipped his jeans off and then pulled his shirt over his head. He tossed them onto the floor. "And now I'm curlin' up in bed—with you, hopefully—and grabbin' a couple o'hours o'sleep."

He pulled back the covers and climbed inside. There is entirely too much estrogen in this house, he thought. He watched her sitting on the edge of the bed for a couple of minutes before reaching his arm out to gently grab her and pull her against him. He couldn't have lain there more than a few minutes with her nestled against him before he was fast asleep.

29

It became one of those dreary days that made Vicki long for a cozy bed and room service. The rain intensified as the morning progressed and though she awakened several times to the sound of droplets hitting the glass panes, the sky remained so overcast that it felt as if the day wouldn't progress beyond pre-dawn.

When at last she awakened to find Dylan gone, she struggled to sit up and look at her watch through bleary eyes. When she realized it was after ten o'clock, she bounded out of bed, rushing into the bathroom to find Dylan stepping out of the shower.

"What are you about?" he said, toweling off.

Her jaw dropped. "It's after ten o'clock. You're just getting up?"

"Best get to the fish house, 'ey?"

Before she could respond, he was moving through the bedroom to the closet. And once she was finished in the bathroom, she found he'd already gone downstairs.

She discovered Brenda in the living room, seated in front of the television set.

"You two lovers must have been having a grand old time," Brenda said, her lip curling slightly. She looked pointedly at her watch.

"We both overslept," Vicki said sheepishly. "How long have you been up?"

"Never really went to sleep."

"Oh?"

"A lot on my mind."

Vicki glanced at the television, where political pundits were battling out their ideologies. "What are you watching?"

"The fall of Rome."

Vicki shook her head. "There's got to be something better on."

Brenda shrugged. "I find it interesting. Entertaining."

"Suit yourself. Did Dylan come this way?"

"You just missed him." She narrowed her eyes. "Does he have a problem with me?"

Vicki felt her spine stiffen. "Not that I know of. Why do you ask?"

"Just wondering. Anyway, when he came downstairs, he wouldn't look me in the eye. I said 'good morning' to him and he just half-waved like a celebrity dismissing a reporter and kept right on walking."

"You're not sensitive now, are you?"

"Me? Hardly." Brenda chuckled. "Just thought it was interesting. Out of character for him, you know what I mean? He always seems to be smiling. Even when his lips aren't, his eyes are." She hesitated. "You two didn't have a tiff, did you?"

Vicki glanced down the hall toward the kitchen as she heard the back door close. "No. Just slept late, is all."

She left Brenda in front of the television and made her way down the hall. Benita was busy in the laundry room and Vicki slipped through the kitchen and out the back door. When she arrived at the fish house, Dylan was unlocking the door.

"Are you okay?" Vicki asked.

"Just grand," he said as the door swung open. He went immediately to the thermostat and turned on the heat. "First time this season," he said. "I'm hopin' it didn't get too chilly for the fishies."

He made his way to the store room in back and emerged a moment later, pulling a dolly. "Would you be alright, Darlin', takin' care of the fishies yourself this mornin'?"

"Dylan."

He made his way to the door and was pulling the dolly onto the brick pathway when she grabbed the door and held it until he looked her in the eye.

"Are you okay?" she asked again.

"Did you not hear me, Darlin'? I said I was grand."

"You don't sound grand."

"Well. That's somethin' I'll need to work on now, isn't it?"

"I'm sorry."

"For what?"

She swallowed as she felt the heat rising in her cheeks. "For doubting you."

He smiled then, but his eyes remained clouded. "It's not that, Vicki." He took a deep breath and glanced into the courtyard. The rain had stopped for the moment but droplets were still falling from overloaded leaves and the roiling clouds appeared as though they could open up again at any moment. "It's this weather. It brings back memories, 'tis all."

Before she could respond, he pulled the dolly the rest of the way through the door. As he turned to go, he hesitated and looked at her again. "I'll get over it. I always do."

She watched him as he made his way to the garage. She wanted to rush after him to entice him into confiding what bothered him so. But her logical self prevailed and once the garage door had been opened and he disappeared inside, she reluctantly turned to caring for the angelfish.

When the door opened a few minutes later, she turned with anticipation, hoping Dylan's melancholy mood had lifted. Instead, Sam marched inside, followed by Chris and Dylan dragging and pushing a cart laden with boxes that appeared to be ready to fall apart.

"What are you doing here?" Vicki asked as Sam stood to the side and watched them.

"Nice to see you, too," he answered.

"It goes in the stock room in the back there," Dylan said. His shoulders hunched as he tried to drag the dolly backward while Chris pushed, revealing just how heavy their load was. He glanced up and caught Vicki watching him. "You wouldn't believe what I found out there." Without waiting for her to respond, he said, "I was up on a ladder, haulin' down thin's from the shelves so's I could repair the buildin', you know how it leans so, and there was a trap door o' sorts in the ceiling. I pushed it to the side and poked me head up and all these boxes were up there. And this isn't all of it. No, there's another two, three loads at least."

Vicki followed them past the fish tanks to the storage room in the back. "What's in there?"

"Don't quite know yet," he answered, starting to huff as he pulled the dolly over the lip in the doorframe. "But what I've seen so far looks to be World War II memorabilia."

Vicki started to turn and almost ran into Sam.

"I'll help you unload that stuff," Sam said, brushing past her.

As Vicki watched the three men stack the boxes along the side wall, her jaw dropped.

"What's wrong with you?" Sam asked when they finished.

"I can't believe you helped."

"What?"

Chris and Dylan turned their attention to Sam.

"I've never seen you do anything like that before," Vicki mused. "That's all."

Sam cleared his throat, his brows knitting together darkly. "You think all I am is a pretty face?"

As he made his way toward the outer room, Dylan burst into laughter.

"Shut up," Sam growled. "I'm here to see her." He thumbed toward Vicki. "Chris and I can help you with the rest of the boxes later. Right now, we've got work to do."

As he headed toward the door of the fish house, Vicki fell in behind him and Dylan's laughter abruptly stopped. In a few short steps, he had pushed past Vicki and was at the door, his broad shoulders almost spanning the doorway.

"Where you think you're goin'?" Dylan asked.

Sam turned to look at him, his brows still gathered. "The house, where it's more comfortable."

Vicki's eyes met Dylan's. Though his remained dark and unreadable, she knew hers must have widened in surprise as she realized the near disaster that was averted. "We can't go in the house," she said. Her own words took her by surprise and as the others turned to stare at her, she realized she hadn't a clue how to stop them.

"No," Dylan said smoothly. "You can't." He turned toward Sam. "Bennie's polishing the floors. Can't walk on 'em. 'Tis why I'm out here, haulin' boxes and Vicki's tendin' fish."

"She's polishing *all* the floors?"

Dylan nodded. "Every last one o' 'em." He gestured for Sam to come back into the main part of the fish house. "So, I'll leave you to it."

"Wait," Sam said as Dylan turned to leave. "Stay. You can observe what she does. There might come a time when I can't get here fast enough and she'll have to run a mission without me."

"But that never happens," Vicki interjected.

"You never know."

"Well," Dylan said, closing the door. "Then let's get to it."

30

Vicki lay prone on the floor, her forearm covering her eyes to block the light from the overhead fixtures. Sam sat across from her; she could tell from the gentle clicks coming from his direction that he was setting up the audio and video equipment to tape her mission.

It wasn't the first time she'd lain on the hard floor of the fish room like this, but the last time she'd done so had been when Dylan had been unaware of her work with the CIA. It felt strange now to have both Dylan and Chris watching her intently as she cleared her mind and prepared herself.

Brenda's image kept popping to the forefront of her mind even before she began the mission and her breathing became deeper, almost as if she was in slumber. She could feel her spirit moving out of the fish house and floating across the back yard, gliding through the closed back door of the house and down the hallway.

She'd expected to find Brenda in the living room, sitting in front of the television with her coffee cup, watching the political pundits. But the room was empty.

She stood near the bottom of the stairs, feeling her sister's vibration as she looked up the darkened stairway.

"Report your location."

Sam's voice was its usual monotone but she could feel his tension. Its intensity was enough to cut through the air.

"Standing at the bottom of a staircase." Her words were slower, more measured, as she contemplated their meaning before she answered. "I'm moving upstairs."

The fish room disappeared around her as she concentrated on the stairs. She seemed to drift upon each one, not truly wanting to move further, fearing she would give away her sister's position but knowing she must provide Sam with something, anything, to keep him sated.

She reached the second floor and reported that she was standing in an upstairs hallway.

"Coordinates," Sam directed.

A series of numbers flashed before her eyes but she shook her head, forcing herself to remain mute.

Then she stepped through Brenda's bedroom door.

Her sister was seated in the corner chair, Vicki's laptop on the ottoman in front of her. As Vicki moved into the center of the room, Brenda looked up, her eyes wide.

"Vicki?" Her voice was tentative. Though she looked toward the center of the room, she seemed to be peering past her shoulder. As Vicki moved out of her line of sight, her sister continued staring at the same point. After a moment, Brenda shuddered as if she had a chill and turned her attention to the screen in front of her.

Vicki moved silently, deliberately toward her, making a wide arc through the room as she came to stand between the chair and the bathroom door. Twice, her sister glanced up as if expecting to see her in flesh and blood. Vicki froze and involuntarily held her breath, although she knew she could not be seen.

After a long moment, Brenda rose and crossed to the doorway. Opening it, she peered into the hall, even taking a couple of steps toward the stairway to squint downstairs. "Vicki?" she called. When there was no answer, she called to Benita.

In her mind's eye, Vicki tried to find Benita but she felt compelled to remain in the bedroom. After a minute, Brenda retreated into the bedroom, closing the door behind her. She wrapped her arms around her body as if chilled and then turned off the overhead fan before returning to the corner chair.

Vicki was standing with her hands on the chair back, examining the screen.

"I'm looking at a computer screen," she said to Sam.

Brenda glanced up, turning to peer into the bathroom behind her.

"It's the same screen I've described before," Vicki continued in a low voice. "A list of congressmen."

She bent over the chair back, narrowing her eyes. The room swam around her as the words on the screen danced. Then the laptop came alive. At the top of the list was Congressman Willo.

She found herself in a wide, pristine hallway. She frowned and looked for Brenda but the bedroom had disappeared. In its place were marbled floors and white walls punctuated by doorways flanked with American flags. Above her was an ornate ceiling with bright lights set a few feet apart and reaching the length of the hall. At the end of the hall was a bright light.

She knew instinctively that the light heralded an outside door. As she shaded her eyes, she made out the hazy images of people walking the hallway toward her, their arms filled with folders or their palms clasping briefcases.

She'd found herself in the halls of Congress.

She peered in the opposite direction at the myriad of flags standing at attention. She began moving, slowly at first and then gaining momentum as it became clear to her where she must go.

"Indicate your position."

"The halls of Congress." Her answer was instantaneous.

She could feel Sam's surprise but he remained silent, waiting for her to continue.

She described the hallway as she glided past staffers and pages. Then she stopped abruptly at a door that looked like all the others. But this one—this one, she knew, was the one she wanted.

She described her movements to Sam as she hesitated and peered at the name beside the door. Congressman Willo.

"Whose office is it?" Sam demanded.

"I—I can't see the name," she said groggily. "I'm going in."

The door was open and as she made her way inside, she could sense a beehive of activity taking place within those walls. The phones rang incessantly as young women hurried to type documents, file paperwork, or rush materials to various offices. She stopped in front of one darkened doorway long enough to view the plaque on the desk: Christopher Sandige.

Then she made her way toward the large office at the end of the short hall. The air grew electric as she approached. She knew before stepping through the closed door that Congressman Willo was on the other side. And she knew he was deep in discussion, his voice tense and deep, growing in intensity as his anxiety increased.

She moved through the door like an apparition and stood near the center of his office.

He was standing behind his desk, his chair pushed back haphazardly as though he'd risen quickly. On the other side of the desk in flanking chairs were two men in dark blue suits. She moved around them, describing them to Sam but remaining mute about the congressman.

"The two agents are in custody," one was saying as if attempting to placate Congressman Willo. "They're being interrogated now."

"She could not have escaped alone," Willo insisted. He was a large man with a chin that fell straight to his collar as if he was lacking a neck. Now the skin waggled as he spoke. "What hold did she have on them? Why did they help her?"

"No one has been able to answer that," the other man said.

"But we're working on it," the first interjected.

"CIA," Vicki breathed.

"CIA?"

"They are CIA officers," she elaborated. She frowned as she drew near, watching the interaction between Willo and the agents with increasing interest.

"They cannot be let go," Willo was saying. "Charge them with spying. Hold them as terrorists. They are accessories. And possibly much more."

"These are good men—"

"*Were* good men," Willo corrected. "*If* they ever were. Leave no stone unturned. I want to know everybody who ever came in contact with them. *Everyone*," he emphasized.

"We're also searching for Carnegie," one of the agents said. "We're closing in on her. We know she's returned home to Lumberton, North Carolina. We've got our best men trying to find her. They *will* find her."

"And this time," the first man added, "we will personally deliver her to you."

"No," Willo said. He straightened his spine, which caused him to look several inches taller. He placed two beefy hands on the desk. "The moment she is captured," he said, leveling his eyes at each man in turn, "eliminate her."

31

Vicki came off the floor before she knew she had returned from her trancelike state. She was halfway to the door before Sam had shut down the equipment and was on his feet. She could feel Chris on her heels but she kept her eyes leveled at Dylan's as she approached the door.

He'd been standing with his back against the wall, one leg bent at the knee to rest a heel against the wall. Now she could see him as if in slow motion, his leg straightening as his eyes searched hers for an explanation.

Sam fumbled for Vicki before she could leave the room. His fingertips caught her blouse and he pulled her backward half a step before she slipped out of his grasp. She kept her eyes locked on Dylan's, beseeching his help. As if in response, he reached out and wrapped his arm around her, pulling her to him and pressing her face against his chest.

"So. Is this the way it goes, then?" he asked. His voice sounded casual but she could feel his heart pounding against her as he combed his fingers through her hair.

"Not quite," Sam said brusquely.

"Are you feelin' faint, Vicki?" Dylan asked smoothly, his arm like an iron vise around her.

"Yes," she managed to say. "I need some fresh air."

"She's always feeling faint afterward," Sam said, his voice revealing his growing impatience. "What did you see?"

Vicki pushed slightly away from Dylan in order to turn toward Sam. Her face felt flushed and hot. "Two CIA agents. They were talking to a congressman—or—or a senator."

"What were they saying?" Sam drew so close to her that he blocked the overhead light.

Vicki felt Dylan's hand tighten on her arm, ready to pull her toward him at a moment's notice. "The two agents that helped her escape will be charged with spying, terrorism—"

"What?"

It was Sam's voice but it could have easily been Dylan, Vicki thought.

"Who were these CIA agents?" Sam pressed.

"I don't know. I didn't recognize them."

Sam pulled out his iPhone and accessed the Internet. He held a picture up to Vicki. As she stared at it, he said, "Was this one of them?"

She recognized the CIA director's photograph. "No."

"Only a handful of people know those agents are in custody. And I'm supervising every one of them." Sam stared at Vicki as though he wanted to climb inside her eyes and read her mind. "And none of them—*none* of them—could go to Congress about this."

Vicki shook her head. "I don't claim to understand what was going on—"

"Why would they involve Congress?" The voice was Chris' now. It was strained and as he came into view, his face was drained of color.

Vicki started to look into his eyes but the pain there was so evident that she looked away. "I don't know."

"Why don't you tell us?" Dylan said. His voice was still casual as if he was discussing dinner plans. Vicki glanced at him to find his eyes leveled directly at Chris. "You work for a congressman, don't you?"

"Yes, but—"

"Congressman Willo did send you here, didn't he?" Sam asked. He backed away from Vicki to stare at Chris. Now the three of them were looking at him for answers.

"He's the one who authorized this mission," Chris said. "He wants to know who is involved in the oil scheme with Brenda Carnegie."

"Spying?" Sam asked. "Terrorism? And an oil scheme? I'm not getting the connection."

"I've got to sit down," Vicki said.

"Get me sketches," Sam said. "I want these CIA agents' faces. Pronto."

"But—"

"Don't you understand, Vicki?" Sam continued. "We've got a mole. And I need to find out who it is. Something's not right here. It's not making sense."

"If she doesn't sit down, she'll faint."

"Then pull up a damn chair," Sam growled. "Or sit on the floor. Can't fall far from there."

"I need air." Vicki tried to push past Dylan but he continued holding her.

"Give her a few minutes," Dylan said. His voice was lower now, polite but firm. "Can you do some sketches, Vicki, once you've had a chance to catch your breath?"

She nodded and tried again to push past him. "Let go of me," she said between clenched teeth.

"Thirty minutes. Chris and I will get some coffee."

"There's a coffee shop at the mall," Dylan said suddenly.

Vicki stopped trying to escape his grip.

Sam looked at his watch. "Thirty minutes."

"Why didn't you let me go?" Vicki almost screamed at Dylan as she slammed the kitchen door behind her.

"Think about what you were doin'," he said. "Had you come toward this house, they'd a'been straight on your heels. You'd 'ave been leadin' 'em right to 'er!"

She stomped down the hallway and came to an abrupt stop at the living room door. Brenda was seated in the corner, watching television. She was bathed in darkening shadows and had she not moved when Vicki entered the doorway, she might have missed her sitting there.

"Turn off that blasted show," Dylan ordered. "I can't stand all that political nonsense."

Brenda muted the show. "Aren't you two in a jovial mood?"

"What did you see?" Dylan asked, turning to Vicki. "And don't give me what you told Sam. I know you saw more. And you knew who you were lookin' at."

"Sam?" Brenda's voice had changed to a hushed tone. She sat perfectly still now, her hands held in her lap.

"Brenda's in danger," Vicki said, the words tumbling out. "It was Congressman Willo. He ordered the CIA to kill her."

"What?" Dylan said. His voice also changed and some of the tension left his face, leaving a stunned expression. "Why?"

"I don't know why." Vicki turned to Brenda. "It's something you know. Something that has to do with oil, an oil scheme—"

"Wait a minute," Brenda said, leaning further back into her chair. Her face was now cloaked in shadows. "Are you telling me that—not only does Dylan work for the CIA but you do, too?"

"You knew Dylan worked for the CIA?" Vicki turned to stare at Dylan.

"Don't look at me. I didn't tell 'er!"

"He didn't have to tell me," Brenda said hotly. "I saw him there. But you—*you*—"

"Well, this has just turned into a big house o' secrets, now hasn't it?" Dylan quipped. "Seems that everybody is hidin' somethin' from everybody else."

"I don't have time to explain," Vicki said, ignoring Dylan and turning to Brenda.

"You've been spying on me!"

"I—"

"It's you, isn't it? When I've been using your computer. You've been right behind me, looking over my shoulder! I knew it was you!" She stood up and walked behind the chair. Both hands grasped the seat back. "You said you were picking me up because—I thought you wanted to reunite—I—I—"

"I did—I do. I want our family back together."

"Before or after I go to prison?"

"Okay," Dylan said, stepping into the room and splaying his large hands. "Let's everybody calm down."

"I'm leaving."

"No, you're not." Dylan stood between Brenda and the door, but she didn't make a move to leave her position behind the chair, as though the furniture was providing some protection.

"She just said they want to kill me." Her face was still in shadow, but her voice belied her frustration. "You think I'm just going to sit here and wait for them to come and get me?"

"Tell us what's going on," Vicki pleaded. "We can't help you if we don't know what's happening."

Brenda laughed. "So you can run back to Sam and tell him?"

"Sam doesn't know they want to kill you," Dylan said. "I can guarantee you that. He didn't know there were CIA agents on the Hill." He glanced at his watch. "He'll be back in a few minutes, wantin' a sketch o' the agents Vicki saw. We don't have time for this discussion now."

"So, I'm supposed to just sit here while she draws her little picture?" Brenda scoffed. "You've got to be kidding me."

"We don't have a choice."

"I've got a choice. I can get the hell out of here before he comes back."

"Where would you go?" Dylan pressed. "What safer place do you have than this?"

"You call this safe?" She chuckled. "How do I know the next time you waltz into this house, Sam doesn't waltz in with you?"

"Where would you go?" he repeated.

She took a deep breath. "I know a place. Along the Lumber River. Used to be a little fishing shack."

"How would you get there?"

"Loan me your car?" Brenda asked. "Or you drive me. All I need is a lift to the river. I can take a canoe from there."

"Alone?" Vicki asked.

Brenda chuckled again but it was sounding forced. "They want to *kill* me, dear sister. What do you think is going to happen to me on the river?"

Neither answered and with an exasperated exhale, Brenda hurried across the room and through the door.

"You're not goin' anywhere!" Dylan bellowed as she took the stairs two at a time. He turned back to Vicki. "Tell 'er she's not goin' anywhere."

Vicki sat down heavily and put her head in her hands. "I don't see how I can stop her."

He stared at her for a moment. "Well, I can bloody well stop 'er," he growled, his voice husky with frustration as his boots hit the stairs.

32

He threw the bedroom door open, ignoring the sound it made as it hit the wall.

Brenda looked up from the bed, her eyes meeting his briefly before returning to the task at hand. In an instant, he registered the duffle bag on the bed, the mouth opened wide to reveal dark clothing. A box of bullets lay beside it, the contents scattered as she deftly removed the clip to his Glock. Finding it full already, she slid it back in with a click before grabbing the bullets and tossing them back into the box.

"You're not goin' anywhere," Dylan said. His breath came fast and heavy as he strode purposefully to the bed and reached for the box. "And you may as well put that gun down 'cause you're not takin' it with you."

"Don't try to stop me, Irish."

He tossed the remaining bullets back into the box and closed the lid before turning to face her. He'd expected to see her with gun in hand, pointing it at his chest. But she'd set it inside the duffle bag and was zipping it.

"Listen to me," he said, grabbing her by both shoulders and turning her so she had no choice but to look him in the eye. She stared at him with eyes that didn't blink—not from fear nor anxiety—and Sam's words rose in his mind. She had nerves of steel. Her chin was lifted defiantly even as he forced her to look at him. "Listen to me," he repeated.

"Talk fast, Irish. Time's a'wasting."

"There's a net over the whole town. You think it's just a few agents you have to avoid. It isn't. They could have satellites focused on every street, every corner. And it wouldn't be the first time they'd focused one on this house."

"Go on."

He realized his hold on her shoulders was enough to bruise her but she hadn't winced. He relaxed his grip but still held her in place. "The moment you poke your head out the door, they'll have you. Your only hope is to stay right here, inside this house."

Her eyes faltered and moved downward as she thought. "Then I'll wait until dark."

"Won't do any good," he insisted. "They've got night vision technology. They'll have you in their sights as clear as if it was day."

She raised one hand to his as if to sling it off her. But instead, her hand lingered on it. "Then what am I to do?" Her voice remained husky and defiant. "Stay here for the rest of my life? Afraid to poke my head out the door or look out a window? Head for the shadows every time the door is opened?"

He looked at her hand on his. Four nails were immaculate while one was missing the false nail. The natural nail looked thin and weak. The image of her cuffed to the chair, the knife embedded in her thigh, rose in his mind. He could feel his heart quicken as he answered. "They won't stay here forever. They can't. They'll have other missions, other priorities. There are only so many satellites and more than enough crime. They'll have to move on. Eventually."

She squeezed his hand. "And what about you? What about her?"

"We'll think o' somethin'," he said. His eyes felt riveted to hers.

"You're risking everything to help me; you realize that, don't you?"

"I'm not seein' as how I've got a choice."

"You could turn me in. Or let me go."

"And face the same consequences, either way? No. There's a third option. Don't rush into anythin'. I've done it meself and it's come to no good. Take it by the day. The hour, even." He took a deep breath and squeezed her shoulders as if to reassure her. "Sam will be back in a matter o' minutes. He'll never suspect we've got you here. He's dependin' on the satellites and the agents to find you in your old haunts. And we both know you won't be at any of 'em."

"But—"

"He's relyin' on your sister to find you in 'er mind. And we know she won't betray you. If anythin', she'll lead 'em somewhere's else."

"And what's in it for you?" She cocked her head and tried to smile slyly but a glimmer of insecurity flicked across her eyes.

"You won't be owin' me anythin', if that's what you're worried about. But you will be owin' your sister. She wouldn't make it in a federal pen, we both know that. And whatever happens, I'll count on you to protect 'er."

She squeezed his hand again. "I'll always insist she didn't know Annie Boyd is really Brenda Carnegie. I don't break under pressure."

"I know you don't."

She took her free hand and raised it to his cheek. Her touch was firm but gentle as she stroked his five o'clock shadow. He kept his hands on each of her shoulders and tried not to notice when her eyes swept from his cheek to his lips.

"So it's settled then?" he said. "You'll stay here."

Her eyes moved upward from his lips to his eyes. "For now. I trust you. But we know I can't stay here forever."

His lips felt parched. "We'll figure somethin' out, the *three* of us."

At the mention of the three of them, she smiled and the old gleam was back in her eyes. "Promise me."

"What?" He wished as soon as he'd said the word that he could take it back.

"Promise me when Vicki breaks your heart, you'll come to me to mend it."

He took a sharp breath, ready to retort even though the words had not yet formed in his mind, when she leaned upward suddenly. Her hand moved swiftly around his neck, forcing his face downward toward hers. With both hands on her shoulders, he shifted to move her further away but her strength was surprising. Instead of forcing her back, she thrust herself closer and her lips found the edge of his mouth. He instantly turned his head as she laughed softly.

"What the—?"

The voice startled them both and he jerked her backward from him as he turned to stare at Vicki in the doorway.

"I hate you!" she screamed as she turned and rushed up the stairs.

Dylan brushed Brenda aside with his arm as he hurried to the doorway after Vicki. "It's not what you're thinkin'!" By the time he'd reached the door, she was already nearing the upstairs bedroom. He glimpsed her back as she dashed inside and slammed the door. The sound reverberated through the stairwell. "I'm gettin' bloody tired o' sayin' that all the time." He hesitated in the doorway. As Brenda's soft laughter reached him, he turned back to her. "Why do you do these things?" When she responded with more laughter, he shook his head. "It's like you're wantin' to be bad!"

She stopped her laughter as he stepped into the hall, his eyes still riveted on the door upstairs. They could hear her muffled cries echoing from under the door and through the halls.

"Well, follow her, you big idiot," Brenda said. "And I'll help you explain."

He stopped at the base of the steps and turned back to her as she neared the bedroom door. "Stay your distance from me," he warned. A movement caught his attention, and he froze, his hand splayed toward her. His head moved away from the bedroom door and toward the downstairs hallway.

"Is everything okay up there?" Chris' voice echoed up the stairs.

"Is Sam w'you?" Dylan said pointedly. In his peripheral vision, he could see Brenda retreating from the bedroom doorway. He took the stairs two at a time until he reached Chris in the downstairs foyer.

"Is Vicki okay?" Chris asked.

"She'll be fine," Dylan said, waving Chris into the living room. Chris took a couple of steps and stopped. "She—she thinks I'm havin' an affair."

"Are you?"

"Hell no, man! Have you lost your senses?"

As Vicki's cries intensified, the two men's eyes wandered from each other to the two flights of stairs leading upward.

"Where's Sam?" Dylan asked, glancing into the living room.

"In the kitchen. With Benita."

"Christ."

"We came back for the—"

Dylan waved off his words. "I know, I know. Look. I've got to go and speak with Vicki, I'm sure you're understandin' that."

"Yes, but—"

"Stay downstairs. Sam, too. This is somethin' I've got to handle by m'self. Man to man, I'm askin' you."

"Sure, but—"

Without waiting for the rest of his words, Dylan raced back upstairs. He didn't even glance in the direction of Brenda's bedroom when he hit the second floor but continued upward to the third.

Moving at full speed, he almost ran into the door when he grabbed the knob and found it locked. He rattled the door knob. "Vicki," he yelled to be heard over her sobs, "unlock this door."

Her sobs began anew.

He listened for a brief moment. When they came no closer to the door, he banged on it. "Open this door right now, Vicki. I'm warnin' you!"

Her sobs exploded into wails.

"I'm not goin' to tell you again, Woman! If you don't open this bloody door right this minute, I'm goin' to bust it down!"

She continued wailing and still came no closer to the door.

"If I bust down this door, you're not gonna like me very much!"

Her cries grew muffled as if she was burying her face into the pillows.

"Open this door!" He pounded once. "Damn it!" Then he rushed down the stairs. Ignoring Brenda sitting in the corner of her bedroom staring at him with wide, confounded eyes, he whirled around to the next flight of stairs only to find himself staring into Chris's. "Damn it!" he said again as his boots hit the foyer.

"What's going on?"

He whirled around to find Sam wandering down the hall from the kitchen, a steaming cup of coffee in his hands.

"You!" he shouted, pointing his finger at Sam. Sam stopped and looked at him as though he'd lost his mind. Then he whirled back to Chris. "And you!" He felt his face flush and he fought to keep from stammering. "Stay here and do not get involved in this!"

Sam froze. "Involved in what?"

"Vicki thinks Dylan is having an affair," Chris offered.

"You're having an affair?" Sam bellowed as Dylan pushed past him to the closet beneath the stairs. "You're cheating on *my daughter*?"

Dylan did a double-take as he grabbed the toolbox from the closet. "I am not havin' an affair. She only thinks I am."

"Why?" When Dylan didn't answer, Sam pressed in a louder, more insistent tone, *"Why?"*

"I don't bloody well know why," Dylan said, finding the electric screwdriver and pushing past Sam to get to the stairs. "Because she's a woman, that's why!"

Sam followed Dylan to the bottom of the steps. "What are you going to do with that? If you hurt her—"

Dylan hesitated long enough to turn and look at Chris before turning his attention to Sam. "I'm not gonna hurt 'er," he said. "I might kill 'er but I'm not gonna hurt 'er." He started to turn back to the stairs, caught a glimpse of Brenda's open doorway and turned back to the men again. "And if you never do another thin' for me in your whole wretched lives, stay out o' this."

Without waiting for a response, he rushed up the stairs. Breathless when he reached his bedroom as much out of frustration and rage than the physical activity, he hesitated only long enough to quiet his hands in an attempt to match up the electric screwdriver with the screw in the door knob. Reversing the direction, the screw was falling out of the knob plate in a few quick seconds, followed quickly by the second one. With one quick pull, he had the knob out of the hallway side and with one pointed jab the knob on the other side fell to the hardwood floor in the bedroom.

He pushed the door open and marched into the room. His cheeks were hot and his eyes stung from anger. As he came toward her, he shook the electric screwdriver at her, his lips twitching with the words he wanted to say but which wouldn't come.

She was standing on the other side of the room, staring at him. Her face was wet, her nose and her eyes red. "Rhett Butler would have kicked the door in," she said simply.

"Rhett Butler had servants to repair the damn door." He shook the screwdriver at her again. "Don't you ever lock me out of any room again; do you hear me, Woman? I will remove every blasted door knob in this house. You'll never be able to close another door, ever again!"

"It's not your house!"

"Well, it's not yours, either!"

They stood facing each other silently. Then they both began speaking at once.

"Why don't you trust me?"

"I saw you kiss her!"

"I did not kiss 'er. I was talkin' 'er into stayin'!"

"I could see that!" she wailed.

"Not in the way that you're thinkin'! I wanted 'er to stay *for you!*"

"I see the way you look at her!"

"What?"

"She's beautiful."

"So what? You're just as beautiful—more beautiful, in my eyes!"

"She's smart."

"So are you, usually. Except for stupid times like this and then you erase all the smartness you ever had." He waved his hands like they were giant erasers.

"She's everything I'm not," she cried. "She's more like you. She's savvy and she—doesn't cry—and she's sexy and she's mysterious—"

"What are you sayin' this for? Are you tryin' to drive me into 'er arms?"

"She's more like you than I'll ever be."

"Maybe I don't want 'er," he bellowed, "because she is precisely just like me! Although, to be quite honest, she takes the unsavoriness to whole new astronomical levels!"

Vicki sobbed loudly, her cries filling the room.

"Is everything okay up there?" Sam's voice was almost drowned out by Vicki's cries.

"Oh, it's just peachy," Dylan yelled. "We'll be down in a jiffy!"

At that, Vicki raced into the bathroom and grabbed the door.

"Don't close that door on me," he shouted. He brandished the screwdriver as though it was a weapon. "I've got me tools, Woman. And I'm not afraid to use it."

She stood in the bathroom, one hand on the door.

"Don't close the door," he said, enunciating each word. He stepped forward. "I'm warnin' you."

She waited until he was within a few feet of the door and with one finger, she slammed it closed.

"She closed the door." He gritted his teeth. In the back of his mind, he could see Brenda sitting in the corner of her bedroom, listening to every word. And just one floor below her were two men that would stop at nothing to find her. All that held them apart was him and he was stuck trying to convince a woman he loved that he truly did love her. "And I thought my family was dysfunctional," he muttered as he found the screw on the bathroom door knob.

When the knobs dropped to the floor on either side and he pushed the door open, he found Vicki sitting on the chair in front of the dressing table.

"Did you not hear me tell you not to close the door?" Dylan said.

"Yes."

"Then why did you close the door?"

"I don't know."

"I swear to God."

She looked like she was ready to burst into tears again. He placed one hand on the side of the doorway to help steady his nerves. But before he could say anything, a man's voice piped up behind him.

"Everything okay in here?"

Vicki's eyes widened and she moved to dry her tears as Dylan turned to face Sam and Chris. Sam still had his cup of coffee in his hands but it didn't appear that he'd drunk any of it. Accustomed to seeing him in total control of every situation, Dylan was surprised to find his face pale, his eyes wide and dark, looking like a man who was completely out of his element. Behind him was Chris, angling to see past the two men to Vicki beyond, his own eyes wide and searching, his brows furrowed with concern.

Dylan turned his back to the men as he faced Vicki. Rolling his eyes at the ceiling, he said in as calm a voice as he could muster, "Vicki, Sam and Chris have come back to get the sketch you promised them."

She didn't respond but continued staring at him.

"And for the record," he said in a louder voice for all three to hear, "I don't cheat. I've done a lot o' thin's in me past that I haven't been proud of. But cheatin' on a woman isn't one o' 'em. Not then. Not now. Not ever." When no one responded, he added, "It's not gonna happen. Are you understandin' me?"

Vicki nodded.

"Well, then," Dylan said, placing the screwdriver on the vanity, "I suppose you'd better get what these gentlemen have come to retrieve."

33

Benita scooped a hefty serving spoon full of potatoes onto Sam's plate.

"It's not a meal without potatoes," Dylan said as he watched her serve up another spoonful for Chris and then for Dylan before returning the pot to the stovetop.

"We're not waiting for Vicki?" Chris asked.

Dylan took a healthy swig of red wine to steady his nerves. "You heard 'er same as I. She said not to wait. She wants to finish up the sketch."

Sam cut through a thick lamb chop, one eye on Benita.

"Days are gettin' shorter," Dylan added, nodding toward the kitchen window. The sky had turned the color of pewter and appeared to be growing darker by the minute. A bush scraped a stray branch against the window as the wind grew in intensity like a spirit trying to enter.

"We'll have rain by morning," Chris said. His voice was barely above a whisper. Though he pushed the food around on his plate, Dylan noted he'd barely eaten any of it.

"Don't care for Irish food, 'ey?"

"What? Oh," Chris shrugged, "it's not that. Food's great. I'm sure. I just… I'm preoccupied."

Sam pointed his fork toward Benita. "Don't worry about talking in front of her. She doesn't speak a word of English."

Dylan caught a glimpse of Benita's eyes cutting toward him before he tore off a piece of bread and rolled it in the juice seeping from the lamb. "Maybe you've told me this before," he said, his eyes narrowing as he turned his attention back to Chris, "but what is it exactly you think this Brenda Carnegie woman can do for you?"

"What she can do for me... Interesting way of phrasing it."

"How else would you put it?"

Chris took a deep breath and set his fork down. "I'm gonna be honest. Maybe I shouldn't be. But I am."

Dylan stole a glance at Sam. He was steadily spooning potatoes into his mouth but his focus was on Chris. The air felt tense as if Sam's antenna had suddenly popped up.

Chris didn't seem to notice the change in the air. "Congressman Willo wants to know who in Congress might be wrapped up in this oil scheme Brenda is involved in. When I was here a few months ago, I had no idea that whatever was going on here in Lumberton reached all the way to Washington—and possibly beyond."

"But," Sam said, slicing off another hunk of lamb, "you cut her off from the computer scheme she was involved in. Maybe *you* didn't," he added, "but law enforcement did. Warrants have been issued. They've been looking for her."

"Yes."

"But obviously," Sam continued, "she's still able to access something. A list of some sort."

"Yes."

"So," Dylan said, "how do you know she's still involved in an oil scheme? Couldn't she 'ave moved onto somethin' else?"

"Whatever it is," Chris said, "it involves Congress."

"Why would CIA agents be meeting with your boss?" Sam asked.

When Dylan turned to look at him, Sam's eyes were so narrowed that they appeared only slightly larger than slits. His hand was resting on the table; he might have thought it was a leisurely gesture except for the subtle thumping of his fingertips on the table.

Chris shook his head. "That worries me."

"How so?" Dylan asked.

"Everything should be going through me. If the Congressman wanted to meet with the CIA directly he could've called my cell phone." He patted the phone on his belt. "I'm sitting here with two of you right now. There's another down the hall."

"Why would he go around you?" Sam asked. His voice was quieter.

Chris shook his head again. "I don't know. I've been asking that same question in my mind. Over and over."

Dylan pushed the potatoes around on his plate. "What will he do with 'er when he gets 'er?"

"Congressman Willo?"

Dylan nodded. "He wants 'er." He looked Chris square in the eye. "You wouldn't be here if he didn't. What's his personal motivation? What will he accomplish when she's apprehended and brought afore him?"

"I don't know." Neither man spoke as they waited for Chris to continue. "I've been so wrapped up in why I wanted her, I haven't thought much about why he wanted her."

"Why do you want her?" Dylan pressed. His voice had grown softer. He noticed Sam's eyes had averted to his plate as though he was very interested in his food. A façade, Dylan thought, and a poorly concealed one at that.

"I said maybe I shouldn't be totally honest," Chris answered, drawing a ragged breath. "But the truth is I'm in love with her. Plain and simple."

Dylan could feel the shadows in the hallway growing longer, deeper.

It was Sam who broke the silence. "Don't you think," he said, his voice unusually smooth, "that's a bit of a conflict of interest?"

"You think?" Chris answered without hesitation. "And you think I haven't thought of that myself? Her knowledge is somehow dangerous to our government. She could be a spy, passing information. I don't know. But there's something—there's something about her—that I can't resist."

"Apparently the agents transporting her to Washington couldn't resist it either." Sam stabbed another piece of meat.

"But what is it?" Dylan pressed. Both men looked at him. "You bedded 'er. Am I right?"

Chris chewed on his bottom lip. "Yes."

"So is the lure of sex with this woman that strong? Strong enough for you to compromise your government—your mission?"

"It's not just—sex." He squirmed uncomfortably in his chair. "I'm in love with her."

"So," Dylan said, "do you think your boss might be noticin' that, perhaps? Do you think he might be goin' around you because he hasn't the faith in you to get the job done?"

Chris shook his head. "He doesn't know—about us."

"What about you?" Sam asked.

"I don't follow you."

"What if Brenda Carnegie waltzed in this door right now?" Sam said.

Dylan almost winced at his words.

"What would you do with her?" Sam pressed.

"I'd talk to her," Chris answered without hesitation.

"You think she'd tell you what she hasn't told anyone else?" Dylan asked.

"I don't know."

"And what if she's a spy?" Sam asked. "What if she's passing information to an enemy? What then? What would win out? Your love for your country or your love for a woman?"

Chris looked at Dylan before looking at Sam. Then his eyes roamed back to Dylan. "I'd help her. Not help her get away—not help her escape the law. But I'd get her the best lawyer I could. I'd be there with her every step of the way."

"You're sounding more like a defense attorney than—"

"I'd make sure she had the best possible defense money could buy."

Dylan let this soak in. When Sam didn't speak, he asked, "And what if Congressman Willo gets to 'er afore you do?"

Chris blinked.

"What then?"

"He'd have her in custody…" Chris said slowly.

"Aye. And would he tell you where she was? Would he allow you to help 'er when he himself was out to nail 'er?"

"You understand," Sam said, "you're putting your career in jeopardy. And maybe a whole lot more."

Chris swallowed.

"I'm gonna have to bump you off this mission," Sam added.

"What?"

"The mission was authorized by a congressman. Not by a congressman's—aid."

"But I brought you the job."

"Under false pretenses."

"But I—"

"If we apprehended her, how could I be assured you're not a spy working with her? Love does strange things to a man. Lust does strange things. And I'm not so sure which one it is with you. And frankly, I don't much care." Sam tapped his fingers on the table again. "I work for Uncle Sam. Feelings be damned. And my responsibility is to this government."

"So, where does that leave me? Where does that leave the mission?"

Dylan could feel Vicki's presence behind him. He was afraid to look in the direction of the hallway, afraid they would stop the conversation before matters were settled, before a course of action had been decided upon. But he could feel her eyes boring into his back.

"I'll have to call the Congressman myself," Sam said. "And get instructions—straight from the horse's mouth."

"But what about them?" Vicki said, striding into the room. She held out an artist's pad, tilting it so they could see the sketch. It appeared similar to a courtroom reporter's rendering, with the penciled lines drawn quick but sure. On one side, she depicted an office with a flag in the background, a non-descript painting on the wall and facing chairs upon which two men were seated.

One had close-cropped hair, almost in a Marine buzz-cut. His face was patrician, his jaw squared, his perfectly straight nose tilted slightly upward. His physique was trim and fit, the suit jacket fitting snugly over his biceps. He faced another man who was slightly older, a swath of white splashed at each temple. His nose ended in a bulb, the nostrils fat. In contrast, his eyes were small and set too close, his chin spongy.

In the center of the sketch was a desk and on the other side stood a man, both hands drawn into fists that rested firmly on the desk top. His mouth was resolutely set, his lips thin, his eyes narrowed. His hair was combed back in an impeccable manner as if he could step before a press corps at any minute and give a flawless performance.

As Dylan's eyes scanned the picture, he was struck by the silence that had enveloped the room. He turned slowly to look at Chris and then at Sam.

Both their faces were drained of color, their eyes wide and unblinking.

They knew the men, Dylan realized. Their expressions were unmistakable.

"Congessman Willo," Vicki said, pointing at the man behind the desk though from the look in their eyes it was clear her spoken identification was not necessary. "I don't know the other two."

"I do," Sam said quietly.

"There's more," she said.

All three men looked at her expectantly. "Congressman Willo's instructions are to kill her."

Dylan turned toward Chris, who looked like he was staring into the face of a monster. Turning to Sam, he said, "So. What do we do now?"

Chris scrambled up so quickly, the chair teetered backward dangerously and might have hit the floor had Dylan's quick reflexes not caught the chair back and held it steady. Though his large hand gripped the wood, his eyes were riveted on the man who was now pacing from one end of the kitchen to the other, his hands jerkily running through his hair.

Sam pushed his chair slowly away from the table. He watched Chris in silence for a moment as the younger man stopped briefly to stare at the darkness gathering beyond the window before resuming his pacing. Benita remained perfectly still at the stove. Then Sam's eyes drifted back to the picture. "You're sure about this?" His question was directed at Vicki.

"That's what I saw."

"Then your mission is over." Sam stood up.

"What?" Vicki's mouth dropped.

"You heard me. Your mission was to find her. You've gone beyond that. Given me even more valuable information." He cut his eyes toward Chris. "Or ammunition."

"But," Vicki stammered, "I don't understand. If my mission was to find her and she's still out there, how can it be over?"

Sam grasped the sketch and rolled it as he spoke. He stood in the middle of the room until Chris paced back around, forcing him to stop and look at him before he said, "Just so you don't get a wild hair up your ass, register this: all of Lumberton is going to be under surveillance. There won't be a dog, a cat, a rabbit, a rat—that doesn't move without us knowing it. We know she's here, we know she's near, I can smell her. I'm deploying every man I trust around this town. And I guarantee you, I will have her by morning."

Chris nodded mutely.

Sam punched the younger man's chest with his forefinger. "Don't even think about doing an end-run around me. Don't even think about it."

His eyes widened. "What are you going to do with her?"

"I'm going to do what my boss tells me I'm going to do." He shook the rolled-up sketch at him. "I'm taking this to the Director."

"You're going to Washington?" Dylan asked.

Sam half-turned toward Dylan and Vicki. "I'm going to Bragg. Getting a helicopter ride to D.C. I'll be back before midnight."

"But—this dragnet you're placing around town—"

Sam held up his hand. "I've got to know from the Director's mouth, staring me in the face, if he authorized these two guys to meet with Willo. Instructions for anybody apprehending Carnegie is simply that: apprehend her. Call me immediately and I'll give further instructions."

Dylan looked from Vicki to Sam. "What's my mission?"

"Your mission," he said, nodding toward Chris, "is babysitting him."

"What?" Chris balled his hands into fists as he stared at Sam.

"I don't want you in Washington," Sam said. "One: I don't know what the hell you're up to. Two: I don't know what could happen to you. So for your protection and mine, you're staying with Bruno here until I get instructions from *my* boss."

"I'm not some *child*," Chris spat, "who needs *babysitting*."

Sam turned to Dylan, who nodded his head. He gave Dylan a quick pat on his shoulder before turning toward the doorway. "You know how to reach me."

With that, he was gone, his footsteps echoing down the hallway as he made his way to the front door.

34

Vicki poured a glass of wine and set it in front of Brenda. They were upstairs in the sitting area of Vicki's bedroom. Dylan had sent up two plates and serving dishes full of potatoes, lamb and vegetables on the dumbwaiter along with a bottle of red wine.

Brenda lifted the glass as though she intended to drink but instead stared into the red liquid as if she was reading tea leaves.

"So I wasn't the only one locked in the bathroom," Vicki said, serving up food for Brenda's plate and sliding it in front of her.

Brenda stared at the food but made no attempt to reach for it.

"Penny for your thoughts?" Vicki said after a few minutes of awkward silence interrupted only by her own chewing.

She continued staring into the glass of wine as if she hadn't heard her.

"Annie?"

She startled at the sound of her girlhood name.

"You look deep in thought," Vicki said softly.

"Maybe I am."

"I'm sorry if you overheard our argument."

She shrugged. "It was hard not to hear."

"I didn't mean—"

"Yes, you did." Before Vicki could respond, Brenda set the glass on the coffee table and continued, "You can trust him, you know."

"Dylan?"

"He loves you very much. I've given him every opportunity to step out of bounds. Not only hasn't he taken me up on it, but he's set me straight. Every single time."

"Why do you do these things?"

She smiled wryly. "He asked me the same thing." She shrugged. "I do it because I'm me."

"You don't always have to walk on the dark side, you know."

She chuckled. "Don't I?"

Vicki sipped her wine in silence.

After a moment, Brenda said, "I was sitting in the chair in the bedroom when they came up the stairs."

"You saw them?"

"No. I heard them talking. I was afraid they'd look in the bedroom, see me sitting there—and you, me and Dylan would all be hauled off. I can take what they dish out. But you couldn't."

"So you hid in the bathroom."

She nodded. "It goes against my grain, to hide. But what else was I gonna do? If there'd been only one of 'em, I might have gotten off a shot—"

"Don't say that."

"Hearing two voices, I ran into the bathroom, locked the door and hoped they passed right by."

"Why does the CIA want you so badly?"

She shrugged.

"Are you involved in terrorism?"

"No," she said without hesitation. "Nothing like that. That I know about, anyway."

Vicki waited for her to continue. When she didn't, she pressed, "What could you have possibly gotten yourself involved in that would cause a congressman to want you killed?"

She chuckled but it sounded forced. "They already tried. Last fall."

"What happened?"

"They sent someone. He killed one of my—partners—but I escaped."

"An assassin?"

She nodded.

"What happened to him?"

She shook her head. "Last I knew, your neighbor—Alec Brodie—was closing in. I think he was arrested. But what they did with him, I truly don't know. I didn't hang around to find out."

Vicki's jaw dropped. "Alec Brodie?"

"Yep."

"But he's—"

"Moved in next door. I know. That's what Dylan and I were doing in my bedroom. We were watching him move in."

"Whatever you're involved in, let us help."

"How do I know everything I tell you won't go straight back to Sam? And, by the way, I'd really like a clarification as to who Sam is."

"I'll make you a deal," Vicki said. "I'll tell you what we do and you come clean with me."

She waved her hand. "You first."

"No. You first. I have to know we can trust you."

"You can't trust me, Sis. That's just the point."

"I saw your computer screens," Vicki said. "First in Argentina. Then here."

"Then why don't you tell me what I'm up to?" Brenda leaned forward and picked up the glass of wine, swirling it gently before taking a healthy swig.

"We know you're involved in an oil scheme."

Brenda laughed. "That's just the tip of the iceberg, Sis."

"You mean—"

"I stumbled on the oil opportunity. It was just a sideline to make a little extra money."

"You took millions."

She shrugged. "Chump change."

"So, if this whole thing doesn't involve oil—what is it all about?"

"You're so naïve."

"That's beside the point."

"You remember when I was little—before we were separated? You know I have a knack for computers."

"You could program circles around anybody."

"Still can. And I get my kicks hacking into things—websites, corporate applications—all over the world. I don't look for anything in particular. I just see what pops up."

"Connect the dots for me, Brenda."

Brenda finished off the glass of wine and poured another. "While I was in college, I got a reputation. You want something hacked into, I'm your gal." She let this soak in before continuing. "So, one day I get an offer. Create a shell corporation—several of them—and make it appear like oil is being sold from one to the other. Bring it right up the chain, as if the transactions are real." She stopped long enough to down another glass of wine. "Last fall a banker I was working with who transferred money into off-shore accounts was murdered. Right here in Robeson County. Alec Brodie was the lead investigator. And as far as I know, just from reading online newspaper accounts, he thinks the computer scam begins and ends with the fake oil companies."

"But you said it doesn't."

She shook her head. "It *begins* with the fake oil companies."

"So, Alec thinks he's looking for you because you've committed white collar computer crime?"

"That's why Alec wants me, yes. But that's not why the CIA wants me."

Vicki waited so long for her to continue that she was afraid Brenda had spilled all she was planning to tell.

"The CIA," she said suddenly, "wants me because I formed a list of members of Congress who are involved in a laundry list of illegal activities."

"How did you do that?"

"The how isn't the question. I'm sure they could care less how I did it. It's who's on the list that's their concern."

"But—what were you planning on doing with it?"

"Selling it to the highest bidder."

"You mean their political opposition?"

"If they were the highest bidder."

"But who else—?"

"Foreign governments. Terrorists. Anybody who wants to see a particular congressman or senator—or president—toppled badly enough to pay a fortune for the information."

Vicki placed her plate on the coffee table, even though the food wasn't half eaten. "So you've been shopping for a buyer for your list?"

"Not for the list. For a name. A single name."

"Whose?"

She shrugged. "Doesn't matter whose. Give me the name of a politician you want to see go away. And I'll give you the goods on him."

"Are you saying that every politician is crooked?" Vicki shook her head in disbelief.

"Of course not. There are some honest ones. But there are enough crooked ones to pad my wallet quite well."

Vicki allowed this information to soak in. Finally, she said, "So, a politician who would order the CIA to kill you…"

"Would be a politician who knows he's on my list," Brenda finished. Her voice was silky and low. "They picked up a—co-worker—of mine, right here in Robeson County. Roughed him up, tried to get him to reveal the location of the file."

"Did he?"

"Of course not. He doesn't know it. No one knows it—except me."

"So, if you're killed—"

"They think if I'm killed, the list dies with me."

"Does it?"

"Just the opposite. If I don't check in to a certain server every so often," she said with a slow smile, "a timer is ticking away."

"And when it reaches a certain point?"

"It goes live. Across the Internet. And into the in-boxes of every major media outlet around the world."

Vicki leaned back and ran both hands through her hair. "That could have enormous implications."

"You think?"

They both sat in silence, each with their own thoughts. Brenda's food remained completely untouched but she reached again for the bottle of wine. "So you see, dear sister," she said at last, "that's why Congressman Willo wants me dead."

"Because he's on the list."

"Now tell me who Sam is."

"Sam," Vicki repeated. "He's the man who adopted me."

Her eyes widened but she waited for Vicki to continue. When she didn't, she prompted, "And?"

"He works for the CIA. You know that already. He's my boss and he's Dylan's boss."

"But you both don't do the same thing."

"I don't know what Dylan does, to be honest. And I want it to stay that way."

Brenda nodded. "Go on."

"Sam is in charge of the psychic unit to which I'm assigned. But I guess he's involved in a lot of things, things that involve Dylan—and a host of other agents."

"What do you know about him?"

"Not much." Now it was Vicki's turn to pour a glass of wine, though she held it in her hands without drinking it. "But," she said abruptly, "if you've put together a list of crooked politicians, you haven't done anything wrong, have you?"

"Apart from hacking into computers all over the world?"

"I mean, you could be of value to our own government."

"If they're willing to pay."

"Surely you're not telling me money means more to you than—than—"

"Political ideology? Of course it does. You don't think I sit in front of the tube watching idiot politicians because I'm enthralled by what they do, do you? I'm watching because I know which ones I have dirt on. And keeping my pulse on the political climate allows me to raise prices, know which countries I can deal with, which guys I want to fall."

"This is sick."

"No, Sister. This is business."

Vicki's hand was sweating against the wine glass even though it was cool in the room.

"Back to Sam," Brenda said. "Is he downstairs with Dylan?"

"Not anymore. He's gone to Washington."

"Why?"

"He doesn't know anything about the agents instructed to kill you."

Brenda chuckled dryly. "Yeah. Right."

"I swear it. He's gone to Langley to speak with the Director."

"About me?"

"Yes."

"And what to do with me."

Vicki nodded.

"And what about you? Are you keeping me here until he gets back? Then you'll hand me over to him?"

"No. We're keeping you here because this is the safest place for you to be."

Brenda nodded, though she appeared unconvinced. She stared into her empty wine glass for a moment. When she looked up, she locked eyes with Vicki's. "And the other guy—the one he was talking to as he came up the stairs. You and Dylan were in here… So who's the other guy?"

35

Dylan stood by the kitchen sink and stared out the window while Chris paced behind him. The days were getting longer but the first vestiges of dusk were beginning to appear. From this vantage point, he could see only a short distance down the side street toward the front of the house before a row of hedges blocked his view. In the other direction, a separate row of hedges and then the fish house prevented him from seeing more than a few yards away.

In his mind's eye, he envisioned the floor plan of the rambling house. Directly above the kitchen was the weight room and above that was his and Vicki's bedroom. Those windows would allow them to monitor the side street and the front and back of the house. Only the side facing Sandy's house would be hidden from view. And that, he reasoned, could be seen from Brenda's bedroom windows or the unfinished space across from his bedroom that was used as storage.

Chris came to stand beside him. "Did you hear me?"

Dylan closed the blinds before turning to face him. "Don't open these blinds."

"Why not?"

"We don't want you seen, that's why not."

"You haven't heard a word I said," Chris said, brushing his hair off his forehead. "I'm not staying here."

"You're wrong about that, mate."

"You can't keep me here."

Dylan slid open a kitchen drawer and slipped his hand toward the back. When he withdrew it, he was holding a Glock.

"Well, maybe you can," Chris added.

Dylan checked the bullets and replaced the clip before placing it in his belt.

"But you shouldn't," Chris said.

"Shouldn't what?"

"Keep me here."

"It's the safest place for you to be until Sam gets back and says differently."

"I don't know why, all the sudden, you two don't trust me."

"It's precautions, tis all." Dylan walked past Chris to the back door, where he locked it and closed the curtains across the window. "And it's for your own protection."

"Protection from what?"

"Why don't you tell me how well you know your boss?" Dylan glanced down the hall toward the front door. Benita had closed and locked it on her way out, just as he'd instructed her to do. He wished he'd had the forethought to have an alarm installed. But how was he to know the house might become their fortress?

"Who? Congressman Willo?"

"He's your boss, isn't he?" Dylan turned to face Chris.

"You don't think—"

"I don't think anythin'. But apparently Sam does. And Vicki does. And that's enough for me."

Chris stopped pacing and put his hands on the chair back. He stared at the table for a long time. It was empty now, cleared of the remnants from dinner, the dishes washed and put away.

Dylan opened the refrigerator and pulled out a couple of Guinness. He set one down in front of Chris before pulling out a chair and making himself comfortable. After a moment's hesitation, Chris joined him, popping the top and taking a quick gulp before speaking.

"I've been in politics my whole life," he said. "Political science major, the whole bit. Worked as an aid on the hill even before I graduated college. I'm a strategist. Do you know what that means?"

"Enlighten me."

"We win elections. Pure and simple."

"I thought the candidate did that."

Chris let out a short snicker. "Winning an election is a business in itself. It means endless polls on every conceivable topic, trying to keep a pulse on where the voters stand. Trying to fit your message to what the voters want to hear. Putting just the right spin on every current event, every appearance, everything the candidate says—no matter how slight."

Dylan started to speak but Chris continued, "It means getting the dirt on your opponents, finding their weak spots, going for the jugular. Making every constituent feel that if their candidate doesn't win—the candidate I'm working for—then the world as we know it will end. Their benefits disappear, their money dries up, their freedoms vanish—"

"But we all know one candidate, no matter how powerful, couldn't wield that much clout."

"We know it. Because we're educated men. But most citizens don't know it."

"So, you're the man behind the candidate."

"Yes. I am the man behind the candidate."

"Then what do you do when your candidate wins?"

"Start planning for the next election. Members of the House serve only two-year terms. It takes a full two years to plan the strategy for their next election, all the while continuing to gather data—on the citizens and on their opponents."

"But this—this mission you're on, with Vicki—you can't be using her abilities to dredge up information on citizens or opponents."

"No. Though it's a thought."

Dylan downed a healthy swig of beer and observed Chris quietly for a moment. Then, "You can't be the only one who works for Congressman Willo."

"Of course not."

"Then why send you here? This case, from what you've told me, has nothin' to do with winnin' an election."

"No."

"Then why—?"

Chris brushed a lock of brown hair off his forehead. "I brought the congressman information about the oil scheme here. I thought it might rear its head on the campaign trail and he needed to know the situation. He's in charge of the subcommittee overseeing oil."

Dylan waited for him to continue. When he didn't, he asked, "So, how did you go from briefin' the congressman to bein' here, pinin' after a woman your boss wants to kill?"

Chris took a deep breath. "If anything happens to her, it's all my fault. I could have stayed quiet. Maybe he would have found out about her and the oil scheme. Maybe not. But once I told him, he wanted me to look into it further, see how deep it went. That's when I started seeing names pop up—"

"Senators and congressmen?"

He nodded. "Couldn't connect the dots. And then—"

Dylan took another drink. "Then what?"

"Every time I started down that road, I thought of Brenda."

Dylan self-consciously glanced behind him but the hall was empty. "What is it about 'er, exactly, that has you so obsessed?"

"It's—oh, it's going to sound strange."

"Try me."

Chris drummed his fingers on the table. "Once, when I was in college, I dreamed up the perfect woman. Blond hair, very pale. Blue eyes. Cheerleader type. Then, I'd flash forward in my mind and see her hobnobbing in Washington, involved in charity events, her hair always straight, always polished, always short. Always impeccably dressed. Playing tennis while I worked. You know the type."

Dylan wanted to say "can't say I do" but he remained silent instead and waited for Chris to continue. After a long moment, he did.

"So I was stranded here in Lumberton last fall and eating dinner alone at a place near here. And I looked across the restaurant and saw this woman sitting there…"

"Blond hair, blue eyes, perfect as a Barbi?"

"Just the opposite. Red hair trying to escape from underneath this newspaper-boy type cap. Eyes a color I've never seen before. Definitely not the type who'd play tennis. Nope, this gal would be more at ease on a shooting range. Or wading through a swamp."

"So you finished your dinner and left."

"Are you kidding? I couldn't get enough of her. The more unruly she got, the more I wanted her."

"So you had dinner with her."

"More than that. Once I asked her to join me—or I joined her—we were never apart. Not until some guy tried to kill us. I diverted his attention long enough for her to get away…" His voice faded away and he finally picked up his beer as though to drink it but set it back down instead. "And I never saw her again."

"So you saved 'er life, and she just disappeared."

"That's right."

Dylan shifted in his seat. "What would you say to 'er if you saw 'er now?"

Chris stared at the beer for a long time without answering.

"I mean, would you say, you ungrateful wench, least you could'a done was say thank you?"

Chris laughed softly. "No. By then, I knew she was neck deep in illegal stuff—the oil scam, computer crime—and I knew the cops were looking for her. They questioned me and let me go. The guy who was trying to kill us—he's in prison now. But never said a word about why he was after us. I always suspected he was hired to kill Brenda and I was just in the wrong place at the wrong time—or the right place at the right time."

"You never answered me, mate."

"Answered you about what?"

"What would you say to 'er?"

Chris stared at his fingers as if his nails held a great deal of interest to him. Then he said, "I'd tell her I love her. I know. It defies all logic. She lives in one world; I live in another. But if she'd just give me a chance, I'd—I'd show her how I could help her, protect her, save her."

"Even if it meant givin' up what you have in Washington?"

"In a heartbeat."

Dylan took a deep breath. "There's somethin' I think you ought to know."

"Yes," a female voice said clearly. "There's something you ought to know."

Both men jerked their heads toward the door. Dylan couldn't help himself; he stared at her unabashed, his eyes taking in her hair cascading over her shoulders in gentle, unruly waves. Her eyes solemn, unblinking. Her expression unreadable, although color was rising in her cheeks. As he drew his eyes downward, he caught the unmistakable rise and fall of her chest as she struggled to breathe normally; the tiniest twitch of her fingers as they hung at her sides.

He pushed back from the table at the same moment as Chris stood up so abruptly his chair teetered on the back legs. Oblivious to its imminent fall, he moved in fluid strides toward Brenda as Dylan grabbed the chair just as it was ready to clatter to the floor.

As Dylan turned around, his eyes caught Vicki's. She'd been standing behind her sister and now as Chris joined them, her eyes were wet. Brenda's eyes, in contrast, remained perfectly dry as she watched him approach her. Her hands balled into a fist and then relaxed only to ball again in the same conflict of emotion that flitted across her eyes. It was as if, Dylan thought, she was unsure how Chris would respond to her presence and she was valiantly trying to hold onto her emotions.

Chris clearly had no such internal discord however, as he strode purposefully across the kitchen and grasped Brenda in his arms, pulling her to him like she weighed no more than a rag doll. One hand gripped her hair, his fingers ensnared in the thick tresses as they moved upward to her head, drawing her face up to his as his lips found hers.

Her own arms remained at her side until she was pressed against him. Then as his lips moved over hers and he thrust his body against hers, both arms moved as if they were suddenly coming alive. Her hands found his back, kneading his waist and then his shoulders until one hand wrapped around his neck and pulled him even closer.

Then they were spinning to the side as Chris backed Brenda against the side of the refrigerator, driving her against the hard surface with unbridled passion. She met his efforts with a husky moan and as he began to pull back, she grabbed his head and pulled him back to her, her eyes opening momentarily to reveal a fire burning from within.

The knowledge that he should not be gawking began to wash over Dylan and he forced himself to draw his eyes away from them. As he moved past them to the doorway they continued their reunion as if they were oblivious of his presence.

As he stepped into the hallway, Vicki moved toward the kitchen but he caught her and pulled her away.

"But—but—" she stuttered, trying to disentangle herself from him.

"No, darlin'," he said gently as he pulled the door closed behind them, "they need to be alone."

36

Her lips were soft and pliable, her breath a sensual blend of cinnamon and mint, her tongue hot and insistent. Chris tried to pull away from her once but she locked her hands into his clothing and dragged him back to her, pressing him against her with such fervor that he felt lost in her embrace.

This was what he had dreamed about for months on end. It was the thought of her in his arms that consumed almost every waking moment; the feel of her mouth on his, her hands exploring his body, her own both soft and firm as she pushed against him. And now that it was reality, he felt as if he'd been thrust into a surreal world that was spinning with relentless fervor. The kitchen lights were harsh, nearly blinding where moments before they hadn't even registered in his mind. He longed to keep his eyes closed, to allow his hands and his body to experience her once again, but something tugged at him, enticing him to draw away again.

She moaned and as her breathing became more labored, he pulled gently back from her. As she tried to grip him tighter, he pressed his lips against her hair, using his hands to bring her closer to him, telling her with his firm grasp that he was not leaving her; that he was only just beginning.

His lips found her ear and he whispered, "Why didn't you call me?"

She stopped moving and tried to push him away from her as she turned her head toward him. He resisted her, surprising himself with his strength. He didn't want to look her in the face and he cursed himself silently for ruining the moment.

"Look at me," she begged, her voice as low and throaty as he'd remembered it. Unable to resist her plea, he reluctantly let her go and turned his face to hers.

Her eyes were like copper glowing with the heat of fire; wide, intelligent, connected. Her face was flushed, her skin dotted with beads of perspiration, her breasts heaving.

"And destroy your life?" she whispered. "I'd hoped you'd forget me. You deserve better than me."

"There was no one else?"

"Of course not."

He stared into her eyes before his own moved over her face, her high cheekbones, her lips, parted and slightly trembling, her chin, tilted upward, defiant. Then he looked back into her eyes where he found an odd mixture of pain and desire. "Don't leave me again," he said. His voice sounded foreign to him, angrier, thick with authority.

"But—"

He shoved her back against the refrigerator so quickly that she gasped. One hand grasped her hair, balling it into his fist with a passion he didn't know he had. "Pay attention, Brenda," he said. He stared into her eyes, daring her to be defiant but she only stared back in surprise. "You're not leaving me again. Not now. Not tomorrow. Not next week or next year."

Confusion splayed across her eyes as her brows knit together. She moved as though to speak but he pushed her against the appliance again. He knew he was hurting her, he knew he was using too much force when he wanted to cajole, but he couldn't help it. When he spoke again, his voice was tense and gravelly. "I've spent months trying to find you. Months in which I thought of no one—nothing—but you. You've consumed every waking minute of every day and every dream I've had has been of you."

He waited for her to respond but her body only relaxed beneath him.

"Don't leave me again," he breathed.

She stared at him, the confusion slipping away, her brows unknotting. Her fingertips massaged his shoulder blades but she made no move to draw him closer nor push him away. Finally she spoke. Her voice was quiet, sensuous, the mere sound of it flicking over his skin. "I won't leave you," she said. "I won't hurt you again."

As he moved toward her again, his arm hit the light switch, plunging them briefly into darkness. He didn't move to turn it on and she remained perfectly still, her eyes cast in shadow. Then as he grew accustomed to the dark, he realized the street light beyond the kitchen window was attempting to find a way into their world. It moved like tentacles between the slats of the blinds, finding its way in through the tiniest of cracks, until it climbed inside and slithered down the walls and across the floor. As he stared at her, her eyes became lighter, revealing abandonment. The unbridled lust was gone but in its place was something else—something he couldn't quite put his finger on. It was somehow deeper than lust, stronger than passion. With a start he realized it was trust.

His hand relaxed his grip on her hair and moved to her jaw. Reluctantly, he dropped his gaze from her eyes to her jawline. As they came to rest on her lips, he found himself moving his thumb over her bottom lip. It remained soft, supple. He glanced into her eyes again to find her looking at him patiently, expectantly.

Both hands moved to her shoulders, feeling the bones underneath, following her collarbone to her neck. He wanted to experience every inch of her, to memorize every flaw in her skin, every curve of her body, every tantalizing breath. As one hand wrapped around the back of her neck against hair now damp with her perspiration, the other found the top of her blouse. It moved downward over the sheer material until it cupped her breast and it lingered there as he felt the quickening beat of her heart against him.

He was gentle now as he inched his fingers over her, kneading her. When she moaned, he looked up instinctively and once his eyes locked onto hers he found himself unable to pry them away. He stared into them as his hands moved downward, exploring her, watching as fresh beads of perspiration broke out across her brow and her upper lip.

And they didn't waver as he found her pants zipper and slid it downward, both hands moving hypnotically to slide them off her rounded hips and onto the floor. She stepped out of them, her eyes still on his, as she matched his actions. Now he was free to run his hands over her hips, to squeeze her and tease her. And as he lifted her up and against the humming refrigerator, she wrapped her legs around his back and locked him to her.

37

Dylan assembled the weapons on the coffee table, mentally checking them off his list. Beside each one was a cache of bullets and with a 15-bullet clip in each one, they had enough to delay or stop an assault.

Vicki sat beside him on the living room sofa. Though she'd watched him carefully, the misty look in her eyes revealed thoughts of her sister. Dylan had tried not to think about it but when the sounds from the kitchen had become intense, he had struggled to maintain his focus.

Now he glanced at his watch. It was dark outside and still hours away from Sam returning from Washington with their instructions.

When he heard the door to the kitchen open, he didn't immediately look up. After a moment, he glanced sideways at Vicki, whose eyes were riveted on the door as Brenda and Chris strolled in.

Brenda's hair was even more a mess than usual. As she breezed past them to the overstuffed chair, he glimpsed at her face. It was reddened and raw, but her features seemed softer. "Well," she said, sauntering past, "aren't you two just full of surprises."

Chris followed her, his sheepish eyes meeting Dylan's as he moved past them. Brenda waited for him to sit in the chair before she perched on its arm. Dylan noted Chris' hand moving possessively to her thigh. Better his problem than mine, he thought.

"What's happening?" Chris said, nodding toward the guns.

Dylan took a deep breath. "We have to assume we could have intruders some time durin' the night."

"Why?" Chris' voice was strained and as he leaned forward, Brenda grasped his hand.

Dylan nodded toward Brenda. "How much have you told 'er?"

"Everything," Vicki answered. "I think."

"Then you know there are those in the CIA who want you dead," he said flatly.

She grew paler but didn't respond.

"And Sam's gone to Washington to speak to the Director, face to face. We know there's a surveillance dragnet over the town."

"But since Sam knows her life is in danger, maybe he called off the surveillance." It was Vicki's voice, strained and dry.

"Even so, it doesn't mean a CIA within the CIA would call it off." He shrugged. "Call it factions, if you wish. We're in one o' 'em. And we don't yet know who's in the others."

"But—why would they come here?" Chris asked.

"Maybe they won't. But we've got to be prepared if they do." He leaned forward and picked up a Sig Sauer from the table. "This one's for you, Vicki."

"I've never fired a gun."

"Yes, you have." He leveled his eyes at her.

"Oh. Yeah," she said as she took it from him.

"You might've forgotten but every time I change me clothes, I'm reminded."

"She doesn't really need a gun," Brenda said. "I'm an expert shot. I won't let anything happen to her."

"You sayin' I can trust you now?"

Brenda rolled off the arm of the chair and reached for a Glock. "This one's mine."

"Suit y'self." Dylan handed the remaining pistol to Chris, who reluctantly took it. Then he passed out the bullets. "Don't set the guns down anywhere. No matter how safe you might be feelin', keep it on you at all times. Are you understandin' me?" He waited for each of them to respond.

"Now, here's what we're gonna do." He glanced at his watch again, although only a few short minutes had passed since the last time he'd looked. A sure sign his nerves were on edge, he thought. "I'm callin' the police."

"Why?" All three of them had spoken in unison.

He held up his hand. "Hear me out. I'm reportin' that someone is sneakin' 'round the house, rattlin' windows and the like. They'll inspect the grounds. Most likely they won't find anyone lurkin' there. But we'll know for sure."

Brenda leaned deeper into the chair as Chris moved forward to wrap his arm around her.

"But even more," Dylan continued, "I'll ask 'em to keep a close watch on the property tonight. There's no guarantees they won't be off tendin' to other business. But if they happen past here, they'll be more likely to take a close look."

He waited until each of them nodded in agreement.

"Soon as I call the police," he continued, "I'm callin' Alec next door."

"But he knows me," Brenda said.

"Alec who?" Chris said then stopped himself. "Alec Brodie, the deputy?"

"One and the same," Dylan answered. "He lives next door to us now. And he's on our blind side. I'll ask him to keep his floodlights turned on. They ought to shine some extra light on that side. And if he's not workin' tonight, if he's home, he'll be more apt to watch out for us."

They all fell silent and waited for him to continue. "The only factor I can't control," he said, fixing his gaze on Brenda, "is you runnin' out on us."

All eyes turned to Brenda. When Chris squeezed her hand, he held it so tightly that she had to gently loosen his grasp. When she spoke, her voice was confident. "I'm done with running."

"Are you now?" Dylan said, one brow raised in disbelief.

Her eyes didn't waver. "Yes. But—" she looked pointedly at Vicki. "I've placed each one of you in harm's way. You could each be risking your lives for me. And I'm not worth it."

Chris and Vicki's voices rose in unison as they protested her words and professed their loyalty to her. When they were finished and Brenda still appeared unconvinced at their course of action, Dylan added, "There's one more thin'. It's our job. It's what we do. Now I want the three o' you to stay together. No matter what. The police might come into the house, at least into the foyer, and the last one they need to see is you, Brenda."

She nodded silently.

"So. Go upstairs to my bedroom. There's a sittin' area there. And windows three sides 'round. Just—" he pointed his finger directly at Brenda "—*you* are not permitted to be near a window. Are you understandin' me?"

"Yes."

"And when the police are here, until I give the all clear, nobody looks out."

He waited until he was confident they all understood. Then he slapped his thigh. "So. As you Yanks say, 'showtime'."

38

The front door was open, allowing a swath of blue lights that flickered and danced across the walls as they penetrated the screen. As Dylan stood in the living room doorway, he could see the brilliant white from Alec's floodlights next door twinkling around the corners of the curtains where the fabric didn't quite meet the wall. After phoning Alec, Sandy had offered to alert the neighbor on the other side of Dylan, who also had floodlights. Now as he looked in the opposite direction, he saw a more yellowed but insistent light peering around the curtains on that side. He made a mental note when this was all over to purchase motion-sensor floodlights for each corner of the main house as well as the fish house.

A brisk knock on the screen door turned his attention to the front porch. The porch light swung with fervor in the growing wind, its buttery glow intermingling with the more zealous blue. He opened the door to a Lumberton police officer just as a gust caught the light door and threatened to snatch it from his hand.

"Come in," he said, gesturing inside. "My, but the wind is strong." In his mind's eye, Dylan pictured his bedroom two flights above him where Vicki, Brenda and Chris waited.

"We investigated the area around your house, Mr. Maguire," the officer said as he entered. He wore a dark blue uniform under which Dylan could clearly see the outline of a bullet proof vest. "I'm glad you cut back all those overgrown hedges. A few months back, they blocked our view of just about every window on the ground floor."

"Aye," Dylan answered. "I thought it was unseemly meself. And quite the security hazard."

"Well, you did a good job. We could see all the windows pretty clearly and nothing seems to have been broken or tampered with." His radio crackled on and he hesitated for a moment while he listened to the dispatcher.

"And the back yard?" Dylan asked when the radio grew silent.

"Checked there thoroughly. That building in the back, what is that?"

"We call it the fish house. It's how we earn our livin', breedin' little fishies."

"Well, it's secure… You say someone was rattling the windows and door knobs, like they were trying to get in?"

"Aye. But you know, it might've been just neighborhood tykes, playin' pranks. You know how they can be."

"I'd feel better if we kept a close eye on it tonight, if it's all the same to you." He fixed Dylan with blue-green eyes.

"I'd appreciate that, I would. Would make us feel safer tonight, knowin' Lumberton's best was keepin' a watchful eye." The screen door opened and they both turned in that direction. "Alec," Dylan said, motioning him inside.

The two officers greeted each other by their first names.

"Are you workin' tonight?" Dylan asked Alec.

"Nope. Off all week, on account of the move. Sandy doesn't like me to smoke in the house so I'll be standing outside off and on for a while. I'll help watch your place."

"Could you keep the floodlight on? Might be nothin' at'all, but Vicki would feel safer. You know how women are."

"Absolutely."

The officer's radio crackled again and they all listened as the officer in the backup vehicle announced he was moving on to another call.

"Busy night, 'ey?" Dylan asked.

"Busy every night."

The other car pulled away from the curb and the officer turned back to Dylan, handing him a card. "Call if you see or hear anything," he said as he made his way to the door. "My guess is, whoever was here has seen all these lights and they've moved on. I don't think they'll be back."

"Thank you," Dylan said as he slipped the card into his pants pocket.

Alec and Dylan watched the officer as he made his way to the car. A moment later, the blue lights were turned off, leaving the foyer in a muted wash of white and yellow lights.

"Where's Vicki?" Alec asked.

"Upstairs." Dylan glanced at his watch. "Headache. I think it was nerves."

"Tell her there's nothing to be nervous about. We watch out for each other around here. You'll have eyes on your place all night long. I can guarantee you that."

"It's nice livin' in a place where neighbors know one another," Dylan said. "Reminds me of me village back home."

"Does it?" Alec looked at Dylan curiously. He'd always looked at him that way, Dylan thought. As if there was more to his story and he thought if he stared at him long enough, it would be written across his forehead.

"I didn't live in the big city, if that's what you mean," Dylan answered. He tried to keep his voice smooth, but he found himself getting rather irritated.

"You told me that once before, I recall."

"Wouldn't be surprised if I did." They gazed at each other for a long moment. It wasn't quite a stare, Dylan thought; they both blinked, both tried to appear casual. But something seemed to be just below the surface.

"Well," Alec said finally as he made a move toward the door, "I'll let you know if I see anything. But I agree with the officer. Whoever was here is long gone. They were probably looking for an easy place to break into. And you've shown them this ain't it."

"Oh," Dylan said as Alec started onto the front porch, "Vicki's uncle will be arrivin' sometime durin' the night. He's flyin' in from out o' town. Don't quite know what time his flight's arrivin'. Wouldn't want you to think he's the intruder."

"Yes, I've met him. Nice guy."

"That he is."

"I thought he lived at Fort Bragg or Fayetteville. Retired military, isn't he?" His eyes narrowed.

"Aye. And he does live in Fayetteville. And it would make more sense for him to go to his own home, now wouldn't it." It was said more as a statement than a question. Dylan could tell by the glimmer in Alec's eyes that he'd verbalized his thoughts almost precisely.

Alec seemed to be waiting for Dylan to continue and the silence stretched on.

"If he's driving his dark sedan, I'll know it when I see it," Alec said abruptly.

"I don't rightly know what he'll be drivin'," Dylan said. "But I'll try to keep an ear open and meet him in the driveway so's you'll know all is well."

They both stepped onto the front porch.

"Wind's kicking up," Alec declared.

"Aye."

"You're sure it wasn't the wind blowing against your windows?"

"That we heard earlier? Could've been. But I don't think so. I've cut most o' the bushes away from the windows." He gestured toward the hedges in front.

"Hm." He sounded unconvinced. Alec lit a cigarette, turning partway around to block the wind until the end glowed red and hot. He stood on the porch, eying the railing and the fresh coat of paint on the decking. He seemed in no hurry to leave and now Dylan felt himself growing impatient. He glanced at his watch again.

"Well, I'm keeping you," Alec said.

"Ooh, no. I've got all night."

Alec continued smoking and Dylan cursed himself for not thinking of a better response. He almost wished Vicki would call him from upstairs but he knew she wouldn't. They would all remain put until he gave them the word that all was right. He'd just begun questioning his own plan when Alec said, "Sandy will be wondering what happened to me."

"That she will," Dylan said, casually leaning one hand against a post. "Don't want 'er thinkin' you've come to harm."

Alec appeared to move slowly as if he was reluctant to leave. When he reached the bottom step, he turned back and glanced past Dylan to the house. Dylan resisted the urge to look behind him. In his mind's eye, he knew all the other man should see was the wide, empty hallway and the stairs leading up to a darkened second floor. After a moment, Alec half shrugged and turned back around.

Dylan waited until he had passed their common property line before forcing himself to move gradually toward the open door. When at last he was inside, he closed the heavy door behind him and breathed a sigh of relief. Then he took the steps two at a time toward the third floor.

39

It was a quarter past two when Chris slid open the bedroom door. "Sam's here," he announced.

Dylan was already halfway across the room before Chris had finished speaking. He'd spent the first half of the night in the living room, listening to the dissipating traffic outside and for the sound of a car door that never came. At midnight, the time they'd prearranged, he switched places with Chris. But when he retired to the sofa in the bedroom, he'd found himself too wired to sleep.

In contrast, the sisters appeared to be sound asleep. They shared the bed and Dylan had looked longingly at it more than once, wishing he was asleep with Vicki in his arms. Instead, he found himself looking at Brenda's still figure under a filmy sheet remembering how she had looked at Chris and how he'd looked at her.

Now as he crossed the room, he glanced in her direction to find her watching him with eyes that were clearly wide awake.

"Stay here," he said in a low voice.

She didn't respond but she made no move to follow him.

He joined Chris and bounded down the stairs. "Stay here," he repeated to Chris as he opened the door and stepped outside.

Sam was halfway to the house from the driveway when he met up with him. Over his shoulder, Dylan could see Alec smoking on his front porch. He half-waved to his neighbor before turning back to Sam.

"What the hell?" Sam said brusquely. His eyes had heavy bags under them.

"Do you have a suitcase?" Dylan asked.

"A what?"

"Suitcase."

"I didn't—oh." He seemed to understand and tossed him the keys. "In the trunk."

"I'll get it for you straight-away," Dylan said in a louder voice, hurrying past him to the sedan. Under Alec's watchful eye, he laboriously pulled out a large suitcase that felt as light as if it was empty.

Sam had stopped on the front porch and was waiting for Dylan. When he finally joined him, they both turned and waved to Alec before entering the house. Dylan switched off the front porch light.

Sam caught a glimpse of Chris standing just inside the living room. "I thought you two would be asleep," he said. His voice was heavy and dry, the voice of a man who was exhausted.

"You're jokin', right?" Dylan said.

Sam looked down the hall toward the kitchen. "Got any coffee?"

Dylan leaned back in his chair and watched as Sam poured himself a cup of steaming coffee. He set the pot on the tray carefully as if he didn't quite trust himself.

Chris sat on the sofa, his hands wrapped around a mug. He blew across the top of the liquid and placed the mug to his lips before he thought better of it and set it down to cool.

Sam leaned back in the sofa and sipped the coffee, seemingly oblivious to its heat.

They each waited expectantly. After a long moment of silence broken only by Sam's periodic heavy sighs, Dylan said, "So, what's it to be?"

"I met with the Director."

"We gathered that."

"Got anything to eat?" Sam said.

"Christ."

"I'll get it," Chris offered.

"In the refrigerator," Dylan said as he watched the other man cross the room. "There's apple pie. Will that do?" His voice sounded exasperated but Sam didn't appear to notice.

"Bring me two slices," he barked. "I've not eaten all night."

The minutes ticked past as they waited for Chris. Dylan watched Sam closely as he continued to sip his coffee. As it cooled, he took to drinking it in larger gulps until he'd downed one mug and then refilled it. He looked like he'd aged considerably. His hair was still mostly jet black, slicked back like a gangster's, but his face was paler, somewhat ashen. The bags under his eyes were not only large but they were dark. And his eyes looked like roadmaps.

Finally, Chris returned with a plate brimming over with a quarter of a pie. "Did you want a slice?" he asked Dylan.

Dylan shook his head and Chris handed the plate to Sam before sitting down. They waited for Sam to speak and Dylan found his impatience growing as time ticked on.

Finally, Sam set the plate down.

"Alright then," Dylan said.

"You got a place I can sleep tonight?" Sam asked.

"Are you gonna be tellin' us what's it to be with Brenda or not?"

Sam did a double-take. Then, "What do you want to know?"

"Christ, man. What did you go all the way to Washington to meet with the director for, if it wasn't for somethin' important? What are we to do if we were to find Brenda Carnegie?"

Sam waited so long to answer that Dylan was beginning to wonder if he'd fallen asleep with his eyes open. Just as he was ready to throw his hands up in frustration, Sam said, "If we were to find her, she's to remain in my custody. Nobody else will question her. Nobody else will transport her."

"But certainly," Chris spoke up, "you can't stay with her forever. What would happen to her?"

Sam shrugged. "We don't know who we can trust. And I don't yet know why I can't trust them."

"Meanin'?" Dylan asked.

"Meaning," Sam answered, "there are too many unanswered questions. What information does she have that's so important we've got some agents helping her escape and others trying to kill her?"

"What if we were able to find the answers? What then? Would she be killed? Tried for treason?"

"She would not be killed," he answered emphatically. "I can tell you that. She'd be questioned. What would happen to her—well, I don't know."

"But the worst would be—?"

"Hell, I don't know."

"Say she's guilty of the highest crime imaginable. What then?"

"The highest crime?"

"Say it's treason. Murder, even. What then?"

Sam thought for a moment. "Suppose she gets the death penalty. It would be after a court of law heard her case. Then she'd no doubt have some high-powered attorney to throw up appeal after appeal. She could sit on death row for twenty years. That's," he added, "if she gets the death penalty. Anything less would be prison time. Hell, it's all speculation right now. I don't fully understand why we're pursuing her."

Dylan took a deep breath and looked at Chris.

"What's going on?" Sam said, looking from one to the other.

"We need to talk," Dylan said.

"I'm listening."

Dylan rose from his seat and crossed into the hallway where he gathered the manila folder that had lain unnoticed on the hall table. When he returned to the room, he handed it to Sam.

"What's this?" Sam said.

"You don't recognize it?"

Sam opened it and looked back at Dylan. "I'm not wearing my reading glasses."

Dylan pulled his glasses from Sam's shirt pocket, opened them and handed them to him. "It's the folder you gave me yesterday," he said as he sat back down. "The one with information on Vicki's sister."

"Yeah, yeah. You said she found her." He made no move to read it.

"I told you then," Dylan said, poorly concealing his growing ire, "that you need to give more thought to Vicki. You've been all she's really had o' a family, and you don't act like you care one whit about 'er."

"I've had a few more important things on my mind lately," Sam retorted. His voice was deep and raspy.

"Well, if you'd cared just one iota about 'er, you'd 'ave at least glanced at it." He jabbed his finger toward it. As Sam opened his mouth, Dylan cut him off. "And if you had, you'd 'ave seen that Brenda Carnegie is Vicki's sister."

The color drained from Sam's face. He shook his glasses as if opening them even though they were fully extended. Then he put them on his face as if he was completely unfamiliar with his own head. Finally, when they were perched just right, he peered over them at Dylan before opening the folder.

"It's all right there," Dylan continued, pointing at the folder again. "Brenda Anne Boyd, Vicki's sister. Adopted in Robeson County by the Carnegie family."

"Her sister Annie—"

"Is Brenda Carnegie."

"Jesus." He skimmed through the folder, obviously reading the material for the first time.

"You received this in an email," Dylan accused, "and you didn't even take the time to read it."

"Jesus," he repeated. After a long moment, he set the folder down in his lap, still open. "But—you said Vicki found her sister."

"She did."

"But—but—" He glanced at the folder in his lap.

"She's here," Chris said.

Sam stared at him, his mouth open.

Dylan spoke more slowly as his ire slipped away and he weighed his words. "She's upstairs, sleepin'. And I'll tell you somethin' right now. She's not leavin' this house without both Chris and me with 'er. You can question 'er all you want right here. And I'm thinkin' she'll cooperate. But she's safe from pryin' eyes here. We can safeguard this house. We can prevent 'er escape—though she's not so keen on escapin' now." He glanced at Chris. "And we can prevent anybody else from grabbin' 'er."

"We had her in custody," Sam said. His voice was strained. "We had her in cuffs. You—you patched her up. You saw her. How can you possibly think you can detain her here in a normal house?"

"Well, first of all, I don't know how normal it is," Dylan said. "But," he waved away his objection, "that was before she was reunited with 'er sister. It was before she was reunited with—him."

Sam turned to stare at Chris. "And what's your role in this?"

"I love her," he said without hesitation. "I don't know what she's done. I don't know why my boss wants her dead. But I can tell you, I will protect her with everything I've got. If she's to be arrested, I'll make sure she's got the best defense money can buy. And I'll be right there in the courtroom every single day."

"You realize this will cost you your job, in all likelihood?" Sam asked.

"There are other jobs. But there's just one—of her."

Sam took off his glasses and set them on the folder in his lap before leaning back against the couch. After a long moment, he took a deep breath. "What makes you think," he said finally, "that she'll cooperate?"

"I can answer that one."

At the sound of the husky voice behind them, they all turned toward the living room door. Brenda made no move to enter. She was dressed in thin, powder blue boxer shorts with a matching sleeveless t-shirt above it. Her feet were bare, and Dylan found his gaze moving downward from her face to shapely legs that looked like they would go on forever. She clearly was not dressed for running.

40

Dylan squeezed Vicki's shoulder in an effort to reassure her. As she half-turned in the chair to look at him, he detected more than a hint of anxiety. Her eyes were clouded, her lips pursed.

He perched on the chair arm. As all eyes focused on Sam, he allowed his to roam the faces of the others. Chris and Brenda had taken Sam's place on the living room couch and it was hard to tell whether Chris was holding Brenda's hands to bolster her courage or if she was clasping his in an act of comfort. They looked equally ill although Brenda appeared to have a better hold on her emotions as they looked at Sam.

"So," Sam said, removing his glasses and squeezing the bridge of his nose. It was obvious he was dead tired. He had a five o'clock shadow that looked a week old and his hair was disheveled from all the times he'd run his hands through it. His eyes settled on Brenda's. "I want to make sure I'm not misunderstanding anything you've told us."

She nodded silently.

"You have compiled a list of politicians who are engaged in unlawful and-or unethical behavior."

"That's right," Brenda said. Despite a lack of sleep, her voice was confident, the added huskiness adding to her allure. "The oil industry is just the tip of the iceberg. I have information on just about every major industry around the world—and our politicians' dealings."

"And you have proof."

"Undeniable proof."

Sam leveled his eyes at her. "Besides the oil industry—"

"Chinese manufacturing, nuclear facilities, illegal drugs, the pharmaceutical industry, oil pipelines…"

It was Chris' voice that interrupted her. "When you think about it, it's really as though she's the NSA all rolled into one person. She's got evidence of so much wrong-doing, she could be extremely valuable to our government."

"There's just one problem," Sam said.

"I sell to the highest bidder," Brenda finished.

The room grew quiet as each of them contemplated her statement. Finally, it was Dylan who broke the silence. "What have you sold thus far and to whom?"

Brenda chuckled but she sounded far from happy. "It would take less time for me to tell you what I *haven't* sold and who I haven't worked with."

There was a collective groan.

"You've given information to the Russians?" Sam asked.

"Not given. Sold." As they digested this information, she added, "And to the Chinese. The North Koreans. The Ukraine. Iranians…"

Sam swore. "Is there anybody you haven't dealt with?"

She shrugged. "A few didn't have enough money."

"And what, precisely, would each o' these governments do with the information you provided?" Dylan asked.

"Not my problem."

"I'd say it *is* your problem," Sam said. It might have been growled but for his weariness. "Help me understand this. The agents who helped you escape—"

"They knew I had information on crooked politicians."

"So they knew the people they were to turn you over to in Washington would most likely—"

A silence hung in the air before Brenda filled it with, "—eliminate me."

Vicki reached for Dylan's hand and held onto it as though it were a lifeline.

"So we're interrogating the wrong people right now," Sam said.

"I'd say so," Brenda answered.

He stared at her for a moment.

"Are you going to do anything about that?" Chris asked. His brows were knit and it was obvious he was deeply worried.

"I'll talk to the Director."

"You'll 'talk' to the Director?" Chris said, incredulous. "This is serious stuff. Those agents were serving their country—"

"We've got bigger problems than those agents," Sam said tiredly.

Chris fell silent and chewed his bottom lip.

"How many politicians are we talkin' about?" Dylan asked. "A dozen? More?"

Brenda leveled her gaze at him. "About a hundred. More or less."

"A hundred?" Sam leaned forward.

"How many are in your government?" Dylan asked.

"Five hundred and thirty-five in Congress," Sam answered.

"Which means—"

"One in every five is crooked," Brenda answered.

"Jesus." Sam rubbed his eyes. Dawn was still a long way off and while each of them undoubtedly preferred to be sleeping, they knew sleep wouldn't come for a very long time yet. "Here's what we do. Once you give us the list, we'll know which ones are involved in illegal activities. Those are presumably the ones who want you killed. We'll do an end-run around them, get to the ones who are not involved—"

Brenda's wry chuckle interrupted him. "What makes you think I'm ready to give you the list?"

Everyone's jaws dropped as they stared at her.

She pulled one lean leg under her as if she was readying herself to watch a relaxing movie. After a moment of silence, she continued, "What do I get in return?"

Now everyone's eyes moved from Brenda to Sam.

"How about your life?" Sam answered. His tone was flat and humorless.

"That's not worth much," Brenda answered without hesitation.

"Annie!" Vicki gasped. It wasn't lost on anyone that she'd used her childhood name for her sister.

"The way I see it," Sam said, "you're in enough trouble to lock you away for the rest of your life. I imagine you've been involved in plenty of computer crimes over the years. But the most significant crimes you've committed are treasonous. You could be put to death for that."

"Like I said, my life's not worth much."

Now Chris, Vicki and Dylan all began protesting. Their voices grew to a fever pitch as they fought to be heard over one another. Only Sam, who leaned back, remained silent.

When their protestations had died down, he waited until Brenda's eyes had turned back to him before saying, "Why don't you tell me what you want?"

Her eyes were level as she answered him. "I don't need money. Lord knows I have enough to live on the rest of my life."

"No doubt you've got millions in offshore accounts."

"No doubt." She waited a moment before continuing, "But I'll tell you what you can give me. Freedom."

The room fell silent as they looked from Brenda to Sam and back again.

"I don't have the authority to make that kind of a deal," Sam said.

She nodded toward his phone. "Then talk to the one who does."

"Depending on the information you've sold and to whom, this may go all the way to the President."

She half-waved toward his phone. "Then I'd start dialing if I were you."

Sam stared at her for a long moment. His eyes were expressionless like an expert poker player. But so were Brenda's.

After a moment, he said, "I'm going to my car."

As he left the house, Dylan took the opportunity to stand up and stretch. Then he gathered the empty cups and drained coffee decanter. Vicki helped him carry the items to the kitchen.

"What do you think will happen?" Vicki said hoarsely.

"I don't know, Darlin'," he said as he set the dirty dishes in the sink. "But it's a bed your sister's made for 'erself."

"We can't let her leave on her own," she moaned quietly. "They'd never stop looking for her. And if the wrong people find her, they'll kill her."

"She won't be leavin'," Dylan said.

"Who's going to stop her?"

"We all will." He took her in his arms and rested his chin on top of her head. His voice sounded more confident than he felt. "None of us want to see harm come to 'er, that's for sure. They'll come to an agreement."

Vicki didn't answer and Dylan closed his eyes. He was dead tired. His muscles ached and he longed for the comfort of the bed, of Vicki's soft curves within his arms, of the sweet sounds of her breathing rhythmically beside him while he drifted into a deep slumber. He was so fatigued that he thought he could fall asleep standing up as long as Vicki remained in place, propping him up.

When the front door opened and closed, he tried to ignore it; tried to disregard the tiny voice inside that said he needed to return to the living room. He didn't want to pay attention to his conscience as it spoke to him of new instructions he'd need to hear. Vicki also made no attempt to move away from him. They both remained like statues frozen in time.

Then he shook his head and pulled away from her. "Sam'll be wantin' to speak to us."

Vicki nodded, her eyes barely meeting his before they both returned to the living room to find Sam in the doorway, putting away his phone. He turned to Brenda. "I have a guarantee for you."

She raised one brow expectantly.

"I guarantee," he continued, "if you don't help us, you will be hunted for the rest of your life—by the bad guys as well as the good ones. You'll die by somebody's hands—whose, I don't know—and it won't be fast and it won't be pretty."

All eyes turned to Brenda.

"Tell me something I don't know," she said.

"I'm authorized to make you one offer. You'll hear it once and you'll either accept it or reject it. But it won't ever be on the table again. Understand?"

She nodded.

"Give us the list. *Give* it," he emphasized, "we won't be paying for it." He let this sink in before continuing. "You're in a lot of hot water; how much only you know. I will do what I can to get your charges reduced, to take the death penalty off the table, and to give you protection from the crooked politicians and their cronies."

"That's a hell of an offer," she said wryly.

He shrugged. "It's all I've got."

"Go higher."

He looked for a moment like he wanted to slap her, though his hands never moved. "I called the Director. He had the President awakened. Because of your crimes, I might add. And the offer I just gave you is as good as it gets."

"And if I refuse?"

"I'll cuff you myself. And you will not get out of my sight until I have personally presented you to the Director. It means you are putting my life—and anybody else's who accompanies us—in danger. They won't hesitate to kill us to get to you."

Brenda stared at Sam in silence before turning to Chris. He shook his head sadly, glanced away and then back at her with a regretful look that bordered on accusatory. She sighed audibly before turning to look at Dylan, who returned her look stone-faced. When she looked at Vicki, her sister burst into tears.

"Ooh," Dylan said, breaking the silence, "now look what you've done. You've gone and made your sister cry. You ought to be ashamed of y'self, Woman."

Brenda watched Vicki without making a move to comfort her. As Dylan wrapped his arm around her and tried to soothe her tears away, Brenda turned back to Sam.

"That's all you've got?" she asked.

"That's it," he said curtly.

"Hell of a choice."

"Life or death, the way I see it."

"Like I said hell of a choice."

The room grew so silent that the ticking of the grandfather clock in the hallway sounded as though it was rising to a crescendo.

"So, if I agree to turn over the list, what then?" Brenda asked.

"Are you agreeing to a deal?"

"I suppose I am, crap deal that it is."

"We still have the same problem we've got right now," Chris interjected. "We'll be watching our backs constantly, waiting for a fringe faction to attack us to get to her."

"We're not going to wait for someone to attack us," Sam said smoothly. "We're taking the fight to them. And we're using her as bait."

41

Dylan drained freshly cooked bacon and sausage on crisp paper towels and then cracked a dozen eggs into the skillet. If he was going to be forced to remain awake, he thought, he may as well eat. And eat like it could be his last meal.

Behind him, Vicki set the plates on the table and then banged around the kitchen.

"Over there," he said, pointing to a wide drawer. "I assume you're goin' for the utensils."

Sam picked up a slice of sweetbread and chewed in silence as he watched Dylan expertly flip the eggs.

Brenda's hand was on the table with Chris' over it. It might have appeared to be a protective gesture, had it not been for Brenda's look of defiance as she watched the others.

Dylan shifted the meat onto a platter alongside the cooked eggs and transferred it to the table. "So," he said, "and we'll fill our bellies and listen to Sam's plan."

"It can't involve using Brenda as 'bait'," Vicki piped up. "She's not a worm on a hook."

"She is to me," Sam said, filling his plate before continuing. "How do you find your buyers, Brenda?"

She placed a healthy helping of eggs on her plate along with a sausage link but didn't make a move to eat any of it. Leaning back in her chair, she answered, "I know certain web sites where I can advertise, places that are visited by people from other countries, people who have the means to pay for the information. People who would know what to do with the data if they had it."

"And how do you advertise? You don't post an ad saying, 'I know Congressman Willo is into illegal activities. Call for more information.' What do you say?"

"It's all in codes."

"What codes?"

She shrugged. "Codes. You learn what they are, what innocuous-sounding words *really* mean to the international traders."

Sam chewed in silence for a moment while the others looked on. "So," he said between slices of bacon, "let's say you put this ad out there. And somebody bites. How do you know who you're dealing with? How do you complete the transaction?"

Brenda's eyes lit up. "I know exactly what you're planning to do." She tore off a chunk of sweetbread and held it just an inch from her mouth while she stared at him. "I'm going to place an ad. One that will attract the people I'm running from. Only instead of conducting the whole thing in secrecy over the Internet, we'll somehow draw them to you." She popped the dough into her mouth and thought for a moment. "But how can we draw them out? It's not usually done that way. It's usually over the wire."

Sam jabbed his finger toward Chris. "That's where he comes in."

"Me?" Chris stopped chewing and looked up like a child whose hand had been caught in the cookie jar.

"How did Congressman Willo come to know about Brenda?"

Chris set down his fork. "Far as I know, it was after I returned to Washington from Lumberton."

"That strike you as odd?"

"Yes… No. It doesn't." Chris glanced at Brenda, his face reddening. "It was me. I told him about you. I told him I—I—it was personal, what I told him. But then, he asked me why you'd disappeared, why it wasn't possible for us to reconnect. And I told him about the oil scheme."

"The oil scheme he is involved in," Brenda finished.

"I'm sorry. I didn't know."

"Pay attention, lovebirds," Sam said gruffly. "Chris, you opened the door for Willo, telling him that Brenda existed. Would he even have known anything before then?"

Chris looked at his plate thoughtfully. "I don't think so."

"What about since then? What has he learned? Who has he learned it from?"

"Me," he answered without hesitation. "I'm the mole. The unwitting mole." He reached for Brenda's hand and squeezed it.

"Well, now you're going to get some wit about you," Sam barked.

"I don't understand."

"You're going to tell Willo we've found Brenda. And she's trying to sell information on the oil scheme." He looked at Brenda with a sideways glance. "Or anything else he's involved in."

"He's involved in a lot of things," Brenda said, her voice dry.

"Then bring out the whole arsenal. Make him think it's life or death for him. Make him send every bit of muscle he's got."

"Then what?" Dylan asked. As all eyes turned to him, he said, "Are we plannin' on sittin' here and waitin' for 'em to surround us? Maybe to paint each one of us as traitors? Are you suggestin' we arm ourselves to the teeth and come out shootin'?"

Sam crammed a slice of bacon in his mouth and talked while he chewed. "That's where your gal comes in. She goes to places around the world, describes everything to us. Why can't we use her to spy on Willo? And his cronies? And while you're at it," he added, "you can find us the ideal spot to draw them to us. A place that's defensible. I'll sketch what I've got in mind and you'll find it."

"So I'll have the bird's eye view as it unfolds," Vicki said. Her plate had remained untouched and now Dylan reached over and swiped a slice of her bacon. She watched him with the eyes of someone whose appetite had vanished.

"And me?" Dylan asked.

"Oh, I've got plans for you."

"So let me guess, why don't you," Dylan said. "Brenda places an ad. Chris alerts Willo. Vicki watches it all unfold—and finds our OK Corral. And you and I will be there presumably with some sort of trusted backup. Am I right now?"

"That's pretty much the plan. I can have any number of trusted agents with a ring around us. They'll never actually get to us before our guys get to them. We're just finding another location as an extra level of security."

"Well, then," Dylan said with a slap of his knee, "With a plan that good and with the talents of all those here 'round me, what could possibly go wrong?"

42

Vicki placed her head on the pillow as Sam pulled a chair beside the bed. It felt strange being in her bedroom without Dylan there. When he was with her, his presence seemed to fill the entire room. Now it felt too large, cold and impersonal. A feeling of total exhaustion washed over her and she wished for a deep, uninterrupted sleep. Even with Dylan downstairs with Chris and Brenda, even without his arms around her in slumber, she could sleep the sleep of the dead.

The morning sun was peeping through the front window. It was going to be a hot day; she could tell by the way the rays stretched far into the bedroom, its heat already searing against her. She placed her arm across her eyes just as Sam rose and tightly closed the draperies, casting the room into shadows that lulled her back to the abyss of slumber.

In her mind's eye, she struggled to see the plan he had drawn. He had been very specific. It had to be a building so they would not be out in the open but he wanted space on all sides; space they could monitor. He wanted it close enough to town so they wouldn't be driving forever on county roads… Something with interior hiding places for them but also an open area where they could easily spot intruders, which seemed a contradiction.

She fought sleep as she blocked out everything else. She felt her breath deepen in rhythmic notes as she lost consciousness of her back against the soft comforter and the pillow beneath her head. She felt as though she was rising, as if there were no roof over her head to block her from meeting the sun and hearing the birds as they awakened.

She hesitated over her neighborhood as she stared downward at the thick green trees, their lush leaves blocking many of the stately homes and occasionally reaching across the street to meet other trees in a handshake of limbs. The terrain here was flat, the ground not rising even a foot, much like the delta alongside mighty rivers.

She rotated slowly while scrutinizing the miles of town meeting country. Street after street of comfortable, dignified homes beckoned to her. Reaching the downtown area, commercial buildings came into view; as she panned the south and southwest, she spotted the courthouse, the Carolina Civic Center's historic theatre just beyond, the downtown shops coming to life and then just a few short blocks over, the mayor walking from his car to City Hall. None of it fit the description Sam had provided.

She continued to levitate and rotate, zooming like a dragonfly in one direction or another, until one building began to form in front of her.

"What do you see?" Sam's voice was firm and low.

From her bird's eye view, she spotted a cylinder-shaped building that appeared almost like a grain silo, but she knew instinctively it was something else. Something unused, something abandoned… Beside it was a large brick building that appeared to be in a state of renovation; as she neared it, she lowered herself to peek into an expansive window.

"Water filtration plant," she said finally. She could feel Sam's surprise though he remained perfectly quiet. "There's a sign in front. There's a picture of a faucet." She chuckled, wondering what Sam would think of something so unexpected. "Southeastern Waterworks. It's going to be remodeled into an art center. But it's empty now."

She continued peering through the windows, moving from one vantage point to the next, her excitement growing. "This is it, Sam." She described in detail the downstairs comprised primarily of a sprawling room that ran the length of the building.

There were pipes throughout that at one time had been used in the water filtration facility but were now being removed as part of the transformation to an art center.

Most of the room was more than two stories high. A second floor catwalk wound its way around the sides, opening to office spaces so as one left an office they found themselves in an open hallway with a railing that separated them from the first floor. It was everything Sam asked for: openness, plenty of broad windows from which they could spot any intruders from all four sides; yet the offices on the second floor provided hiding space should they need it. She traveled to the third floor, which was smaller than the first two, but provided a breathtaking view of the town below.

As she continued to describe it, Sam interrupted. "What is around this building?"

She zoomed upward and floated above it. "The back of the facility has something akin to a patio and then just beyond it is the Lumber River." She turned in the other direction. "There are front grounds fairly close to the road."

"No homes nearby?"

"Directly across the street are a couple of parking lots. It's close to a residential neighborhood, but there isn't a house directly next to it. No, wait. There is an old home you could walk to but it's beyond some trees…"

"Latitude and longitude."

"I can give you the precise address," Vicki said as she peered at the sign in front of the building. She rattled it off.

"Good girl," Sam said. "Come on back now."

She turned away from the plant and into the direct sun as she moved eastward toward home. Their house appeared silent and sleepy from afar, the roof sparkling with dew, the newspaper beckoning at the edge of the porch, a bird's nest just beyond her window filled with bald babies chirping for the mother gathering worms nearby.

"Come back, Vicki," Sam said, his voice firmer.

Vicki smiled. "Walking in the door now." She glided through the front door, her head nearly bumping the porch roof. Once inside, she heard voices coming from the kitchen. She floated down the hallway, her feet barely brushing the hardwood floor.

The light beckoned to her from the kitchen and as she passed through the open doorway, she found Benita had arrived. The blinds were open, revealing the fresh sunlight, the trim hedges and a slice of the side street.

Chris had finished breakfast and was leaning back, appearing more relaxed than Vicki had ever seen him. Brenda was finishing her meal at a snail's pace and seemed deep in thought.

Dylan was seated at the table with his back to the door, telling Benita she wouldn't be needed for the rest of the day. He stopped himself in mid-sentence. His voice changed, and he started to turn. "Oh, Vicki, darl—" He stopped, the last word still on his lips as he stared at the doorway.

"She's upstairs," Chris said quizzically as he watched Dylan continue to stare at the doorway. As Vicki slipped into the kitchen, he seemed to follow her movement with a slight tilt of his head.

"Cut it out, Vicki," Brenda said, looking up from her plate.

Vicki chuckled softly while Benita muttered something in Spanish as she left through the back door.

"Stop playing games," Sam ordered, his voice brusque. "Get back here. Now."

"What did you say that for, I wonder?" Dylan asked, turning to face Brenda.

"You feel her," Brenda said. "I know you do. I can see it in your face."

"See who?" Chris asked.

"Vicki."

"But she's—" he hesitated "—upstairs?"

Vicki stopped at Dylan's knee. God, he is so handsome, she thought as she stared into his face. She extended one finger and ran it along his jawline, feeling his five o'clock shadow as it tickled her skin. Immediately, he raised his hand and brushed his face as though it itched.

"What is she doin'?" he asked.

"Ask her," Brenda answered.

"You can talk to 'er?" he said.

"She'll hear you. I don't know if you'll hear her. I've never been able to."

"What are you doin', Vicki?" Dylan asked. The color was draining from his face.

"Vicki." Sam's voice was louder now. "I gave you a direct order. Stop the games and open your eyes. *Now.*"

Dylan's face wavered in front of her as if it was turning into a watercolor. She reached to his arm and tugged on it before moving a few feet away. As she continued slowly toward the kitchen door, beckoning him to follow her, he rose suddenly. With a few quick steps, he was at the door and peering down the hallway. She continued to move toward the front door, backing away from him as she watched, mesmerized.

"Dylan?" Chris called from the kitchen.

"I can't see 'er," Dylan said, "but I can feel 'er. And she wants me to follow 'er."

Abruptly, he broke into a run, racing up the stairs and bursting through the bedroom door. Startled, Sam bolted from his chair and stared at Dylan. But Dylan was halfway across the room, heading for Vicki's body as it lay prone on the bed.

"Somethin's wrong," he said as he reached for her.

"Don't touch her," Sam warned. "She's got to come back naturally."

"But—"

Vicki opened her eyes. They were heavy and she was dead tired.

"What were you doing?" Sam demanded.

"Aye," Dylan said, sitting on the edge of the bed, "what did you think you were doin'? You scared the wits half out o' me!"

"I had to see if I could do it," Vicki said, rising slowly.

"Playing games!" Sam shouted.

"No," Vicki said, grabbing Dylan's hand. "I wasn't. I had to know if you could feel me. If I—see something—I had to know if I could warn you."

"Warn me?"

She swallowed. "I'll be watching you. And I had to know if I touched you, if you could feel me." She reached for his right arm. "A touch here means look to your right. A tug means go to your right."

"That's impossible," Sam scoffed. "You're not really there."

"Same thing on the left side."

Dylan nodded. "I'm understandin' you now."

"A touch on the back means look behind you—a tug—"

"—means go behind me."

"And a touch on your chest—"

"—look right in front o' me."

"And this," she said, running her finger along his lips—

He knit his brows and shook his head.

"—means I love you."

"Ah, isn't that sweet," Sam said sarcastically. "A little love pat in the middle of a sting."

Vicki leaned in and kissed Dylan where her finger had been.

"I feel like I'm with a bunch of rabbits," Sam growled as he made his way to the bedroom door. "I'll be downstairs with Brenda." As he closed the door behind him, he added, "If you care."

43

Dylan stood on the catwalk and studied the room below. "You don't think bein' in town will make the operation riskier?" he asked.

"I want it to be accessible," Sam answered as he spread out a map. He pulled out his cell phone and dialed a number as he pointed to the map. "Yeah," he said into the phone, "Sam here." He waited a few seconds before continuing, "I'll need a unit at Luther Britt Park." He tapped the map as Dylan nodded in understanding. "Another north of the park, east of it, and south of it. Director's orders. Your Eyes Only. And a mobile satellite unit set up at—" he hesitated and pulled out a sheet of paper before rattling off the address. "Electronics? Yeah. From the parking lot on the other side of the Lumber River. You got me in view?"

Dylan strode to the broad windows that ran along the back of the building. A thick row of lush trees separated the property from the Lumber River. He didn't like it. The trees were too thick as if they had not been trimmed in years, their branches low, the undergrowth too concealing. With the windows uncovered, it meant operatives could watch Sam, Dylan and Chris unhindered by obstructions or the privacy of draperies.

Shortly after Sam hung up the phone, a white paint truck pulled into the parking lot on the other side of the river. Dylan moved from one window to the next in an effort to keep an eye on them.

Two men dressed in white uniforms with white caps unloaded two commercial sized paint buckets. Dylan used a pair of Sam's binoculars to watch as each removed what appeared to be paint brushes and rollers before one locked the truck. As they made their way toward the footbridge over the river, he turned to Sam, who had joined him.

"They're ours, I'm hopin'?" Dylan asked.

"Go downstairs and let them in. I want everything unloaded up here, the office on the corner."

As Dylan descended the stairs, he kept a watchful eye on them. They knew exactly which door to go to, he thought, the one least likely to be seen by prying eyes. The trees hung low over the footbridge at this narrow point in the river and continued with a tight canopy until the men were just a few feet from a concrete patio of sorts. Dylan slid open a delivery door.

The men sprinted toward the building.

"Where are we going?" one asked as soon as they were inside. Dylan recognized him as Max, one of the agents who had raided Brenda's house.

Dylan pointed to the stairs. "Office on the corner. Sam's waitin' for you." He paused to peer into the park-like area as he heard the men's heavy boots on the stairs. The area behind the building was quiet and peaceful, the only sign of life the tree limbs swaying. Tranquil and idyllic, he thought. Something gnawed at him and after a moment, he shook his head as if to clear his brain. He didn't know why he felt uneasy but he did. Why did Vicki and Sam think this was a defensible location?

He heard Sam barking orders and he climbed the stairs with a watchful eye on the windows. He could view quite a bit of the main street as well as a side street in front of the building. It was the thickness of the trees that concerned him, he thought. They were abundant enough to form a generous canopy, which sheltered the ground from the satellites until one was within a few yards of the building.

He glanced into the office when he reached the second floor. The paint buckets were open and the men were quickly removing and assembling computer equipment. Soon wires, screens and keyboards were scattered everywhere. It looked like one massive jumble to him but they appeared to know exactly what they were doing. They made two additional trips to the truck to retrieve more paint buckets which were filled with still more electronic surveillance equipment.

His services weren't needed there, he knew; the electronics were mind-boggling to him. And so was the whole plan to ensnare the rogue agents within the CIA. For all he knew, the agents who were busy installing this mess could be the very ones who would turn on them.

He fingered his pistol in the holster beneath his jacket. Chris, Brenda and Vicki were back at the house and though it was only a few minutes' walk, he had a growing uneasiness that he was in the wrong place—and a mounting concern that he needed to be in the right place. He leaned against the balcony and studied the floor below him for the umpteenth time. They'd taught this very thing in the CIA training—securing buildings, finding weak spots, eliminating risk, and he mentally checked off the items in the list as he thought of all the possible scenarios.

When he returned to the office, the equipment was set up and Sam was fine-tuning the satellite locations. Eight screens were mounted in a U-shaped display, each with its own keyboard. As he moved from one to another, he adjusted latitudes and longitudes until he could view various locations.

The last monitor was divided into a dozen smaller screens and as Dylan peered over Sam's shoulder, he realized the "painters" were applying wireless cameras at every corner of the building, providing them with angles of every inch of the surrounding property.

As the time ticked slowly past, he found himself itching to get this thing over and done with.

The two men returned to the office and peered at the monitors alongside Sam.

"Okay," one said finally. "We'll have these same coordinates on our monitors in the truck."

"And you'll be at Luther Britt Park," Sam answered.

"Affirmative. It will take us three minutes to get here. There's an old tobacco warehouse just south of here; we have another unit setting up there. A third is in a parking lot east of here, just a block from Vicki's house."

"And north?"

"A vacant home along the river, set beneath the trees, also very close to Vicki's house."

"Okay," Sam said. He looked at his watch. "Countdown. Five hours."

They synchronized their watches and tested their earpieces and communications devices. Then the men were gone as rapidly as they had appeared.

Sam sat at the desk for a moment before turning to Dylan. "Let's get back to the house. Brenda should have her work ready for us."

"What about this place?" Dylan asked. He waved toward the equipment. "It's a lot o' equipment to leave unattended."

Sam chuckled. "Are you kidding me? Anybody coming within a mile of this place will be picked up on monitors at several locations. They'd be surrounded before they had a chance to cross the threshold."

"What about those who are renovatin', remodelin'?"

"I went by City Hall earlier today. They were quite eager to talk about this place. I acted like I was interested in donating money to the new art gallery." He started down the steps as Dylan followed. "Next phase doesn't start for another month. In the meantime, the place is vacant."

"It'll make a nice art gallery, I'm thinkin'," Dylan said as they reached the ground floor.

"It will, won't it?" Sam looked around. "That took a lot of vision; turning an old water filtration facility into an art gallery."

"I'll have to make plans to attend the grand openin'," Dylan said, following Sam to a side door. They stepped outside, secured the door and moved under the treeline until they'd reached a neighborhood a block away. Then they crossed a property that appeared to be abandoned before reaching the street.

"Remind me to get a dog," Sam growled as he broke into a jog.

"Why's that?"

"I can walk a damn dog and nobody'll be suspicious. I can't take but so much of this jogging."

44

They crowded around the kitchen table, shoulder to shoulder, to peer at a screen only Brenda understood.

"You see, the way this works," she was saying, "when you give me the word, I'll upload this to the servers. On the surface, it looks like a simple advertisement for sex aids."

"All the things you could've advertised and you think o' that?" Dylan blurted.

"Not what you think. People are so turned *off* by ads like this, they gloss over them. If it was really good stuff, they might poke around. And that's what we don't want."

"Then how does it work?" Sam asked.

"Hidden in the ad are code words. This one right here," she pointed the mouse, "means I have information on oil. This word says I've got blackmail information. And this one says it's on the man in charge of the subcommittee. This one identifies him as American."

"You're jokin' me," Dylan said, leaning past Sam to see. "How does one get all that from this little ad, I wonder?"

Brenda smiled. "They're in the business of knowing what it means. Clear and simple."

"And the rest of the ad, that email address—" Sam interjected.

"It's one I set up this afternoon. They'll email me and use certain code words. I'll respond with other code words. And if we reach a deal, they'll get the information and I'll get the money wired to an offshore account."

Dylan narrowed his eyes, a subtle movement that was not lost on Brenda.

"*If* this was really going down," she added.

"So on my word," Sam said, "we'll set the trap."

"There's more," Brenda continued. "You see, if I depend entirely on someone seeing the ad today, responding today and following the trail, it's a long-shot."

They waited for her to continue. Finally, Sam said, "So?"

"So," she said, shrugging, "I've improved our odds."

"I'm almost afraid to ask how," Dylan said.

"Kind of a little…worm."

"Oh, Lord."

"Purely to benefit us. You see, when the ad is placed and it appears online, the whole thing won't be visible. Enough will be there to whet someone's appetite—someone who knows what the ad really says. So when they click on the hyperlink, the worm takes effect."

"What does it do?" Sam asked.

"It follows the trail. Within milliseconds, it will tell me the computer that clicked on it and where it's located, right down to the street address."

"All that from a hyperlink?"

"When you're good, you're good."

Sam stroked his chin. "Fascinating."

"That's not all."

"There's more?"

"The worm also pings Russian and Chinese servers."

"What?" Sam leaned in to stare into Brenda's face.

"The CIA and NSA regularly monitor them. So I've made it look like I want to sell to the Russians or the Chinese. Of course, we could get offers from overseas… But I'll also know Intelligence here has been alerted instantly."

"You're amazing," Sam said in a low voice.

"I know."

Vicki shook her head. "I don't understand any of it."

"You don't have to," Sam answered. "You just need to know when I give the word and this is uploaded that it's time for you to watch Congressman Willo. After Chris calls him, that is, to make sure he knows the ad is on the street."

They had begun to disburse when Sam turned back to Brenda. "Tell me."

"Yes?"

"Why is it that you never did this sort of stuff for the government?"

She half-smiled. "Do I strike you as the kind of gal who goes to work in a cubicle every day?"

Sam gazed at her for a moment before replying, his expression changing in so many subtle ways that it was clear a myriad of thoughts were racing through his mind. "No," he said finally. "You certainly do not."

She shrugged. "Well, there you have it."

"You know, there are private companies that employ hackers like you just to do this sort of thing—as government contractors."

"Like I said… Oh, by the way," she interrupted herself. "I'm only putting this out there for oil. There are more than a hundred politicians involved in all kinds of things. I don't want them and their cronies—or henchmen—converging on us all at once."

"Willo is the one I want right now," Sam said. "And this ad—if they trace it—?"

"It leads them to the address you gave me. I'm cyber-hopping so it can't be traced back to this house."

He nodded. "Good." Then he turned to the others. "Get a couple of hours' sleep, if you can. It's going to be a long night and I need each of you fresh and rested… Mind if I catch a snooze on your couch, Vicki?"

"Be my guest. Or you're welcome to one of the bedrooms."

"Couch will do fine." He looked at his watch. "Two and a half hours. Meet here and we'll get this ball rolling."

45

Dylan absent-mindedly stroked Vicki's arm as he listened to her rhythmic breathing. They lay on their sides, her back pressed against him in slumber, his arm thrown over her protectively. Her skin felt like fine silk and her hair smelled as sweet and pure as any garden.

She'd fallen asleep almost immediately. He marveled at that ability. His brain was buzzing with all that had happened and all that lay before them. His eyes wandered around the room; although they had closed the draperies, he could still feel the daylight peeking around the corners and the shadows that crept across the room seemed woefully inept. The wall clock sounded loud and rude in the stillness.

He was so tired his body felt numb yet sleep would not come. Each time he closed his eyes, his mind raced through the plan Sam had laid out: Vicki and Brenda would remain at the house. Brenda would have the laptop, ready to upload the ad when Sam gave her the green light. Vicki would be ready to go into her trance-like state to monitor Congressman Willo's activities.

Chris, Sam and Dylan would be at the Waterworks Regional Art Center, surrounded on all four sides yet a mile away by other operatives. When the program was online and ready, Chris would telephone Willo and inform him that Sam had intercepted the ad. That would prompt the congressman to move fast, contacting his inner circle at the CIA and setting in motion the rest of the night's events.

That's where Dylan's mind began to buzz.

Everything up to that point would be things they could control. But once Willo had his own team involved, he couldn't figure out how they could possibly maintain control. The glaring weakness of a defensive position lay in not knowing what the offense would do. There were too many things that could go wrong.

If the program Brenda uploaded spread like a virus internationally as she claimed, it could be picked up by hundreds of operatives all over the world. How would they possibly know which were the good guys and which ones were rogue? What if a team of Russians showed up? Or began contacting her, trying to buy the information? What then?

In his mind's eye, he remembered walking into her bedroom after raiding her house to find her half-clothed. Her voice echoed in his mind, husky and silky at the same time: "Rule number one, Irish. You can't trust me."

She'd proven time and again that she couldn't be trusted. She lied, she connived, she misled. Two teams were positioned close enough to the house to be here within two minutes. And Sam was stationing one operative inside. But Dylan would feel far more comfortable if he was left there to protect them.

Brenda had been willing to steal from her own sister and flee while Vicki slept. Then Chris showed up, they had a romp in the kitchen, and now she's supposedly ready to settle down. It made absolutely no sense.

And he didn't trust her.

But assuming Brenda did as she was instructed, what if Vicki was not able to follow Congressman Willo's movements? He didn't know enough of her past missions to know if she had ever failed. But what if, in their time of need, she tried to find his location and couldn't? What if they were blindsided?

In fact, he continued thinking, what if she was busy monitoring Willo while his cohorts were tightening a trap around *them*? He didn't know how three men could defend themselves if their defenses were penetrated. Sam had chosen the

Waterworks as a last stand but was a last stand really necessary? Couldn't they have eased out a sting operation?

He let out a heavy sigh and closed his eyes tighter, trying to block out his worries. But the more he struggled to rest, the more his brain buzzed.

Sam had four units, he reminded himself. Each had two to four men assigned to it so it wouldn't be Sam, Chris and himself waiting like worms on a hook. They had a noose ready to tighten when the time came.

But how, precisely, was that noose to tighten?

He cursed his inability to relax. He would need his wits about him and dawn might be a long time in coming.

He flattened his chest against Vicki's back, tightening his grip on her as he held her closer. She moaned softly but her steady breathing told him he hadn't awakened her. She didn't have the toughness her sister had. He couldn't imagine her tied up, sleep deprived, questioned for hours on end. The mere thought threatened to drive him crazy.

He'd brought up their vulnerability time and again but Sam was confident the outer rings of operatives would prevent anyone from reaching the house or the Waterworks.

How could they have a shoot-out without involving the local police? Oh, his mind was jumping in every direction. He didn't even know yet what he would be compelled to do. Murder? Dumping bodies in the Lumber River? Apprehending, cuffing, transporting fellow agents to Washington? Who could they trust and who might be spies?

Congressman Willo was a powerful man, one of the senior politicians with more than thirty years in Washington behind him. He'd risen from that status as freshman congressman with little or no voice to one of the most influential politicians in the country. There had even been talk of him running for president in the next election. How could they possibly go up against him? How many powerful allies might he have?

Even if they managed to apprehend the agents working for him, could they make any charges stick? Could Willo survive any media onslaught and come out on top? What would happen to them all if he survived politically and legally?

He swore under his breath and rolled over on his back. Sensing his movement, Vicki turned around and draped her leg across him. As she nestled her head in the crook of his arm, he stared at the ceiling.

Sam didn't seem to be the kind of operative who went off half-cocked. And he did have the total backing of the director of the CIA, he told himself. At least, that's what the director led Sam to believe. But what if this was really a sting against them? How could they know the director hadn't immediately pulled in the other operatives and they were, at this very moment, ready to launch an assault against them?

He thought of Sam downstairs, nestled into the sofa, and wondered if he was sleeping or if his brain was humming as frenetically as Dylan's. Was he, at this very moment, going through every last detail, making sure he'd thought of everything? Dylan sure hoped so. He'd rather be on the team of the man dotting every *i* and crossing every *t* than the man who slept soundly and didn't have his ducks in a row.

His mind wandered from the living room to the second floor where Brenda and Chris were presumably resting. Were they asleep as Vicki was? Or were they lying awake talking? Was one of them fast asleep while the other was thinking through every scenario just as Dylan was?

His eyes felt like sandpaper and he knew he would regret it if he didn't get some sleep.

So this was America, he thought. His life had become so complicated after moving here. This time last year… He felt a sharp pain in his heart as he thought of where he was, what he was trying to overcome, what he was struggling to move past. It had been the carrot of America that had enticed him to keep on living, to keep on caring, to keep on hoping. To *try*.

How ironic that he missed Ireland so much. He was here, in the land of opportunity, with a job paying more than he ever dreamed possible. He had a woman who was clearly in love with him and he was equally smitten with her. So why did he long for Ireland?

It was immensely preferable to this, he thought. What was worse, after all—not knowing if he would make it through the day emotionally—or physically?

It was what it was, he thought. He glanced down at Vicki asleep in his arms, her hair streaming out across the bed, her face free of worry because he was there to protect her. If he hadn't come to America, he wouldn't have her, he reminded himself. But could he protect her now?

After covering almost every conceivable *what if*, he felt himself beginning to drift off to the deep sleep he craved when he heard the sound of heavy footsteps on the stairs.

It was time.

46

They gathered in the sitting area of the master bedroom. The laptop sat innocuously on the coffee table, the browser open and ready for Brenda to upload the ad and embedded program. Although she sat directly in front of it, her eyes were not on the screen but instead were following Sam's every movement. Her eyes were narrowed, her brow slightly furrowed, her mind obviously moving through one scenario after another.

Dylan sat on the other side of the coffee table. Though his arm was casually encircling Vicki's neck, his fingers absent-mindedly exploring the skin on a shoulder laid bare by a summery halter top, his mind was riveted on Brenda. He kept his own eyes narrowed in an attempt to conceal his thoughts, but his mind was flooded with her voice: "Rule number one, Irish: you can't trust me." It seemed to grow in intensity until he could think of nothing else.

He watched Chris, half-perched on the arm of the sofa beside Brenda, as he leaned down and whispered something only she could hear. Her eyes brightened and she turned toward him, a half-smile on her lips.

Dylan didn't buy it. Not for one second.

Sam handed out earpieces to everyone. "I have them tuned to a secure frequency," he said as they each received them. "This is how we'll communicate. It's how I'll instruct you when to upload the program, Brenda."

She nodded and moved her massive volume of hair to the side while she inserted it in her ear.

"And it's how I'll communicate with you, Vicki. Brenda, once you've uploaded the ad your job will be to observe Vicki. I want you two to stay together. If, for whatever reason, Vicki isn't able to communicate with me I'll need you here to monitor her."

"That's why we're in this room," Brenda said. "She'll get comfortable on the bed while I upload this puppy. Then I'll move over there where I can keep an eye on her."

"I should've installed security cameras 'round the house," Dylan said. He was surprised at the sound of his own voice; he hadn't meant to express his concern aloud.

"Why?" Sam turned to look at him. "We have satellites trained to watch the house from every angle. And we have one operative downstairs now, and others who can be here in an instant."

"That might be, but I'd feel better if I called Alec and asked 'im to keep an eye on thin's just for good measure."

"That might only arouse his suspicion," Vicki said.

"I agree. He'll wonder if you're so worried about her, why you're leaving her here alone," Brenda said. "Remember, he doesn't know I'm here. Anyway, we'll be fine. We're staying in this room together. And if anything did happen, all I'd have to do is talk on this thing."

"That's right," Sam agreed. "Whatever is said on your mike will be picked up by all of us-the operative downstairs, the teams nearby, and the three of us."

Dylan had a growing concern that each of them could have their hands more than full with the events of the evening and he wondered how any one of them could possibly be spared to return here. But as he looked at Vicki's trusting face, he realized it was better to keep his insecurities to himself. "I'll check the doors as we leave," he said instead, "and make sure everythin' is tight and buttoned down. And I'll leave some lights on."

"What about the dragnet you have around Lumberton?" Chris asked. "Won't they pick up that the three of us have moved from here to the art center?"

"I took care of that this afternoon," Sam said. "I told them to redirect the satellites to Pembroke, about fifteen or twenty miles from here."

"How'd you do that, I wonder?" Dylan asked.

"I told them I had intelligence indicating Brenda had been sighted there. She was entering a beauty shop, presumably to get all that red hair chopped off."

Brenda's face paled. "It isn't lost on me that you're all in this because of me."

"Don't start thinking we're doing this for you," Sam said gruffly. "Crimes are being committed against this country. That's why I'm here. And that's why we're doing this. And you, young lady, are helping us serve our country."

"Is it too late for me to renegotiate our deal?" she said flippantly.

Sam raised one brow but didn't answer.

Chris squeezed her shoulder. "Whatever happens, I'll stand by you."

"Let's take things one day at a time," Sam barked. "Focus on what we're doing tonight." He glanced at his watch. "Time for the three of us to get moving. With any luck, we'll be back in six to eight hours. And we'll all celebrate and get a good night's sleep—not necessarily in that order."

Dylan pulled Vicki to her feet. Placing one finger under her chin, he raised it so she was looking into his eyes. "I'm wantin' you to be careful," he said in a low voice.

"Don't be silly. It's you guys who should be careful. I'll be somewhere else in my mind—but in my mind only. I won't be in any danger."

"If you are—if you even think you are—let me know. I'll be back here straight-away."

"I'll be okay," she murmured as he bowed to kiss her.

"Christ," Sam said. "You'd think you two were going off to war. We'll be back in a few hours."

Dylan reluctantly pulled away from Vicki. Out of the corner of his eye, he saw Chris doing the same thing. He glanced down at her once more. "I'll be back soon," he said. He tried to make his voice sound more confident than he was. Her reassuring smile said she believed him. Or maybe, he thought, she was as good an actor as he was trying to be.

As he made his way around the sofa, he stopped in front of Brenda. Chris was already heading toward the door where Sam waited impatiently. Brenda looked up at him expectantly. "Take care of your sister," Dylan said. His voice was low and fervent.

"Of course."

"Make sure you do," he answered in a hoarse whisper only Brenda could hear, "or I swear to God—" He left the rest of the sentence hanging and didn't wait for her response before heading to the open doorway.

Sam had moved to the top of the stairs and once Dylan's head emerged from the bedroom, he and Chris started their descent. Dylan was halfway down behind them when Vicki called out to him.

"Aye?" he said, turning around.

Vicki was standing in the hallway outside the bedroom door. Her mouth opened and closed as if the words were on the edge of her tongue but she'd thought better of saying them. He made a move to ascend the stairs to her when she spoke. "Be careful."

He stopped. Her face was partly in shadow but he had a gut feeling that she'd wanted to say more. "Don't you worry about me, lass," he said, forcing his voice to sound more carefree than he felt. "I'll be back home to you faster than you think."

With that, he was down the stairs to recheck the back door before rushing to catch up with Sam and Chris.

47

Vicki fluffed the pillow before she lay down. She had a queasy feeling in the pit of her stomach. Glancing up, she caught a glimpse of doubt in Brenda's eyes as she watched her.

"Will they be okay?" Vicki asked.

"Of course they will," Brenda answered without hesitation. Her eyes were dark now as she turned away.

Vicki made herself comfortable as Brenda grabbed a chair and dragged it to the side of the bed.

"Your program—?"

"It's ready. Soon as Sam gives the word, it'll take just seconds to upload."

Vicki nodded. She peeked across the room at the laptop sitting on the coffee table. It felt like a live being now, an accomplice in their scheme. Then she forced herself to look away, to lie on her back and face the ceiling. After a few shaky breaths, she raised her forearm over her eyes. It was as much an effort to clear her mind as it was to block the light. She focused on a white light that she hoped would prevent her worries from escalating.

When Sam's voice sounded in her earpiece, it was as though he was sitting right beside her rather than a few minutes away. "Vicki, are you ready?"

"Yes," she said. Her throat felt constricted. "I'm ready."

"Brenda?"

"Ready when you are."

"Vicki, we're going to start with you," Sam said. His voice was monotone; the same bored intonation she was accustomed to. It suddenly dawned on her that perhaps he had been trained to sound so impassive. Certainly in a mission with such high stakes, it was soothing to hear a lackluster voice so devoid of expression.

"Ready," she said simply.

"Go to Congressman Willo. Tell me where he is."

She expelled a deep, hot breath and concentrated on blocking out everything around her. Within seconds, she was soaring over Lumberton and heading northward. Then in the blink of an eye, she was inside Congressman Willo's office. He was seated at his massive desk, reading papers, a pair of glasses perched precariously on the end of his nose. His leather chair was so tall that it seemed to swallow him, though he was a large man. She described him to Sam and then rotated slowly in the room. No one else was there. His office door was open. Directly outside was a desk but its occupant was nowhere to be seen.

Elsewhere in his suite of offices she heard the sound of laughter and banter, bringing an image of employees gathered around the water cooler. She turned back to Willo's room.

"Brenda," Sam said. "You're up."

In the back of her mind, Vicki registered Brenda rising from the chair beside the bed and walking purposefully across the room. She tried to remain in the congressman's office even as she heard the sound of her sister's nails clinking against the keyboard.

"It's uploaded." Brenda's voice sounded strained. She remained at the keyboard.

"Willo is still reading," Vicki said.

"Chris," Sam directed, "make the call."

Vicki watched as the congressman's phone began to ring. He glanced at his office phone and realizing the sound was coming from his cell phone, reached into his pocket to retrieve it. He glimpsed at the screen and then pressed a button. "Yes?"

"I just got a call from Sam," Chris said. Though Vicki was standing in front of Willo, she heard Chris' voice through her earpiece.

"Sam."

"Sam Mizzoli, the CIA guy I'm working with here."

"Yeah, yeah." Willo's voice sounded distracted but Vicki noted he instantly put down his paperwork and removed his glasses. He leaned forward into the phone as Chris continued.

"His tech guys got a hit on some Internet traffic."

"It's her?"

Chris hesitated and Vicki could feel the wheels churning. She couldn't see Brenda across the room but she felt her presence and knew she was listening attentively. "Yes. She's trying to sell information."

"What information?"

"We don't know yet. It's all in code, and the decoders are working on it. But it has your name in it and something about oil."

Willo continued leaning forward intently. A long silence elapsed. "Yes?" he said finally.

"That's all I know right now."

Another silence ensued. "Keep me up to date," Willo said abruptly.

"What is he doing?" Sam's voice came through Vicki's earpiece. She described the congressman as he clicked off the cell phone. He sat for a moment, idling fingering the phone as if deep in thought.

Then he buzzed his assistant.

An attractive young woman scurried away from her colleagues and answered the intercom at her desk. "Yes, sir?"

"Get me the vice president."

"Yes, sir."

Vicki could feel her heartbeat pounding in her temples as she described the scene to Sam.

Within seconds, the intercom on Congressman Willo's desk buzzed. "Yes?"

"The vice president is on the phone, sir," his assistant announced.

He reached for the phone. "Mr. Vice President."

He paused and then participated in a brief exchange of cordialities. Then, "The CIA has picked up activity from Brenda Carnegie. She might be trying to sell information." Another pause followed by, "I don't know. They're deciphering it now. My name is in it; they know that. And she mentions oil."

Willo's face reddened. "Yes, I know. I'm on it."

He held the phone halfway between his face and the desk. It was apparent the vice president had already hung up. Then he raised the receiver back to his ear as he clicked the phone for a dial tone. A moment later, he was dialing. "Congressman Willo here. Is the director available?"

Vicki felt her face growing flush. Time seemed to stand still. And as she relayed the congressman's words back to Sam, she could feel the wheels turning.

"One of your men just picked up some traffic," Willo was saying. "Can you tell me where it came from?"

Willo leaned back in his chair and rotated it slowly until he faced the window. It seemed as though it took forever for him to speak again, during which time she felt as if all of them were holding their breath. Finally, he turned back around and grabbed a pen and a note pad. "And you said that website was—?" He scribbled something. "The vice president has issued orders," he continued. "Take down the ad. Brenda Carnegie is to be disposed of on sight."

Their conversation ended, Willo then placed another call. He repeated the web site address and the ad. "Trace it," he directed. "I want her dead." He clicked the phone off but again dangled it for a long moment. Then he replaced it in the cradle, rotated his chair and stared out the window once more.

"Vicki." Sam's voice remained monotone.

"Yes."

"Find the CIA director's office."

"I have activity." It was Brenda's voice. "The ad is being downloaded."

Vicki sought to move out of the congressman's office and soar above the city but she felt sluggish, like a projectile running out of fuel. She wobbled above the city, turning in each direction as she tried to find her internal compass. Then she was inside a long corridor, moving between a set of pristine white walls, gazing at glistening white tiles beneath her feet. She stopped at the end of the hallway and stared at the massive wood door. She wanted to go inside but now the door felt as if it had more substance or her body had substance or… She squeezed her eyes tightly as she struggled through the door. It hurt as she passed through, almost as if she could feel the wood splintering inside her.

"Focus, Vicki," Sam was saying. "Describe where you are."

She described the director's office.

"Is he alone?"

"Yes. He's on the phone."

"Who is he talking to?"

She hesitated. "I think he's on hold."

She could feel their collective breathing as they waited for her to continue. The walls were beginning to fade in and out and now she saw the dresser against the far wall in her bedroom, could hear Brenda's nails clicking once more against the keyboard.

"Mr. President," the director said.

Vicki relayed the words back to Sam.

"Moscow," Brenda announced suddenly, her voice betraying her excitement. "Beijing. Pyongyang. Langley. Langley," she repeated as if the location was just now sinking in. "Langley."

The sunlight hit Vicki full in the face. She groaned audibly as she struggled to sit up. The sun was setting, the waning light shining stubbornly around the draperies as it sought to pierce her eyes. She was gone—he was gone—the conversation lost in the atmosphere.

48

Dylan stood just outside Sam's door, his eyes wandering from one expansive window to the next. Though the sun's rays remained strong as they tumbled across the floor in the last vestiges of daylight, he could clearly see black clouds forming in the distance. He watched them for a moment, gauging their direction, as he listened to Sam and Vicki through his earpiece.

There had been one other time in his life in which he felt a pull so intense, so insistent, that he could not ignore it. Now that feeling was screaming at him to go to Vicki, even if all he did was stare at her while she spoke in her dream-like state. It was taking all his willpower to keep from rushing out the door to her.

When Brenda interrupted Vicki's session, he inwardly groaned as he glanced over his shoulder at Sam. He watched him as he expertly managed two earpieces at once, providing instructions to the CIA teams who surrounded them as well as Vicki's remote viewing session.

Sam swore in frustration. "Vicki, get your cell phone." The air was still and musty; he wiped perspiration from his brow as he glanced up to meet Dylan's gaze. His eyes were ringed in pink, aggravated by a lack of sleep. For the first time, Dylan noted pallor in the man's face that made him wonder if Sam was all that healthy.

"Got it," Vicki answered.

"Call me. We're doing your session over our cells."

"That won't open us to eavesdroppers?"

"We don't have a choice. Brenda, stay on this frequency. Vicki, cut off your earpiece."

Dylan felt his chest tighten. He didn't like the thought of Vicki getting separated from the rest of them even if she was establishing an alternate form of communication. He watched Chris as he wandered across the spacious center room downstairs; he walked deliberately, peering furtively out each window while he listened. His movements were tense and stiff, and Dylan realized this was a far cry from the desk job he was probably accustomed to. He just might be wondering what he'd gotten himself into, he thought.

Sam's cell phone rang, disrupting his thoughts. "Go back," Sam was saying now, "I've got to know what the director is doing. Who he's talking to; what they're saying."

As he fell silent, waiting for Vicki to re-enter her trance-like state, Dylan stepped to the door and leaned his forearm against the doorframe. He hoped the casualness of his gesture masked his inner turmoil. "We're not expectin' men to travel here from Langley, are we? Or for the congressman to come here to Lumberton?"

Sam shook his head. "They have operatives in the field, same as we do. They'll be issuing directives. Whoever is nearest will be closing in. The others will follow until they've received word the mission is complete."

"Meanin'…" Dylan hesitated.

"Meaning Brenda is dead or captured," Sam answered bluntly.

"We've got company," Chris announced.

Sam turned to the monitors while Dylan straddled the threshold, watching through the window as below him, Chris pointed.

Dylan glanced back at the controls and screens as Sam said, "This is exactly what we want to happen."

How could that be, Dylan wondered. Shouldn't the noose 'ave tightened before they got this close?

Chris backed away from the windows, moving into the shadows of the cavernous room.

"Unit Alfa," Sam said into his second microphone. "Status."

"Unit Alfa," came the instant response. "Two men. One at the north end. One on your backside."

Dylan passed behind Sam to peer out the window to the grounds below. Directly beneath them was a concrete deck surrounded by a metal railing. It overlooked the narrow and winding Lumber River, whose water appeared as black as oil as it snaked lazily past. A thick canopy of trees draped over the shores as if trying to touch in the middle. He strained to see into the murky shadows but couldn't. His breath came steady and deep as he waited for any sign of movement.

"Unit Bravo," Sam said behind him. "Status."

"Unit Bravo. Individual in back giving hand signals. We don't have a visual on his accomplice."

"Unit Alfa," the first group broke in. "Target to your north is not in the line of sight of the backside target."

"Unit Charlie," Sam said. "Status."

The line was quiet.

"Unit Charlie," Sam repeated. "Status."

Dylan turned from the window to watch Sam's expression as the seconds ticked by. His face remained immobile. Only his fingers tapping silently against the top of the desk revealed his concern.

"Unit Delta." Again, he was met with silence. He pulled the map closer to him, where thick black X's marked the locations of the four teams. "Unit Delta. Status."

"Vicki," Sam said, switching to his cell, "status."

"Trying to locate the director. He's no longer in his office."

"Brenda," Sam said, "status."

"Getting pings from all over the world," she answered. Her voice was hushed and Dylan imagined her sitting on the sofa a few feet from the bed, trying to remain quiet while Vicki concentrated on her mission.

"Unit Charlie," Sam said again. "Status."

There was no response.

"Where was that unit?" Dylan asked.

"Tobacco warehouse off Water Street."

"North or south?"

Their eyes met. "South."

Dylan stepped into the room and pointed at one of the monitors. "Can you be my eyes?" he asked as he pointed to the man waiting along the edge of some trees at their northern border.

Sam nodded. "I want him alive—if possible."

Dylan reached across the desk and grabbed a roll of duct tape. "You mind?"

"Take it." Sam turned back to the monitors and tried in vain to raise the third and fourth units as Dylan slipped the roll into his cargo pants before heading for the stairs.

"Where'd he go?" Dylan asked Chris as they converged at the north end of the building.

"There's a roofline through those trees," Chris said, pointing. "Looks like a house."

"I see it."

"Last time I spotted him, he was in between the hedges separating the properties."

Dylan nodded. "Then that's where I'll be."

"What do I do?" Chris asked as Dylan made his way to a door on the east side.

"Get the binoculars and get upstairs where you have a better view all the way 'round. Tell me who you see and where you see 'em."

With that, he was out the door and sprinting toward cover. He couldn't assume there was only one man to the north, he thought as he dashed around a hedge to emerge onto a residential side street. If they were professionals, they would be working in teams of two or more.

From this vantage point, he could see the old water sedimentation tank, a large concrete structure that loomed over an otherwise peaceful neighborhood. It was situated just a few yards from a sizable Queen Anne home in such need of repair that it appeared abandoned.

He slowed until he reached the end of the thick hedge, where he came to an abrupt stop. The sun that had shone so brightly just a short while ago was soon to be a memory on the distant horizon, taking the last remnants of light with it. He took in the street lamps' yellow glow. It wouldn't be long, he reasoned, before darkness would descend and they would illuminate the area in which he stood.

He turned his attention toward the decaying house. A movement caught his eye and he narrowed them instinctively to focus in the waning light. A man hovered near the edge of a crumbling porch in a futile attempt to use it as cover. A black wire dangled from his ear across a white collar. Dylan's first inclination was to move further away, double around in between two other houses and approach from the other side. But something held him in check and he remained fixed to his location while his eyes continued to scan the area.

He almost missed the second man but for a slight movement near the tank. He was dressed in a black jumpsuit that blended into the lengthening shadows. His black gloves caressed the concrete tank as he lingered just beyond the light of the street lamp.

As if on cue, Chris said in a low voice, "I can't see anyone on the north end anymore. The man on the west side is remaining stationary."

Dylan didn't respond. Glancing at the man in the light shirt, he backed away against the hedge line, retracing his steps until he was on the other side of the tank.

"I can see you," Chris said. His voice sounded tense.

"I'm on the south side," Dylan whispered.

There was such a long silence that he could almost feel Chris' mind attempting to process the information, knowing full well that he was on the north side. He closed his eyes momentarily in a wordless silent prayer. Then Chris said, "Roger."

Dylan stepped forward with the grace of a cat, his feet landing securely on the ground beneath him so silently that not even a twig cracked beneath his weight. In his mind's eye, he memorized the placement of the house, the porch, the accomplice… And hoped the man in black was still in place.

He stopped at a precise location. One more step and he was certain he would be visible to them both. He waited with bated breath; sure the man could hear his heart beating.

Then a shadowy figure shifted into his line of sight.

With one swift kick, his heavy boot connected with the man's temple, throwing him into the concrete wall. As the unconscious man went down, Dylan swiftly rifled through his pockets. Finding several sets of zip-tie cuffs, he quickly bound his hands and feet together behind his back like a trussed-up pig waiting for slaughter. He slapped a piece of duct tape across his face, sealing his lips, and ripped the earpiece from his ear, securing it into his own. As it fit neatly inside his ear, he was surprised to hear Sam's voice. His hunch had been correct.

He slipped back behind the hedge, retracing his steps until he was once again on the side street in view of the deteriorating home.

"Brenda." Sam's voice sounded in his left ear. "Status."

"Making a list of IP addresses," she answered. "My ad was pretty popular at Langley—and at NSA."

"Roger," Sam said. "Vicki. Status."

"Not having any luck finding the director," Vicki answered. Her voice crackled and Dylan realized he was listening to her through the cell phone's speaker—and so were the other operatives.

"Change your target to the vice president or president."

"Roger."

"Unit Alfa," Sam said next. Dylan listened in stereo through both earpieces now as he continued, "Status."

"Two operatives on the west side. One under the second story patio. The other in the treeline."

"Dylan. Status."

Dylan watched the man's back as he huddled against the aged house. He had no doubt that he was also listening to Sam's status checks. What he didn't know was whether this team had taken out Unit Charlie and seized their communication devices—or if this *was* Unit Charlie in a counter maneuver.

"Dylan," Sam repeated. "Status."

It was too risky to answer now, even in a whisper. Instead, he ignored Sam's call and edged closer. His foot hit something round and slippery, almost causing him to lose his balance and he caught himself, instinctively holding his breath as he watched the man just a few yards away. Glancing down, he found his foot against a giant magnolia pod thick with algae. Taking in the uneven ground between the two men, he continued to inch forward.

Dylan was within a few steps of him when he turned, bringing them face to face.

49

Somewhere in the distance, Vicki's mind registered a roll of thunder. But inside the Oval Office was calm and serene. The president sat behind the desk, his eyes riveted on the papers in front of him. She floated through the office, feeling more like an intruder than she ever had before, almost expecting Secret Service agents to come through the doors at either side of the room and whisk her away to an interrogation room.

She described him to Sam, who was unusually silent. Her training had never included an operation such as this one, and she wasn't sure what to expect. She knew her handler's attentions were split between her and others, and she had no way of knowing how much he heard and how much he was able to process.

Vicki continued around the desk until she was peering over the president's shoulder at the paperwork that held his attention. A CIA operative was off the radar, his last known location along the eastern coast of Ireland. For a moment, she forgot her own mission as she read the circumstances: he'd been on a covert assignment that had begun in Berlin. He'd followed his target, a known terrorist, to London. Hoping to connect the man with other terrorists, he'd watched him for weeks as he went about his business. Then one day, the man took a ferry to Dublin and the operative followed. Once ashore, they were both lost—simply vanished from all surveillance.

She processed this information with what she knew of Brenda's activities. It couldn't be related, she concluded. But she relayed the information back to Sam.

"Find the vice president," Sam responded without further comment.

Instantly, she moved through the corridors, using her internal radar to find the location of the vice president. Another clap of thunder sounded; this one closer and more urgent. Her eyes remained closed in the bedroom, but she could feel Brenda's startled figure looking up from her computer and toward the window. A flash of lightning soared through the darkening sky, poking around the draperies and searing Vicki's lids.

She struggled to remain in Washington even as her body lurched toward home. As she redoubled her concentration, she felt a beacon drawing her toward the Eisenhower Executive Office Building like a homing device, pulling her closer to her target.

The energy in the room shifted and she felt split once more. Something wasn't right. She hesitated outside the ceremonial office of the vice president but her thoughts felt hijacked by events in her home. As she stared at the closed door, she felt her body twisting around, almost against her will. And as she turned, she found herself staring at her own bedroom.

Brenda's face had lost all color. She sat motionless, her hands frozen in the air above her laptop's keyboard as she stared at the closed bedroom door. The door knob was still sitting on the floor where it had fallen the previous day and now Vicki felt as though that whole scene had been immature and unnecessary—and now it meant they could not lock the door.

The vice president's office was lost. Though the bedroom was dim, the light emanating from the laptop screen felt like daggers piercing her eyelids and she felt an eye migraine coming on. Rising unsteadily to her elbows on the bed, she stared at Brenda through narrowed eyes. "How long was I out?" she asked. Her voice sounded distant to her as though she was listening to herself through a long tunnel.

Brenda shook her head silently as she came to her feet. She approached the bed, her eyes still riveted on the door.

"How long was I out?" Vicki repeated.

"I don't know," Brenda mumbled. "Maybe an hour."

She fell back against the pillow. No wonder she was exhausted. Sam had always been careful to bring her back within twenty minutes. Why did he keep her out there so much longer? She answered herself as quickly as she asked the question: because he needed her. She was their eyes and ears. She held the key. She always held the key.

She felt Brenda's apprehension as she made her way along the side of the bed. As Vicki peered at her, her expression caused something deep within her to awaken. She labored to rise but Brenda waved her back down.

"What is it?" Vicki asked.

"I thought I heard something." Brenda said.

"Like what?"

"Probably the guy downstairs, the agent they left here." Brenda approached the door. She stopped when her fingers wrapped through the hole where the door knob once was.

"Sam," Vicki said into her cell phone.

She was met with silence.

"Sam," she repeated. Turning onto her side, she pulled the phone away from her ear and stared at the screen. It was on; they should have been connected. Why wasn't he answering?

"Garrett," Brenda said, using the agent's name stationed downstairs. She shook her head at Vicki. He was not responding to her through his earpiece. "Garrett," she said more forcefully. "Status." She shook her head once more.

Vicki wobbled as she sat on the edge of the bed. The room spun and she held her head in her hands, trying to stabilize herself. She felt as though she'd been hurling through the air at a hundred miles an hour, and now that her skin had stopped, her insides continued to zoom. It was a crazy feeling akin to a wicked hangover.

As she struggled to focus on Brenda, she spotted a pistol in her hand. With her free hand, she slowly cracked the door open. Then she cocked her head, listening.

Vicki struggled to rise but though her feet were touching the floor, she couldn't feel the rug beneath her. Her legs felt like liquid and unable to support her. Helpless, she watched Brenda slide the door open until it could go no further. She stood in the doorway, staring into the hall, searching for any sign of movement.

Then she stepped into the hall.

"No," Vicki said. She tried to jut out her arm to stop her but she felt like it was moving through a heavy current. Though her efforts should have propelled her off the bed and to the door, her arm barely moved. This was what she had feared, what she had always feared: complete helplessness.

"Stay there," Brenda said. She squared her jaw. "I'm sure it's nothing." A gust of wind rattled the shutters outside the bedroom window and they both looked in that direction. "It's probably the wind I heard," she said, stating the obvious. The lights flickered, casting them into blackness before a stubborn hum kicked back on.

"I'm just going to check it out. Keep trying to raise Sam, will you?"

"Don't go," Vicki managed to say. As Brenda turned once more to face her, she said, "We have to stay together."

Her sister hesitated. Then, "I won't let anything happen to you. I promise."

Vicki wanted to ask her how she could promise such a thing when she was leaving her alone but Brenda was through the door before she could utter a word. A wicked clap of thunder sounded as a flash of lightning lit up the room. Then the power snapped off. She peered into the hallway, trying to find her sister through the darkness, but she couldn't.

She closed her eyes and tried to gather her wits. She had to stand up. She had to move to the hallway, to watch her sister, to have her back. She opened her eyes once more. Somewhere in the recesses of her mind, she remembered her pistol. She turned toward the nightstand but the movement seared into her eyes and she closed them as nausea threatened to overcome her.

The seconds ticked by and a wave of rain pelted against the windows, drowning out any other sounds that might have struggled to reach her. She opened her eyes, forcing herself to look at the clock and note the time but the effort caused her to fall backward on the bed, the pistol just outside her grasp.

She felt as if her eyes had been closed for only seconds before she steadied her roiling stomach and forced herself to sit up again. Clutching the bed just behind her back to keep herself from falling once more, she looked again at the clock. Fifteen minutes had passed. That couldn't be right, she thought.

There was no sign of Brenda. She tried to focus on the hallway, to see through the blackness, to force the electricity back on through sheer willpower. But she was met only with the rising sound of the storm outside her windows, whipping against the house in a growing fury.

Painfully, she dropped her legs over the side of the bed, trying to feel the floor beneath her feet. She managed to reach to the nightstand and grip the pistol. Taking a deep breath, she placed one foot firmly on the rug, followed by the other one. Then she took a deep breath and stood.

Her ankles buckled beneath her. As she fell to the floor, the pistol flew from her hands. She heard it clatter on the hardwood but in the murky darkness, she couldn't see where it had gone. She couldn't see anything, she realized with a sick feeling. She was falling, her knees crumpling, her back hitting the wood rail along the side of the bed, causing her to lurch forward until her head bounced off the hardwood at the edge of the rug.

She thought she heard something; footsteps perhaps. She lay on the floor with one ear pressed against the hardwood, staring into the hallway as the darkness surrounded her.

50

The rain arrived in a vicious torrent as the man took the first swing, striking out with a vengeance with a direct aim at Dylan's face. Dylan instinctively threw up his forearm, blocking the blow from reaching his nose but absorbing the full brunt of the smaller man's force against his arm. They remained locked for a brief moment as Dylan stared into the man's night vision lenses.

With the storm came darkness, sudden and total, leaving Dylan squinting in a futile effort to see more clearly.

When they separated, he threw the next punch, hitting the apparatus with an uppercut that knocked the lenses onto his opponent's forehead, where they dangled precariously. The violent impact with the equipment cut into his knuckle and into the man's face, spraying them both with blood. But the searing pain Dylan felt was secondary to meeting his goal. Now he could look into his opponent's eyes as he fought him: they were gray-green, wide and surprised for a fleeting moment before a well-rehearsed veil enveloped them, leaving behind a hardened stare that left Dylan with no doubt as to his intentions.

The man's left fist jutted out with a direct shot to his chin but again Dylan deflected it, only to find his opponent's right fist in a well-coordinated hook that met his torso with punishing accuracy. He felt the air whoosh out of him as he doubled over from the blow to his liver and he stumbled backward before catching himself. As he struggled to regain his breath, the agonizing pain shouted that the blow had also reinjured his cracked ribs.

Pain had often been both his enemy and his friend. In Ireland, he'd funneled his anger, his frustration and all of his emotional suffering into fighting. When the physical pain settled in, he forgot everything else—the torture of losing the only family he'd ever known, of burying his future along with those he loved the most, of all the cruel twists that fate had screwed into him. All that was left was an unbridled fury, a mounting rage that coursed through his veins instinctively like a rabid animal.

Now he could feel the blood rushing to his head along with the familiar feeling that he might explode if he didn't strike out again and again.

His leg shot out, smacking the man directly in the chest with his steel-toed cowboy boot. An unearthly sound escaped his opponent's mouth as he struggled to stay on his feet; a strange mixture of air rushing out of his body along with a guttural pain-filled cry.

But as Dylan attempted to kick him again in the same region, the man grabbed his ankle with both his hands, rotating it with such power that in another second, he knew the bone would snap. He let out a roar as he came off his other foot, knocking the man backward as they both staggered, locked together in a vicious embrace.

The man had no choice but to let go of Dylan or risk falling. The second both feet hit the ground, Dylan pulled back his arm and swung with an uppercut meant to connect with his chin, but he was blocked by the man's powerful forearm. They were locked once more, their faces inches apart, both sets of eyes unblinking and murderous. Dylan was by far the larger of the two; his head towered above the other man, his shoulders were broader, his arms stretched further. But he knew it wasn't size that would determine the winner; it was tactics.

The man stepped backward and to the side, releasing the locked embrace. Now they circled one another, gauging their opponent's body language, trying to determine what the other might try next, and calculating their next moves as the storm soaked them both to the skin.

Dylan used his height and long legs to his advantage as he kicked the man in his kneecap with a speed and brutality that stunned the smaller man. A loud crack resounded through the air as he started to buckle. Dylan quickly followed up with a kick to the man's jaw. A tooth flew from his mouth as blood spurted forth and he collapsed on the muddy ground.

Dylan stared at him as he writhed and groaned. How many would be sent? How many would he be required to fight? He quickly pushed those thoughts from his mind as he bent over him, jerking the zip-tie cuffs from where they dangled on the man's belt. Obviously, he would need to requisition similar items from Sam, he thought as he tried to brush a combination of sweat and water from his brow. His hair was sopping now and hanging in folds as it fell across his forehead.

His opponent was lying on his right side now with one arm twisted under him and his legs rotated like pretzels. Dylan grabbed the wrist closest to him and hurriedly secured it with the zip-tie cuff. Then he straddled the man as he bent to turn him onto his stomach so he could secure his other wrist.

He saw the pistol as soon as he flipped him. The black metal was unmistakable; the barrel staring at him with obvious intent. In a fraction of a second, it registered that it was planned: the twisted body, the right hand underneath where the man could easily grab his weapon and use it to eliminate him.

Like a slow-motion movie, he heard the click of the safety at the same time as he watched the finger pulling the trigger, releasing the bullet with an ear-shattering boom.

51

Vicki's psyche felt suspended; in her mind's eye, she pictured her body in a vast ocean, her arms out to the side, her hair spread out around her head like a halo as she sank slowly toward the ocean floor. From somewhere outside her, she heard her name over and over again. Someone was calling to her, someone whose voice she didn't recognize, someone urging her to open her eyes, to swim to the surface.

Like a drowning woman suddenly regaining consciousness, she gasped, the sound of her own struggle awakening her further.

She was lying on the bedroom floor. The house was deathly quiet, filled with the stillness that envelops a home when all the normal humming from appliances suddenly cease. She raised her head and tried to peer through the darkness as she attempted to pull herself out of her stupor.

Brenda.

She hadn't returned; of that she was certain. Her sister would never have left her on the floor, disheveled and unconscious.

The thought awakened something deep inside her and she pulled herself to her knees. She was no longer shaking. She looked at the clock but couldn't remember when she'd first tried to memorize the time, and then couldn't decide how many minutes she'd been knocked out.

She stood, extending her hands out beside her to catch herself if she teetered but she was steady. She stepped to the doorway, intent on calling to Brenda, when something inside her warned her to remain silent.

Vicki took a half-step into the hallway and peered below. The stairs led to the second floor and continued on to the front foyer. A break in the black clouds allowed a full moon to peer through the stained glass sidelites on either side of the front door, and now a muted rainbow of light struggled across the hardwood floor.

A shadow emerged at the entrance to the living room and her breath caught in her throat. It moved methodically as if the person was moving steadily toward the doorway. It was too large and too hulking to be either Brenda or Garrett.

She retreated to the bedroom doorway and continued to stare below her, her eyes fixed on the shadow as it continued to grow.

Then a man emerged.

He was tall with broad shoulders and an expansive chest. Though he was dressed in black from neck to toe, she could gauge his size by the way he filled the doorway. A glint of metal shone at his side. As his head turned slowly, taking in his surroundings, she realized he was wearing night vision goggles.

She backed into the bedroom and closed the door. Though she'd tried to remain quiet, she knew immediately that he'd heard her; she could feel his head turning upward, staring at the steps.

She held her breath and listened through the wood door, a door too heavy and solid for her to hear much at all. But then they started: the unmistakable sound of boots on the stairs. They came steadily, neither dragging nor in a hurry but precisely, one boot after the other as the sound carried up the stairs and grew ever closer.

Panicked, she hurled around. She was on the third floor, she thought in a whirlwind of realizations. The third floor, with aged windows that might very well be painted shut and if they weren't, her only salvation might be to jump to the ground looming below—and perhaps right into the hands of an accomplice.

The boots grew louder in the still air, and she rushed to the bathroom only to hurry right back out. He could come through the bedroom door and he could also walk right into the bathroom.

There was nothing to hold off the man, even for mere seconds. And she knew he would not give up until he had her.

In a split second, her mind raced through the possibilities—under the bed, beneath hanging clothes, in the bathtub, under the bathroom sink—all seemed completely ludicrous. She was stuck like a cornered mouse.

Her eyes fell on the dumbwaiter.

Without a moment's hesitation, she was there, sliding the door open and climbing inside. She pulled the door closed behind her, plunging her into pitch blackness. She felt for the ropes that suspended it and began lowering herself just as she heard the door open above her.

She found herself seated on a stainless steel tray, her knees drawn up beneath her chin, the shaft so narrow that she realized she could easily get stuck if a wayward knee or elbow were to jut out at just the wrong moment. Had she been a larger person, she would have found herself hopelessly wedged in. As it was, her shoulders brushed against either side as she continued lowering herself. It felt painstakingly slow as she heard the man's heavy footsteps wandering the room, throwing open the closet and bathroom doors with unbridled force.

She only knew when she passed the second floor bedroom by the way one shoulder caught against a piece of metal, tearing her clothing and ripping into her flesh. She bit her lip until she tasted blood, terrified of crying out and giving away her position. Her hands were raw from handling the rope and her breath was labored. At any moment, she expected the man to open the dumbwaiter door and peer down at her, catching her inside walls from which she could not escape.

She should have reached the kitchen by now but the dumbwaiter continued into what felt like a bottomless pit. Then if it was possible, the air around her became even blacker and she realized she had reached an open area. Gingerly, she held out one hand while she grasped the rope with the other; there was no wall around her now.

She tried to adjust to the darkness but the room did not appear to have any windows. She cautiously allowed one leg to dangle over the side and was surprised when it touched something. It wasn't solid like the floor but something piled up—something as black as the darkness itself.

With a start, she realized she was in a coal cellar.

But where was the door? She raced through the ground floor in her mind, but couldn't remember ever seeing a door leading to a cellar. Then was there a door outside?

Brenda.

She looked up but saw only blackness above her. The house was silent again, which was more frightening than the man's movements through the bedroom. Now she had no clue where he was.

As her eyes adjusted, she realized she was in a small room about twenty feet square. Just a few feet above her was the dumbwaiter door leading into the kitchen. She had to find Brenda.

She stood on the stainless shelf created by the dumbwaiter and tried to balance her feet so she didn't topple into the coal. Carefully, silently, she pushed the door leading into the kitchen aside. It was the same size opening as the one in the bedroom; so small that as she placed her hands on the lip and hauled herself upward and through it, both shoulders at once halted her progress. She had to angle her body so her shoulders crept through at the upper left and bottom right corners.

She spotted Brenda as soon as her feet were on the kitchen floor.

She was face-down, blood flowing from her head and pooling beside her. Vicki rushed to her side, calling her name in a hoarse whisper but she did not respond. Panicked, she realized her wrists were bound behind her back.

Vicki rolled her onto her back, eliciting a semi-conscious moan from her. She was alive, she thought, both relieved and alarmed. How serious was her injury? She shifted her mass of red hair to the side and tried to find the wound, hoping it had not been inflicted by a gunshot. She took in her full figure—her clothes disheveled, her skin pale, her ankles bound together with a heavy plastic wire. She appeared to have just the one wound, she realized as she refocused on her head. But how serious was it?

A gust of damp air hit her full in the face and she realized with a start that the kitchen door leading into the back yard was wide open. She scrambled to her feet. The chain across the door had been unlatched from the inside, the deadbolt disengaged and with no sign of forced entry.

Lying just outside the door was Garrett's lifeless body.

She had barely turned back toward Brenda when a fist seemed to fly out of nowhere, catching her at her temple and knocking her off her feet. As she fell across her sister's body, her vision was filled with the blurry image of a man stepping toward her with plastic zip-tie cuffs.

52

Dylan crept along the tree line on the west side of the Waterworks, peering around a cluster of pine branches heavy with rainwater that seemed intent on impeding his progress. His right ear was ringing incessantly and he wondered if the eardrum had burst. He still didn't know how he'd managed to move so quickly, but judging from the rip in his shirt and the blood on his arm, he'd only managed to shift perhaps a few inches at best before the bullet had grazed his skin. Even worse than that searing pain was the sharp agony that seemed to rip his ear apart.

He'd reacted like a madman, breaking the man's wrist as he wrenched the gun free from him and pummeling his face until he lay unconscious. Only after he had secured him with the zip-tie cuffs, binding his wrists together behind his back and then joining them with his trussed ankles, had he taken the time to touch his ear.

The sharp pain had dissipated, leaving behind a throbbing ache. But when he touched his ear and felt the liquid oozing over his hand, he fully expected to find himself covered in blood. He even wondered if the bullet had found his ear and clipped it off. But when he looked at his hand, he found it covered in clear liquid.

He felt his heart racing and forced himself to get a steel grip on his emotions. There was no time to ponder whether his eardrum had burst. As he moved stealthily along the back side of the building, he noted two men creeping toward the back door from the opposite direction. His eyes panned the area between them and the Lumber River, searching for others. When he detected no additional movement, he began his progress toward the men.

It was no longer necessary to remain in the shadows; as the storm had rolled in, everything had been cast in shades of black and gray. He was within fifty feet of them as they broke open the back door and entered like a swat team ready to engage or apprehend.

He climbed onto the concrete patio that jutted toward the Lumber River, slipping between the metal rails and drawing his pistol as he approached the back door. His eyes constantly panned the windows, where the interior of the Waterworks now lay dark and still.

Then he was slipping past the door as it dangled from its hinges, his movement so silent that he could hear the beat of his own heart. He stood for a moment while his eyes adjusted, taking in the renovation equipment sprawled throughout the main floor. Ladders with painter's sheets stored atop them, the material spilling over the sides, now seemed good hiding places for a gunman, as did drywall and plywood stacked against the wall or leaning against beams.

He heard Sam's voice echoing through the empty chamber. "Unit Alfa," he was saying, "status." When there was no response, he repeated it a second time and then a third before switching to Unit Bravo.

Dylan crept along the outer wall, the giant, dormant water pipes becoming his shield.

No one had responded to Sam's calls to Unit Bravo and he switched to Unit Charlie and then to Unit Delta.

Dylan's chest grew tight as he realized none of the units were responding. His imagination threatened to overcome him as his mind raced through the myriad of possibilities: that all their units had been taken out, the members killed or apprehended, leaving only three men—Chris, Sam and himself. Then just as quickly, he considered the likelihood that the units had been working against them all along. For all he knew, as he continued his slow movement through the plant, the two men he was trying to find now were the very units that Sam was frantically calling.

He reached the far end of the plant and glanced upward to the second floor. The center was completely open, leaving only the sides in a type of catwalk with railing that provided no chance at concealment. He strained his eyes as he tried to view the staircase at the opposite end; it appeared to be empty.

Outside, the street lamps flickered and then went out, leaving the exterior in total darkness. He hadn't realized until then just how much light they had allowed inside; now, without it, the blue light emanating from Sam's makeshift office was like a beacon. He'd had the forethought to supply the equipment with a generator, assuming the power had been cut during the restoration of the building, and now the sound of it hummed and echoed in the cavernous chamber.

He took a half-step forward when a bolt of lightning raced through the night sky, lighting up the interior like a row of floodlights at a football stadium. In those crucial seconds, he clearly spotted a shadow reaching out from the second floor wall and melting over the banister just outside Sam's office and another shadow on the ground floor not twenty feet from him.

Then in the next instant, the light was replaced with a growl of thunder and total darkness.

His eyes remained riveted on the location where he'd seen the closest shadow. His body seemed suspended in time. He continued to hear Sam calling out to each of the units as well as Dylan, and receiving no response from anyone. Then he realized in the blackness that had them all enveloped, the blue light from Sam's office had ceased as well. The generator had stopped its incessant humming and the screens had gone black.

In its place was the realization that Sam was in his corner office upstairs, Chris was nowhere to be seen, and two men—one of whom was only steps away from him—were there to kill them.

53

She was pinned against the refrigerator door, her breath coming fast and shallow, as the man grabbed both her wrists in his. She felt like she was being attacked by an alien as she stared dumbfounded at him. A pair of night vision goggles dominated his face, the green lenses appearing like twin neon lights at the end of long black tubes, the straps holding it in place clutching both his chin and the top of his head.

He easily slipped one end of the plastic zip-tie cuffs over one wrist and pulled it taut. He was large and muscular, easily outsizing her, and she realized with a sinking heart that she was no match for him. She tried vainly to struggle free but he only chuckled at her efforts, his amused laughter conveying just how futile her exertions were.

He made a move as if to turn her around. In seconds, he would have her second wrist bound to the first one, both securely joined behind her back. Then no doubt her ankles would be similarly trussed and she would be at his mercy.

Out of the corner of her eye, she caught Brenda's eyes open and staring at her, wide-eyed and stunned. She was unable to help her, unable to do more than move with painstaking sluggishness.

Vicki felt terror welling up inside her, panic that she was so helpless, that she had no choice but to be tied up like a pig going to slaughter.

All your feet are doin' is keepin' you vertical.

The sound of Dylan's voice was so strong she almost expected to see him standing before her.

She stared into the surreal green lenses. Then with all the strength she could muster, she brought her heel down hard. His boots were steel-toed and her heel landed with the crack of bone so loud that the man stopped turning her. She cried out with the pain, screamed with the frustration that she hadn't even fazed him while she probably had broken her own bone.

Gritting her teeth against the agony, she forced herself to use the same foot to kick him in his shin. As her bare toe connected through his pants to his leg, he stumbled back half a step but regained his traction and grasped her wrists with more intensity.

It felt as if her life was playing out before her in slow motion: Brenda staring at her through dazed eyes, the man starting to twirl her around to grasp her free wrist, and her knee jerking upwards, slamming into his groin with all the viciousness she could muster.

He let out a primal shriek that didn't sound remotely human. As he doubled over in pain, he lost his grip on her. She brought her knee up once more, smashing into the bridge of his nose with a savagery she never knew she had.

He fell backward, his knees buckling under him.

She was on him like a madwoman, tearing his pistol out of the holster at his side, fearing that at any second he would grab her again and wreak vengeance upon her. Then she was rolling away from him, across the floor until Brenda's still body stopped her movement.

He was coming to his feet, his night vision goggles out of kilter, groaning in a tone that had changed from pain to rage. As he threw himself toward her, his lips curled cruelly and his groan became a roar.

She fired the pistol, hitting him in the chest. She screamed as he toppled with a ferocity that caused the floor to shake beneath her.

Quickly, she moved to untie Brenda but the zip-tie cuffs couldn't be budged.

Then she heard a voice. She stopped to listen, her own breath coming so fast and hard that it almost obscured it. Then the blood drained from her face as she realized the sound was coming from an earpiece the man was wearing. She shoved his body onto its side so she could tear the piece away from him. As she inserted it into her own ear, she heard another man asking where he was and telling him he was coming to help him.

He wasn't alone.

She stared at Brenda, who was moving her lips as if trying to speak but no sound was coming out. She was bleeding out across the kitchen floor, unable to run, unable to move, unable to speak.

Of course he's not alone, Vicki thought, her breath catching in her throat. And his partner was coming for them.

54

Chris emerged from a downstairs office, seemingly unaware that anyone else was on the ground floor. Dylan watched him as he wandered through the center of the room. His eyes were fixated on the windows at the front of the building, and Dylan tore his own eyes away from Chris in an attempt to discover what he was looking at. But the only thing he could see was the rain, now driving nearly sideways across the road a short distance from the building.

Dylan was painfully aware that a third man hovered somewhere between Chris and himself and another was upstairs, perhaps watching Chris down below or preparing to enter Sam's office. Three against two wasn't normally bad odds. But something told him Chris hadn't been in too many scraps and Sam was aging.

He remained perfectly still as his eyes roamed the area where he'd seen the shadow. There was no sound of movement and no visual evidence of the intruder. He longed for the lightning to return as a vital aid to discovering where his enemy lay.

Chris leaned his forearm on a window frame and peered outside. From his forward stance, he appeared to be straining to see. Apparently not finding what he was looking for, he continued moving slowly from one window to the next, stopping in turn to scrutinize the area just outside.

Dylan turned his head toward Sam's office. He could barely see the banister in the darkness and nothing beyond it. The blue light that had illuminated Sam's door was still gone, leaving behind nothing but a cavernous blackness. With the screens off, Sam had also fallen silent. He longed to tell him that he had returned but he dared not speak.

Chris continued moving toward Dylan, oblivious that he was pressed against the far wall, his entire body in the deepest shadows.

He inched closer to the location where the shadow had emerged. Keeping his back pressed against the wall, he continued his slow progress until he was against a short partition. Judging from Chris' location, the proximity of the front windows, and his own hiding spot, the intruder had to be hiding just on the other side. They were inches away from each other, but only Dylan knew he was there.

He fingered the pistol he still held in his hand. His fingers were wet with rain and sweat. He had to assume the intruder was not only armed but ready to fire and any sudden movement might bring a volley of shots. But as he watched Chris grow ever closer, he knew in another moment fate would step in. And his job was to mold it to his advantage.

Then Chris glanced in his direction. His eyes grew wide and his mouth opened as if to speak. But before he could talk, the man between them sprang forward, tackling Chris and sending them both reeling across the floor. Instinctively, Dylan lunged forward, racing to Chris' aid as shouts rained down on them from above. Somewhere in the back of his mind, he registered Sam's voice, something crashing and breaking on the floor above, and another man bellowing. Then a shot rang out and Sam's voice was immediately stilled.

Dylan grabbed Chris' assailant from behind, his strong hands hauling him off his feet and slinging him away from the leaner man.

"Get your hands in the air!" Dylan shouted, training his pistol on him.

The man began to comply, raising both hands on either side of his head.

But before Dylan could step toward him, disarm him and cuff him, he was thrust to the floor with the seeming force of a locomotive. He knew even before he was able to roll over that the second man had jumped from the catwalk, landing on his back. More than two hundred pounds had overtaken him, a mixture of beefy brawn and electronic equipment and now he was struggling to throw the man off him so he could rise once more.

His pistol had flown out of his hand and now he punched with both hands at whatever part of his assailant's body he could reach. Then the man had both of his hands on Dylan's throat. Instinctively, he reached his hands atop his, trying to pry them loose before he lost consciousness. In the dark recesses of his mind, he could hear Chris fighting the other man.

Then he forced himself to loosen his own grip on the man's hands, which caused him to tighten his hold around Dylan's throat. With an attempted roar that erupted as a choked gurgle, Dylan plunged two thick fingers up the man's nostrils as if he was trying to reach the depths of his sinuses. With his other hand, he ripped off the night vision goggles and thrust his middle finger into the man's soft eyeball, twisting it as he did so.

The effect was immediate: the hands flew off Dylan's throat as the man staggered backward, trying to escape the pain. As they disengaged and Dylan's fingers were pulled away, he found both hands dripping in blood. He spotted his pistol a few feet away and managed to half-roll and half-propel himself to the weapon. When he'd grabbed it and reeled around, he expected to see his assailant ready to go at it again. But the man was lying on the floor, his hands covering his face and moaning.

Dylan came to his feet and took two swift steps toward the man. Standing over him, he raised the pistol. With an exploding rage, he struck him on the side of the temple with the butt of the gun. His head lolled to the side, one eye closing while the other remained half open but unseeing and oozing.

Then he turned his attention to Chris, who was being relentlessly pummeled. Though he was stumbling backward as he was hit repeatedly in the head, he was managing to stay on his feet. His fists were raised and in between his head lolling to the right and then to the left, he was swinging at the air between them.

Dylan took a deep breath. He was dead tired and not in the mood for another scuffle. Raising his pistol, he fired it once, hitting the man in the shoulder blade, the sound causing excruciating pain in his injured ear. The assailant crumpled like an inflatable doll, falling at Chris' feet as he stared at him in stunned silence.

"You're damn lucky Sam wanted you all alive," he muttered as he cuffed him.

Then both men faced Sam's office, now deadly silent.

55

Vicki knelt at Brenda's head as she yanked her blouse off. "Brenda, can you hear me?"

Her sister tried to nod but then closed her eyes tightly. A single tear escaped and ran down her cheek.

"Listen to me, Brenda," she whispered as she wrapped her blouse around her head, "we've got to get out of here."

Her eyes opened once more and she croaked out a single word: "Go."

"Not without you." Vicki rose and grasped her sister under both arms. She dragged her across the floor, hoping the material around Brenda's head would help to stop the bleeding and also prevent a wide swath of blood from leading the others straight to them.

The man on the communication device had fallen silent, which worried her. She couldn't hear him in the house and had no way of knowing if he was on the third floor, making his way down the stairs—or if he was standing just a few feet from her. She had to hurry and pulling Brenda's almost lifeless body was sapping her strength more than she could have imagined.

Finally they reached the dumbwaiter. She angled her around so her feet could go through first and caught a glimpse of the terror in Brenda's face. "Don't worry," she said. "I'll be right behind you."

She shoved her legs through like she was a weighted rag doll, and then pushed the rest of her body into the small opening.

"Jay?" the man's voice was in stereo and Vicki realized with a start that she'd heard him on her earpiece and in the hallway outside the kitchen.

She scrambled into the dumbwaiter, her feet finding Brenda's body below her as she heard him moving toward them, his boots heavy on the hardwood floor. "Forgive me," she mouthed as she landed on her sister's body. Then she struggled to her feet and grabbed the door with shaking hands, sliding it shut just as he entered the kitchen.

Vicki peered through a tiny slit at the edge of the door. She watched him race to the other man's side, rolling him over and checking for a pulse. Like his partner, he wore night vision goggles that obscured his facial features but she had no doubt that it was the man she'd seen at the living room doorway.

She slowly slid the door all the way closed and sank to the floor beside Brenda, pulling her head into her lap. She had no way of knowing whether Brenda's body was twisted like a pretzel under her and even if it was, she couldn't move her. She felt her lap growing wet and as she ran her hand over Brenda's face, she felt the tears racing down her cheek.

She still didn't know if she'd been shot or if she'd suffered a severe blow. But she'd never seen Brenda cry before, even during times that would have had a grown man bawling and her heart broke as she held her. She could be dying right there in her arms and there was nothing she could do about it.

She listened as the man moved around the kitchen. She pictured the blood on the floor, the open doorway, the dead man. *Please,* she prayed, *please believe we escaped through the back door. Please leave.*

As her eyes adjusted to the darkness, she realized it was her own body that was distorted, her legs sprawled out in opposite directions, both bent at the knee, her feet twisted. Brenda lay on her side, curled nearly into a fetal position, her ankles still securely bound, her hands tied behind her back, her face turned upward.

Vicki stared into her eyes. She wanted to tell her it would be okay; she wanted to assure her she would get help for them. But the man was painfully close and she dared not utter a sound. Her heart was beating so strongly that her chest hurt and she was certain he would hear it. He could be moving toward the dumbwaiter at that moment, and all she could do was sit there like a trapped animal.

Because she *was* trapped.

She squeezed her eyes shut in a fruitless attempt to blot out the image of the man in the kitchen. Where was Dylan? Worry was beginning to overtake her—worry that she no longer heard Sam, Chris or Dylan in her earpiece; worry that Dylan had been captured and could not come to her aid; worry that they could remain in the cellar for hours or days before they could safely escape. She looked down at Brenda, whose eyes were open and watching her silently. Worry that her sister would die there in her arms.

"Put your hands in the air!"

The sound of the man's voice startled them both, causing Vicki to jump and jolt Brenda's head. As they both stared upward, expecting the man to be hovering above them, Vicki realized the dumbwaiter door was still closed.

Then who was talking?

"I said put your hands in the air! *Now!*"

The voice was just feet from them.

Then shots rang out and Vicki plunged her head downward over her sister, covering her with her own body, each one reverberating so close to them that she was certain she'd been hit.

And then seconds later there was nothing but silence.

56

Four men lay bound and gagged, their bodies strewn from the abandoned house next door to the water tower to the first floor of the building. But now as Chris and Dylan rushed up the stairs toward Sam's office, they were interested in only one man. The storm was ending, leaving the cavernous structure as quiet as a tomb and as black as pitch. They felt their way up the stairs and to the end of the corridor just as the street lamps flickered and came on.

"Can you see anything?" Chris asked, his voice revealing the panic they both shared.

Dylan felt stunned by the night's events and wondered what course of action he would take if they found Sam dead in his office. Everything had gone horribly awry and though he wouldn't admit it aloud, it was time to consider the unthinkable.

They stopped at the door as they both peered inside, narrowing their eyes in an attempt to see. As Dylan's adjusted, he found the computer screens strewn throughout the office and the wires stretched taut across the floor. Sam's chair was turned upside down in a corner of the room.

As Dylan stepped inside, something cracked beneath his foot and he stopped to stare at the floor. It was covered in blood and water and broken glass shards. The dampness in the air soaked into his skin and he instinctively looked for the source. It didn't take more than a few seconds to realize the window had been busted out. He quickly crossed the room and looked outside expecting to find Sam's body on the concrete patio below, but it was empty except for fallen glass.

Turning back to the office, his eyes met Chris'. Their thoughts were mirrored in their faces—where was Sam?

He was halfway across the room when he heard a low moaning. He stopped and held up his hand, cautioning Chris to remain silent.

Hurriedly, he dropped to his knees and looked under the desk. The knee hole was darker than pitch and as he strained to see he found Sam's body crumpled into a fetal position. He was tucked in the very back of the desk, his dark clothes blending into the deep shadows. He made no attempt to reach for Dylan or speak, as if he didn't know he was there. But as his intermittent moaning continued, Dylan sprang into action.

He swept the remaining equipment off the desk with two wide strokes and then turned the desk on its end. As the furniture fell away, so did Sam. With an agonized groan, he sprawled across the floor, leaving a pool of blood that continued to grow.

"Sam!" Dylan said, dropping to his knees and slapping his cheeks in an attempt to rouse him.

He was met with a low moan.

"Sam, it's Dylan and Chris. We'll get you out o' here. Are you shot?"

Sam's eyes opened wide enough to display a spark of recognition before they closed again.

"Stay with me, Sam," Dylan urged. "Don't go to sleep. You're not done yet. We've work to do." He thought the mention of work to the workaholic would be a tonic that would further rouse him but Sam lay still as the blood continued to pool.

Dylan stood and almost ripped off his own shirt before kneeling again and wrapping it securely around Sam's head, tying it tight. The blood seeped through the thin material. He turned to Chris. "We've got to get him out o' here. He needs a doctor. Fast."

Chris opened his mouth to respond and then closed it. His eyes had caught something beyond Dylan and now they both turned to stare out the open window. Dylan rose to his feet.

"We've got company," Chris said.

"How many do you count?"

"Three—no, four."

"Same as me." He watched the men in dark clothing as they scurried across the bridge toward the building. "You're sure there's not more?"

Chris hesitated. "I don't think so."

Something grasped Dylan's ankle and he recoiled as he stared downward. Sam had rolled toward him, grabbing his ankle with desperate strength. His bloodshot eyes were open, revealing his misery.

"We're gettin' you out o' here," Dylan said.

Chris raced through the doorway to peer over the banister at the floor below.

"No," Sam croaked. His voice was dry and his fingers tightened around Dylan's ankle, tugging him into coming closer.

Dylan knelt.

"I'm not going to make it," Sam said laboriously.

"You won't be the judge o' that."

"Leave me here."

"I'll not be leavin' you."

Sam's fingers tightened around his pants leg. "Go to Vicki. Save her, Dylan."

Dylan stared into Sam's eyes at the mention of her.

"She needs you," Sam said, his fingers loosening as if the mere effort of holding on was too difficult. "Tell her—tell her I love her. I always have."

Dylan's jaw dropped. "I refuse to tell 'er," he heard himself saying. "You'll be tellin' her y'self."

"I'm a dead man," Sam said, his hand dropping back to the floor. "Leave me. Save yourself. And save Vicki."

"They're coming in," Chris said in a stage whisper.

Dylan rose, glancing at Sam as his eyes closed once more before rushing into the open hallway. "Which door?"

Chris pointed.

"Then take these stairs. We'll go out the door on the side. We've got to get to the girls."

Chris glimpsed into Sam's office, where his body lay still, before giving Dylan a fleeting look. Nodding, he rushed to the top of the stairs, Dylan on his heels.

Dylan had taken one step downward before he froze. In a fraction of a second, he hurled around and dashed back to Sam's office. Sliding one arm under his knees and the other under his torso, he lifted the man in his arms and carried him to the stairs. Glancing down as he descended, he was met with Sam's open eyes, questioning and baffled. "I'll not be leavin' you," Dylan said simply.

57

Vicki pressed her ear close to the edge of the dumbwaiter door, listening to the men as they talked. She would have been through that door in a heartbeat had she heard Dylan's lilting Irish brogue, but as she listened to the flurry of southern accents she realized with a sinking heart that he wasn't there. He hadn't come to her rescue and coming close on the heels of that realization was a growing fearfulness that he might at that very moment be fighting for his own life.

The men spoke without the emotion one might expect of human beings standing over two dead men. They reminded her of Sam as they carried on an analytical discussion involving the exact location of the crumpled bodies, their weapons, their black clothing and night vision goggles. One interrupted to mention he was late for dinner and needed to call his wife.

It felt bizarre to listen to the men talk so casually while her sister lay in a heap at her feet, her once gorgeous hair now matted in dried blood.

As the electricity kicked back on, bringing with it the sounds of appliances humming, she picked out one voice as it rose above the others. She cocked her head as if the gesture could allow her to hear him more clearly. He recounted his movements as he'd stepped onto his front porch to smoke, only to find a shadowy figure moving around his neighbor's house. Alec, Vicki thought as her heart began to race. She pressed her ear against the slim opening between the wall and the door as he told of calling the Lumberton police department while he went back inside his house and grabbed his service weapon. The man was gone when he came back outside; but he walked around the perimeter until he reached the back door. He found it gaping open, one man dead on the steps and another man staring out the back door with his weapon pointed directly at Alec's chest.

Vicki knelt beside Brenda. She was covered in a fine layer of coal dust that settled in the fine lines around her eyes, nose and mouth.

"Annie," Vicki whispered, her mouth close to her sister's ear. When she didn't respond, she tried again, "Brenda. It's me, Vicki."

But she remained motionless, her eyes closed.

Vicki felt for her pulse as she tried to quiet her own racing heartbeat. Brenda's was faint; so sluggish it reminded her of a battery losing its charge. The blood was almost dry now, but she didn't know if that was good news or bad: it meant the bleeding had stopped but having never encountered a situation like this, she didn't know if it meant something even more ominous—something she dared not think about.

But even as she resisted the thought, she knew she had to face their options and no matter what her course of action would be, the result could be a life-altering decision. She could remain silent and save Brenda from being arrested only to run the very real risk of having her die in the cellar. Or she could attempt to save her life even if it meant Brenda would go to prison.

Her sister might hate her for the choice she was bound to make.

Vicki rose slowly, gently placing Brenda's head against the cold floor. She took a deep breath and slowly slid the dumbwaiter door just enough to peek through the hairline opening.

Alec stood just a few feet from her. He was speaking to three men, easily identifiable by their uniforms as Lumberton police officers. Her heart sank and rose simultaneously; they would know precisely what to do, but they would also know—and Alec would know—that Brenda was a wanted woman.

She fought the panic growing within her as she began to slide the door open further. Alec turned and recoiled, his eyes widening. As she watched the others turn toward her with the same stunned expressions, she realized what a sight she made. With the harsh kitchen light pouring into the tiny opening, she caught a glimpse of her hand in front of her face, her fingers wrapped around the metal door as she inched it open, blackened with coal dust and coated in dried blood.

"Alec," she managed to croak.

"Vicki?" He stood perfectly still as he stared at her. Then his brain visibly kicked into gear and he shot toward her. "Vicki, are you alright?"

She nodded.

"What are you doing in there?" he asked as he grabbed her arm.

"Hiding," she said, "from *him*."

He placed a strong hand under each of her arms and hauled her up and out of the small opening. As she tumbled onto the floor, she tried to shield her eyes from the piercing light but found herself smearing the coal dust across her face.

They were all talking at once: one officer was calling for an ambulance, another was assisting Alec in carrying Vicki to a cleared spot and a third was communicating with the dispatcher. In spite of her vigorous protest, they seemed determined that they knew what was best for her—until she started to scream.

"What the—" Alec began.

"I'm not alone," Vicki said, coming off the floor.

"Dylan—?"

"No. My sister. She's been shot." She pointed toward the dumbwaiter. "I got her into the cellar." Despite her best efforts, her bottom lip began to tremble. "I'm afraid she's dying."

The last word had barely escaped her lips before all of the men were at the dumbwaiter door. One of the officers jumped into the cellar and shouted back to the others. "She's alive. Is the ambulance on the way?"

"The ambulance is here," one of the other officers said, relaying information from the dispatcher. "They're sending them to the back door."

“Alec,” Vicki said, tugging on her neighbor’s sleeve. With every touch of the fabric, she wiped coal dust onto him but she forced herself to look into his eyes.

“She’ll be okay,” he said, though she could clearly see the doubt in his eyes.

“Alec,” she repeated, forcing her voice to remain firm, “my sister—”

He stared back at her expectantly.

Somewhere in the back of her mind, it registered that paramedics were entering the kitchen with a stretcher and one was climbing into the cellar with a medical kit. They were here, she thought. Six of them—Alec, three police officers and two paramedics. The hospital was five minutes away. They would save her. They had to save her.

“Yes?” Alec said hesitantly.

“My sister—she’s Brenda Carnegie.”

58

Chris urgently waved for Dylan to hurry as he kept a wary eye on the opposite end of the building. Carrying a full-grown man down the open staircase felt like waving a flag announcing he was there. Once both feet were on the ground floor and they had made it into the shadows, he breathed a deep sigh of relief.

"We can't make it to the door," Chris whispered hoarsely.

Dylan glanced at the outer door before turning his attention to the four men entering the building at the opposite end. He slipped further into the shadows and placed Sam on the floor, his back propped up against the wall. Chris was right. As the men entered, one issued hand signals to the others. Even from this distance, the intent was clear: they were splitting up, each man taking a different route through the building.

He watched helplessly as one man took the staircase at the far end, moving up the steps in the darkness. Like the men Dylan had overtaken, they were dressed in black and wore night vision goggles, giving them the dual advantage of seeing clearly without being clearly visible themselves.

Another moved stealthily toward the front of the building, his pistol in his hand as he expertly checked around every fixture. A third made his way through the center of the building, using the old water filtration pipes as added protection as he made his way to the farthest corner. The fourth waited until all were well on their way before ascending the stairs and moving in the opposite direction from the first man as he reached the second floor.

Dylan and Chris waited silently, almost shoulder to shoulder as they nestled into a corner. The shadows were an illusion, Dylan thought. With the night vision goggles, they would see them plain as day; all one needed was to look in their direction.

At their feet, Sam remained where he was placed. Dylan glanced at him. His face was ashen and his eyes closed, and if it weren't for the corner wall catching him, he might have toppled to the side.

Dylan pulled out his pistol and watched as Chris did the same. He motioned for him to remain silent and then nodded in the direction of the closest man. Chris returned his nod.

They had no choice.

They would wait until the man was close enough to attack. Once a gun was fired, no doubt the others would rush to his aid. He could try to knock him out without the gun first, he reasoned, but he would have no way of knowing if that was possible until the last second. And then he'd have to hope that Chris didn't panic and shoot them both in the melee.

He narrowed his eyes and tried to gauge the location of each man. The two upstairs were opening office doors on either side of the building, searching in each room. One would soon be upon the corner office just above them. One man was methodically moving through the far end of the building on the ground floor but could reach them in seconds. They all could reach them in seconds, Dylan realized. And then what? They would fight wave after wave of men until they were too exhausted to continue or they were wounded or dead?

It was suicide. In setting the trap, they had trapped themselves.

He pressed himself flat against the wall, his face to the side, watching and waiting for the closest man to round the corner. He could hear him; though he moved stealthily, the huge building was largely silent. In another moment, he would be close enough to hear their breathing and then it would begin all over again.

There was no time to think about the soreness settling into his muscles, the tenderness where he'd been pummeled in the previous fights, the pain in his ribs or his ear, or the exhaustion that waited at the edge to overtake him. Sam's words haunted him and now he found himself forcefully pushing thoughts of Vicki out of his head. He had to hope they were safe. Brenda could protect her sister, he told himself. And whatever her shortcomings were, he had to have faith that when it mattered, she would do what it took to keep Vicki from harm.

He could see the toe of the man's boot now and he made a motion to Chris that he was going to try and cold-cock him. Chris raised his pistol as backup and nodded.

One more step, Dylan thought as he felt his whole body tensing. One more step…

He felt a sudden tug against his right arm and he jerked his head back toward Chris.

"What?" Chris mouthed.

Dylan turned back toward the man. His foot had not moved. Again he started to raise his arm. Again, he felt a tug, this time stronger than the first.

He turned back to Chris, his brows knitted together, the rage building.

But Chris was standing in the same position as he had been; a puzzled expression on his face.

With a start, Dylan realized it was Vicki. He lowered his weapon as a shout came from above. "Sam's not here."

The foot rotated away from Dylan.

"He's got to be here," the other said from upstairs. "They couldn't have taken him. We've got eyes on the building."

"The room's been sacked. Looks like a struggle. And there's blood all over the floor."

"Then he's wounded," the man nearest Dylan shouted. Instinctively, Dylan pressed himself even flatter against the wall as he listened. "Can you follow the blood? We've got to get to him before it's too late."

Dylan glanced at Chris and wondered if he wore the same bewildered expression he saw on his face.

The first man upstairs swore. "I knew he needed more backup."

"We were assured of more backup," the other answered.

"Fan out. We've got to find him. If the others capture him, you know what they'll do…"

What the bloody hell, Dylan thought as he stared at Chris. He glanced down at Sam, who was still out cold. He mentally calculated the distance and route to the door, but knew even if he made it through he couldn't get Sam to safety without detection. Especially if they had eyes on the building.

But who were "they"?

"There's blood on the stairs," one man called out. A blue beam from a flashlight illuminated the steps toward the floor. "It's dripped all the way down."

Dylan glanced at the floor beneath him. There were more than drips in the corner. He had no doubt the bloody trail was leading them straight to them.

He felt another tug on his arm, this time directing him into the open. This had better be you, Vicki, he thought as he took a deep breath. Then he shouted, "Identify y'selves!"

He could hear the men's boots shuffling and could only imagine that each one was ducking for cover while trying to identify the source. The man closest to them would know he was in close proximity and Dylan envisioned him giving hand signals to the others. As he peered across the building to the fourth man, he could clearly see the glint of metal as he turned to face them.

It was all over, he realized. With his night vision goggles, he could see them as plain as if they'd had a spotlight trained on them.

The man furthest away made a hand signal that Dylan couldn't quite comprehend before ducking behind a metal beam. "Are you Dylan Maguire?" the man shouted.

"I am," Dylan shouted back.

"Is Sam with you?"

Dylan glanced at Chris, who was still holding his pistol, preparing to use it at any second. "Yes. And he's injured."

"We're Unit Alfa," the man closest to them said. His voice was loud and echoed through the building. "We're here to help."

"If you're Unit Alfa, where 'ave you been?" Dylan demanded.

"Two of us are from Unit Alfa," the closest man replied. He spoke loud enough for the others to hear. Dylan spotted movement above and he glared upward as one of the men upstairs made his way around the banister while he eyed them below. "We were attacked. Two of us went down. They knocked out our communication."

"Who are the other two?"

"Unit Charlie," the man upstairs called down.

"Unit Bravo," said the other man upstairs.

"We're here to help," said the closest man.

It could be a trap. He could put down his weapon and step forward and be shot down in a hail of gunfire. Or they could apprehend him, take him to a secretive location and torture him. And Chris' and Sam's fate were now interlocked with his own.

He looked back at Chris, who was nodding as he lowered his weapon.

Dylan turned back toward the open space. Or he could fight them, one by one; he could resist until the result was exactly the same: he was killed or apprehended.

"We're comin' out," Dylan shouted.

59

He spotted the crime scene tape across the back door as soon as he slipped through the break in the hedges. It was impossible to miss; the bright yellow tape glowed in the dim light of the distant street lamp.

Now that the storm had passed, the ground was saturated, making his progress slippery. He hesitated as he stared upward at the windows on the back side of the house. There was a soft light in his bedroom window and a softer one on the second floor as if emanating from a side room. The kitchen light was brighter, the radiance seeping between the slats on the blinds, beckoning him inside.

An owl hooted nearby and a dog barked in the distance.

Dylan glanced behind him at the two men who had followed him. He nodded silently and they responded in kind. He slipped on the night vision goggles they'd given him and quietly made his way to the back door, slipping around the tape to make it appear undisturbed. Dried blood pooled on the steps.

The back door was locked, as he'd expected it to be, and as he reached for his key, he was surprised to find his hand trembling. He willed himself to regain control and slid the key in the lock. The door opened easily and he skimmed past it. Once the others were inside, they closed the door behind them.

He felt the heat rising in his cheeks as he faced the blood splattered across the kitchen floor. Small folded numbers on crisp cardboard sat strategically around the room. He turned around slowly as his mind raced through all the possibilities. As he did so, he spotted the open dumbwaiter and he made his way to the opening and peered inside. Finding the tray was somewhere beneath him, he hauled it up and secured it at the kitchen level.

The tray had markings on it akin to scuffmarks. In his mind's eye, he pictured Vicki and Brenda in the bedroom, one or both of them piling onto the dumbwaiter and escaping inside the walls to the floors below. He considered the urgency and fearfulness required for them to attempt such an escape.

"Lumberton police," one of the others, a man named Troy, said quietly.

The second man holstered his pistol. "That means they've already swept the house." His name was Dwight. He removed his goggles as he peered upward at the kitchen light. "No need for these."

Dylan's mouth was dry as he moved into the hallway. There were no signs of a scuffle there or in the dining room or living room. Peering up the stairs, he noticed the doors to Brenda's bedroom and the room he shared with Vicki open, the lights shining across the hardwood floors.

He took the steps two at a time as the others followed more slowly. At each turn, he again noted no signs of a fight. But when he reached the top floor and saw the door knob lying on the floor where he'd pushed it through a day earlier, the pounding in his temples grew. Stepping inside, he took in the disheveled bed and items strewn about the room. He found himself walking straight toward the dumbwaiter, which he opened as though thinking someone was on the other side.

But he knew she wasn't there. She'd made it to the kitchen, even into the cellar below it. But where was she now?

The pounding in his head continued to intensify until he thought his brain was going to explode. Where was she?

A sudden banging grabbed his attention and he whirled back toward the bedroom door. Making his way to the hallway, he peered down the stairs. Troy was standing in the living room doorway. At Dylan's appearance, he motioned toward the front door and drew his gun.

Dylan stepped across the top of the staircase, moving to the other side of the banister as a key was jingled in the lock and the front door opened.

"Hands in the air!" Troy shouted.

"Alec!" Dylan yelled almost simultaneously, his voice echoing down the open staircase. "It's okay," he said as he rushed down the stairs. "He's a sheriff's deputy."

He reached the front foyer to find Alec frozen with his hands in the air, his eyes taking in the man dressed in black, another one joining him, and finally Dylan.

"It's okay," Dylan said again and Troy lowered his weapon. Turning back to Alec, he said, "What happened here?"

Alec lowered his hands and warily studied Troy and then Dwight. "Who are these guys?"

"Federal officers," Dylan said.

Alec nodded. "I'm not surprised."

His mouth was dry and his voice sounded hoarse as he said, "Have you seen Vicki?"

"Just left her. She asked me to come back here and wait for you."

"Is she alright?"

"She's fine. Her sister's a bit worse for the wear."

"B—" Dylan began before catching himself.

"Brenda Carnegie?" Alec said. "That the name on the tip of your tongue?"

Dylan nodded.

"She was hit in the back of the head. Blunt force trauma. She'll be okay—eventually. She's got a concussion but they've got her stabilized."

"Where is she?"

"Southeastern Regional Medical Center. So is Vicki. She didn't want to leave her sister but she's worried about you."

"I've got to get to 'er."

"I'll drive you." He took in the other two men with a wary eye. "You two coming along?"

"No," Dwight said. "We've got some people waiting for us."

"I bet you do."

Dylan hurriedly shook each of their hands. "I'm goin' to run."

"Go," Troy said.

Alec and Dylan stepped onto the front porch. After Dylan closed the door behind him, Alec said, "Look, Dylan. I don't know who you guys are. And I don't know what you're doing here. All I know is Southeastern is crawling with feds. They've got security around Vicki and Brenda like they were each the First Lady."

Dylan breathed a sigh of relief. "That's music to me ears, mate."

They descended the steps to the sidewalk and made their way toward Alec's driveway. "Those guys gonna be okay?"

"Who? The ones in me house? Aye. They'll be fine. They'll let themselves out, they will."

"You know," Alec continued, "Brenda Carnegie is in a whole lot of trouble."

Dylan nodded silently.

"I placed her under arrest. Want to hear the charges?"

"I don't need to. I'm sure she's facin' a prison sentence."

"You knew she was wanted?"

They reached Alec's car and Dylan opened his door and leaned on the roof as he peered at Alec. Alec's gray eyes were narrowed and his face dark.

"I suspected as much," Dylan answered.

"Yeah. Well, I've been hunting for her these last few months. She's wanted in connection with a double homicide and some computer crimes."

Dylan shifted his eyes downward. "Vicki's not involved in it, I can tell you that."

"I have no reason to suspect she was."

"It's goin' to be a regular family reunion at the hospital, you know."

"Oh?"

"Vicki's Uncle Sam was taken there as well."

"Her 'uncle' huh?"

Dylan met his eyes. "Aye. Her uncle."

"Like I said, I have no idea who you guys are…" His voice faded and he looked expectantly at Dylan as though waiting for an explanation.

"What happened back there?" Dylan asked instead. He nodded toward the house. "The blood in the kitchen."

"Get in," Alec said as he opened his door. "I'll explain on the way."

60

Dylan poked his head through the doorway to find Sam sitting up in the hospital bed, his head bandaged and a blood pressure cuff around his arm.

"It's the same as it was the last time you checked it," he growled at the nurse. "Get that thing off me. And don't come back."

Dylan stepped inside, gently pulling Vicki behind him. He was bruised almost from head to toe but he told himself he was no sorer than he'd been after any of his boxing matches back home. The mantra did nothing to ease his pain but he continued repeating the thought. To his relief, Vicki's only injury was a fractured heel, and if he had to wait on her hand and foot until it was healed, he would do just that.

Spotting them, Sam barked, "Get me some coffee. This stuff is crap."

Dylan picked up the cup from the hospital tray straddling Sam's lap and sipped it. "It tastes perfectly fine to me."

"Then you drink it."

"Well, as luck would 'ave it," Dylan answered, pulling a bag from behind his back, "Bennie made you a good breakfast." As Vicki helped to arrange it on his plate, he added, "It's your favorites. Rashers, sausage, eggs, biscuits, and sweetbreads." He pulled out a cup. "And coffee." Then another cup, adding, "and orange juice."

"Where are the pancakes?" Sam snarled.

The nurse rolled her eyes as she removed the blood pressure cuff. "His pressure is too high," she told Dylan. "Way too high."

"Now you hear that?" Dylan chided. "You're makin' y'self crazy and gettin' y'self sick. And most likely, 'alf the staff here. You need to be behavin' y'self."

Sam grumbled something he couldn't decipher.

"Sam, seriously," Vicki added, "you need to calm down. Relax."

"I think I liked you better when you thought you were dyin', if you want my opinion about it."

"I don't," Sam said, but his voice had less of an edge to it as he ate. After a moment, he motioned toward the chairs. "Have a seat. I've got another assignment for you."

"You've got to be kidding me," Vicki said, pulling up a chair. "The last thing you need to be doing is working. Good grief."

"Hold on a moment," Dylan interjected, though he also pulled up a chair. "Brenda's room is empty. Why is that?"

Sam leveled his eyes at Vicki as he answered. "As of this moment, Brenda is in federal custody."

"CIA?"

"FBI."

"Why are they involved?" Dylan asked.

"They have jurisdiction. Pure and simple."

"But you can get her off," Vicki said, adding, "like you did Dylan."

"Now wait just a moment, Woman. I'm thinkin' he didn't quite 'get me off' 'ere. I'm thinkin' he pushed me into a no-win situation where I might 'ave been killed. That's no deal, if you want to know the truth o' the matter."

"Sam," Vicki pleaded.

"Don't beg," Sam growled. "It's not becoming. Anyway," he continued, relishing a bite of sweetbread, "I can't help her."

"What do you mean, you can't help her?"

Dylan squeezed Vicki's shoulder in what he hoped was a reassuring gesture, but as Sam continued, Vicki's face continued to fall.

"Brenda's in a lot of trouble. She's facing a host of local charges—which are not minor charges, by the way, including a connection with a double homicide." He let that sink in. Then, "She's also got a laundry list of charges facing her federally. So right now, the FBI trumps local law enforcement."

"But she helped us. She told us about Congressman Willo."

Sam attacked a sausage link. "You read the papers this morning?"

Both shook their heads.

"Willo was arrested last evening. So was the Vice President. Of course, both are out now—booked and released. Both will fight the charges with all they've got. But my guess is both will resign."

"And the president?"

"He was not involved—at least as far as we know."

"And the director?"

"Definitely not involved. He was sending another wave of agents, too, but our man here had everything under control."

"I wouldn't 'ave put it that way at'al," Dylan said. "And the next time you put a plan together, Sam, do me a favor and leave me out o' it."

"I didn't pull my weight, either," Vicki said glumly.

"Sure you did. Without you, we wouldn't have known about the veep."

"So, where is Brenda now?"

Sam shrugged. "Federal custody. It's all I know. She's got a concussion so my guess is she's in some infirmary in a federal prison somewhere."

"But can't you make a deal?" Vicki pressed. "She gave us the list—"

"Whoa," Sam said, holding up his hand. "She didn't give us the list. In fact, she claims now she doesn't have one."

"What?" Dylan said, his face reddening.

"You heard me."

"Are you sayin' to me," Dylan said, his voice rising, "that she now claims she has no list of senators and congressman, politicians and their dirty deals?"

"That is exactly what I'm saying."

"It's the concussion," Vicki said. "She's lost her memory. She's…"

Dylan's anger was growing by the second, choking out Vicki's words. There had been no evidence of a forced entry. He had locked the house himself as they were leaving and when he and Vicki returned home together from the hospital he had checked and rechecked every door and every window. He'd lain awake after a long, hot shower and tried to reconstruct Brenda's movements. Had she gone downstairs to flee yet again, leaving her sister alone and vulnerable? Was Garrett dead when she arrived downstairs or had she been forced to eliminate him? Had she arranged for someone to pick her up and help her escape? And had that person turned on her, attempting to kill her? Or had she opened the kitchen door to find someone else standing there instead?

She'd promised to take care of Vicki. She'd looked him square in the eyes and promised him. And she'd abandoned her.

Rule number one, Irish, the words echoed in his mind, *don't trust me.*

Sam was waving away Vicki's protests. "It doesn't matter. You got the list. Remember? You read it right off her screen and it was all caught on tape. We'll get the others."

"With a better plan next time, I'm hopin'," Dylan added.

Sam ignored him as he continued, "Anyway, it's out of my hands. I know you love your sister," he added, leveling his eyes once more at Vicki, "and I promise I'll stay on top of her case and let you know what's happening."

"And Chris?"

"Chris has vowed to help her. God only knows why, but he has. And as it turns out, he has a lot of time on his hands."

"He was fired?" Dylan asked.

"Resigned. Wouldn't you?"

Dylan fell silent. The woman had a hold on that bloke that he simply couldn't understand.

"Well," Dylan said, slapping his knee before rising and helping Vicki to her feet, "we'll leave you to your breakfast. We'll bring your lunch and your supper, too," he said before Sam could interject, "but I need to get this young lass home where I can take care o' 'er."

As they made their way to the door, Vicki stopped suddenly and turned around. "And Sam."

"Yeah?" He looked up from his plate.

"I love you, too."

"Huh?"

Vicki glanced at Dylan, who nodded his head in encouragement. "Dylan told me you said you loved me."

"I was delirious." He waved his hand. "Now get outta here."

As they walked down the hall, Dylan said, "Proof positive the man will live forever. The mean ones always do."

61

It was a delightful morning. The sun was shining in all its glory and though it was well into autumn, the temperature was a balmy 82 degrees. Dylan had taken the opportunity to open the door to the fish house, allowing it to air out. Now the slight breeze caressed his skin, bringing with it an exotic mixture of aromas. The boxwood was particularly fragrant and even the gardenia and tea tree bushes filled the air with their bouquet.

He loved the sunshine, the warmth and the endless blue skies.

He glanced down the aisle at Vicki, who was busy feeding the angelfish. They would soon have another shipment ready to take to the post. Their business was booming, which had been a surprise to both of them.

Nearly eight weeks had passed. Eight weeks filled with mornings in the fish house, afternoons exploring tourist sites in North Carolina, and evenings filled with—he glanced at Vicki again—unbridled passion. A man simply couldn't ask for more, he thought.

His hearing had largely returned and the prognosis was for his ear to heal completely. His bruises had long ago disappeared. Even Vicki's fractured foot seemed completely healed; she never complained about it and it didn't appear to have affected her activities.

He'd never had medical insurance before and with the past two months quiet and idyllic he was appreciating the income and benefits from the CIA that much more. He wondered if he'd come to the United States a few years earlier if *she'd* still be alive. No doubt she would be, he thought. All she'd needed was medical attention and living here, she would have received that.

He shook his head as if to clear his thoughts. He'd promised himself he wouldn't think about her. Not now. Not ever.

And he would never have met Vicki had things been different.

Chris called each afternoon to keep them informed of the latest news with Brenda, though the conversations generally were the same; she remained in a maximum security federal prison awaiting trial. Considered a flight risk—though he couldn't imagine why, he thought wryly—she'd been denied bail.

Vicki had come to accept the predicament her sister was in. Though she longed for things to be different, she understood there was little or nothing she could do.

Dylan continued to report in each day to the CIA as did Vicki but his only assignments had been in the form of additional training.

"You know," Vicki said, interrupting his thoughts, "there's been something I've been meaning to ask you."

"Oh?" He stopped his water test and peered at her. "And what would that be, I wonder?"

"The coal cellar."

"What about it?"

"There were no windows down there. And no door."

"Ah, that. Well, you remember when I was renovatin' the exterior and addin' new siding?"

"Yes."

"I covered up the windows."

"Why did you do that?"

"Security. I knew no one was likely to use that cellar for anythin' and why 'ave the vulnerability if it wasn't necessary?"

"Hhmm." She went back to feeding the fish. Then, "But what about the door?"

"There were two. One led outside, which is what the coal trucks used when they filled it. Though it wasn't really quite a door but an openin' o' sorts. That one I put siding o'er. The other one, leadin' into the kitchen, is still there."

"It can't be—"

"Oh, but it is. Ever walked into the pantry?"

"I've peeked in there—"

"Aye. And that's all you've done."

"Benita always cooks. Or you do when she's not here."

"And in the back o' the pantry," he continued, "is a broom closet. The door to the cellar is in there."

"So, I could have hidden in the cellar through the broom closet."

"Aye."

"And if Alec hadn't come along when he did, the intruder could have found me by opening the door to the broom closet and discovering the other door to the cellar."

"I suppose he could 'ave. But it's best not to think about the thin's that might have been."

Before she could answer, they heard a man's voice calling out to them.

"In here!" Dylan shouted in return.

Sam poked his head through the open door. "Thought I'd find you two in here. Got a chair?"

Dylan motioned to a chair set beside the door. "It's all yours."

He watched as Sam sat down heavily and mopped his brow. His head had been shaved for his surgery; now that the bandages had been removed, they could clearly see the incision healing along one side of his head. His hair was beginning to grow back but the spiky hairs were a big change from his customary long black hair that he liked to comb straight back. He also walked with a cane which he claimed was just for balance until he was completely healed, but Dylan wondered if he'd been hurt far worse than he allowed them to believe.

Now he held up a packet of papers. "Take it."

Dylan retrieved the bundle as Vicki came alongside him.

"What is it?" she asked.

"Real estate title. It's yours."

Dylan opened the envelope and rifled through the papers as Vicki looked on. He didn't understand it but one thing stood out. "It's in both our names."

"You got a problem with that?" Sam demanded.

"No; no, not at'al. It's just—taken me by surprise, is all."

"The CIA paid for it. Laurel Maguire's nephew had no idea what she owned so we got it for a song. Lock, stock and barrel."

"So, we're completely clear of him now?" Vicki asked.

"That's right."

Dylan had taken the papers to the doorway, where he studied them intently under the bright sunlight. "I've never owned anythin' like this a'fore," he mused quietly. "No one in my family has ever owned property."

Sam leveled his eyes at Vicki as if daring her to defy him. "I figured it was only right, giving him equal ownership. He's done a lot to this place."

"You did the right thing," Vicki said. She joined Dylan in the doorway and gently squeezed his arm. He didn't look up but continued staring at the official-looking documents.

"I'll 'ave to read the whole thin'," he announced.

"Don't worry about it," Sam growled. "Our best attorneys looked it over. It's all there."

"No," Dylan said quietly, "I must look o'er them. It's me duty as a landowner." He looked at Vicki. "I'm a landowner now."

She pointed to the paperwork. "All point seven acres."

"And the house."

"And the fish house."

"And the garage."

"I've been meaning to talk to you about that," Sam said. "You know it's about to fall over?"

"Aye. I've emptied it out. Everythin' is in the store room there." He motioned toward the back of the room. "I'll most likely knock it down and build a new one."

"I bought something myself," Sam said.

"What did you buy?" Vicki asked, smiling.

He patted his shirt pocket. "I bought a stake in the new Waterworks Art Center."

"You did not."

He looked taken aback. "I'll have you know, I enjoy art."

"I never said you didn't."

"I bought a staff workroom."

"You did what?"

"Yeah. I donated a certain amount and one of the workrooms will have my name on it."

"Are you serious?"

"Of course I'm serious."

"You bought a workroom. In an art gallery. In Lumberton."

He looked at her blankly.

"Why on earth would you do that?" she asked.

"I want to invest in my new home town."

"Your new *what?*" Now it was Dylan's turn to stare at him.

"You heard me." He patted his shirt pocket again. "I bought a home here, too."

Dylan glanced at his packet of papers and then at Sam's shirt pocket. "Just how much do you think you can fit in that pocket?"

Sam chuckled. "They're getting the paperwork ready for me to sign. I bought it this morning on the courthouse steps."

"I'm not following you," Vicki said.

"A certain house went up for auction—non-payment of taxes—and I bought it."

"You bought a house. Here in Lumberton."

"Why does that surprise you? You think I live in a box?"

"No, but—"

"Wait a minute," Dylan interjected. "You didn't buy a certain house on Elm Street, did you?"

Sam looked at him without answering.

"About ten blocks up the street?"

"I don't get it," Vicki said.

"He bought your sister's house."

"You—"

"Not for her, I want you to understand that," Sam said. "I bought it for me, personally." He shrugged. "It's the right size. Small yard, easy to keep up. Close to family."

"Ah, close to family," Vicki repeated.

"Aye, close to family," Dylan said, his voice no-nonsense. "I suppose now we'll have you here on Christmas mornin' and Thanksgivin' and Easter supper—"

"The thought had occurred to me."

"Oh, that's just lovely," Dylan said, his voice bordering on sarcasm.

Sam waved his hand as if to dismiss him. "Don't worry. I know you two need your time alone. But that's not why I came."

"There's more?"

"Enough of this idle chit-chat. We've got work to do."

"Which one o' us?"

Sam thumbed toward Vicki. "That one. You remember the report you saw the president going over, the one with the missing operative?"

"Of course I remember."

"We need you to find him. We've heard nothing from him in weeks and the operatives on the ground have covered the case from all angles. They have no idea where he might be—or even if he's still in the same country."

"So, it looks like I have my next assignment."

"You got a problem working with me?" Sam barked.

"Of course not. Why would you ask that?"

"The director thinks I'm getting old. My reflexes aren't the same as they used to be."

"He's not forcing you out?"

"Not yet. But I think, in the next year or two, maybe sooner, you might have a different boss."

"Oh, no." Vicki's brows furrowed.

"For now, I'm limited to psychic missions."

"So," Dylan interrupted, "I'll leave you two to your next mission."

"Stay here," Sam said, coming to his feet. "Vicki and I will go in the house. You finish your—" he waved his hand toward the fish tanks "—whatever you do."

Dylan watched them as they made their way to the house and then turned his attention to the paperwork he still held in his hand. He owned a house. And not just any house, but Aunt

Laurel's house. Nearly four thousand square feet. A mansion. And almost a whole acre.

Then he started toward the driveway like a thunderbolt. He couldn't simply walk in the house and toss these papers onto the kitchen table. He needed a box at the bank where it could be stored safely and protected against fire and floods and—all sorts of catastrophes. And he'd have to make a copy of it, to boot; otherwise, he'd have nothing to study.

As he rounded the break in the hedges, he caught sight of the garage again as it leaned dangerously toward one side. And now that he owned it, he thought, he couldn't afford another moment's rest. He had work to do.

The Southeastern Waterworks Regional Art Center is a real project in Lumberton, North Carolina. The Water Street Water Filtration Plant was designed in 1946 by William C. Olsen, Consulting Engineers of Raleigh. The building was constructed on the Lumber River in the downtown commercial district and dedicated to the McNeill family of Lumberton in 1952. An addition was constructed several years later to meet increased demand. The property was abandoned in 1990 when a larger treatment facility was built less than a mile upriver.

The community's vision is to transform an abandoned though light-filled industrial building into a central gathering place with open artist studios, event space for up to 1,000 people, galleries, workshops, outdoor amphitheater, gardens and dining on the river.

The advantages of having a gallery space on the river are coveted in small rural communities like Lumberton and may seem at first to be a luxury that Robeson County could not afford. It is through the foresight and innovative commitment of the City of Lumberton that Southeastern Waterworks Regional Art Center will receive the 6,000 square foot building on the Natural and Historic Lumber River, to become a centerpiece of a new Downtown Riverwalk, also in the works.

For this purpose, the generous citizens of Lumberton, North Carolina are marshaling all their resources, including the prospect of building a solar farm to provide ongoing funding for the center through the sale of sustainable energy.

This groundbreaking collaboration connects municipal government, the private arts sector and renewable energy. The strong commitment of the City of Lumberton is evidence that both her leadership and her public understands the great value of moving energy back into our historic downtown.

To stay abreast of the progress of the Southeastern Waterworks Regional Art Center, visit www.waterworksart.org.

Information provided by Rebekah Thompson of Lumberton, North Carolina, who first conceived the idea of turning the filtration plant into a regional art center.

About the Author

p.m.terrell is the pen name for Patricia McClelland Terrell, the award-winning, internationally acclaimed author of more than fourteen books in four genres: contemporary suspense, historical suspense, computer how-to and non-fiction.

Prior to writing full-time, she founded two computer companies in the Washington, DC Metropolitan Area: McClelland Enterprises, Inc. and Continental Software Development Corporation. Among her clients were the Central Intelligence Agency, United States Secret Service, U.S. Information Agency, and Department of Defense. Her specialties were in white collar computer crimes and computer intelligence.

A full-time author since 2002, *Black Swamp Mysteries* is her first series, inspired by the success of *Exit 22*, released in 2008. *Vicki's Key* was a top five finalist in the 2012 International Book Awards and 2012 USA Book Awards nominee. The series will have six main characters whose lives are forever intertwined through events or family ties: Dylan Maguire, Vicki Boyd, Brenda Carnegie, Christopher Sandige, Alec Brodie and Sandy Stuart.

For more information visit the author's website at www.pmterrell.com, follow her on Twitter at @pmterrell, her blog at www.pmterrell.blogspot.com, and on Facebook under author.p.m.terrell.

Other Books in the
Black Swamp Mysteries Series

Exit 22 (2008)

Christopher Sandige is a political strategist on his way from Washington to Florida when he is involved in an automobile accident at Exit 22 in North Carolina. Stranded for the weekend, he meets a beautiful but mysterious woman and becomes embroiled in a double homicide. He now must decide whether to trust the woman he is falling in love with even as evidence mounts against her and he is swept into a world of shell corporations, bank fraud and the oil industry. Now he is being pursued by a dogged homicide detective and a hired assassin – one who wants to arrest him and the other wants to kill him. And time is running out.

Vicki's Key (2011)

After a botched mission, Vicki Boyd leaves the CIA and moves to a new town to work for an elderly lady. But when she arrives, she finds that Laurel Maguire has suffered a stroke and is confined to her third floor bedroom and her nephew has arrived from Ireland to care for her. Vicki quickly falls in love with the charming Dylan Maguire but all is not what it seems to be in Aunt Laurel's rambling old home. And when the CIA arrive to recruit her for one more mission, she finds her past and her future are about to collide—in murder.

Dylan's Song (2013)

Dylan Maguire receives word that his grandmother is on her deathbed in *Dylan's Song*. Vicki Boyd accompanies him to Ireland along with a CIA assignment from Sam to locate a CIA operative who disappeared near Dublin. Soon after they arrive in Ireland, he is assaulted by men accusing him of murder, opening a door to a past he thought he had turned his back on forever. Now Vicki is discovering the real reason he fled Ireland for America—while harboring a secret of her own.